the
mother's
secret

BOOKS BY KATE HEWITT

the mother's secret

KATE HEWITT

bookouture

Published by Bookouture in 2023

An imprint of Storyfire Ltd.
Carmelite House
50 Victoria Embankment
London EC4Y 0DZ

www.bookouture.com

ISBN: 978-1-83790-289-7
eBook ISBN: 978-1-83790-288-0

To Emma, thank you for the writing retreats and all the brainstorming chats! This book wouldn't have happened without either.

PROLOGUE

I never knew what I was capable of, until now.

I never realized both the rage and the despair I would feel—coursing through me, clenching my fists, making a howl rise in my chest and out my throat—if I ever let it escape, but I didn't. I *didn't*.

Sometimes I wonder if I should have. If we'd all be better off if I had.

And yet, no. Never. I *didn't*, and so I shouldn't be here, sitting on a hard plastic chair in Hawley's tiny police station, staring at the wanted poster of a crazy-eyed guy with several weeks' stubble and wild hair. *That's* the kind of person who ends up being taken in for questioning, maybe even arrested.

But not me. *Not me.*

I've always been nice. What a bland word that is, and yet I cling to it now. I'm the kind of woman who gets along with everybody, who wants to like and be liked. If anything, I've been looked over, even invisible, and yet here I am, under suspicion. Under arrest.

I don't know how much trouble I'm in, except that it's bad. Already I can hear their accusations, so coldly stated. I can see their flat-eyed stares, pursed lips, folded arms. *You had the care of a minor, a vulnerable person. You abused your authority. You crossed the line.*

And no matter how much I protest my innocence, how much I plead or weep or beg or explain, they won't believe me. They've already made their assumptions, passed their judgments. They think they know what happened, and this feels like a formality, even if it shouldn't be.

But how did this happen? How did this happen to *me*?

I look again at the guy with the wild hair and eyes, staring straight at the camera; from here, I can't read the small print underneath saying what he's wanted for. Armed robbery, maybe? Assault? Nothing like what I did, and I didn't even do it.

At least... I don't think I did.

The door opens, and a police officer stands there, as unsmiling as I expected, staring me down. I swallow, rubbing my damp hands along my thighs, as I meet her flat glare. She looks as if she already dislikes me, and I can't really blame her, because the trouble is, maybe she's right to.

Maybe I really do belong here, after all.

CHAPTER 1

LAURA

I never knew trees could be so dark. They stretch along the side of the road, stately evergreens, standing so closely together that it's like an impenetrable wall of green and brown, all the way to the sky. It's a beautiful, blue-skied day, but these trees block out all the sunlight, so I feel as if we're going through a tunnel. I am reminded of the William Wordsworth poem I teach to tenth-graders—*continuous as the stars that shine/and twinkle on the milky way/they stretched in never-ending line/along the margin of a bay*. But Wordsworth was writing about sun-bright daffodils that tossed their heads "in sprightly dance" and lifted his heart with joy; not these dark, dark trees, that fill me with a swirling dread.

"We're almost there," Allan announces in the voice of a TV presenter or an airline steward. He is so very cheerful, chipper, and part of me wants to throttle him.

You agreed to this.

I know I did; I reminded myself often enough as we packed up our little house back in suburban Connecticut—the first one we'd ever owned and that we've now rented out—as I said goodbye to our daughter Katherine, not quite sixteen but already out of the house, thanks to this move. She'll be living with family friends so she can stay at the Leabrook School, where we spent five mostly happy years, Allan as deputy head, me as an English teacher.

And while she stays back there, we are now moving to northern Maine, to a town with a population of less than two thousand, so my husband can take up the position of head-master of a school I'd never even heard of, not until six months ago. And even then, I don't know that I particularly wanted to hear about it, a place so close to the Canadian border that apparently some of the road signs are in French; a place when people ask and you say "Maine," they reply, "Oh, Portland?" and you have to say, "No, four hours farther north than that." Four *hours*.

I turn to look out the window as I breathe in and out, telling myself yet again to banish my negative thoughts. They circle like a flock of dark crows in my mind, but I am trying not to let them settle.

I can see my reflection in the window, because the trees make it that dark; my hair like a straight brown curtain around my face and eyes like black holes, with a wide-eyed, dazed expression I am trying to shake. The lines of strain between my nose and mouth that have deepened in the last few months are visible even in the darkened glass; I look gaunt, older than my forty-seven years.

I gave myself a stern talking-to several months ago, insisting that I was not going to be down about this move, because I knew how much Allan had wanted to be a headmaster. He's climbed the never-ending ladder of academic leadership rung by tedious rung—head of department, housemaster, deputy head. Now he's got the prize—or least the first one. One of the ways he convinced me to agree to this move at all was by explaining that it was simply a step onto a better headship, at a bigger, more prestigious school. We'll stay for two years at least, so our son

Tucker, attending on a rugby scholarship, can graduate. And after that? I'm hoping we'll go back to Connecticut. Or Massachusetts, New York, New Jersey, even. I can be flexible, within reason. But right now, two years, as a *minimum*, feels like a very long time to spend so far away from everything. Especially from our daughter, and in some ways from our son, since he will no longer be living with us but boarding at the school.

"Laura?" Allan glances at me, and I realize I haven't responded to his chirpy comment. I haven't said something enthusiastic about the fact that, finally, after seven hours, we've almost reached our destination. We've been driving down Route 11 for hours, with nothing, *nothing*, but tall evergreens on either side of the road. They make me want to loosen my collar, even though I'm only wearing a T-shirt, or scratch at my skin, pull my hair. I don't think it's a normal reaction, but I'm a suburban girl at heart, and it's been well over three hours since we left Portland, which felt like the last outpost of civilization. And we still have another twenty miles to go.

"I'll be glad to stretch my legs," I say, a bit woodenly. I need to stop these negative thoughts, I know I do, but they crowd in, jostling for space in my brain, because the truth is, when Allan first told me that the headship of the Wilderness School—yes, that really is its name—was coming up, I thought he was joking. A move to Maine, and not just Maine, which is already far away, but *northern* Maine? We're New Englanders, yes, but we're not *crazy*.

Maine is beautiful for vacations, for visiting Portland and up to Bar Harbor if you've got the time, and Freeport for the outlets. I've done all that, oohed and aahed at the magnificent scenery, the mountains, and yes, the *trees*, but then I've always breathed a sigh of relief to head back to civilization. Suburbia.

But now we're going to live here. Tucker is already up here, for pre-season rugby training; Allan moved him into his dorm three days ago. We could have all moved up then; Allan wanted to, and it would certainly have been more convenient, but I was dragging my feet, finishing last-minute things. Not wanting to say goodbye to our little house, which I'd made into our home, the first real home we'd ever had in twenty years of school living. And not wanting to say goodbye to my daughter, even though Katherine seemed excited to live with her best friend Molly. I think they're envisioning enacting *Gilmour Girls* together, minus the mom. Or at least, minus me.

Molly's mother, Elise, is a close friend; I wouldn't entrust my daughter to her otherwise, but it still feels strange, to let go when I'm not ready, when I didn't think I would have to. And I know that Elise isn't as much a stickler for rules as I am; she lets Molly have her phone in her bedroom at night, although I've told her, as clearly as I can, that Katherine can't have hers. But it worries me, this seemingly little thing, now completely out of my control, along with so much else. How could I have left my daughter?

"Ah," Allan says in satisfaction, and he turns off Route 11, which cuts through Maine from north to south, onto an even narrower road that leads to Hawley and the Wilderness School, which sits on its paltry outskirts. I've only been to the school once before, in February, after Allan had been offered the position. I could have accompanied him for the second round of interviews a month earlier, and maybe I should have, but Katherine had midterms and Tucker had a basketball game, and it didn't feel like the right time to leave them, even just for a couple of days.

Anyway, seeing the school in February was hard enough—a foot and a half of snow, the temperature hovering just above zero, with a cutting wind coming from off the Appalachians— the Appalachian Trail ends a hundred miles *south*, which seems crazy in itself. The visit was a blur of handshakes and chitchat, touring the buildings, trying not to shiver, wanting to go home with a desperation I tried not to let myself feel.

As we drive through the town now—two streets and a traffic light—to the school, I acknowledge fairly that it is much more pleasant at the end of August, when everything is green and lush, the day warm and sunny. At least we've had a break from the trees; as we turned off Route 11, the evergreens were replaced by rolling fields, the occasional barn, of weathered red painted wood.

"The town's meant to have a nice Italian," Allan remarks.

It's not the first time he's mentioned Mario's, the pizzeria that is supposed to make me think we've entered a booming metropolis. That, as well as an old-fashioned movie theater, a hardware store, a public library, a hipster-styled coffee shop and a box-like Price Chopper on the town's edge, is pretty much the extent of Hawley's offerings; I suppose it's more than some places.

We've reached the school now, which is a somewhat jarring mix of New England brick and limestone, everything pillared and porticoed, and a handful of single-story shingle buildings that were put up in the 1970s, back when the school attempted to reinvent itself as an outdoorsy type of place, offering rock climbing, hiking, camping, that sort of thing. It was the head-master's vision of the time, and it lasted about fifteen years, before expensive insurance policies and dwindling interest made the school rely instead on beefing up its quota of international boarding students. It seems there is still a remnant of that spirit left, though; the incoming ninth-graders, Allan has told me, do a week's camping up on Mount Katahdin in the spring. But mostly, the Wilderness School—renamed during that period in the 1970s—has yet to find its niche, its vision, and that, I suppose, is where my husband comes in.

He drives slowly down the main drive, which sweeps up to the Westcott Building, named after the founder. This part of the school is comfortingly familiar, like so many other schools where we've worked—a gracious, green quad, beautiful buildings, if a tiny bit on the neglected side. But beyond are those squat buildings of dark brown shingle, and then the forest starts to creep in at the edges of the campus, and when I look at all that darkness, it feels hard to breathe.

I'm overreacting. I know I am. It really is beautiful, and the headmaster's house, where we'll live, is beautiful, too, far nicer than any other school housing we've lived in before. Allan pulls up to it now; it sits directly behind the Westcott Building, on the way to the school dormitories, right in the middle of the campus. It's called Webb House, because it's named after Josiah Webb, a Maine-born chocolatier who gave a lot of money to the school, a long time ago. It's three stories of gracious brick, with an imposing front door and a lot of history and tradition attached to it. The entire downstairs is furnished with historic antiques and oil paintings, and the living and dining rooms are often used for receptions for trustees, prospective parents, honor students. When I'd asked Allan if we had to have those kinds of events in our home, he'd looked startled, maybe even a bit disapproving.

"It's part of the school's tradition, Laura, and you've always liked having people over."

Yes, friends, I thought. Casual kitchen suppers or family barbecues. Not this kind of potentially pretentious, highbrow *entertaining*. But that, apparently, as wife to the headmaster, is what I'll be expected to do. When I'd asked if there was a teaching job for me, even something just part-time, Allan had suggested that I spend the first year getting used to "my new role." I'd known I would be giving up my old job, but I'd still hoped for something new, something more than my *role* as headmaster's wife, which would involve no more, I assumed, than smiling and standing by Allan's side, hosting the odd tea or dinner. Hardly a full-time, or even a part-time, job.

Although, to be fair, none of it is an entirely unfamiliar idea; when he was a housemaster, we lived in an apartment attached to a boarding house by a fire door and we regularly had students hanging out in our kitchen. I enjoyed it—the sense of busyness, young people coming and going, a kitchen filled with chat and laughter. I'd wanted more children, once upon a time, but it never happened, and this felt, in a way, like the next best thing.

I've done other hosting, as well, over the years; when Allan was department head, I had all the teachers in the history department over for pre-Christmas drinks and nibbles, or summer barbecues; when he was deputy head, I hosted the annual "fun day" for the children of faculty. So, it would be unreasonable, I know, to think that hosting teas and dinners and receptions for various interested parties and stakeholders in the Wilderness School is somehow beyond or beneath me, because I know it isn't. But when I did all that other stuff, I also had a *job*, teaching English, which I love. And now I don't, because apparently there is no job for me at this school, and I'm not sure if there ever will be, since the staff turnover is apparently pretty low. Allan told me that many of the teachers here are Maine born and bred, and they hardly ever leave, but I am still trying to hold onto some hope that I'll find a job eventually. Allan wouldn't ask me to give up *that* much, I've told myself, even though he pretty much already has.

We step out of the car in front of the house; there is no one about, although I hear a whistle blow from the rugby pitch, on the far side of campus. School starts in three days, although some of the students have already arrived, for pre-season training.

"Well, Mrs. Haile?" Allan asks in a jolly tone which I am trying not to let annoy me. Since becoming headmaster, he's adopted this tone of jocular bonhomie, like a character he inhabits, and while I understand the impulse, I wonder how long it will last.

"Ready," I reply as brightly as I can, and we mount the three steps to the shiny black door, and then step inside, into a house that feels like a museum. None of the rooms on the ground floor, save maybe for the kitchen, are allowed to be changed at all. There are five bedrooms on the second floor, and we've decided we'll make one of those our own private living room, but it still feels strange, to have a downstairs we'll have access to, but isn't really ours. The third floor is attics, useful only for storage.

The kitchen is cavernous, with industrial-sized equipment, to cater for all the lunches and dinners and teas hosted here, but it's the only kitchen the place has, so presumably I will have to use it, too. Allan sold this to me as a plus when we toured the house back in February, marveling at how big the dishwasher was, the twelve-burner stove that took up half a wall, the enormous fridge, as if these aspects would somehow be convenient for us, now an unexpected household of two. I could only think how this kitchen could never be considered cozy, or someplace I wanted to spend any of my time; being in it feels like working in a cafeteria. In fact, none of the rooms downstairs feel like a place I could call home.

I am reminded of all that now as I walk through the empty rooms downstairs. They smell of lavender and lemon polish, which is pleasant, but I know there is absolutely no way I will be able to put my stamp on any of them. Not that I have ever been all that big into interior design, but since we had our own house for the first time back at Leabrook, it feels hard to return to the golden handcuffs of school housing—a lovely, rent-free home, but something that will never truly be ours, not even a little bit.

I'm certainly used to living in houses that aren't our own, which is part and parcel of working for a boarding school, and I know we've been lucky, to have been provided housing, a lot of it very decent, all along. I tell myself that as I head up the sweeping staircase in the grand foyer, to the floor we will call our own.

The five bedrooms are all large, square, and gracious; they have tiled fireplaces and long, sashed windows overlooking Westcott House and the quad on one side, and the sweeping hills and forests on the other. As I walk through the empty rooms, my mood begins to lift; these rooms alone are twice as big as some of the places we've lived. I can make them homey, cozy, once we have our own furniture, our own things, and the view really is breathtaking.

I hear Allan come up the stairs, each one creaking under his step, and I turn from the view to smile at him as he comes into the first bedroom, across from the staircase, facing the front.

"What do you think about this one for a living room?" I ask him, my voice almost as jocular as his has been. "It's got such a nice view."

"They all have amazing views," Allan replies, and although he's essentially agreeing with me, it *almost* feels like a rebuke. Or maybe that's just me, because I know how ungenerous and resentful my thoughts have been about this move, and I want to make up for it now. At least, I want to try. I want this move to work for us, even if I've been resistant. I'm going to try harder, now that we are here.

"Maybe the one in the back for the master?" I continue, as I cross the room and head into the hallway, which is wide and long enough to put a bowling alley in. When the kids were little, we might have; I could have set plastic pins up on one end, had them use a playground ball, made a real game of it. The thought gives me a pang of nostalgia, of bittersweet memories of those happier times.

This is the first time we've moved without the kids—yes, Tucker is here, but his scholarship paid for him to be a boarder, and so we've become empty-nesters in one fell swoop, three years before I thought we would have to.

The room on the far end, facing the forest, is the most private. There are no adjoining bathrooms to any of the bedrooms, just one large one in the hall, complete with a claw-foot tub, a pedestal sink, and a shower cubicle that someone shoehorned into the corner. The whole place is a mixture of grandiose and budget, typical of a lot of small boarding schools that started with money but no longer have much left.

"Yes, this one looks good," Allan says as he strolls into the room with a smile. He comes toward me and, somewhat to my surprise, slides his arms around my waist, drawing me against him, my back to his chest. We haven't touched very much in recent weeks, maybe even months, because life has been so busy, and Allan has been so focused.

Nine months ago, he applied for the headship at Leabrook; he wasn't even granted an interview despite being deputy head, and I know the snub both hurt him and made him feel like he had no choice but to leave. The Wilderness School was the next one in New England to come up with a headship vacancy, and their approbation has been a balm to his wounded soul—and ego. But it's meant a very busy few months, between applications, interviews, and then winding things down in Connecticut. We might be empty-nesters now, but we haven't spent a lot of time together lately.

"I like this room," Allan murmurs, and nuzzles my neck; the feel of his lips on my skin is strangely shocking, considering we've been married for twenty-three years.

I laugh and pat his hand before stepping lightly away. I know Allan is pretty much thrilled about this move, and I'll get there, I *will*, but not quite yet.

"When does the moving truck arrive?" I ask.

"I got a text when I was downstairs. They should be here in about twenty minutes."

"Great." I want something to do, to take my mind off the future, which feels as empty as these yawning rooms. I have no job, no children at home, and this role as headmaster's wife I'm meant to step into feels foreign and strange. Not to mention I'm forty-seven, with all that entails—hot flashes, wrinkles, hormonal swings, the fear of being called a Karen if I so much as raise my voice. But I really am going to focus on the positives, for my sake as well as Allan's.

As I head downstairs, I try to think of them. *Fresh air. Space to think, to breathe.* Life was busy, maybe too busy, back in Connecticut; three years ago, I started working full-time and, on top of helping my elderly parents whenever I could and parenting two teenagers, it felt like a lot. Now that they've moved into a townhouse in an assisted living community outside Boston, I'm not needed as much; I suspect our move prompted theirs, although they said they'd been thinking about it for a while. I'm just not sure I believe them.

But slowing down, at least for a little while, could be a good thing for me. Maybe I'll get into walking, or hiking, even, up in the mountains. Are there bears in Maine? Probably, but it's not something I've googled. Still, maybe it would be good for me, to be a little less suburban. A little less busy.

And yet as I wander through the formal rooms downstairs with their oil paintings—a small one even by Winslow Homer—and the teak tables and desks inlaid with leather, the sofas made by the rococo master John Henry Belter, everything *just so*, I feel an emptiness sweep through me again. A sense of grief swamps me, because I feel as if I have lost everything—my children, my parents, my home, my job. The only thing left, I think, is my husband, who is now whistling as he comes down the stairs.

I walk slowly toward the living room window that faces the Westcott Building. When we came in February, there were students streaming to and from classes, right in front of the windows. I worried we'd feel the lack of privacy, but I suppose we'll spend most of our time upstairs.

In two days' time there will be a welcome barbecue on the quad for us and all the faculty; the day after that, there is a tea for new parents, right here in this room; and the day after that, there is another barbecue, this time for all the boarding students. It feels like a lot, but I tell myself it will help me to meet people, to get into the swing of things, which I definitely need to do.

I hear a sudden burst of laughter as a gang of boys stroll across the lawn, joking and jostling each other, ruddy-cheeked and tousle-haired. They have just come from rugby practice, and I see my son among their number, and my heart both softens and swells. He was thrilled to make this move, because at a small school like Wilderness he can play on the varsity team; at Leabrook, he was a bench-warmer on the junior varsity football team—they didn't even have rugby.

I watch him chat to a brown-haired boy on his left, both of them brimming with vitality, with youth and innocence, and I tell myself—*again*—that this is a good thing for my family. A good move.

And then I turn from the window to prepare for when the moving truck arrives, and our new life actually begins.

CHAPTER 2

RACHEL

The baby is crying. Again.

I know I need to stop thinking of him that way, as *the baby*.

"*Nathan,*" Kyle told me, six days ago, before he left to go up north. "His name is Nathan."

I know that, of course I do. It's just that for some reason I keep calling him *the baby*. It's easier that way, somehow. If I call him the baby, I can think of him as something *other*, a separate entity. If I think of him as Nathan, as my son, then I feel guilty for what I don't feel. So, it's *the baby* who is crying right now—a shrill, desperate, endless shrieking at four o'clock in the morning, having only slept for forty-five minutes; I might have managed twenty. It's not *Nathan*, my son, whom I love and who is only six weeks old—fragile, vulnerable, beloved. *The baby* is something else entirely.

His shrieks have become that desperate, warbling throttle; it makes me hope he might give up, except he never does. I've let him cry for forty-five minutes—Kyle woke up then—and he never stopped, not once, not even, it seemed, to take a breath.

Somehow, I drag myself out of bed. I have been lying on my stomach, breasts full, eyes scrunched shut, body utterly leaden.

I walk, in a stupor, down the hall toward his bedroom. Three months ago, I decorated it in a tasteful palette of taupe and cream; what a joke. What kind of ignoramus decorates their baby's nursery in shades that show every stain—the leaking from me, both the milk from my breasts and the blood from my uterus, as well as from Nathan, the dribbling, curd-like spit-ups and the vast, viscous, mustard-yellow poos. There is so much *liquid*. I am mired in it, a swamp of bodily fluids. No one tells you these things. No one likes to admit how *gross* having a baby is. At least no one I know.

My mother, the self-proclaimed font of all maternal wisdom, thinks having a baby makes you the next best thing to the Virgin Mary. Saintly. Holy. In the process of perfection. At least, it did for her—although, funnily enough, I certainly didn't see her that way when I was growing up. She was in a constant state of resentful dissatisfaction, blaming me for my father leaving, and basically for everything else, as well.

I walk into the nursery, and I pick the baby up like he's a fragile parcel, carefully draping him over my shoulder and gently patting his back. His crying continues; if anything, the shrieks became more desperate, more furious, as if my picking him up has actually enraged him further. A mother at the only baby group Hawley offers, which I've dragged myself to twice so far, has said how nice it is to be "the magic person." Those were the words she used. When I stared at her blankly, she explained, "You know, the person who can always stop them crying. Who they always want." She laughed then, a self-conscious, little tinkle. "But sometimes it can be a bit tiring, right?" she added that in what I think was meant to be a conspiratorial whisper.

Right. I know all about *tiring*, but I don't know anything about being the magic person, because I'm not. I never have been. The baby—Nathan—doesn't stop crying for me. Sometimes, like now, he seems only to cry harder, as if he senses my fear, or my weariness, or maybe the indifference I try not to let myself feel, because, right now, as I sway where I stand, tired in absolutely every aching muscle of my body, I don't even *care* about this child, I just want him to go to sleep.

I don't tell anyone any of these things, of course. I laughed along with that other mom, her cherubic six-month-old perched on her hip, chubby hands patting her face as she pretended to nibble her little fingers and the baby squealed with laughter, and I nodded. "Yeah, yeah, the magic person," I said, as if agreeing.

"Ssh, baby, sssh," I say now. I rub his back in rhythmic circles and then I do the only thing that I've found that seems to stop his crying—deep squats. The kind that makes my thighs burn and my breath catch, and that's not even taking into consideration that I am six weeks postpartum and *still* bleeding.

After about thirty squats, his crying begins to lessen, just a little, turning into snuffles and jerky little sobs. After another twenty or so, I half-stagger toward the glider in the corner and ease myself into it. Nathan snuffles at my shirt and I put him to my breast, wincing slightly as he hunts for my nipple with greedy urgency. Something else no one tells you—breastfeeding *hurts*. Apparently, it will stop hurting eventually, when my nipples toughen up to something like rhinoceros hide, but right now, when he latches on, my toes curl. I breathe deeply, in and out, and then make myself relax. Nathan softens against me, and I stroke his head as my eyes drift shut.

For a few minutes, I can almost let myself feel contented— I'm comfortable, he's quiet. I can let that be enough, at least until morning, when it all starts again and the day stretches in front of me, totally empty and yet so frustratingly *full*—of feeds and diaper changes and walking back and forth, comforting a crying baby.

But I'm not going to think about all that now. Instead, I find myself thinking, as I often do in these moments, about my old classroom, of its long, sashed windows facing the rugby pitch, the rows of books in the little library of recommended reads, classics as well as contemporary novels, that I encourage students to take out, of the impressionist and modern art posters on the wall, to give them an added dose of culture. The *peacefulness* of it, at the end of the day, sunlight slanting through the window, the distant sound of students or teachers in the corridor as I sit at my desk and have a moment to myself, reveling in what I've accomplished, the shaping of young minds, because I *did* make that kind of difference, even if it sounds soppy.

Thinking of it all soothes me, even as it creates an ache of longing deep inside me. I miss that classroom so much. I miss who I was when I was inside it.

Tomorrow—really, today—is the day of the Wilderness School's welcome back barbecue for the faculty. It's the first time in ten years, since I started at the school, that I won't be going, because I'm on maternity leave for another four months, until January. My closest friend at the school, Deidre, left for a job down south at the end of last year, and I can't imagine being at any school event without her; we'd always stick together, lamenting the weak iced tea and tasteless food, shaking our heads at all the school gossip and backbiting.

Liz Pollard, the Head of English and single, childless and fiftyish, has sent me a congratulations card but not come to visit, and she didn't suggest I turn up, baby in tow, to say hello to everyone, although I probably could, if I wanted to. I'm not sure I do. I'm not sure I want my colleagues seeing me like this, tired and frazzled and *depleted*.

I really thought I'd have this baby thing down. I absolutely breezed through pregnancy—no morning sickness, only gained seventeen pounds, and I had the neatest little baby bump imaginable underneath my tailored dresses. I didn't even need to wear maternity clothes until the third trimester. I read the books, I took the prenatal vitamins and the folic acid, I did yoga. I had a birth plan, which pretty much went as I wanted it to—gentle music, all natural, twelve hours from start to finish, and only the last hour was hard. My memory of that hour is blurry, but I know I alternately wept and screamed, said I hated Kyle and that I loved him, all the while feeling as if my body were being wrenched apart—quite literally, as it turned out. Pretty normal stuff, though, for a woman in labor, or so I told myself.

It was everything *after* that that really threw me for a loop—not that I've said as much to Kyle, or anyone else. Not that I've even *thought* as much, except now, when I'm half-asleep and the room is quiet, the sky just starting to lighten at the edges, and I am vacillating between fragile contentment and total despair.

How do women *do* this? How do they like it? How do they survive it? Admittedly, most have a husband or partner on hand, and I don't, not as of six days ago, at least. Kyle works as a logger up north; he starts at the end of the summer and finishes up in mid-March, although he gets a few short breaks in between, to come home and see his family; he promised he'd come home in a week or two, but right now that feels like forever. It was fine when I was teaching full-time; we love each other, but we both like our space, too. But now? When we have this tiny, fragile, demanding human being to take care of? It's not so great.

Still, the only way to make it work financially, while I'm on maternity leave, is for Kyle to do one last season. After that, he said, he'll find something else, although I don't know what that will be. In any case, before the baby was born, I told him it was fine. I thought it would be.

It's been six days, and I still have over six months until he comes home. I cannot even let myself imagine it, the utter *endlessness* of it. Instead, I chop up my time into manageable bite-size portions, the way the baby books tell you to do with table food, once you start introducing it to your baby, which, of course, shouldn't be until at *least* nine months. I can handle this morning: I will shower, I will clean the kitchen, which I know is a sticky mess of greasy pans and plates and bowls with crusted-on food, and I will feed the baby, probably three or four times. And that is one whole half-day I will have gotten through. I can manage that. I think.

I must fall asleep, because I wake slowly, blinking, the sunlight warm on my face. The nursery looks ethereal in the morning light, with its blond wood and neutral colors seeming almost to glow. It looks like some Scandi fantasy of what a nursery should look like, minus all the mess and stains, of course. That was probably the look I was going for, back when I decorated it. I can't remember anymore.

I glance down at Nathan, and for a second an emotion flickers through me like one of those silvery minnows in the Penobscot River—in his free time, Kyle likes to go fly-fishing. The baby's cheek is round and soft, and his lashes, fanning that plump, perfect cheek, are golden and curly. His mouth is pursed like a little rosebud, a milk bubble frothing at the corner of his Cupid's bow lips. I start to smile, and then Nathan startles awake, like he's been prodded or poked, his skinny little arms suddenly flailing, his deep blue eyes widening in shock and then his tiny face screwing up with rage as he begins to shriek. That emotion I felt, whatever it was, slips away.

I try to soothe him, cuddling him, patting him on the back, draping him over my shoulder for a burp, but it all feels half-hearted, like I'm just going through the motions—probably because I am. I don't actually believe any of these things will make him stop crying. Eventually, I feed him again, because that at least seems to work, at least for a little while, and I close my eyes, trying to enjoy the sunshine that is warm on my face.

Amazingly, when he finishes nursing half an hour later, he

has fallen asleep, and even more amazingly, I manage to lay him down in his crib, slowly, *so* slowly, like I am handling a precious antique crossed with a live grenade. My back is aching, my thighs burning as I half-squat over the crib, gently, so gently, easing myself away from him, because so often, the second my hands leave his body, his eyes open, and the screaming starts. Again.

This time, though, it doesn't. He lets out a shuddery little sigh while I hold my breath, and then his breathing evens out. He's asleep. He's actually asleep, in his own crib. This is a miracle, and not even a minor one.

I tiptoe out of the room, everything in me tensing for the sudden squawk of his cry, but it doesn't come. I crawl into my own bed and curl up, scrunch my eyes shut. So often I am too tense to sleep, but for once, I let myself drift off, and it feels wonderful.

I wake two hours later, which is another miracle. For a second, lying there, the room quiet around me, I wonder if he's actually dead. When has he ever slept for two hours? Then I hear his cry, not a shriek, but a grizzle, and an emotion floods through me—relief? Maybe.

I get out of bed, feeling almost human in a way I haven't for six long weeks. I go into the nursery and peer into his crib.

"Well, hello there, little man." I sound uncharacteristically cheerful, and Nathan peers at me quizzically before his mouth suddenly turns up in a delighted grin, shocking me. He's actually *beaming*, his little face lit up, and I feel as if I could cry. Right now, *I* am the magic person. "Hello, hello," I murmur, and then I pick him up, nuzzling his head as I draw him close. He smells of spit-up and sour milk, but I don't care. Am I finally starting to *get* this baby thing? The OB did tell me that it could take some time, to bond with the baby, but she sounded like she had to say it, like she'd never seen a case where it had actually happened like that.

But maybe that's what happening with me. I hold this thought close, like a secret, a treasure, as I change Nathan into a fresh diaper and onesie. I press a kiss to his tummy, something I haven't done before, and he kicks his legs in joy. Then I settle him into his bouncy chair and take it into the bathroom, so I can actually have a shower—my first in three days.

He gurgles happily to himself as I step under the spray, close my eyes and let the hot water sluice over me. Sometimes I cry in the shower, because it's the only place where I can pretend that I'm not, but today I don't feel the need.

I am just soaping my hair when Nathan's happy gurgles turn to grizzling sounds, and then, before I can rinse my hair, agonized shrieks, like someone is pulling out his little baby toenails.

I tell myself to ignore it, just for thirty seconds so I can finish washing, but then, suddenly, the shrieks turn to splutters, so he sounds like he is choking. When I poke my head around the shower curtain, his face is bright red, his eyes are bulging, and panic seizes me. I trip over the rim of the bathtub, nearly sprawling right on top of him, and snatch him up into my arms, but my hands are wet and slippery and I almost drop him. Meanwhile, he's still choking. What can a newborn baby who only drinks breastmilk be choking *on*?

I don't know whether to pat his back or give him the baby Heimlich—although I seem to have forgotten how to do that, from the course I took—and so I am simply standing there, naked and dripping wet, holding my choking baby, my mind blurred with panic, when he suddenly vomits half-digested milk all over me.

At least he starts breathing again, and crying, a shriek of complete distress like no other I've heard, and I cradle him to me as I half-stumble, half-walk into the nursery and collapse, still naked and dripping, into the glider.

After a few minutes, Nathan calms down, snuffling against

me. I close my eyes, my body weak with the aftermath of total terror. I still have soap in my hair, and I am covered in baby sick. And it is at that moment that the front doorbell rings.

It's barely eight o'clock in the morning, but I know who it is. My eighty-year-old neighbor, Gladys, who thinks nothing of wandering right into my living room after ringing the doorbell, because that, to her, is fair warning. Unfortunately, I must have forgotten to lock the door last night, because I hear her open it and then call out, "Hello? Rachel?"

I close my eyes. I am sitting butt naked, covered in soap and sick, and my neighbor does not have the social awareness not to walk right into this nursery. She's a widow, old and lonely, and I feel sorry for her. Usually.

"Hi, Gladys," I call out, trying to keep my voice cheerful. "I'm just getting changed—"

"Don't mind me, dear. I just came to see if you wanted anything from Price Chopper...?"

"No, I'm fine—"

"Are you sure?"

I can hear her coming down the hall, and I scramble up from the glider, throw the cream blanket draped over the back across my shoulders. It's not big enough to cover, well, anything.

"I'm sure," I call back, sounding desperate and maybe even a little crazed now. "Really, really sure." Even if I did need anything, I'd want to go myself. The last thing I want is to be deprived of my one big outing of the day.

"They've got those butterscotch pudding cups on sale," Gladys continues. She's right outside the door. "Two for three."

"That's okay, Gladys—"

"They're so tasty, aren't they?"

The knob is turning. This woman has no boundaries whatsoever. "Gladys," I say, as firmly as I can, lunging over to the door to press my hand against it, Nathan in my other arm, carried like a football. "Sorry, but I'm just getting changed."

"In the nursery?" She sounds confused. She must be standing right outside the door, maybe even with her eye pressed to the crack between the door and the wall.

"Yes, in the nursery." I can't think of an explanation, and frankly, I don't need to give her one. "I'll come by later, okay? Maybe we can watch *Who Wants to Be a Millionaire?*" Gladys loves game shows.

"Oh..." She sounds disappointed, enough to make me feel guilty. Gladys was probably looking forward to a chat, a cup of coffee, and a cuddle with Nathan. Normally I don't mind her coming by so much; it breaks up the boredom at least, but not right now. "Are you sure you don't want some pudding cups?" she asks, a bit plaintively.

I haven't had butterscotch pudding since I was about six. It was my mother's idea of a fancy dessert. "That's really kind of you, Gladys, but I'm okay. I'll see you later?"

"All right, dear." I hear how she's trying to rally, and it makes me feel even guiltier. "I'll see you later, then," she says, and shuffles off.

I breathe a sigh of relief, and then I change Nathan, and settle him back in his seat, and then manage to rinse off—again—in the space of ten seconds. As I'm getting dressed, I stare at my reflection in the mirror. My hair, once so dark and shiny, looks lank and flat. Clumps have come out in the drain, which apparently is normal after giving birth, but no less alarming. I would have once called my eyes a "warm brown", but now they look dazed, empty, like I'm just a little bit dead inside. My skin is pasty; I didn't get a tan this summer, the way I normally would, when I'd be out and about, busy and active. As for my body... my stomach is a slack, sagging, empty sack; I still can't even fit into what I used to call my fat clothes. Amazing how my tiny, neat bump morphed into this. I feel fatter now than I did when I was nine months pregnant. How is that even possible?

With a sigh, I turn away from the mirror. Better not to look at all, not yet, not until I can handle it better. Nathan still seems happy in his seat; he's found his hand, and he's gnawing his fist experimentally.

I watch him for a moment, and suddenly I can't stand the thought of the empty day stretching in front of me. Cleaning the kitchen and feeding Nathan and watching *Who Wants to Be a Millionaire* with Gladys. Cluster feeding—that's what the books call it—Nathan until midnight, with the vain hope that it will actually make him sleep for longer than forty-five minutes. I already know it won't. And then having to do it all again tomorrow, on basically no sleep at all.

I close my eyes and then I open them again, to see Nathan giving me another gummy grin. This one heartens me, but not as much as the first one did. Suddenly, I decide, with a surge of determination I haven't felt since my son was born, that I'm not going to have another empty day in front of me.

Today I am going to go to the school's barbecue.

CHAPTER 3

LAURA

I study my reflection in the mirror, wondering if I've managed headmaster's-wife chic appropriately. My usual style is a fortyish woman's version of funky, with patterned skirts, knee-high boots, colorful tights, but I've tried for something streamlined and more tailored today, for the school's barbecue.

I'm wearing a knee-length khaki skirt that has been in the back of my closet for about fifteen years, and a sleeveless blue cotton blouse, a sweater in darker blue knotted loosely over my shoulders. My hair, which I usually leave loose around my face or else pulled up into an artfully messy bun, is in a sleek ponytail. I don't look myself, but then again, I don't really feel like myself, either.

We've been at the Wilderness School for two days, mainly unpacking our stuff, although last night we went over to the deputy head's house, on the other side of campus, for a wine and cheese evening. There were a few others there from the senior leadership team, with their wives—the entire team is male, ostensibly because the school is all boys, but it still felt a bit like a throwback to the 1950s, although I did my best to take it in my stride, chatting and nodding and smiling until my

cheeks ached. My mother, an academic who fought in the feminist trenches in the 1960s, would have been horrified. She'd
also probably be horrified by my outfit, the way I'm deliberately changing myself to suit a perceived—and stereotypical
—role.

"It's a little bit Stepford wife, isn't it, Laura?" she'd remark. I
can practically hear her voice now, her head cocked to one side,
her assessing gaze sweeping over me.

And yes, it *is* a little bit Stepford wife, I'll be the first to
admit that. But I know how important it is for Allan to start on
the right foot, to make a good impression, something he finds
anxiety-inducing, even if he never admits as much. He didn't
grow up in the elite world of boarding schools, not even a small
and shabby boarding school like this one. His family is firmly
working class, from Stamford, Connecticut, and he went to the
local high school, and then to the University of Connecticut,
branch campus. He worked hard to smooth out his rough edges,
to make it seem as if he fits into the world of golf clubs and
horse-riding lessons, but I wonder if he ever truly will.

I admire my husband for how far he has come, how much
he's achieved. I, meanwhile, grew up upper middle class, with
all the privilege that comes with it, accepting my education at a
first-rate girls' boarding school without even thinking about it,
walking into the freshman class of a Little Ivy as if it was my
birthright. My mother has always lamented how little I've made
of my education—teaching high-school English is not, in her
view, aspirational enough. When I was working part-time, she
used to call it my "little job." She wasn't impressed that I wasn't
walking to a full-time role at Wilderness, but I tried not to draw
attention to the absence of a job.

"Laura?" Allan's voice floats down the hall and I turn away
from my reflection, smoothing down my hair one last time. Our
bedroom is still full of boxes, although I've managed to unpack
at least half of our clothes. Allan has been busy with various

meetings and introductions, so I've mostly been on my own these last two days, and it's felt more than a little lonely.

I texted Katherine, to see how she was getting on, and while she replied quickly, she didn't take up my offer of a video call. The only glimpses I've had of my son is when he walked by the headmaster's house from or on the way to the rugby pitch, in a gang of boys, but at least he waved once. I am struggling not to feel isolated, adrift, although I tell myself I just need to get used to this new normal. Friends, familiarity, will come with time. I've moved enough to know that, yet it's hard to trust it now.

"Hey." I step out into the hallway and Allan eyes me up and down before nodding in approval.

"You look very nice."

"Thank you." His attitude—that up-and down glance—seemed to suggest I needed his approval, which irritates me, but I tell myself not to be so contrary. I wore this outfit for that very purpose, after all. I know how much he wants to make a good impression at this barbecue for all the faculty, and I'm doing my best to live up to my husband's expectation of what a headmaster's wife is *supposed* to look like, even though I'm not sure that's even a thing, anymore. But maybe it is here, because even after just two days, I sense that Hawley, Maine, is a little behind the cultural zeitgeist.

Based on the spattering of comments I heard at the wine and cheese night yesterday, the school seems to be run as an uneasy mix of traditional British boarding school circa the mid-twentieth century and 1970s progressive, outdoor education. I'm not sure how well those two styles go together, so I can't yet imagine how it's going to manifest itself day to day, but I did learn that they use the old British terms for grades—form one, form two, all the way to lower and upper sixth. Tucker is, therefore, in lower sixth, which sounds strange, but the senior leadership team seemed to see it as a point of pride that they are different from other schools.

"Shall we go?" I ask Allan as he straightens the French cuffs of his shirt. He's wearing a new suit for the occasion, made of cream linen, with a light blue shirt. He's a handsome man, with a charismatic presence, both which work to his favor in school settings. His dark, wavy hair is graying at the temples, which only makes him look more distinguished, and his hazel eyes still sparkle with humor and vitality. His face is chiseled, with a jawline that is every bit as sculpted as it was twenty-five years ago, when we first started dating. He runs every morning at 5 a.m., followed by some weightlifting, and so even though he's approaching fifty, his tall, lean body is muscled and trim. Today, he certainly looks the part of headmaster—handsome, confident, dynamic.

"Yes, let's go." He gives me a quick, slightly distracted smile, and then we head down the stairs.

Outside, the sky has turned a bit overcast, and although it's only the first of September, the air feels not chilly, not precisely, but not warm, either. It's a reminder of just how far north we are—a mere hundred miles from the Canadian border.

A marquee has been set up on the quad, and the catering staff have brought out long tables lined with metal serving trays. It's a hog roast rather than an actual barbecue, and the pig, glistening brown, is rotating slowly on a spit in its own tent. I look away from it queasily to survey the gathering crowd.

Allan shepherds me along, his hand on the small of my back; we're early, and so there are only about a dozen or so people milling around, and I don't recognize any of them, except for Stephen Wilcox, the deputy head in charge of academics, and Ted Lytton, the director of wellbeing, inclusivity, and all that jazz. I smile at them both and they smile back, barely.

I'm afraid they might have decided when they met me last night that I was boring, and in truth I wouldn't blame them, because last night I *felt* boring. I didn't talk about anything that interested or was important to me; I was too worried about making a good impression. Now it feels as if the moment to be myself has passed, and as Allan and I greet them, they end up chatting to him, not me, and even though that stings at first, simply because of the principle of it, I find I'm not that bothered, because the truth is, I don't really care about all the shop talk. Maybe I should—I did, when I *taught* at a school—but now I feel a disconnect and I let my mind wander, along with my gaze, as the quad starts filling up with faculty and their families.

There is a table set up for face painting that a dozen or so children have already lined up for, and another one with a man blowing up balloons and twisting them into shapes. Apparently, the headmaster's wife usually organizes the children's activities, but I didn't know that until yesterday, and so thankfully someone else made all the arrangements. I was told this at last night's wine and cheese evening, with the obvious expectation that next year I would take it on—something I can't even think about yet.

The two deputy heads have, most likely unthinkingly, angled their bodies away from me as they talk to Allan, and so, after a decent interval, I murmur my excuses and walk away, grateful to be on my own. Already I know this evening is going to be full of making chitchat with strangers, and although it's just about the last thing I feel like doing now, I straighten, determined to give it my best effort.

I head over to the drinks table, where one of the catering staff is pouring glasses of iced tea and lemonade, and I take an iced tea with murmured thanks.

"Have you been working here long?" I ask her brightly, practicing my chitchat, and the young woman, barely older than Tucker with her blond hair pulled back into a tight ponytail, looks startled.

"Just started this summer, after I finished high school," she replies cautiously. "But my mom and aunt have worked for the school for, like, forever."

"Oh, wonderful." I take a sip of my iced tea; it's weak, almost tasteless, like barely flavored water. I can't think of anything else to say and so, with a small, conciliatory sort of smile, I move off.

The trouble is, I realize as I look around, everyone here knows each other, and they're having those post-summer reunions that all teachers like to have, catching up on vacations, respective families, changes at the school, all that stuff. They don't want to meet someone new, suffer through the necessary pleasantries, and I don't blame them.

A toddler with sticky hands outstretched stumbles toward me, almost barreling into my legs, and I move past with a little laugh.

"Careful there, sweetheart," I say in a jolly tone I recognize as my husband's. The father, chasing her, barely gives me a distracted smile as he hurries by.

I look around for someone—*anyone*—to talk to, but they are all huddled in tight little knots, chatting animatedly, oblivious to me. It feels like entering the school cafeteria in seventh grade, except worse. My hand is slippery on my glass, and I take another sip of the terrible iced tea just to have something to do.

Someone... anyone...

Then I see a woman standing alone on the edge of the quad. She's pushing one of those outrageously expensive designer strollers, the kind that can turn into a car seat or a Moses basket or, who knows, a helicopter. Her hands are clenched on the steering wheel, and she is looking around, seeming a little lost and dejected.

With determination, I start walking toward her. She doesn't see me coming until I'm almost on top of her, and then she looks startled, taking an involuntary step back.

"Hel-*lo!*" I sound way too cheery, almost manic, and I quickly moderate my tone. "Are you a teacher at the school? I'm afraid I'm new here, so I'm just trying to learn everyone's name." I hold out my hand to shake. "I'm Laura Haile, the new headmaster's wife."

"Oh." She takes my hand limply, looking a little wary. She's a pretty woman, with the same coloring I have, brown eyes and hair, but she looks incredibly tired; the concealer she has not rubbed in all the way has not covered the dark circles under her eyes. Her hair, tucked behind her ears, looks lank and a little greasy, and her clothes are shapeless and crumpled, hiding what looks like a lumpy, postpartum, figure. "I'm Rachel Masters."

"Hi, Rachel." I peek over the brim of the stroller, arranging my features into a parody of surprise, as if I wasn't expecting a baby to be in there. "Oh, how absolutely sweet! How old?" I turn to her expectantly. I kind of hate myself right now, but I'm not sure how else to be.

"Um, he's six weeks." She tucks her hair behind her ears, although it's unnecessary. "I'm on maternity leave, but I teach English at the school. I'll be back in January."

"Oh, wonderful," I enthuse, even as I feel a stab of envy I didn't expect. I won't be going back to teaching English in January. "Did you know I teach English, too?" Of course she doesn't know. "Not here, though," I add quickly. "Not right now, anyway." I smile even more brightly to cover my own deep disappointment.

"Oh... right." She looks like she doesn't know what to do with that information. She tucks her hair behind her ears again, a nervous twitch. "What grades?"

"I've done all the grades, from seventh to twelfth, but mainly ninth and tenth grade, more recently. We were at Leabrook School before this—do you know it?"

She nods. "Yeah, sure."

"How long have you been at Wilderness?" I learned last night that's what they call the school—not the Wilderness School, ever, but just Wilderness, which, considering how I feel about the place, seems apt.

"Ten years. I haven't taught anywhere else."

"Oh, wow, amazing." I try to hide my horror at the thought of staying in this place for ten whole years. "What brought you up to Maine?"

She gives me a look like I'm stupid, although she masks it quickly. "I'm from Portland."

"Oh, of course." *Not* being from Maine is the anomaly here, I've learned. "Well, I haven't spent much time in Maine before this, but I'm looking forward to exploring the area."

"Do you hike?" she asks, and I can tell from her tone that she does, or used to.

"A bit?" I give what I hope is a tinkling little laugh. "I'll have to do more of it now, though." I decide it's time to change the subject. "So, what's this little man's name?" I'm assuming the baby is a boy, since he is wearing blue, although these days you never know. Some parents deliberately dress their girls in blue, their boys in pink, to disrupt gender norms, and, it seems, to confuse people.

"Nathan."

There is something about her tone that sounds a little flat, a little off, but maybe she's just tired. "Is he a good baby?" I ask, before remembering that you're not supposed to call babies good or bad anymore; the whole landscape of parenting—and mothering in particular—has changed. "How's the sleep?"

"Oh, it's..." She stops, and for a second, I think she might cry. Her face freezes, and she draws a slow, deliberate breath. "Not that great, to be honest."

"Oh, I'm sorry." For the first time, I truly warm to this woman; I feel a deep empathy for her. Tucker was a terrible sleeper. For eighteen months, I basically existed in a fugue state. The mothers I met in the baby group said I was a different person once he finally started sleeping, and it was true, I was. I was myself again. "It's so tough, isn't it?" I tell her, a throb of memory in my voice, and she blinks, seeming startled by my understanding. "No one tells you about the sleep deprivation," I continue. "It's like you know it in *theory*, but to experience it is something else entirely. It's... unimaginable. No wonder they use it as a method of torture." I have a memory of lying in bed, listening to Tucker cry, and physically being unable to get up for several minutes. I was simply too tired.

To my surprise, Rachel's whole face lights up, transforming her from an exhausted, worn-out woman to someone who must be beautiful. Her eyes go from mud-brown to rich amber, and a flush enters her cheeks. "It *is*," she says, with so much feeling that I think she must be having a truly hard time. "It really is."

Just then, baby Nathan starts to grizzle, and a look of panic flashes across Rachel's face, followed by an even more heartrending despair.

"Oh..." she says, futilely, and I know exactly how she's feeling—that this moment of adult conversation is slipping away, that the baby's needs will subsume her, again.

"Is he hungry?" I ask, and she shrugs, disconsolate now.

"I fed him twenty minutes ago, right before I came."

"Why don't I take him for a bit, then?" I suggest, realizing after the words are out of my mouth, that this is a bit presumptuous. This woman barely knows me, but I know how she's feeling, that sense of exhaustion, of feeling so depressingly trapped. "I can walk around the quad with him, if you like? I've had two of my own, and while the baby stage was a long time ago, there are some things you never forget. You probably want to catch up with some of your colleagues...?"

"Oh..." She looks longingly toward a knot of teachers, and I know she's feeling like she has to refuse, like it's the done thing, because it usually is. You don't let strangers wander off with your baby, even if you want to. Desperately.

"I'll bring him back to you after a few minutes," I suggest, wondering why I'm pressing so much. I don't even want to hold a fussy baby, do I? And yet I want to feel useful, for Rachel's sake as well as my own, because since we arrived at this school, I've felt like a spare part. At least now I can be helpful to someone.

"Oh... okay," she says, the word slipping out of her like it surprises her. "If you're sure you don't mind."

"Not at all," I assure her, almost merrily, and then she is undoing the five-point harness and lifting him out of the stroller. He really is *tiny*, dressed in a pale blue onesie and khaki overalls that swim on his small frame.

"He doesn't fit into zero to three months sizes yet," Rachel says, like an apology.

"He's adorable," I reply firmly, and then I take this little scrap of humanity into my hands. I remember to support his head and neck, at least, but for a second, I am panicked, because he's so very light, and I haven't held a newborn baby in a very long time. I bring him to my chest, one hand behind his head, the other cradling his body. "What a total sweetie," I tell her, a reassurance. I start bouncing back and forth on my feet a little, the way I did with Tucker and Katherine. The grizzling noises he was making stop, at least for a few seconds, which fills me with relief. "Go and enjoy yourself," I tell her, genuinely glad I can help her out in this way. "We'll be absolutely fine."

Rachel smiles at me, her eyes lighting up again, and one hand flutters by her side, as if she wants to reach out and touch me. "Thank you," she says, sounding so heartfelt that my own spirits lift.

As she walks away toward her colleagues, I hope I've found a new friend.

CHAPTER 4

RACHEL

I walk away from the headmaster's wife—I can't actually remember her name—and my arms feel weightless, like they could float up to the sky. My body feels weirdly weightless, too, like I've lost my center of gravity, like I'm walking on the moon.

It feels completely disorientating, and, I realize, totally wonderful. I'm *free*.

I make my way toward the three other English teachers at the school—Liz Pollard, the department head, John Fowler, who teaches the junior years, and Anthony Weiss, who is the former head of department, approaching retirement, part-time, and teaches only Advanced Placement classes.

"Hey," I greet them, my tone a cross between shy and jubilant.

"Rachel!" Liz does a theatrical double take as she turns, one hand pressed to her ample chest. "You're out and about *already*?"

"Well," I reply, managing a small laugh, "it has been six weeks."

"Six weeks, really?" Liz's eyes widen and she shakes her head slowly. "I can't believe it."

I can, I think, because every single day of those six weeks has been hard-won, drawing blood.

"Yep, well, it has been," I say, and there is the very slightest edge to my voice, because, as a single, childless woman, Liz has been a bit passively aggressively sneering of my maternal state. When I first told her I was pregnant, her way of congratulating me was to say, "I suppose the population needs to reproduce."

"How's the... baby?" Anthony asks, and I can tell he can't remember if I've had a boy or girl. I've known these people for ten years, have taught alongside them the whole while, so you would think they could bestir themselves a little more about the fact that I gave birth, but the truth is, I'm not surprised. The world doesn't exist outside the school for Liz or Anthony, and John has two little kids of his own, and lives an hour away. He gives me a sympathetic smile, and I am grateful for it.

"Nathan is doing well," I tell Anthony, with a slight emphasis on my son's name.

"Where is he?" Liz looks around, as if she expects to see a baby suddenly appear out of the ether.

"The headmaster's wife is holding him for a bit." I glance around, and I see her with Nathan out of the corner of my eye. She's walking along the buffet tables, jiggling Nathan and pointing out the different foods to him.

"Laura?" Liz fills in, and there is something slightly repressive, almost condemning about her tone, I'm not sure what. Liz isn't the friendliest toward other women; having taught at a boys' school for the entire thirty years of her career, maybe she's used to being one of the only females around. In any case, she's never truly warmed to me, nor I to her.

"Yes, Laura." I nod, glad to be reminded of her name. "She seems nice. She used to be an English teacher."

"Did she?" Liz sniffs, sounding dubious. "I suppose you haven't heard about the absolute debacle your replacement has been?" she adds, changing the subject with something like relish. Everyone likes a bit of gossip. "I don't know *what* we're going to do."

"No, I haven't heard, what?" I fold my arms, fighting against an urge to clasp them around a baby I am not holding. While I feel intoxicatingly liberated, I also feel weirdly bereft, almost naked, without Nathan. It's been less than five minutes.

"She's just gone and pulled out," Liz says, with the same relish, even though it surely means more hassle for her and the other English faculty to be down one teacher. "Her boyfriend's accepted a job in San Francisco, and at the last minute she decided she has to go with him."

"What?" For a second, I can't believe it. "You mean, my job is... available?" My mind starts to race, leaping ahead to possible scenarios.

"We'll have to scramble for a sub," Liz continues. "With all of us covering the classes until someone suitable can be found. It's a complete pain, to be perfectly frank."

Who? I wonder. Wilderness doesn't get a ton of applicants for any position advertised, because of its remoteness. When I first moved here, I thought I'd stay for only a couple of years before moving on, but then I fell in love with the school, with the area, and soon after that I met Kyle.

"If you're really stuck..." I begin, trying to think of how to frame what I'm going to say in a way that sounds reasonable, but before I can, Liz jumps in.

"Don't worry, we'll figure it out." She gives me a decidedly patronizing smile. "You just enjoy this special time with your baby." I'm pretty sure she's already forgotten his name.

The conversation moves on then, and I know I've lost my opportunity to suggest what I was immediately thinking—that I could come back early. It was more Kyle's idea than mine to take maternity leave till January, although I did read how important those early weeks and months can be. Still, when I was pregnant, I had no idea my life was going to be like this.

I want my job back. I *need* my job back.

"Who's going to do the hiring?" I break in, even though they're taking about something totally different now—the yearly trip to Boston the eleventh-graders take every October that the English faculty chaperones. Anthony and my cover were meant to be the ones going.

Anthony purses his lips and Liz looks slightly annoyed at my interruption. "Probably the new head. He seems to be pretty... keen." She, Anthony, and John all exchange knowing glances, and Anthony smirks a little, which makes me wonder what that is all about. Is the new headmaster too eager or something? I think of Laura's overbright voice. She definitely seemed to be making quite the effort and, while I appreciate it, I think I know what Liz means, at least in relation to the headmaster's wife. It felt like she was trying too hard, and yet I really do appreciate her offering to take Nathan. It's more than anyone else has done.

"Okay, well." I swallow down what I want to say, that he won't have to hire anyone because I'll take my old job back, because I'm not sure I want to see everyone else's reaction just now.

Liz's gaze flicks to my chest and then up again, and her mouth twists in a grimace. "Um, maybe you should go find Nathan, Rachel?" she asks, and that's when I feel the damp patch on my shirt. I'm leaking milk.

I turn and walk away from them blindly, conscious of their whispers and clucks. Liz and Anthony, at least, aren't even trying to hide their disdain, but I know I shouldn't be all that surprised. Anthony has always been a little smugly superior; he's been at the school for forty years, and when I started, aged twenty-three, he acted as if I was this unpredictable, outrageously emotional wreck, no matter how I behaved, simply because I was a woman. I've heard he was against the hiring of female teachers at all, back in the 70s when the school had something of a rebranding.

As for Liz, well, she's from the same mold, even though she is a woman; solidarity of the sexes is not a thing with her.

And John? He's always been quiet, even weak. Whenever I've had to go to battle for something he agrees with in principle —like including more diverse authors in the curriculum—he has stayed quiet, refusing to ruffle any feathers.

No, I'm not surprised by any of their reactions, although I am a little hurt. For four years, Deidre was my ally in the department, as well as a true friend—and I miss her now more than ever, even more than I expected to. There's no one to laugh with, or exchange that knowing smirk, that subtle eyeroll, when Anthony makes one of his sexist comments or Liz goes all bombastic.

I knew I'd be lonely without Deidre, just as I was before she came, but I didn't let myself think about how it would feel. I suddenly find myself looking for Laura, even though I barely know her, and when I see her standing by the buffet, she catches my eye and waves, hoisting Nathan a little higher, and I smile faintly and wave back.

Laura continues to move down the buffet, jiggling Nathan, and a weary sigh escapes me as I glance at the crowd milling around the quad. A couple of people catch my eye and wave, but no one makes a move to come over to me. They weren't expecting me to be here, I know, and I can tell they're not quite sure what to do with me now. I could make a big fuss of introducing Nathan to everyone, but I don't actually want to do that just now, because I wanted to save it for a day when school had already started, so I could come into the classroom. I suppose I can do that anyway, but I have a feeling people will think it's a bit much. It's a baby, not the Second Coming.

I've given ten years of my life to this place, I think, so why do I feel so alone right now?

Then I hear someone call my name, and I turn to see Kate, a part-time PE teacher, jog over to me. "It's so good to see you," she enthuses, and I am heartened. We've always gotten along, have gone out for drinks at the one bar in town on occasions. Her department is even more male-dominated than mine. "How are you?" she asks, and her gaze drops to my chest and then zooms back up again, which reminds me that I am leaking milk.

"I'm feeling pretty proud that I made it here at all," I say jokingly, except I am actually serious. I fold my arms across my chest to hide the milk stain.

"You should be," Kate replies firmly. She has three boys, all out of the house now, and I have a feeling the baby years are a very distant memory for her. She isn't about to empathize about sleep deprivation the way Laura did; surprisingly, I felt like the new headmaster's wife really got it. It was a little embarrassing, how grateful I was, that she seemed to understand. "Where is your little baby?" Kate asks, looking around.

"Over there." I point to where Laura is doing the jiggle and bounce baby dance, by herself. "The headmaster's wife was kind enough to take him for a bit."

"She seems really nice," Kate says in agreement, and my glance moves over the crowd, looking for Laura's other half.

"What about the head?" I ask. "What do you think of him?" I had met him briefly, when he came here last winter, after he'd accepted the position. I didn't do anything more than shake his hand, but he seemed very friendly, smooth and assured, maybe a little too much. I suppose I met his wife then too, but I can't remember her from that time.

"Yeah, he seems, *you know*..." She makes a little face. "Very head-like."

I know what she means—headmasters come and go at a school like this one, a lowly rung on the ladder climbing ever higher, to bigger and better schools. They're always looking for a way to make their mark as swiftly as possible—get a couple of kids into Ivy Leagues, or raise the money for a new building, and then move on.

"Don't they have a son at the school?" I ask, recalling that tidbit of information from somewhere.

"Yeah, he's a junior." No one actually uses the terms the school insists upon—forms, rather than grades. It's so pretentious for a place like this. "Boarding, on a rugby scholarship."

"So, they'll be here for two years at least?" I half-joke, and Kate shrugs.

"Who knows?"

"Well, at least he seems nice, right?" I've spotted him now, moving along a line of teachers, shaking hands with each one like he's the President of the United States.

"It's his first headship," Kate says, like an explanation, and maybe it is. Heads can be so self-important, especially early on in their career. We've both seen it, lived it.

"I should go get Nathan," I tell her, a farewell. My breasts are feeling heavy and tight, and I am conscious of the still-damp milk stain on my shirt. As much as I dread heading home, I know I can't really hang around here much longer without embarrassing myself, if I haven't already.

"Okay, well, stop by the school, sometime, okay? Don't be a stranger." Kate gives me a cheery wave and then heads off, and even though she was super friendly, I can't help but think she's relieved to be shot of me. Or maybe I'm just being paranoid.

I make my way over to Laura, my steps slowing as I get closer. I had maybe ten minutes of time away from Nathan, and now that I'm facing the rest of the day, the evening, my whole *life*, with him, the dread is setting in, along with the deep and unutterable loneliness.

"Hey." I try to pitch my voice bright. "Thanks for taking care of him, Laura. I hope he wasn't too much trouble?"

"Not at all," Laura assures me. "He didn't make a peep,

actually." She's still jiggling him quite vigorously, and I'm not surprised he didn't cry. He looks a little dazed by the perpetual motion.

"I'll take him now," I say, and I hold my arms out. Laura hands him over quickly enough, and as my arms close around the familiar shape of him, feel the small but solid weight of him against me, something settles inside me, a rightness, but also a heaviness, the feelings inextricably intertwined. "Thank you," I tell her, and she gives a little laugh.

"Oh, it was nice to hold a little baby again. It's been a long time. And," she adds conspiratorially, leaning a little closer, "it kept me from having to make chitchat with a bunch of strangers, although I know I should." She lets out a little laugh, seeming embarrassed for admitting as much.

I'm surprised; she seems so assured to me, as assured as her husband. She must be in her late forties, but she looks good, her hair is thick and only faintly stranded with gray, and the tailored clothes she is wearing suit her trim, athletic figure. I wouldn't have thought she'd be someone who dreaded small talk.

"Just a lot of names to remember," she adds, like an explanation, and I nod.

"Yeah, it can be hard at first, I guess." When I came here, I was so excited to finally be teaching, I don't remember being lonely, but I must have been. In fact, I know I was, because I met Kyle when I went out to a bar by myself as I had no one to go with. And when Deidre came, six years after I started, I realized afresh just how alone I'd felt at this school. Now it's back to square one—for me as well as for Laura.

"Yes, it always takes time, doesn't it? To get used to a new place. You just have to be patient. I need to remember that." She smiles and nods, as if she wants to shrug off her earlier remark. "What about you? Are you enjoying your maternity leave?"

No, would be the honest answer, I realize. Absolutely and completely not. But I can't say that, obviously, so I smile and jiggle Nathan a little, the way she was a few moments ago. "It's an adjustment," I tell her, and she nods in immediate understanding.

"I never knew how the days could feel so long, and yet I still struggled to find the time to brush my teeth." Laura laughs.

I feel a rush of gratitude, again, that she really gets it. "Exactly," I agree.

She must hear the throb of emotion in my voice, because she says suddenly, "Would you like to come over for a coffee one day? Or herbal tea, if you're off caffeine? I'm meant to be hosting the new parents' tea tomorrow, but perhaps the day after that?"

"Um, sure." I am surprised and a little taken aback by the invitation; I don't think I exchanged more than a dozen words with the last headmaster's wife, and she and her husband were here for six years. He stayed a little longer than most, wanting to make it till his retirement.

"Around eleven?" Laura asks, eyebrows raised expectantly. "Will that work with his sleep schedule?"

Sleep schedule? As if. "Sure," I say, and I give a little nod of farewell. "Thank you. I'm looking forward to it."

As I head back to the stroller I parked at the edge of the quad, I realize I really am.

CHAPTER 5

LAURA

Once again, I am staring at my reflection, wondering if I look the part that I struggle to play. It is the new parents' tea in twenty minutes, where I will pour drinks and make chitchat with forty strangers for an hour and a half.

Today, on this gray day with the rain streaking steadily down the windows, I have opted for a no less tailored look than the barbecue last night, but a little warmer—gray pants, a white turtleneck sweater, understated gold jewelry. If I want to keep playing this role, I'm going to have to get some new clothes, because this is the extent of my wardrobe for the so-called sophisticated look.

I wonder why I don't want to wear my usual clothes—a brightly patterned midi skirt, a cute little cardigan—and I know it is both because I don't want Allan to disapprove, although he would never say he did, and because I don't want this role to be the real me. I want to separate myself from it somehow; it feels easier, even if it isn't, to act like a headmaster's wife rather than to actually be one. When I go downstairs, I can inhabit that role in a way that I can't here, and I don't even want to. I want to be myself, even if I'm not sure who that is. What it isn't, though, is the Stepford version of a headmaster's wife.

According to Allan, the barbecue was a success. He met just about everyone, gladhanding all the way, while I, after handing baby Nathan back to his mother, managed to chat to a few people, mainly part-time teachers and the catering staff, which felt a little easier than approaching the old guard, all of whom looked as if they'd already decided to be unimpressed by everything, including me. Still, I made an effort, smiling, nodding, offering pleasantries, enthusing about the school, the town, the state of Maine. I must have mentioned wanting to go hiking at least a dozen times. I even started to believe myself.

As Allan and I walked back home in the chilly twilight, my legs and back aching from standing for so long, he was practically fizzing with enthusiasm.

"What I like about this school," he told me, "is that it has a clear sense of history and tradition, but there's also room for improvement and progress, which is exciting." This was the gist of the supposedly impromptu speech he gave to the faculty back in February.

"So, you can make your mark," I filled in for him, meaning to sound enthusiastic, and he looked slightly affronted.

"I wouldn't say that, not exactly. It's not about making my mark, but *improving* the institution itself, for its own sake, rather than mine."

"You don't need to talk to me like that, you know," I told him, and I'd meant to sound gently teasing. "I'm not one of the staff you have to impress."

"I'm not trying to *impress* anyone, Laura," he said, clearly miffed.

Somehow I was hitting all the wrong notes without meaning to. "I didn't mean anything by it," I tried to explain as we walked across the darkened foyer, up to the second floor. "Only that you can be honest with me, Allan."

"I thought I was," he replied, and I stifled a groan.

We didn't used to argue like this. We used to laugh about stuff, quite a lot, even; I can't remember the number of times I met Allan's wry gaze across a room and knew we were thinking the exact same thing. Sometimes, if I was talking to a tricky teacher or demanding parent, Allan would pull a face from afar, and it would take all my self-control not to burst out laughing.

He never took himself too seriously, before becoming a headmaster, and that was something I loved about him. There was an earnestness to him, to get it right in a world that felt foreign, but it was tempered with a self-deprecating ruefulness that made him warm and approachable.

However, since becoming headmaster, Allan seems to have decided he needs a certain kind of gravitas.

I decided to try a different tack. "That head of English was pretty fearsome, wasn't she? Quite the dragon, breathing brimstone and Shakespeare quotations." I didn't particularly relish the thought of being under her, if I did take a job here one day, although that prospect seemed unlikely, considering the staff turnover rate was so low, and an English teacher had left just last year; they had managed to cover her position without making a new hire, which said something about the school's budget.

"Maybe," Allan allowed, with a very small smile that reminded me of how he used to be, if only a little, "but I'm sure she knows her field."

It seemed like that was the closest we were going to get to a moment of solidarity, and I decided to take it as a win. Allan no doubt felt like he needed to start on a serious note, make sure everyone respected the role. I understood that, but I wish he could be a bit more real, a bit more himself, with me. As we headed to bed, I told myself all we needed was a little time, for *both* of us to get used to our roles.

It's a reminder I need this morning, when I am doing my

best not to dread this tea. I don't even know why I'm dreading it so much; I have done things like this before, more or less, in other schools. Maybe it's because those were off my own bat, and I hadn't been expected to do them. Or maybe it's because Allan's attitude has become so changed, so seemingly contrived and put on, since arriving here, although I know it was happening before then, since he was appointed. It's like he studied the headmaster's character in *Tom Brown's School Days*, or maybe Mr. Banks in *Mary Poppins*, and decided that's how he would be. Not, of course, that I would tell him any such thing, but I can't help but think it. My husband didn't used to be so... pompous.

It feels disloyal and mean, even to think that way, to use that word, but the truth is, I can't help it. Allan irritates me now.

Stop, Laura! Stop thinking this way!

I glare at my reflection, a bit of self-scolding that I know I need. These negative thoughts don't help me, or Allan, or my marriage. I can't let myself give in to them.

Straightening my shoulders, smiling in determination, I turn from the mirror.

Downstairs, the catering staff has taken over the kitchen; there are one hundred and twenty scones laid out on trays, along with little dishes of clotted cream and strawberry jam. The school, I have discovered, has a thing about acting like it's in England.

"Everything all right in here?" I ask Diane, who is in charge, and she barely looks up from the tray of mini pains au chocolat she is putting into the industrial-sized oven.

"Everything's fine, Mrs. Haile."

I told her to call me Laura, but she hasn't, so far. I don't think Allan has asked for any of the catering or grounds staff to call him anything but Mr. Haile, but that's understandable, I suppose. I can practically hear him telling me about the importance of his role, garnering respect.

As I turn away from busy Diane, I am pulled up short by the pettiness of my own thoughts. Why am I thinking about my husband, the man I love, this way? And I love Allan, I do. We met at Columbia, in New York, where we were both training to be teachers. I noticed his suave handsomeness right away, of course, and it made me suspicious, turned me off. But over the next few weeks and months I saw how shy he was, how charming he could be, in such a self-effacing way, and after that, I fell in love with him in about five minutes. I need the reminder of our past, of how Allan used to be and how I need to believe he still is, now.

I walk out of the kitchen, leaving the catering staff to do their thing, as I check that the living room is in pristine condition, which, of course, it is; the housekeeping staff come in to clean the whole ground floor three times a week. Subtle uplighting on every oil painting, it feels like a museum, but I suppose it means I don't have to keep our living space tidy for guests.

There, I think, almost proudly. *I've thought of something good about this place, this situation.*

Now, if only I can think of another...

Actually, hosting the tea turns out to be surprisingly pleasant. The parents who come in are both uncertain, having left their children for the first time, and eager for reassurance, and as I pour tea and pass out scones, I listen to them and commiserate, because I certainly know how it feels to leave your children. I've barely heard from Katherine since we arrived, and even though Tucker is just down the road, in one of the boarding houses, it feels like he's operating in a separate universe. I texted him to ask to have dinner with us later this week and he seemed unenthusiastic about the idea, although maybe I was reading too much into a text. I know I can't really blame him; being the headmaster's kid has to be hard enough, but I want to spend time with my son.

Tonight, I'm finally going to video-call Katherine, if she remembers, and I can't wait. It's only been three days since we've seen her, but with the moving and the meeting people, it feels like an age, an epoch. A text, even a flurry of texts, just isn't the same; I want to see her face, hear her voice, gauge her expression and tone. Then, and maybe only then, will I actually feel okay about leaving her behind—not that she'd see it that way. She was thrilled to stay, which, I admit, stung just a little, even as I understood it, and was glad her life wasn't being disrupted... the way mine was.

As the parents start to leave, looking forlorn at having to say the final goodbyes, I help the catering stuff clear up. It doesn't take long, and then the rest of the day stretches in front of me, and I have absolutely nothing to do.

I could unpack the last few boxes, of course, or organize books or clothes or papers a bit more. I could walk into town, which I haven't done yet, or I could walk around campus, say hello to the boarders who have moved in today. I could find Tucker and see if he wants to get an ice cream or a Coke with me. I doubt he will, but he might take pity on his poor old mother, at least.

I don't do any of those things, though. I head upstairs to our living room, in the room facing front. Our furniture all fits—the deep, L-shaped sofa, the coffee table, the bookshelves, the TV. I feel a little more grounded in here, in a space that feels a little more like my own. But I'm still restless, unsure what to do, wishing I had friends to see, lessons to plan, *something*. I didn't realize how much purpose my job gave me until I didn't have it anymore, although, of course, it's not just my job, it's my children, my friends, my parents being nearby. It's *everything*.

Don't do this, Laura.

These kinds of thoughts are a rabbit hole I don't want to go down, because I know I'll disappear, and so I pull on a light jacket, change my flats for walking shoes, and head outside, into the fresh air.

The rain has stopped and the sky is clearing to a fragile blue, and simply being out here lifts my spirits. It *is* beautiful, even the dark trees, and I am glad I can see and appreciate that.

The campus is coming to life, as it always does in September; some students are kicking a soccer ball on the lawn between two of the boarding houses. Others are still moving in, with suitcases and duffel bags, and others are sprawled on the grass or gathered in groups, chatting.

I walk past the boarding houses, smiling at anyone whose eye I catch; some of the boys smile back, a bit uncertainly, while others just look away, like they don't know how to respond to me. I'm not fazed; I got the same reaction as a teacher.

It isn't until I'm halfway to the rugby pitch, where Tucker and the rest of the team are practicing, that I realize what is different about the whole, seemingly pastoral scene. There are no girls.

Of course, I knew Wilderness was a boys' school when Allan first applied, although I was a bit bemused by the news—I didn't think there were many single-sex boarding schools left, outside of military academies and maybe the Deep South. But I didn't think about it much then, and certainly not in the way I *feel* it now—there are boys everywhere. Boys jostling, joking, jeering; boys messing around, being rough or ducking away from those being rough; boys wrestling, guffawing, being both loud and physical, all of it unsoftened by the presence of girls. I'm not sure how much difference it makes, but I'm definitely aware of it in a way I didn't expect to be.

As I pass the humanities building, I see Liz Pollard, the head of English, come out, walking like she has somewhere important she needs to be.

"Laura!" She smiles at me in a way that feels patronizing.

Last night, when I was introduced to her, I had a sense she'd dismissed me before I'd so much as spoken, and so I stayed pretty quiet. Now, I am determined to make more effort. "Hello, Liz. Everything ready for classes day after tomorrow?"

She rolls her eyes theatrically. "Not really. We've had a real wrench in the works."

"Oh?"

"I'm actually just heading over to meet with your husband about it. The woman we hired for maternity cover has decided she can't take the job. *Very* last minute." She huffs importantly.

I find myself staring at her, dumbfounded. "So, you're down one English teacher?"

"Well, yes, but we placed a last-minute advertisement yesterday, and we're going over applications this afternoon. Fingers crossed we'll have someone in place by the end of the month, and we'll just have to cover as best as we can till then." She gives me a sunny smile, the kind that says *this isn't your concern*, and starts to walk by.

I let her, because I am reeling too much from what she has said, and in any case it's not her I want to talk to, it's my husband. There's a need for an English teacher and he didn't even *ask* me?

I vacillate between an incredulous fury and a worse, deeper hurt. It is so obvious to me that I could be the replacement. Yet, Allan is trawling the internet looking for no-hopers who don't have a job in September of a school year? *Seriously?*

There is no point going to confront him now, because Liz Pollard will be meeting with him, so I keep walking toward the rugby pitch, hoping I can be distracted by the sight of my son. I've barely seen him since we arrived, except from a distance, in a gang of rugby boys. The fact that Wilderness offered rugby at all was a major draw of the school; most American boarding schools offer football instead of this rougher, less padded version, but Tucker has always loved it, ever since he joined a rugby club when he was seven, begun by a British teacher at the school where Allan was working. Throughout the years, Tucker has always found some way to play it, even though it's not a particularly popular sport in this country. Playing varsity rugby is, quite literally, a dream come true for him.

Not so much for me—seeing the boys collide and crunch always makes me wince. Tucker has already suffered a concussion and two broken fingers over the course of his rugby career. Still, I've tried to come to just about every match, to cheer him on, because I know how important the sport is to him.

Now, I stand at the edge of the field, pulling my jacket more closely around me, because the pitch is less sheltered than the rest of the campus, and the wind sweeps across it, chillier than I would have expected for early September. I spot Tucker right away, jogging along the side of the pitch; even after three years, I still don't really understand the game, so I watch as they pass the ball, tackle and scrum, without really knowing what is going on.

I catch Tucker's eye and wave, not too wildly, and he gives me a little nod that seems to be all the acknowledgement I am going to get.

The boy next to him catches my eye, as well; he says something to Tucker, laughs, and then looks straight at me. There is something bold and assessing about his gaze, resting on mine for no more than a split second, and I feel oddly unsettled by the tiny exchange.

Before I can even process it, they are both jogging back down the pitch, and my gaze instinctively tracks the unknown boy—he's powerfully built, over six feet, with short brown hair and hazel eyes—I could see their color even from across the pitch.

I look away, even more unsettled, determined to dismiss him and his bold stare. Hopefully, Tucker will make some good friends on the team.

I watch for another fifteen minutes or so, shivering slightly in the breeze, before I turn away and head back to the house, but as I reach it, I suddenly swerve for the main building, where the headmaster's office is. I am, I realize, determined to talk to Allan about the English teacher position. I want to know, at least, why he didn't even tell me about it.

By the time I get there, he's alone, or so his assistant, Helen, a fiftyish woman with a very strong Maine accent, tells me. I flash her a quick smile, tap once on the door, and then slip into the study.

Allan is sitting behind the desk, his forefinger pressed to his chin as he studies the screen of his laptop, a slight furrow between his straight, dark brows. He looks up when I come in, his expression of concentration morphing into surprise, and, I fear, the tiniest bit of irritation.

"Laura!" My name is more a question than a greeting.

"Hey." I smile, determined to be casual. "How is your day going?"

"Fine. Busy."

He sounds wary, and I decide to cut to the chase. We didn't use to play these games, where we framed our words, carefully pitched our tones. That wasn't how we operated at all, and I am determined not to play them now. "I ran into Liz Pollard earlier. She said the teacher who had been hired for maternity cover—" *Rachel's* maternity cover, I realize suddenly— "is a no-show."

"That's right." He sounds even warier.

"I can cover it, Allan," I say quietly. Firmly. And then I wait.

Allan lets out a short little sigh. "There are appropriate channels for this kind of thing, Laura, as you very well know—"

"Yes," I cut across him, "but it seems like a no-brainer, to me." I keep my voice pleasant. I can't believe we're almost arguing about this; it's so *obvious* to me. "I am a qualified, experienced English teacher," I point out, "and I'm already here.

Why would you go through all the HR red tape and recruiting if you don't have to, especially for a subpar candidate, which is all you'll surely get at this late stage, when school is about to start?"

"We actually have two decent candidates—"

"Allan." I move forward, place my hands flat on his desk, and force him to look at me. "What's going on? Why didn't you tell me about this position? Why didn't you even consider me?"

His mouth tightens, pursing up like a prune. "Laura, be reasonable. I don't want to be accused of nepotism the very minute I arrive—"

"That would be a valid concern if you'd shoehorned me into a job, made a space for me that wasn't there." My voice throbs with emotion, with intensity, because he *knows* this. When a full-time job came up at Leabrook after he'd been made deputy head, he recommended me for it. It was no big deal. Why is this any different? "But there's a *need*," I continue, striving to sound reasonable, "a very obvious and urgent need, and I can fill it. This *isn't* a big deal. This is obvious, to everyone, it seems, except you."

He is quiet for a moment. "Your name didn't come up in discussions."

I absorb this, refuse to let it hurt. Yet. "Why would it, if they don't know that I'm an English teacher?" I lean forward, forcing him to meet my gaze. "I'm assuming you haven't told anyone?"

He looks away. "I can't remember if I mentioned it."

I whirl away from the desk, struggling against a sudden and surprising tidal wave of fury. I can feel it poised to crash over me, drag me under. I take a deep breath, let it out. "I don't understand why you're being like this," I say, as much to myself as to him. "If we were at Leabrook, you wouldn't have thought twice about putting my name forward. I know you wouldn't have, because you *did*, once upon a time." And, I realize, he would have been excited for me. We were a *team*, supporting and encouraging each other. Why does it feel like that has changed?

"But we're not at Leabrook," he replies in a measured voice that irritates me all the more. He's refusing to get riled about this, and meanwhile I am fuming.

"So, what's the big difference?" I turn around. "Just that you're the oh-so important headmaster now?"

His mouth tightens again. "I'm glad to know what you really think of my job."

"Come on, Allan!" The words explode out of me. "Be *honest*. Why don't you want me to take this job? This can't just be about the fear of being seen as nepotistic, because I know people would understand. Couples are hired by the same school all the time, especially in remote places like this. It makes *sense*."

He is silent for a long moment.

"I didn't realize it was so important to you," he finally says. "I suppose... I suppose I thought you'd appreciate the time to settle into a new place. Figure out your new role."

What role? I think, but don't say, because as I stand there, staring at him, his slightly supercilious glare turning into a thoughtful frown, a hint of sorrow in his eyes, I know Allan is right, at least in part. I loved my job, but it wasn't as important to me, back at Leabrook, when I had so much else going on—my parents, my children, my life—as it is now, when I feel like I have nothing. It was just one piece of a varied and complex puzzle. But now, when those other crucial pieces have been taken from me, teaching has become everything. The *only* thing. And yet, for a second, I can see things from Allan's perspective, or almost; I realize I might be acting a bit over the top, when all we're talking about is a single term of teaching.

But I feel it, all the same.

"I don't know why I can't do both," I say as levelly as possible. I try to smile.

"It's a full-time position, Laura—"

"And I don't have anything else going on, save hosting a tea once in a while. Even with that, the catering staff do most of the work. Come on, Allan." The smile I've managed to find threatens to slide off my lips. "I don't want to be some kind of Stepford wife here."

"I never asked you to," he says, and I believe he means what he says. "That's not what this was meant to be about at all." He stops, blowing out a breath, and then slowly he shakes his head. "If it's so important to you, I'll mention it to Liz," he finally says, on a sigh. "She's the one making the hire, but I can certainly recommend you." He finds a smile as he looks at me directly, but his eyes, normally flashing with charismatic fire, look droopy and sad. "You're a good teacher, Laura. I know that."

I've won, I realize distantly, as I gaze back at him, but as I stare at my husband, it doesn't feel like it.

CHAPTER 6

RACHEL

I do my best to make sure Nathan is fed and bathed and dressed by ten-thirty, so I can walk to the headmaster's house, without him screaming the whole way, by eleven. It feels strange, to have something to look forward to in the day, an actual interaction with another person—besides Gladys, that is. The night after the barbecue, I sat with her through two episodes of *Who Wants to Be a Millionaire* and took home a six-pack of butterscotch pudding cups. I ate three of them, methodically and without any real enjoyment, at two in the morning, after Nathan had been crying for half an hour.

But that was last night, in the dazed blur of sleep deprivation and despair, which I can swat away in the morning light, after I've managed to have a shower, blow-dried my hair, put on some mascara and lip gloss. I feel human; I feel *good*. More like myself, the self I used to be.

Before I had Nathan, I was pretty well turned out. I am still one of the youngest teachers at Wilderness, and I liked to dress smartly—tailored skirts or trousers, turtleneck sweaters or crisp blouses. Always heels, although fairly low ones, as appropriate to my position. Hair blown out or pulled up elegantly, discreet jewelry.

I used to feel powerful, walking into a classroom, twenty-five pairs of eyes on me as I pivoted smartly toward the white-board. Just about every other teacher at the school was stuffy, old, boring, the kind who had crumpled tissues in their cardigan pocket, popped throat lozenges as they droned on, nasal and uninterested in what they themselves had to say. I liked being different—interesting, exciting, young, current.

Now, I just feel drab—but at least a little less drab today than normal.

As I push Nathan in the stroller along Main Street, past the movie theater and the hardware store, the drugstore and the coffee shop, there is a little spring in my step. I am actually *going* somewhere, and it is not the library or Price Chopper, which are pretty much the only two places I've been in the last six weeks.

As I approach the imposing headmaster's house, though, nerves flutter in my belly; I don't actually *know* Laura Haile, and I feel out of practice with making small talk with a stranger. There is a good chance I will embarrass myself, by either leaking breastmilk or tears, or both. Nathan might scream or need to be fed, and I haven't yet got the hang of breastfeeding in public, at least not without flashing my boobs and wrangling with the hooks and straps of my nursing bra, which feels like a piece of high-tech military gear. I'm pretty sure Laura will be laidback about it all, laughing and sympathetic, fetching me a blanket, a glass of water, but I also know I'll be embarrassed all the same.

She opens the door before I've even pressed the doorbell, as if she's been waiting for me.

"Hel-*lo!*"

That jolly voice. It makes me jump, just a little. "Hi..."

"Come in, come in." Laura steps aside, waving me through. "Do you want to bring the stroller inside or leave it outside?"

"I can leave it outside." I am a little embarrassed by the stroller, which cost a fortune, and was Kyle's idea. Maybe he thought it would turn me into the kind of mother he wants me to be.

I turn away from her to unclasp Nathan's seat; I've done it a fair few times, but I fumble every time, just as I do now, with the various hooks, clamps, and levers.

"Folding up a stroller was always my Waterloo," Laura remarks with a laugh. "They can be such impossible contraptions, can't they?"

"Yes." I give her a quick smile as I turn, car seat finally in hand. I am sweating. "Thanks for having me over."

"My pleasure! It's nice to be able to get to know you. Come through, come through."

I step into the massive foyer, turning instinctively to head into the formal living room with its fancy sofas and antiques, but Laura stops me, her fingers brushing my arm.

"I thought we'd go upstairs. We've set up our own little living room up there. That room"—she nods toward the living room—"feels so formal. If that's okay?"

"Sure." I realize I am curious to see her private living space.

She leads the way, up the grand, sweeping staircase, to the second floor, where I've never been. Its dimensions are as imposing as the downstairs, but without the grandeur; there are a few framed photographs and paintings propped against the walls, the art looking modern and surprisingly funky, but not much else.

"We haven't got around to hanging those yet," Laura says with a little laugh. "It always takes so long to feel really settled somewhere, doesn't it? I must admit, when it comes to unpacking, I run out of steam after a couple of days."

She leads me into a bedroom that has been turning into a

living room, with an L-shaped sofa that has definitely seen better days but looks squashy and comfortable. There is a photograph, propped on the fireplace mantle, of two children, maybe eight and ten years old. It's one of those professional photos, taken in a studio; the children looked posed, their smiles fixed, their wide-eyed gazes a little deer-in-the-headlights.

"That's an old photo," Laura says, following my gaze. "Teenagers don't like having their photo taken so much, which is a bit ironic, considering the number of selfies they snap and post online everywhere." Her laugh trails off into a sigh, and then she turns to me with as fixed a smile as the ones in the photograph. "What can I get you? Tea? Coffee? Something cold?"

"Herbal tea, if you have it, thank you," I tell her. I love coffee, but I'm off caffeine in the vain hope that it will help Nathan sleep. He is already starting to fidget in his car seat, and he lets out an exploratory squeak as Laura turns to the door.

"Be back in a jiff," she tells me. "Make yourself comfortable."

I prowl around the room, curious to learn more about Laura and her family, but there isn't that much more to see. There is an empty bookshelf with a box of books next to it, and a heap of small, framed photos on the window seat that feels invasive to look through. I settle myself on the sofa, Nathan's car seat next to me on the floor, and jiggle it with one foot.

After this coffee with Laura, I'm going to stop by the headmaster's office and drop off my résumé. I thought about it last night for a long time, and although I haven't talked to Kyle about it yet, even though he called last night, it makes sense to go back to work if they need me, which I think they do.

I know I don't actually need to hand in my résumé like an off-the-street applicant, but since the new head won't have ever seen it, I figured it couldn't hurt to remind him of how long I've been at the school, my decade of faithful service.

I looked up the laws online last night, and if I want to go back early from maternity leave, I technically have to give the school eight weeks' notice. But surely this is more about helping the school out than doing something for myself? They need a replacement, and I know they can't have hired anyone yet. I'm bailing them out of a tight spot; they'll be grateful.

The prospect of going back to work gives me a thrill of excitement, as well as of trepidation. Can I manage full-time teaching, with Nathan to care for? I called Busy Bees yesterday, Hawley's only daycare possibility; he'd already been signed up for January, but, miraculously, they said they have a space now. It could all work out. Although I can't quite imagine teaching full-time on the amount of sleep I'm currently getting, but I'm half-hoping, once Nathan is in daycare, that he'll sleep better. The nursery workers will know how to manage a baby more than I do.

The trouble is, I know Kyle won't be thrilled by the idea of me going back to work so soon; his mom stayed at home until he went to kindergarten. Still, I'm sure I can talk him around and, in any case, it's my life, not his. He'll call again tomorrow night —we try to speak every forty-eight hours or so—and I know I should mention it then... if it really is a possibility. I am hoping, more than I should maybe, that it is.

"Here we are," Laura sings out, brandishing a tea tray worthy of a restaurant—there is a teapot, with a cup and saucer, a French press with another cup and saucer, and bowls of lemon and sugar, a jug of milk and a plate of scones with cream and jam. "Leftover from the tea yesterday," she says with a nod to the scones, "but they were quite tasty. I'm sure you've had them a million times before. If Wilderness is anything like the schools we've been at, they serve the same things at every single function."

"Yep," I say with a huff of surprised acknowledgement. I realize she reminds me of Deidre, just a bit older, with her laughing wryness. I can picture myself joking with her at one of the interminable school events, standing on the sidelines the way Deidre and I did, whispering under our breath and trying not to burst into giggles. "Scones and pains au chocolat for any teatime function, and a hog roast for barbecues. If they do a fancy supper, it's always chicken Dijon."

She nods knowingly as she pours my tea and her coffee. "Sounds about right. Leabrook did roast beef with peppercorn sauce. Every. Single. Time."

"Fancy," I say, pursing my lips in mock admiration, and she laughs, a clear sound. "It's quite a well-known school, isn't it?" I continue. "Leabrook?" Somewhere in Connecticut, I think. Every year, a couple boys from Wilderness leave after tenth grade, to go to a "better" boarding school. A school like Leabrook.

"I suppose," she replies as she hands me my tea. "Better known than this, anyway." She puts her hand over her mouth, wincing theatrically. "Sorry, sorry. I didn't mean... Sometimes these things slip out." She grimaces, shaking her head. "I'm trying to get used to everything, honestly."

I am not offended; she was only stating the obvious, after all, but I am curious about her attitude. I suppose it must be quite a big adjustment. "Were you happy at Leabrook?" I ask.

"Yes. Very happy." She takes a sip of her coffee, her expression turning drawn, a little sad.

I glance at the photo on the mantle. "How old is your daughter now?" I ask, thinking she must be in college since she's obviously not here.

"Sixteen in November. She stayed at Leabrook. She's living with friends." I can tell Laura is trying to keep her tone upbeat, but the way she says it makes it sound as if her daughter has died. That has to be really hard, leaving your child behind. I wonder if Laura wanted to come here at all.

"And your son is here, a student?" I ask.

"Yes, a junior. That is, lower sixth." She makes a face, and I laugh.

"We all say eleventh grade or junior. Only the real dinosaurs use forms."

"Ah, right, good to know. I must have met a few dinosaurs recently, then." She lets out a laugh then, almost like a guffaw, and I find myself laughing again, too. My cheeks hurt from smiling; I haven't smiled this much in six weeks, and I feel lighter inside than I can remember in a long while. It's a good feeling, one that buoys me. I forgot I could feel this way—easy in someone's company, enjoying a chat. It was how I felt with Deidre, and I am surprised but gratified to feel it with the headmaster's wife, of all people.

"You'll get used to it here," I tell her, like a promise. "Wilderness does take some getting used to, I know. It's kind of its own world. Maybe it's the remoteness."

"It does feel like entering a bit of a time warp," she admits. "Like I've stumbled upon Sleepy Hollow or something."

"Hopefully no headless horsemen," I reply, gently teasing. I feel sorry for her; this move had to have been hard on several levels.

Nathan has started to grizzle a bit more, and I decide to risk taking him out, even though it means he might fuss more, and I'll probably have to feed him. I am bent over, unbuckling the straps of his seat—something else I always fumble with—when Laura continues, confessing in a rush, sounding shyly pleased.

"I shouldn't sound as if I'm complaining. It's so beautiful here, and actually I'm excited, because I'm going to be teaching, after all." She gives a little giggle, almost like a young girl, and as I pick Nathan up and straighten, bringing him to my body, I see she is blushing.

"You are?" I ask a bit woodenly. I think I know what is coming, and yet I resist the idea, especially as we've been

getting along so well. Maybe she's going to teach music or something. An extracurricular club, even. *Anything but...*

"Yes, your job, as it happens," she tells me, with another
little laugh, as if I will find that funny, and maybe I should.
"The maternity cover bailed at the last minute, and they obviously needed someone, so I stepped in. I'm glad, to be honest. I
didn't want to be twiddling my thumbs for a whole semester."

Now *I'll* be the one twiddling, I think, as I pat Nathan's
back methodically. He squirms against me, starting to grizzle
and fuss all the more. I am trying to school my face into a
friendly expression, even though a sense of futile rage is
coursing through me, an unrelenting river of despair. I can't
blame Laura for stealing my job... and yet that is exactly how it
feels. "Wow." I force a smile. "Well, I'm glad it all worked out."

"Is there anything you can tell me?" she asks, leaning
forward. "Any tips or tricks?" Her face is animated, her eyes
alight.

She must be in her late forties, but she really is a striking
woman—good bone structure, thick hair, nice figure. I feel a
rush of envy, not just for the fact that she's taking my job, but
for who she is, *where* she is, in life. She's way past all this messy
baby stuff; her breasts aren't leaking, and she is not going to be
up eight times tonight with a crying baby. Her days aren't
stretching in front of her, endless and empty, save for feeding,
changing, not sleeping. Her children are grown up, more or less,
and they don't need her anymore. Frankly, that all sounds
pretty wonderful to me.

"Umm..." My mind blanks. Part of me doesn't even want to
help Laura, even though I know that's unfair. Nathan squirms
against me and I fight a sudden, overwhelming urge to scream—
or burst into tears. "It's always good to have a firm hand," I
finally say. My voice feels as if it is coming from outside of
myself. "Boys, on their own, can be a bit rowdy, especially with
a female teacher." I think of how I used to stand at the front of

the classroom, hands on hips, a friendly but appraising gaze in place. Feeling on top of the world. "You need to let them know who's boss right away."

She looks intrigued, as well as a little nervous. She nibbles her lip for a second before asking, "How did you do that? Especially when you started out? You must have been pretty young—"

"Twenty-three." I had to work extra hard to prove myself—not just to the students, but to the other teachers. And I did it, by sheer effort—and I want the opportunity to do it again. It's only one semester, I tell myself, but right now that feels like it might as well be the rest of my life.

Nathan has started to cry, proper howls. I'm going to have to feed him, something I really don't want to do right now, with all the palaver it will entail.

"Is he hungry?" Laura asks, her face softened into sympathy. "Do you need to feed him?"

"Yes, probably." I feel miserable, and still far too close to tears; there is a lump in my throat that hurts to speak past.

"Would you like a blanket? Or a glass of water?" she offers, just as I thought she would, and for some contrary reason, it almost makes me angry.

Before I can respond, Laura rises from her seat and takes a soft cashmere throw from the back of the sofa and hands it to me; I'm worried I'll get it dirty, but I drape it over my shoulder all the same while Nathan continues to squirm and shriek.

"Shall I take him while you get yourself organized?" she asks, already reaching for the baby. "I remember what a to-do it was, especially at the beginning. No one ever tells you that breastfeeding might be natural, but it doesn't *feel* natural."

"Amen to that," I mutter.

She scoops up Nathan while I fuss and fumble with my stupid bra. I am blinking back tears, both in disappointment at knowing I will not be able to take back my job, and the sheer futility of my life right now. I don't want to be here, grappling with my bra, needing to feed my baby, feeling so frazzled and messy and out of control, everything such hard work. I don't want Laura Haile, who seems so nice and normal and understanding, to be the one to take my job. I'd almost rather it wasn't her, if someone had to do it, although I'm not even sure why.

By the time I've managed to haul my boob out of my bra, Laura has returned with a glass of water, which she sets on the table by my seat, and then hands me Nathan, discreetly looking away as I manage to get him to latch on and then cover myself modestly with the soft blanket.

"I hope you didn't think you needed the blanket for my sake," she says with an apologetic little laugh. "I just thought sometimes women like a little privacy, but *I* don't mind either way, I promise."

"It's fine," I say, because right now that's all I can manage.

Laura is quiet, and the only sound is Nathan's guzzling, which is ridiculously, cringingly loud. He sounds like a trucker downing a can of Budweiser. I'm just waiting for the sound of the can being crushed, his loud burp.

"Do you have family nearby?" Laura asks, and now her tone is gentle. She must sense my fragility. Hell, she must *see* it.

"My mom is in Portland, but she works full-time," I say. Much to her own bitterness and regret; if my dad had stuck around, as she's told me many times, she wouldn't still have to be a secretary aged sixty-two. "My husband Kyle's parents are only twenty minutes away, and they come by every so often, but they work, too." His mother is a nurse in the ER, working all hours, and his dad is a plumber. I don't think they've ever really known what to do with me, a self-proclaimed career woman, who went to college, to boot; when I took maternity leave, my mother-in-law seemed relieved, like she now knew where to place me, except the problem is, I haven't lived up to her expectations—or Kyle's.

"What about other moms?" Laura asks. "In Hawley?"

I shrug; I hate feeling so pathetic. "There's a baby group I go to." Hawley's only one, and all of twice, but maybe I'll make more of an effort, especially now I won't be going back to my job until January. The injustice of it burns, even though I know it's not really unfair. Nathan is still tiny, and I did request leave until January, which was actually a compromise between Kyle and me; he wanted me to take the whole year off.

It's just I'd gotten my hopes up; I'd pictured myself striding into school in one of my smart outfits, even though I know I wouldn't actually fit into those clothes right now. I'd seen myself as I'd once been, in control and on top of everything, smart and sophisticated, and not as I am now, a frazzled mess, with milk-stained clothes, a leaking body, a fussy baby.

Just then, Nathan pops off my breast, and milk jets into the air, spattering the coffee table with drops. He lets out a roar of fury and briefly I close my eyes. Perfect. Just perfect.

Laura laughs easily and takes a napkin from the tea tray to wipe away the drops, while I try to get Nathan to latch back on.

"I remember finding it so hard," she remarks, "at the beginning. I felt as if I wasn't in control of my own body. It was so... unsettling."

"Yeah." That's *exactly* how it feels, but I can't say anything more, because I am too close to embarrassing myself—by crying or screaming, I'm not sure which. Something, though. I am very close to doing something.

"What about your husband?" she asks. "Does he work at the school?"

I almost laugh at that. Kyle, at the school? He barely managed to finish high school, scraping by with Cs and Ds, maybe one hard-earned B. We're very different that way, but it hasn't bothered me. Kyle's great in other ways—good with any kind of DIY, a big bear-like guy, competent and capable, who makes me feel small and safe. I didn't think I'd ever fall for a guy like that, but I did. He slid onto the bar stool next to me and ordered a beer, then turned to me with a quiet smile and said, "I don't think I know you." Something about the way his brown eyes glinted, his dark head cocked to one side, the simple *solidness* of him, hooked me right then and there. Already he felt like someone I could trust.

"No, Kyle owns his own landscaping business," I tell her. "But, in the fall, he heads up north and works for one of the big timber companies, as a logger."

"Oh, really?" She looks surprised. "Do you know, I didn't realize there was still logging in Maine... but I guess there must be. There are so many trees."

I nod, ignoring the sarcastic little voice inside me that remarks what an incredibly astute observation that is. It isn't Laura's fault that I'm angry at her for taking my job. "Yes, up in the north woods, there's still plenty going on. Most loggers are freelance now, like Kyle. They have their own separate businesses in the summertime."

"So, when will he be back?"

"He tries to come back about every other weekend, and then a longer stretch over Thanksgiving and Christmas, and then back for good in late March." I speak matter-of-factly, but I feel that yawning pit opening up inside me. Six months. Six months of basically being a single mother to a very demanding infant.

"Goodness, so you're all on your own?" Laura looks sympathetic, but also a little horrified. "That must be hard. If there's anything I can do to help..."

Yeah, give me my job back. I bite my lip, hard enough to hurt, to keep from actually saying such a thing, because I am that desperate. If I begged her, I wonder if Laura would agree to give up my job. I think she might, and I am actually tempted to try. A few tears, while Nathan is crying? I could guilt her into it, if I really wanted to.

I don't, though, because I know it doesn't work that way, and I don't want to embarrass myself any more than I already have. And if Kyle knew I was even thinking about going to work so soon, he'd be disappointed—and worse, he'd be hurt.

So I force a smile and then I look down at Nathan, who is still guzzling like his life depends on it, and try not to let the tears still crowding my eyes fall. The only thing worse than Laura taking my job is her knowing how much it hurts me, and taking it anyway.

"Thanks," I tell her, forcing an uplift to my voice that I don't remotely feel. "I'll keep that in mind."

CHAPTER 7

LAURA

I take a deep breath, letting it billow through me, buoying my confidence.

You need to show them who's boss.

Rachel's words echo through my mind. It's hard to picture her walking confidently into a classroom; she seems so tired and dispirited now, barely put together, but that's what new motherhood can do to you; I remember it well, even after all these years, and I feel sorry for her.

But I don't want to think about Rachel now; I need to focus on the present. Focus on the twenty-five eleventh grade boys on the other side of that door, waiting for me. Tucker isn't one of them, which is probably for the best, but I will teach him later in the day.

I press my hand to the door, anchor myself in this moment. Breathe deeply again, because I need to.

Why am I so nervous? I've been a teacher for over twenty years, admittedly with some large gaps to stay at home with Tucker and then Katherine, and part-time for a lot of it, but still. I know my way around a classroom. I'm teaching a unit on

poetry for the months of September and October, which I *love*.
I've got this.

No, it's not my own ability that is making me nervous right
now; it's everyone else's attitude toward it. Allan might have
told me I'm a good teacher, but I don't think he managed to
convince Liz Pollard, even though she agreed to hire me. The
other supposedly worthy candidate wasn't that accomplished,
after all. Still, Liz seemed very dubious of my skills when she
handed over the eleventh-grade syllabus, heaving several sighs
as she warned me that "you might find we do things a bit differently here."

As if Wilderness would have a better English department
than Leabrook. I knew she was just trying to throw her weight
around, and my résumé *is* a little patchy, thanks to long breaks
for child-rearing, but still. I resisted the urge to big myself up,
knowing she wouldn't appreciate it. I wanted to make a good
impression, even though, for whatever reason, it already felt like
a lost cause. Liz Pollard had taken against me from the moment
we met. Maybe she's like that with everyone, the kind of person
who always needs to feel just that little bit superior. I don't
want to picture her supercilious expression now, as I am about
to step into the classroom.

The bell has already rung. I am going to be late. I straighten
my shoulders and then open the door.

If I'm hoping for some kind of inspiring *Dead Poets Society*
moment, I don't get it. I wasn't really hoping for that, of course;
just about every teacher I know actually hates that movie,
because Robin Williams is not really a good teacher; he is self-
ish, narcissistic, and irresponsible. But kids love it, and I suppose
we all secretly crave that kind of starry-eyed approbation he
engenders in them.

What I get now, though, is twenty-five boys slouching in
their seats, smirking at me. At least, that's what it feels like.
There's a smell of testosterone in the air, a metallic tang of

sweat mixed with the cloying scent of cheap body spray, a whiff of sports socks, unwashed hair. The smell of boyhood—that is, boyhood that is on the cusp of manhood, overpowering and aggressive.

The smell catches at the back of my throat. I'm used to smelly classrooms; I taught seventh-graders last year, many of whom had yet to figure out the benefits of deodorant on their burgeoning bodies. This, however, feels different. The smell isn't just overpowering, it's... menacing.

Or maybe I'm being fanciful, because I feel so vulnerable right now. I have so much to prove.

I walk briskly across the room and open a window. Behind me, I hear someone stifle a laugh, and I tense.

"There. That's a little better," I say as I turn around. I scan the room, not meaning to meet anyone's gaze quite yet, but a boy in the second row is staring at me so boldly that my gaze is unwillingly caught by his. I immediately recognize him as the boy from rugby, who looked at me before, and then laughed and said something to Tucker. Even from across the classroom, his gaze seems to drill directly into mine.

I feel my cheeks warm, and it takes me at least a second too long to look away, around the room at the rest of the boys.

"So." I walk slowly to the desk, place my hand on it to steady myself, and turn around. This time as I gaze around the classroom, I avoid the boy with the unnerving, direct gaze, his hazel eyes glinting knowingly. "My name is Mrs. Haile, and I'll be covering Mrs. Masters' classes until she returns from maternity leave in January."

I sling my bag off my shoulder and reach for the register I printed out this morning. My throat feels dry as I start reading out the names and get various "here"s in response—some sullen, some bored, some quiet, one barely suppressing laughter. Still, I feel myself start to relax into it—this, at least, is familiar.

Then I call, "Ben Lane" and I know whose voice it is, even before I look up.

"Here." His voice is quiet, deep, and very assured. There's something so *knowing* about his tone, almost intimate, without any juvenile smirk or jeer.

I look up, and once again I'm looking at those unblinking hazel eyes—Ben Lane—who is staring straight at me, a hint of challenge in his gaze, his chin slightly lifted, a faint smile curving his mouth. This time, I am not disconcerted; I am annoyed. If he wants to play these little power games, he has picked the wrong woman.

I flick my gaze away, deliberately indifferent, and then return to the register. "Mark Lyndsey?"

"Here."

And so it goes on.

By the time I get to the end of the list, I am tense again, and struggling not to be. "Right." I put the register on the desk and look up with a bright smile. I do not look at Ben Lane. "We're starting a unit on poetry, moving through the various ages and stages, from the early 1800s, the start of Romanticism, to contemporary poetry, including works by the current Poet Laureate—anyone know who that is?"

I wait, but no one says a word. No one's expression has even changed, except perhaps to slacken into boredom.

"Something to learn," I murmur as I move to the book-shelves running along one whole wall of the classroom; there are a couple stacks of poetry anthologies there, looking old and dusty. I nod toward the boy closest to me. "Could you help me pass these out, please?"

The first two poems on the syllabus are from the Goth-ic/Romantic period—"Annabel Lee" by Edgar Allan Poe and "O Captain! My Captain" by Walt Whitman. I decided to start with the Poe because I didn't want to invoke *Dead Poets Society* on my first day, but as I flip open the anthology to find it, I feel a frisson of unease, maybe even of regret. The poem is both romantic and macabre; will these boys be able to handle it without being silly?

Of course, I can handle some silliness. I've done *Romeo and Juliet* with seventh-graders; Lady Macbeth's "unsex me here" speech with giggling ninth-grade girls. I've talked about the homoerotic overtones in Oscar Wilde's *The Picture of Dorian Gray* with a class of squirming seniors; "Annabel Lee" is positively tame in comparison to any of those. Besides, kids these days are far more sanguine and knowledgeable about all this stuff—sex, gender, consent, balances of power, all of it—and very little fazes or shocks them anymore. In fact, it can be a little disconcerting, when the students you are teaching are less bothered by the material than you are.

So, I can handle this. I know I can. I take a quick, steadying breath, as discreetly as I can, and then smile at the class.

"We're looking at 'Annabel Lee' by Edgar Allan Poe. Does anyone know anything about Poe?" I raise my eyebrows, cock my head. Wait.

Boys shuffle in their seats, look around; one clears his throat. A few whisper, titter. They're not behaving that badly, all things considered, but I still feel nervous, and my smile turns fixed.

"Anything at all?" I ask lightly. "Have you ever read anything by him before?" Most kids read a Poe short story in seventh or eighth grade—*The Purloined Letter* or *The Cask of Amontillado.*

"I think we read something, once," a boy from the back volunteers.

"A poem or a short story?" I ask, with more enthusiasm than necessary, as I am so grateful for a response at last.

He shrugs.

I persevere. "Do you remember what it was like? In content or tone?"

Another shrug.

The rest of the class remains silent in a way that is starting to feel oppressive.

Accidentally, I catch Ben Lane's eye; he's smiling at me, almost in sympathy. I look away quickly. The kids at Leabrook were more switched on than this, more willing to answer, to postulate and surmise, to engage and debate. They were well read, in comparison, but maybe these boys are being difficult on purpose, testing the new teacher with their reticence. Never mind. I can handle this. I *can*.

"Well, let me give you a quick summary of Edgar Allan Poe's life," I say as I put the anthology down on the desk and perch on its corner. My knee-length skirt rides up a little, and I tug it down; I can tell the boys notice. I wore one of my old outfits that I felt confident in—patterned skirt, purple tights, knee-length leather boots, with a turtleneck sweater, but now I wonder if it looks like I'm trying too hard to be funky. Relevant. Everything feels like a potential minefield, a misstep waiting to be taken.

"He was born in Boston, the child of actors, in 1809," I begin, scanning the classroom without actually looking anyone directly in the eye. "His father abandoned the family when he was a year old, when his mother died, and he was taken in by a couple in Richmond, Virginia." I pause, and once again I find myself looking at Ben Lane. I don't mean to; it's as if my gaze is drawn to his. He is paying attention, his expression almost rapt, and I am heartened by his response. Maybe he's not going to be as difficult as I feared, and so I continue, my voice gaining energy, emotion. "He left the University of Virginia after one year, due to gambling debts," I continue, my voice growing stronger, "and married his thirteen-year-old cousin in 1836, when he was twenty-seven." This gets the predictable ripple of responses—titters, murmurs, indrawn breath, but nothing I can't cope with. "She died eleven years later, of tuberculosis, and he died a short while after that, when he was just forty, found in a gutter in Baltimore." I pause, my gaze moving around each boy; they are all, more or less, looking interested, or at least not completely bored. "His last words were, according to the attending physician, 'Lord, help my poor soul.'"

Another pause; I can't tell if I am losing them or not. I do not look at Ben Lane.

"So," I ask, reaching for the anthology again. "Considering all that, what do you suppose his poems might be like?"

Silence. I can wait, I tell myself. I have waited out many a quiet classroom, with a smile fixed on my face, but it would have been nice if there was at least a spark of interest, from *someone*. Usually by this time there would be; I thought they'd seemed more engaged, but maybe I was wrong.

I count to ten, then twenty, then thirty. A couple of boys shift in their seats; one boy leans over and whispers something to another. He chuckles softly, glancing at me. I feel frustration lick through me, and worse, a curdling kind of embarrassment. I tamp both down.

"Okay, why don't we read the poem and you can see for yourselves?" I suggest, and the slight harshness of my tone tells me that any control I had in this classroom is already starting to slip away from me. I take another steadying breath, this one audible, and then glance at the register. "Luke Atlee, you can read the first stanza." I search the classroom for the boy in question, but, of course, I don't know who he is, and for an agonized second I wonder if I'm going to get mass resistance, where no boy tells me his name or reads aloud, and they all think it's a great big joke.

Then, thankfully, Luke Atlee starts with the first stanza, speaking in a monotone. "*It was many and many a year ago/In a kingdom by the sea...*"

I breathe a silent sigh of relief.

Somehow, we get through the first verse. I pick a different

boy to read each stanza, and when they've finished, I put the anthology down and give them all a bracing smile.

"So, what do you think?" I ask.

They look surprised by the question; I suspect this is not the way English is normally taught at the school, and I wonder if I'm channeling a little *Dead Poets Society*, after all. I want them to think for themselves, not just memorize the standard lit crit and parrot it back at me.

"Dude's a pedo," someone says from the back, and this is followed by a burst of laughter from around the classroom, like gunfire.

"Why do you say that?" I ask. It's not the most erudite observation, but I've got to work with what I've got.

"Well, you said he married his thirteen-year-old cousin, right?" the boy says. I locate him this time, and I can tell right away he's the class clown; freckled and slight, he's lounging in his seat as he keeps looking at the boys around him, gauging their interest and approval, clearly craving it. "So that kind of says it all."

"Well, actually, there is some evidence that Poe's relationship with his wife was strictly platonic," I reply, keeping my voice light and even. "Although many believe this poem, 'Annabel Lee', was based on his wife, Virginia Clemm, so you are right there."

"So," another voice drawls thoughtfully, and I know, before I turn, that it's Ben Lane. He's sprawled in his seat, khaki-clad legs stretched out in front of him, the material hugging his muscular thighs, his head resting on his hand, his thumb and forefinger framing his face. I keep my expression interested, engaged, but with a little, instinctive vestige of chilly reserve. "When he writes 'we loved with a love that was more than love' what is he talking about?" he asks, his eyebrows raised. "Having a sleepover?"

His arrogant, laughing gaze challenges me, dares me to

respond. There's something far too suggestive in his stare, and I am seriously annoyed by it.

"Well," I reply levelly, "if you read the next line, where it refers to their love being coveted by the seraphs, what do you think that might imply?"

"That it must have been some pretty awesome sex," he drawls right back at me, and before I can respond, the class erupts into great guffaws of laughter, echoing through the room.

It has only gone on for a second or two before the door bursts open, and Liz Pollard stands there, buxom chest puffed out in outrage, hands on ample hips. "Boys, *boys*!" she thunders. "Behave yourselves! I will not have this kind of commotion in a classroom! Where is your teacher?" She turns to me, her eyes widening theatrically when she sees me. "Mrs. Haile," she says in surprise. "Considering all the mayhem, I thought you must have stepped out of the room."

Yeah, right, I think. I have more than a sneaking suspicion that Liz was waiting outside the classroom, eavesdropping and hoping for a chance to sweep in like an avenging angel, putting me in my place, embarrassing me in front of my students.

"We were just having a rather rousing discussion about 'Annabel Lee,'" I tell her as mildly as I can, as if I am not seriously irritated that she has interrupted my class and, deliberately, I think, humiliated me. It is an absolute no-no among teachers, to throw your weight around like this in another teacher's class. She must know this. "So maybe," I add, the very slightest edge entering my voice, "you could let us get on with it?"

As soon as the words are out of my mouth, I know they're the wrong ones. I meant to say them playfully, but I didn't, and it's obvious now that I've made an enemy for life, because I've humiliated her, just as she humiliated me.

Liz's eyes narrow to slits as she regards me and then she gives an exaggerated, theatrical bow. "By all means," she says, her voice filled with derision, and she stalks out of the class-room, closing the door behind her with enough energy to almost count as a slam. A few boys snicker as they exchange gleeful looks, entertained by the drama.

I feel completely drained. The class isn't even half over yet. I turn back to the anthology, but I don't even want to talk about "Annabel Lee" anymore. I was hoping to draw out the themes of love and tragedy, trauma and grief, the dark overtones, the symbolism of the angel... but I got stuck on "Poe's a pedo" and it went downhill from there. I'm usually savvier than that, even with a class that is giving me grief.

Still, I try to rally. To redeem. "Let's look at the opening line," I say, keeping my gaze on the text in front of me, unwilling to so much as lift my head and meet anyone's gaze. "What does it remind you of?"

Finally, thankfully, some lovely student throws me a bone. "A fairy tale?" he guesses, and I could practically weep with relief.

"Yes, a fairy tale!" I try to moderate my voice. I feel the sense of speculative glee start to recede, like a malevolent tide. "Why do you think that is?" I ask, and my voice comes out both cheerful and firm. I've clawed back control, if only just.

Somehow, I manage to stumble through the rest of the class without getting mired in talk about pedophilia or sex, and by the end it feels like I've made some headway. I smile at the boys as they file out without actually meeting anyone's eyes, least of all Ben Lane's.

Why does he bother me so much? Maybe it's the boldness of his stare; maybe it's the fact that for a sixteen- or seventeen-year-old, he looks like a man—over six feet and muscular. There's something potent, almost vaguely threatening about him, but I tell myself I'm being fanciful. I'm just used to teaching younger kids, in classes of both boys and girls; last year, I taught all seventh- and eighth-graders, a lot of them prepubescent, skinny and small. They seem like mere infants compared to these gangly boys, many of whom have broad shoulders, stubble on their chin, a leashed sense of power, of aggression, even when leaving my classroom, which still smells. So why has Ben in particular got under my skin? I've taught older kids before, if not all that recently. This shouldn't feel that different, that hard.

On shaky legs, I go to the window and crack it open a few inches further. I breathe in the fresh air and close my eyes; I am already exhausted, and I have four more classes to get through today, including one with my own son in it. I can do this, I tell myself, yet again. I can.

But as I picture Ben's laughing gaze again, I'm not sure I believe myself.

CHAPTER 8

RACHEL

I am half-sprawled on Gladys's ancient sofa, Nathan sleeping on top of me, watching reruns of *Jeopardy!* and trying not to move in case I wake him up. He's come down with a cold somehow, and he has been furious about his blocked nose, and also sleeping even worse than usual. I'd feel sorry for his obvious anguish if I weren't so tired. Next to me, Gladys is muttering the answers to the questions under her breath.

"Who is Andrew Jackson," she fires back for $600 in American Presidents. "What is the milk frog," she adds triumphantly, for $800 in The Amazon.

I close my eyes. It's been a week since I've had coffee with Laura, and my frail dreams of going back to work died before I could even begin to breathe life into them. After I left her, I walked straight back home, crumpled up my résumé and threw it into the recycling bin while Nathan woke up and started to scream. I felt stupid for believing it could work, furious with Laura, even though I knew it wasn't fair, and worst of all, hopeless.

It's that sense of hopelessness that is the hardest to bear. I grabbed Nathan from his seat, abruptly enough to make him yowl louder, pacing the room like something caged for a few minutes before I made myself calm down. I pressed a kiss to his head and then slumped onto the sofa to feed him. Story of my life now, on endless loop.

It felt even harder to go back to my empty, endless days after I'd had that brief glimpse of what my life could be—my job back, my purpose back, *myself* back. It was as simple as that, as starkly black and white, even if Kyle didn't see it.

We video-chatted the following night, while I fed Nathan.

"How's my little buddy?" Kyle asked, his dark eyes screwed up as he peered at the screen of his phone while I angled mine down to Nathan guzzling away.

"Always hungry," I told Kyle. "Always feeding."

"He's like a little tanker." Kyle sounded proud of even this feat—the ability to breastfeed. How about *my* ability to be a human milking machine?

After I gave birth, Kyle was wonderful. He kissed me, with tears in his eyes, and told me I was the most incredible woman on earth. And for a few seconds, sweaty and triumphant, my newborn baby cradled in my arms, I *felt* like the most incredible woman on earth.

Unfortunately, I've been disappointing everybody ever since.

"He's had a stuffy nose," I told Kyle, "and a little bit of a cold, but I think he's doing better now."

"How are you doing?" Kyle asked as I angled the phone back to my face rather than my baby and boob. His expression was soft with concern, his eyes drooping at the corners, which made me more honest than I would normally be.

"I'm really tired. He's still not sleeping, and it feels like a kind of torture sometimes. Sleep deprivation, right?" I joked-but-not-joked. "Isn't that actually a form of torture?" I think of what Laura said, and feel a pang of something like affection for her, or at least affinity.

Kyle's lips tightened, his eyes flashing what looked like irritation as he nodded his acceptance, but I knew I probably shouldn't have said anything. He doesn't like it when I complain about Nathan—and that's how he sees it, *complaining* rather than being honest. His mother, apparently, was a saint or a superhero, maybe something of both. According to Kyle, when he was little, she was never tired, never impatient, certainly never hopeless, although I haven't told him about feeling that. According to his mother, Kyle slept through the night at two weeks. If both are true, they almost certainly relate.

"You need to get him on a schedule," he said, which is what his mother says, and makes me want to scream.

"You know I would if I could," I replied, as mildly as possible. "Unfortunately, he's not a clock I can wind."

"That's not what I mean, Rachel, and you know it." Now he sounded annoyed, and I closed my eyes briefly, even though he could see me on his screen, and my reaction would probably just irritate him further, another sign I am not coping as I should —as I always have done before, and as he clearly needed and expected me to.

"I do know. I'm sorry," I said as I opened my eyes, although I wasn't exactly sure what I was apologizing for.

"If you need help," Kyle suggested, "my mom could come down on the weekend..."

Whenever Kyle talks about me "needing help", he makes it sound, without meaning to, I think, like I'm not coping when I should absolutely be able to. When everyone else, including his mom, does, easily.

"I'm fine, Kyle," I said as I stroked Nathan's head. "I just need more sleep."

I did not particularly want his mother, Tracy, coming over "to help." She has done a few times since Nathan was born, and she tends to give me lots of unwanted advice, usually with the attitude of someone who has done this all before but better, and then she offers to do something like scrub the toilet or mop the kitchen floor, when what I really want her to do is hold the baby so I can sleep, uninterrupted, for just a couple of hours. That would be heaven, but Tracy rarely offers to hold Nathan, beyond a quick, thirty-second cuddle. She'd much rather be doing something, which is an impulse I understand, but it's not all that helpful.

I never say any of this to Kyle, though, and I didn't that night. I just smiled and asked him how he was, how the logging was going.

"We're doing some underwater logging," he told me. "Which is pretty cool."

"Wow, yeah." I tried to muster some enthusiasm. I knew already that some lumber companies focus on retrieving logs that were cut around two hundred years ago, and then sank in one of Maine's big lakes during a log drive. Thanks to the cold, fresh water and its lack of oxygen, the wood has been preserved and people can pay good money for that kind of quality timber. "Are you still coming home the weekend after next?"

"Yeah, hoping to." In the past, Kyle has tried to come home one or two weekends out of four, but now with Nathan here, he said he'd come back more. I hoped he really meant it.

"Okay, great," I managed, and Kyle just nodded.

He's never been a big talker, and I long ago accepted he's never going to be much of an emoter, either. And, generally, I've been okay with the way Kyle is. When I was in college, naïve and idealistic, I thought I wanted an academic guy—the kind with hipster glasses and a scruffy beard, who made ironic quips and loved the classics. I dated a couple of guys like that, and realized pretty quickly that their so-called depth was actually depressingly shallow.

Kyle was the opposite of that in every way—the classic still waters run deep. Unlike those other guys, Kyle didn't have arrogance or attitude. We'd only gone on a couple of dates when I mentioned I wasn't able to change the lightbulb in my bathroom because I couldn't manage to unscrew the fixture. He came over, unasked, with a stepladder, screwdriver, and a new lightbulb. He changed the bulb in my bathroom and checked all the others, in a solid, silent sort of way, needing no thanks, just wanting to take care of me.

I was old enough to realize that was the kind of guy you could trust, the kind of guy you could spend your life with. Kyle has always made me feel safe, protected, cherished... until I had Nathan. Until I showed him that I wasn't the competent, capable can-do woman he'd married. And he doesn't even know the dark truth of it all—that I cry in the shower, that sometimes I fantasize about getting in my car and just driving away, heading north, through the trees, that I spend hours imagining myself in my classroom, childless. I'm not about to tell him, not when he looks disappointed when I simply say I'm tired.

"I should probably go," I said, even though I didn't have anything to do, anywhere to go. "You look like you need some sleep, too." I tried to smile as Kyle nodded grudgingly.

"Yeah, I guess." He paused, and something flitted across his face—sadness? Regret? It made me tense. Had I disappointed him again, without even knowing it? "I love you," he said, surprising me, because he didn't say it that often, and when he did, I knew he meant it.

A lump formed in my throat, and I swallowed past it. I never let myself cry unless I'm in the shower. "I love you, too," I said, and as I disconnected the call, the silence in our little ranch house felt endless, rippling outward in invisible waves, like I was the only person left in the entire world.

. . .

The next six days passed pretty much the same, because since Nathan was born, nothing ever seems to change.

Nathan cried, slept, ate. So did I—although less of the sleep. I went for walks with him in the stroller, through town, to the public library, although not the baby group, and a couple of times to the edge of campus, to watch the students walking between buildings. Classes started a couple of days ago, and I wondered how Laura was getting on with my job. I had a guilty sort of hope she might be struggling, and then tried to banish that mean thought. I considered bringing Nathan for the big show-and-tell at school, but I wasn't ready. I wanted to save it for when I felt more put together, and also because I knew I had one, maybe two, baby visits to the school before people would wonder why I kept showing up. I didn't want to waste one, not in the very first week.

So I stood at the edge of quad and watched as boys joked and jostled each other—my tenth-graders, my favorite class, now juniors, all of them looking so much older, like proper men, striding along in their khakis and blue blazers, school ties and pale blue button-down shirts. I'd taught that class since they started at Wilderness, and last spring, Liz decided I could keep going, see them all the way to senior year, when Anthony would take over the AP class. I missed that class, those boys, the sense that I was helping them, guiding them. I missed *everything*.

After another ten minutes of just watching, some of the boys who didn't know me started glancing over, wondering who I was. I saw John Fowler on the other side of the quad, talking with some teacher, and I knew I didn't want him or any of the faculty to see me skulking around, looking desperate and needy.

I turned and walked back to my house, to my messy kitchen, to an overflowing diaper pail, to the monotony of my life.

. . .

It's Final Jeopardy now, Gladys's favorite, but, to my surprise, she reaches for the remote control—I showed her how to use it, a couple of years ago—and turns it off, before giving me a serious, slightly beady look. "How are you, Rachel?" she asks. "Really?"

It's the *really* that gets me, like she knows, or at least suspects, and so I decide to give her a small, sanitized version of the truth.

"Oh, you know." I try to smile. "It can be hard sometimes."

"Yes." She nods solemnly. Gladys had a son named Mark who died fifteen years ago, when he was only forty, of pancreatic cancer. Apparently, it was drawn out and painful; she nursed him while he wasted away. I never feel like I can complain about how hard parenting is when Gladys has lost her only child and is now all alone in the world; her husband died ten years ago, before I met her. "If you ever want me to look after him," she says, her wrinkled face creased in a smile, "you know I'd love to."

"That's so kind of you, Gladys." I smile without actually accepting her generous offer, because Gladys is a bit unsteady on her feet, as well as a little forgetful. As much as I would love for her, or at least someone, to look after Nathan, for a little while, I don't quite trust her to be alone with him. She'd forget about him, or drop him, or put him in the oven by accident. Well, maybe not the last one, but I still can't do it, and I know Kyle wouldn't want me to, either.

"I should put this little guy to bed," I tell her, finally allowing myself to move a millimeter on the sofa. Nathan immediately startles awake, revealing the total fiction of my statement —he's not going to bed, probably not for hours and hours, and therefore, neither am I, even though everything in me is aching with exhaustion. I feel jet-lagged, like I've been on a non-stop flight to Australia with no sleep. It's okay to feel that way when you're on the vacation of a lifetime, but day after day? Not so much.

"All right, then," Gladys says, rising from the sofa with an audible creak of her joints. "Come for a coffee tomorrow? And a cuddle?"

I nod obediently as she stretches her scrawny arms toward Nathan and I let her take him for a moment, even though she holds him the way you would a dripping towel, away from her body, and I'm semi-afraid she might drop him right on the floor.

"Sleep for your mama, eh, baby boy?" she says, her fingers digging into his little stomach, so he squawks.

I take him back swiftly, bringing him against my body. "Thanks, Gladys. See you soon."

Back at my house, I feed him—again—and then, while he seems content to sit in his bouncy seat, I clean the kitchen, abandoning the effort after five minutes to surf the internet instead. I look up jobs online, teaching jobs at schools all around the world, which is pointless, and worse, unhelpful, because I am imagining myself teaching English in Malaysia—huge salary and housing provided—or at a girls' school in Honolulu, or a day school outside Chicago—anywhere but here. Anything but *this*.

Nathan starts crying after about ten minutes, and I swear under my breath as I slam my laptop shut, a sudden surge of fury flashing through me like a streak of lightning. I read on a blog, I can't remember which one, "I never knew what rage was until I was a parent," and I thought, *yes*. I wasn't an angry person before I had Nathan, but there are times when the complete constancy of his demands, his utter neediness, the total lack of sleep, has me practically gnashing my teeth with rage.

That, apparently, is more normal than the despair—it's mentioned in the parenting books, and the advice is always: leave the baby to cry and take a moment for yourself if you need. Walk around, call someone, breathe. Whatever it takes.

But what if it takes something else? Something more?

In any case, Nathan's crying is short-lived, and after just a couple of howls, he subsides, gnawing on his fist, his eyes wide and unblinking as he stares at me crouched in front of his bouncy seat.

I stare back at him, and my breathing slows. Something in me settles. "We can't go on like this, little man," I tell him. "*I* can't."

Nathan continues to stare at me as he works his baby gums over his fist. It's too early for him to get teeth, but he's really going for it.

A sigh escapes me, slow and long. Then I straighten, and before I can overthink it, I open my laptop again, going through my emails until I come across one from Tamara Watson, who is the school's HR person. I hit reply.

Hey Tamara,

I hope you're well. I just wanted to let you know I'm free for any subbing if it's needed this semester—Busy Bees has space for Nathan, so I have some flexibility.

Thanks, Rachel

My fingers hover over the keyboard and then, resolutely, I press send. A day or two a week of doing something else sounds like heaven right now, and subbing isn't the same as teaching; there would be no lesson plans, no marking, no prep. I'd just have to show up and manage a classroom—twenty-five teenagers versus one baby? No contest.

And maybe, *maybe* Laura won't work out. She seemed a little uncertain, like she was used to younger kids. Maybe she'll rethink it, back out and be a headmaster's wife again.

My heart lightens as I imagine it. I see myself sitting at a desk, my hands folded in front of me, everything so blessedly *quiet*. I can call Busy Bees again, explain the situation, tell them

I need some flexibility—the flexibility that I already assured Tamara of.

It could work, I tell myself. Even if I end up just subbing. A day or two a week, which would probably be the most I'd do, is *not* a big deal. I wouldn't even have to tell Kyle.

I am still thinking about it, imagining myself at the front of a classroom, as Nathan begins to cry.

CHAPTER 9

LAURA

I have been teaching for a week and I am exhausted, the way I was back when I first started teaching, when every lesson felt endless, and I put so much into planning, each class felt like offering my students a piece of my soul, so by the end of a school day, there was little left; I felt like wisps of cotton, blowing on a breeze, all the essential parts of me scattered.

I eventually grew out of that level of emotional investment, as every teacher does, but somehow, I've fallen back into the trap of caring too much, or maybe just feeling too insecure. Every class I've taken has been a challenge, but no more so than the first group of eleventh-grade boys, where "Annabel Lee" felt like my Waterloo. Never mind what I told Rachel about folding up a stroller; facing those boys'—and in particular Ben Lane's—laughing gazes threatens to be my defeat.

Not that I would ever admit as much, to anyone, and certainly not to Liz Pollard.

She came up to me in the staffroom on that first day, while I was getting a coffee and doing my best to avoid chitchat or eye contact. I felt too strung out, and I didn't trust myself to give the necessarily careless replies.

"Is 11A too much for you, Laura?" she asked straight off, no nonsense, cutting to the chase in a way that felt utterly brutal.

I forced a smile, a tilt of my chin. "Not at all, Liz," I replied in as confident and casual a tone as I could muster. "We were just having a... robust discussion." I kept my smile, even as she eyed me with blatant skepticism, and worse, an unpalatable mixture of pity and dislike.

"*Robust*," she repeated, and I nodded.

"Robust."

She eyed me appraisingly, looking like she was debating whether to give me another withering putdown, but, thankfully, she didn't. She just nodded slowly and then turned away.

Fortunately, things did get better, after that first class, if only a little. I taught "Annabel Lee" twice more, including to my own son, introducing the subject matter with a dispassionate briskness that hardly did the poem justice, but was as much as I could manage while still being effective. Then two sets of ninth-graders, learning how to write a persuasive letter, and I was done for the day, only to repeat it all tomorrow. Like most schools, Wilderness taught English to every class every day. I'd always thought it sensible, but right now, it felt like an exquisite, finely tuned torture, with no respite or reprieve.

Allan asked me how that first day went, but in a preoccupied way, like he wasn't altogether interested in the answer, so I gave him the minimum of reply. He has seemed genuinely glad for me, that Liz decided to give me the job, and we've put the argument about it behind us. The last thing I want to do, though, is imply that I'm finding it challenging.

When I video-chatted with Katherine—she'd postponed our chat from the other night—she didn't ask at all, and she didn't volunteer much about her own first day of school, either.

"It's fine, Mom," said with a smile to take the sting from her good-natured eyeroll. "It's all fine."

"Any plans for the weekend?" I asked brightly, and she

shrugged, looking away, twirling a lock of strawberry blond hair around one finger. I gazed at her familiar, beloved face—the scattering of freckles across her nose that I knew she hated, the blue eyes the same as Allan's, everything about her reminding me of a flower unfurling, on the cusp of womanhood—a description that would make her roll her eyes all the more. "No?" I pressed, keeping my voice bright.

"Not really," she answered, which was no answer at all.

I decided to let it drop, because if anything was going on, Katherine clearly wasn't telling me.

I felt that frustrating sense of slipping away, the loss of control that was total, even if I was trying to pretend that it wasn't. After our abbreviated chat, I ended up texting Elise, to get a bit more information about what might be going on, and she replied—blithely, it seemed—that both Katherine and Molly were going to a classmate's sweet sixteen party that weekend. The plans Katherine clearly didn't want to tell me about.

What kind of party? I texted, to which I got an eyeroll emoji which is the reaction I'd expect from Katherine, but not my friend who is meant to be in charge.

A slumber party!! Don't worry, Laura. It'll be fine. Plus two heart and kissy face emojis, which did not make me feel any better, although I appreciated Elise was doing her best. I couldn't resent her for parenting my child when I could not.

Still, I wanted more information; Allan and I have always been strict about sleepovers, because, unfortunately, you can't necessarily trust other parents, and you only learn that the hard way. But Katherine is fifteen, almost sixteen; I know I can't manage her social life forever, nor should I. Still, I wanted to know—would there be alcohol? Boys? Whose house were they going to? Would the parents be present?

I mentioned it all to Allan over dinner; we both had a full day of school the next day and he seemed tired, the lines on his face drawn, his phone resting next to his plate, which was normally a no-no for our family. Maybe our no-phones-at-the-table rule had changed, now we were essentially empty-nesters.

"Why don't you call Elise and ask for more details?" he suggested, as if this were both obvious and easy. "And then you can call the parents in question, if you need to."

"Yes, maybe I will," I replied, even though I knew it wasn't that simple. If I demanded details, names and phone numbers, Elise would take it as a criticism of her parenting. I was already realizing what a high-wire act it was going to be, balancing a friendship with the responsibilities of motherhood. I had to tread carefully, both for my daughter's sake as well as my friendship with Elise.

In any case, it was only Wednesday, and I had two more days of classes to get through before I had to worry about the party.

By the time Friday came around, I was too tired even to care anymore, but I made myself call Katherine, deciding it was better to ask her directly.

"Mom?" She sounded hassled as soon as she picked up, which I tried not to let hurt. Just a few months ago, Katherine had felt like my best friend; we had spa days together, and many Saturdays were spent wandering around one of Connecticut's cute little towns, or watching Netflix, or just hanging out. In the evenings, as I was getting ready for bed, Katherine would often come in and sprawl on Allan's and my bed, legs in the air, impish smile firmly in place.

"Is this a good time?" she'd tease, because she knew, no matter how late it was, I was always up for a chat. I always wanted to be available for my children.

But now, it seemed, my child didn't want to be available for me, and that kind of easy affection felt as distant as the moon.

"I just wanted a few more details about the party this weekend," I told her, keeping my voice as light as I could. "Just so I know what's going on."

This seemingly reasonable request was met with a theatrical groan. "*Mom*. Why? It's just a party."

Katherine had been to all of two parties at the end of last year, at houses I knew, with parents whose numbers were in my phone, and she was picked up at midnight by Allan or me.

"Who's going to this party?" I asked.

Another huff. "People."

"Come on, Katherine." I tried to sound wry rather than worried, but I don't think I quite managed it. "Don't make this harder than it has to be. I'm not giving you the third degree here. I just want some basic information."

Eventually, I got out of her that the party was at the house of Emma Price, a girl in her class I didn't actually know all that well and that I didn't think Katherine was particularly friendly with. She was one of those blond, bubbly in-girls; my daughter wasn't quite at her level, which was absolutely fine by me. So it gave me pause that Katherine was going, that she'd been invited at all.

"How many girls are going?" I asked, and Katherine told me that she didn't know.

"Will the parents be there?"

"Yes."

"Any boys?"

A sulky silence before she finally admitted, "Some, but they're not sleeping over."

I let out a breath. It all sounded reasonable, but I still felt panicky, unsure. Maybe it was just being so far away, knowing there was nothing I could do about any of it, and knowing that Katherine surely knew that, too.

"All right, well, please be sensible and safe, okay? And call Elise if anything feels off or out of the ordinary or... anything. Or call me," I added hurriedly. "We're not that far away—"

"Yeah," Katherine scoffed, "like *seven* hours. You were the one who chose to move, not me." Even though she'd been excited about living with Molly, I knew I couldn't blame Katherine for feeling abandoned; *I* felt abandoned, and I was the one who had left.

"I can still be there for you, Katherine," I said quietly, and she let out a huff.

"Yeah, whatever."

I closed my eyes, fighting against an urge to cry, to scream, to get in the car and go get my daughter, simply because I hated being so far away. It was a *party*, I reminded myself. Nothing more. I did not have to freak out about it. "Okay, well, still," I said. "Call me on Sunday and let me know how it went."

"Okay," Katherine said, grudgingly. She used to love giving me all the details of her life, relating conversations, arguments, jokes; now she parted with any information sparingly, doling it out in paltry amounts.

"I love you," I said, meaning it utterly.

"Love you too," Katherine replied, and hung up.

By Saturday, I feel as if I have limped to the finish line, trying my best not to show it, just in case Allan gives me a sanctimonious I-told-you-so, which he thankfully doesn't. In fact, we celebrated the end of our first week with a bottle of wine and takeout from Mario's last night—his idea.

As I lay in his arms later, counting the stars in the endless night sky I could see out the window, I told myself we're both relaxing into our roles. The newness and uncertainty would surely wear off. Eventually.

Saturday was bright and clear, and that afternoon was Tucker's first rugby match, against another Maine boarding school.

"I didn't know there were any boarding schools in Maine before coming here," I teased Allan that morning. "Never mind two."

"There's actually a fair few," he replied, mildly enough, but with a set to his mouth that made me wonder if I had annoyed him. How quickly and easily the fragile equanimity we'd found last night could start to fracture.

"I'm sure there are," I murmured, conciliatory.

He gave a brief nod, like he was accepting my apology.

We headed to the rugby match separately; Allan had to meet some alumni who had come for the match, while I was on my own. I'd thought, fleetingly, of inviting Rachel to go with me; she seemed lonely, and I could use a friend, but I realized I didn't get her number when we had coffee, so I have no way of getting in touch with her again. In any case, maybe it would seem weird; she seemed a little brittle and touchy by the end of our time together. I'd started to wonder if I'd said something wrong.

Quite a few students and just a handful of teachers are all heading to the pitch; rugby is Wilderness's main fall sport, another one of its British-inspired quirks, since they don't do football, although apparently basketball is big in winter, base-ball in summer.

I'm both excited and nervous about seeing my son play; rugby can be so violent. You'd think in these days of strenuous health and safety measures, it would have been banned, or at least regulated, but every time I see Tucker and his teammates crash into one another, I have to wince. It looks like it *hurts*.

I stand on the side of the pitch by myself, arms folded, trying to smile as I locate Tucker in the scrum. He catches my eye and I wave; he nods and looks away. Then I feel someone else's eyes on me, and reluctantly, unwillingly, even, my gaze moves over to another boy on the pitch. Ben Lane.

What is it about him that unnerves me? I wonder as I keep my gaze moving, not letting it rest on his for so much as a millisecond, even though I can sense he is still staring at me. Is it his boldness? Besides that stupid sex joke on the first day, he hasn't said or done anything inappropriate, nothing I could actually call him out for. But it *feels* like he has, simply by the way he *looks* at me, although even that isn't all that suggestive. More... *intense*, I suppose, although I could hardly explain it to anyone. I don't even want to think about it, to myself.

I have always been scrupulously careful with my students, especially in these times, when a simple pat on the shoulder can be taken the wrong way, and everything becomes a matter of consent, of power balances—or imbalances, as the case may be. I never want to put so much as a pinky toe wrong, and I won't. I know I won't.

It's just because I'm used to younger students, in a coed setting, I tell myself. Liz Pollard was right, in one respect; they do things differently here. At least, things *feel* different.

I angle my body slightly away from the boys, and cast my gaze down the pitch, a faint smile on my face as if I am looking at something. I wonder if Ben Lane realizes how hard I have to try not to look at him, and I also wonder why it is so hard, when it never has been before. Why does this one student affect me so much? What is it about him? I suppose I am hypersensitive to everything, thanks to the perfect storm of challenging elements —a new school, a new position, my children as good as gone, Allan's stress and focus on his job, even these trees.

They loom above the pitch, dark and menacing, and they're just *trees*. I suppress an urge to shiver; it's not that cold. It's a beautiful day, in a beautiful setting, and I am watching my son play a sport he loves. What do I really have to worry or complain about?

A sudden crunching sound from the pitch, followed by a scream, has me whirling back around. *Tucker...*

There is a mess of boys on the ground, a spill of arms and legs so I can't tell one boy from another, but, thankfully, it's not my son who is hurt. He is standing on the edge of the scrum, his hands on his thighs, breathing hard.

The coach blows his whistle, and a few people head onto the pitch, to check on the boys.

My stomach roils; some of the boys have scrambled up, but one is still lying sprawled on his back on the pitch, his hands to his head. I hope he isn't seriously hurt.

A few moments later, the coach comes off the pitch with his arm around the boy's shoulders. He is hobbling, blood streaming from a long cut on his thigh, and he's holding one hand to his head.

It's Ben Lane.

The coach guides Ben to a bench on the side, but there's no one else around to attend to him, and I feel a flicker of annoyance, even outrage. *Yeah, they do things differently here*, I think. There's no nurse or matron to check for injuries? During a *rugby* match?

I glance around for some other teachers or people in charge, but few teachers seem to come to the matches on their day off, and Allan is far down the pitch, by some bleachers, talking to the oh-so important alumni. I'm not sure he's even noticed that a student has been so badly injured.

One of the boarding house assistants checks on Ben, but he looks like he's about seventeen himself, and he clearly doesn't know what to do. He flutters his hands uselessly and then pats Ben's shoulder before moving off.

I hear a burst of laughter from farther down the field; it's from one of the alumni, chatting with my husband, jangling change in his pocket and barely looking at the match, which has already started again.

Ben sits doubled over, his elbows braced on his knees, his head in his hands. He reminds me of Tucker.

Somewhat against my better judgment, based on my previous interactions with this boy, I find myself walking over to him. "Ben," I ask quietly, "are you okay?"

He doesn't even look up; he just gives a little shake of his head and then lets out a groan. My annoyance turns to alarm. The school is being utterly irresponsible here; why can no one even see this save for me? He might be seriously injured; he might have a concussion.

"I think you need to go to the nurse's office," I tell him.

Ben barely seems to take it in, not even lifting his head.

Again, I feel a shaft of motherly concern; this really could be Tucker, and someone needs to take care of him. "Would you like me to walk you there?" I ask gently.

After a second, he nods, and when it's clear he needs help getting up from the bench, I hook my arm through his and help him to rise; he staggers a bit and then straightens, my arm still linked with his. It's the closest I've ever been to him, or any student here.

I glance at the boarding house assistant, who has darted forward again, looking nervous. He's been working here less than a week; I can't help but feel sorry for him.

"I'm going to take this student to the nurse's office," I state firmly, and he nods in relief.

No one else notices as we walk away from the pitch, my arm around Ben's shoulders as he hobbles along. Right now, he is not a threat, or an annoyance, but just a boy. A boy who needs someone to help, and so I do.

CHAPTER 10

RACHEL

I watch Laura walk Ben Lane back towards the boarding house, my hands gripping Nathan's stroller just a little too tightly.

She didn't notice me here at the match; no one has. Sometimes I wonder if having a baby makes you invisible... at least until the baby cries, that is. Then you get all the covert glares, the eyerolls, the barely concealed resentment that you—or your baby—are being so noisy, so distracting. But, today, thankfully, Nathan has fallen asleep in his stroller, and I've been standing at the edge of field, unnoticed by everyone, until I started to wonder if I really *was* invisible; if I held up my hand in front of my face, would I even see it? The essence, the *reality* of me, felt as if it was bleeding out, right here into the grass.

I wasn't going to come today; I thought it might look weird, to just show up randomly at a match, but I saw it on the school's website and a bunch of the rugby boys were in my English class. Ben Lane, the one who got hurt, was one of my favorites. I know teachers aren't supposed to have favorites, but secretly you always do, and I liked Ben from the moment I met him—a bit impish but with a good heart, and a tough background to boot.

I remember him starting in ninth grade, seeming so small—

he had a late growth spurt—yet not homesick, the way so many other boys were. When I asked him if he missed home, the look he gave me was surprise mingled with scorn. "No," he said. "Not at all." Later, I learned he was one Wilderness's "charity boys," taken from foster care. Every year, five percent of the ninth-grade intake are meant to be from such backgrounds; it's in the school's charter. Ben is sadly one of only a few success stories of that program; many of them struggle to adjust to life here, and more often than not they've left the school before senior year.

Besides that, though, I came today because I was also hoping to see Tamara, since I received her depressingly brief reply to my email, but, of course, she's not at the match. Hardly anyone is; it's a cold, windy day, despite being early September, and most teachers are at home on a Saturday. They only come out for the big matches, not an early, unimportant one like this.

Which makes it sting all the more, that I can be invisible even in a small crowd. Do any of the boys even recognize me? Have I changed that much? As I stand there watching, I realize they're the ones I really wanted to talk to, not the teachers.

I miss my students. I miss who I was with them—smart, funny, on the ball.

A sigh escapes me, and I glance again, toward the road that heads back to the boarding houses. Laura and Ben are just two little specks in the distance now.

I think of Tamara's email, short and breezy: *Hey Rachel! Thanks for the heads-up. I'll keep you in mind. Best, Tamara.*

I've read it a dozen times already, analyzing every word, undecided if it's a brushoff or just a quick, positive response that should hearten me. There's no one I can talk to about it—not Kyle, not Gladys, not Deidre, who is over a thousand miles away, and not any of the friends I haven't yet made among the baby group. Kyle keeps telling me to get to know them, but I'm not sure I want to. I don't want to talk about breastfeeding and co-sleeping and quality time. I really don't.

I glance again down the road; Laura and Ben are gone. Worry flickers through me; Ben looked like he was really hurt. I bet Laura is taking him to the nurse's office, but the nurse doesn't come in on weekends anymore; she has to be called on her cell. Laura probably doesn't know that.

I hesitate, and then look around the field. The match is still going, with a handful of half-interested spectators; Laura's husband is chatting to what looks like some potential donors, moneyed alumni he's trying to flatter. He's not even watching the match.

And no one is looking at me.

I start walking back to the rest of campus, bumping the stroller down over the curb and onto the road. I can at least tell Laura that the nurse won't be in her office.

It feels a little... not *wrong*, no, but suspect, maybe, to walk along the road, to be in the heart of the school campus. Technically, visitors have to register at reception, in the Westcott Building. They can't just wander around wherever they like.

But I'm not really a visitor, am I? Even if I am, *technically*, this term, at least. And anyway, it's a Saturday, and the place feels like a ghost town; Wilderness is sixty percent boarding, and most of those boys look to be away, probably on a day trip to Bangor or somewhere. They always like to start the semester with a big trip, wow the boarders with an outing to Acadia or Splashtown, even though both are two hours away.

As I walk along, everything feels empty, and as the sounds of the match fade behind me, I almost feel as if I am alone. I keep walking.

The nurse's office is locked, just as I thought it would be. There used to be someone on duty pretty much all the time, but budget cuts have meant this office is unused more often than not; emergencies can be dealt with at the walk-in center twenty minutes outside of town.

I hesitate outside her darkened office, and then abruptly turn and head to the senior boarding house. Maybe Laura took Ben back there. I start walking, although I'm not even sure why I'm trying to track them down.

I haven't had much reason ever to go into the boarding houses, although I've certainly known where they were. I've dropped things off for boys there on occasion—missed homework assignments and the like. But they still feel like unfamiliar, foreign places as I punch in the key code that hasn't changed in my ten years of teaching and step into the entrance hall.

Both boarding houses are large, solid colonial structures that have been added onto over the years, mainly about fifty or sixty years ago. The smell is equal parts institution and boy—sweat, dirty socks, cleaning fluid, and a lingering odor of burnt popcorn. I know the boys are allowed to make their own snacks in the houses' kitchens.

I leave Nathan sleeping in his stroller in the hall as I step around a heap of cleats and sneakers—all which have named cubbies to put them in—and walk quietly, almost on my tiptoes, into the lounge. I don't know why I'm being so quiet, why I'm not calling out a concerned hello, but the atmosphere in the house feels hushed, strangely secretive. There are no boarders around, or housemasters, and I'm not even sure that Laura and Ben are here, either.

The lounge is certainly empty—a mess of pillows and discarded hoodies on the sofas, some empty game cases on the coffee table. The smell of socks is stronger in here.

Where are they? I turn toward the kitchen, and as I come to the doorway, my breath bottles in my chest, freezes in my lungs.

Ben is sitting on the countertop, legs out in a typical man sprawl, and Laura is standing between them. Her hand is on his bare thigh and Ben's hand is clamped over hers.

My breath comes out in a startled rush, and Laura jumps a little and then whirls around.

"*Rachel*." Laura puts one hand to her chest, a flush coloring her cheeks. A guilty flush? For a second, I can't believe what I've seen. "I was just trying to clean up Ben here." She steps aside, and then I see there is a long, bloody gash on the side of his thigh, and she's holding some cotton gauze in her other hand. I find now I am flushing too, in embarrassment for my own thoughts, the assumptions I rushed to. "It's a nasty one," she says, and then she frowns a little. "What are you doing here?"

What *am* I doing here? Why did I follow Laura and Ben?

"I saw Ben got hurt and I thought I'd see if I could help," I explain stiffly. I take a step into the room. "How are you, Ben?"

He glances up, not really meeting my eye, before he looks down again. "Okay, Mrs. Masters," he mumbles.

"I don't know if he'll need stitches," Laura says. "And he also got a bad bump to the head. I'm worried he might have a concussion."

"He should go to Cary." I speak decisively.

Laura frowns, her brows drawing together quizzically. "Cary?"

"It's the nearest hospital, about an hour away. They do X-rays, MRIs, that type of thing."

Laura blows out a breath. "All right. Is there someone in boarding to take him?"

I look around the empty kitchen with a shrug. "They must all be on a day trip."

A look of something almost like annoyance flashes across Laura's face; her lips tighten and her eyes spark. "There has to be *someone* on duty, surely."

I shrug again. There should be, of course, but that doesn't mean it always happens. Wilderness has always been notoriously short-staffed, cutting corners whenever and however they can. "One of the assistants, back at the match, probably is," I tell her. "You could talk to him."

"I doubt he can even drive." She shakes her head and mutters something under her breath; I hear the word *ridiculous*. "I'm just going to make a call," she says, more to Ben than to me, and she steps out of the room, into the hall.

Ben is still sitting on the countertop, legs sprawled, head bowed. It does look like a nasty gash; I think it will need a couple of paper stitches, at the least.

"Are you all right, Ben?" I ask quietly. "Looks like you took a real beating out there."

He lets out a sound that is half groan, half sigh, and shakes his head.

I take a few steps toward him. "You're supposed to tell me 'you should see the other guy,'" I tease gently, and even with his head bowed, I see the faintest smile curve his lips.

Laura steps back into the room, her movements brisk, her voice matter-of-fact. "Okay, Ben, I'm going to take you to Cary," she announces. "Hopefully you'll get an X-ray there for your head, and maybe some stitches. I'll bring my car around. Are you okay to wait here for a couple of minutes?"

"I can stay with him," I offer quickly, and Laura glances at me, rather appraisingly, I think. I have no idea what's going through her mind, but I feel uncomfortable, all the same. Does she suspect I've wanted my job—her job, now—back? Does she know how desperate I am to do something, *anything*, other than go back to my house and take care of my own son? It's not something I like to admit, even to myself, and yet I know it's true.

"Thanks, Rachel," she says, after a beat, and she smiles at me.

As soon as she's gone, I turn to Ben with a smile. "Do you want some other clothes?" I ask. "It might be cold in the hospital. I could get you a sweatshirt or something."

His head still bowed, he shrugs and then nods, and I ask

him what room he's in. He tells me the number, and after checking on Nathan, who, miraculously, is still asleep, I head upstairs. Younger boys are four or even six to a room, but eleventh-graders have only one roommate, and twelfth-graders get singles.

I find Ben's room; one side is a complete mess of clothes, papers, and toiletries, the other side is military-neat, the bed made with precision, everything put away exactly. I am a little surprised to discover it is this side that is Ben's. I find his Wilderness hoodie folded in a drawer under his bed.

When I come back downstairs, he's managed to slide off the counter and is standing by the door.

"Thanks, Mrs. Masters," he says when I hand him the sweatshirt.

"It's okay, Ben. I hope everything gets sorted out." I smile, even though he's not looking at me. "I miss teaching you guys," I tell him with a little laugh, and he makes no reply. I struggle not to feel embarrassed by the admission.

From the hall comes a squawk-like cry—Nathan. Ben glances up, startled.

"My son," I explain, and then gently tease, "You do remember I went on maternity leave?"

To my surprise, Ben blushes. "Um, yeah," he half-mumbles.

Nathan cries again, and so I go get him, scooping him up and cradling him in my arm as I come back into the kitchen. "Here he is," I say proudly, but if I hoped a sixteen-year-old boy, as one of my former students, would take an interest in my son, I am sadly disappointed. Ben barely looks at Nathan, and he doesn't say a word. Nathan continues to cry, and I try to hush him, wishing I hadn't picked him up. Wishing, even, that I hadn't come back to the boarding house, at all. What am I doing here, really?

Ben shifts from foot to foot, deliberately not looking at me. Nathan's cries are turning shrill.

"I think he wants to be fed," I blurt, and then wish the very ground could swallow me whole. Why on earth did I say such a thing to a student?

Ben is doing his best to pretend I don't exist, and I can't blame him.

Thankfully, after a few more torturous seconds, Rachel comes back in, a little breathless, keys in hand.

"All right, Ben—" She breaks off to glance at me. "Oh, dear, poor little Nathan. Is he okay?"

"Yeah," I mutter, patting Nathan's back. "He's fine."

"You ready to go?" Laura asks Ben. "Do you think you can walk out to my car?"

He nods and Laura waits; it takes me a second to realize she is waiting for me to go first, because, of course, I shouldn't be in the boarding house on my own. I shouldn't really be here at all.

I fumble with the straps and buckles of his seat as I put Nathan back in the stroller, with him shrieking all the while. Then I mutter an apology as I bump the stroller through the door. I wait until Laura and Ben are out of the house and in her car, driving away, before I start pushing the stroller toward home.

I'm not invisible now, with Nathan screaming; as I walk across campus and then through town, every person I pass gives me either an irritable or darkly suspicious look. I can practically hear the question running like tickertape through their mind—
what's wrong with you that your baby is crying that much?

It doesn't help that I'm not even trying to soothe Nathan, or smile at him, or even to pretend to do either; I just keep pushing the stroller, putting one foot in front of another, resolutely, all the way home.

Back home, I take Nathan out of the stroller—he's soaked in sweat and tears from his angry exertions—and collapse on the sofa before putting him to the breast.

I close my eyes as he drinks greedily and I fight a sudden,

sweeping wave of despair. It's one o'clock in the afternoon and I
have the whole day stretching emptily in front of me, and every
day after that.

My mind drifts to that strange scene in the kitchen—Laura
standing between Ben's thighs, his hand on hers—although now
I'm half-wondering if I really saw that at all. Did Laura seem
nervous, like she was hiding something, or am I imagining that,
too? Something about the scenario seemed off, but I don't know
if it's just my sleep-deprived brain jumping to conclusions. I've
never seen Ben act inappropriately or provocatively with a
teacher before; he certainly hasn't with me. Yes, he can be a
high-spirited, sometimes even a bit sly, but not... *suggestive*.
And yet that's exactly what that little scene looked like. If it
wasn't on Ben's initiative, who, after all, was injured and ill, was
it on Laura's?

It's foolish to dwell on it, because obviously I have no
answers, and who knows when I'll see either of them again.
There's no good reason for me to go back on campus, and Tamara's email seems obvious now; she was fobbing me off, placating
me because she probably sensed my desperation. It leaks out of
me, like poison, infecting everyone. She's not going to call me.
She's probably already forgotten my email, or if she does
remember it, it will be with a shake of her head, a twist of her
lips. *Poor Rachel.*

Which is why it is such a surprise, when at nine-thirty on
Monday morning, when I'm still in my pajamas, half-lying on
the sofa watching dumb daytime TV as Nathan feeds yet again,
my phone rings.

"Rachel? It's Tamara, at school."

"Oh, hey—" The enthusiasm in my voice is entirely real yet
sounds over-the-top and artificial.

"It turns out we do have a need," Tamara explains in the
briskly chirpy tone of everyone I've ever known in HR.
"Although not for a substitute teacher. We're down one staff in

the senior boarding house rather suddenly, and we could really use a matron. I know it's not your usual MO, and the pay will, of course, be less, but I thought I'd give you a call to see if you're interested...?"

Interested in being a *matron*—a cross between a house-keeper and a nurse, with a dash of substitute mother thrown in? I know, roughly, what matrons do—the laundry, the tidying up, the giving of medication, the confiscating of cell phones. That sort of thing. The pay is dire.

"What would the hours be?" I ask.

"Tuesdays and Fridays, 1 till 8 p.m., until the October break, preferably, maybe a little bit longer."

The hours are not entirely conducive to home life, but what is my home life? Busy Bees said they had space, and I know they're open till eight. I could do it, at a pinch.

Kyle would be asking me why—why such menial work, for such low pay. I'm a qualified teacher, for heaven's sake. I have a master's degree.

And yet...

"Sure," I tell Tamara, far too cheerfully. "I'd be happy to help out."

"Oh wow, thanks so much, Rachel." Tamara is gushing a bit, sounding surprised, and no wonder. What teacher wants to step in as a matron, for less than half the pay? "You're an absolute lifesaver."

No, I think, as I end the call and Nathan starts to squirm, needing to be burped. *I'm not the lifesaver, Tamara. You are.*

CHAPTER 11

LAURA

I didn't do anything wrong. It's what I keep repeating to myself as I drive to Cary Medical Center, Ben in the passenger seat next to me. His head is bowed, his leg still bloody, and he hasn't spoken since we got in the car. I don't want to speak to him. I can't.

All I can think about is the moment Rachel walked into the kitchen... or, really, the moment just before.

My heart rate starts galloping again at the memory and I take a couple of shallow breaths, trying not to hyperventilate. *How did that happen?*

The trouble is, I don't *know* what happened, if anything. Even now, just minutes later, it feels surreal, hazy. I'd walked Ben to the nurse's office, which was empty, and he suggested he go back to the boarding house. The gash on his leg was dripping blood and I knew I couldn't leave him alone. We went into the kitchen; I told him I'd clean up his leg. I found gauze and rubbing alcohol in a cupboard; he heaved himself up onto the counter.

I was so focused on tending his wound, mainly because I'm not brilliant when it comes to blood and I wanted to seem no-

nonsense, in control. Matronly, if not downright maternal. I said something, I can't remember what. *This might sting a little...* And then I started to dab the gash on his thigh, suddenly conscious of how high up it was on his leg, how unsettlingly intimate it felt.

I could hear him breathing. I could feel his breath, warm on my cheek. I dabbed at the wound and then, suddenly, with no warning, he trapped my hand with his, hard against his thigh, his palm covering the back of my hand completely. I felt his warm skin, the taut muscle underneath, the bristle of hairs, and it was as if my senses were on high alert, my nerve endings tingling to alarmed, aware life. Then I made the mistake of looking up, first in surprise by his sudden movement, but then as my gaze met his, I felt...

I don't know what I felt. I don't want to think about what I felt. A jolt. A jolt of something. I don't know what. *I don't know what.* The moment felt suspended, and yet it could only have been a second, half a second, maybe.

And then Rachel walked in.

I release my breath in a decidedly shaky sigh. Ben looks up.

"Relax, Mrs. H," he says in a low voice, and I stiffen. He has never called me Mrs. H before. Nobody has.

"I'm fine, Ben," I say in my most teacherly tone. "I'm more worried about you. I think you might have a concussion." I am speaking to him as if he is about six. My eyes remain fixed firmly on the road.

"She didn't see anything," he says, and it's as if I've put my finger in an electric socket, shockwaves ricocheting through my body.

My hands tighten on the steering wheel until my fingers ache. My brain buzzes. I cannot think of what to say, and yet I have to say *something*. I can't let this moment pass; I absolutely cannot become complicit in whatever he's thinking happened, because it didn't happen. It absolutely *didn't*. Nothing did.

"I don't know what you're talking about," I state crisply, and out of the corner of my eye, I see Ben smirk, an upward tilt of his lips that oozes satisfaction. I shouldn't have said that, I realize. I should have coldly asked just what he thinks Mrs. Masters might have seen, put him firmly in his place. Instead, he's looking like he's enjoying this, and concussion aside, he probably is. I can picture him bragging to his friends.

I made Mrs. Haile so aggy. It was hysterical. I was pretending to flirt with her. LOL. Such a joke. She must be, like, fifty.

Or something like that. Whatever the teenaged boy slang is these days. I know, I absolutely *know*, that this must all be a joke to Ben, but it's not to me. This kind of thing is how a teacher loses her job. Ends up in court—or worse.

Maybe, though, I'm being paranoid. My position at the school still feels insecure; *I* still feel insecure. I'm annoyed that Allan asked me to drive Ben to the hospital, that he seems irritated that I'd called him at all, when I'd ducked out of the kitchen, needing a moment to compose myself. I'm frustrated that I'm in this situation in the first place, when I definitely shouldn't be. The school should have more staff. There should be structures in place. I shouldn't even be in this car, alone with a student. I know that, and yet here I am.

I decide to ignore Ben for the rest of the journey. It feels the safest choice, even if an entire hour together in the car seems a fraught—and frightening—prospect. It's only been five minutes.

After another ten minutes of blessed silence, Ben suddenly grabs my arm, making me jerk the wheel and give a little yelp as we start to veer off the road.

"What are you doing?" I exclaim as I manage to right the car, my heart pounding.

"I'm going to yak!"

"*What?*"

"I'm going to be sick!" he cries, and with a couple of jolting bumps, I pull onto the side of the road.

Ben throws open his car door and vomits out the side, his shoulders heaving.

Once again, he's a boy like any other, like my own son. I put my hand on his shoulder. "You okay?" I ask quietly, even though he obviously isn't.

He retches a few more times and then slowly straightens before he slumps back into his seat. "Sorry," he mumbles, his eyes closed.

I reach across him to close his door and then straighten, running a hand through my hair. I feel shaky, in all sorts of ways. He probably does have a concussion; vomiting can be a symptom of one. What happened before—*and nothing did*—pales into irrelevance in light of this. He needs to be seen by a medical professional as soon as possible.

"Are you all right for me to keep driving?" I ask, and he nods, his eyes still closed.

Drawing a steadying breath, I check behind me—the road is completely empty—and then pull back onto it. We keep driving.

Forty-five minutes later, I pull into the parking lot of Cary Medical Center. Ben has barely spoken since he threw up, and I am feeling pretty worried. Even as I fret about his physical condition, the memory of that moment worries me. My hand on his thigh. His hand on mine.

Don't worry, Mrs. H, she didn't see anything.

I'll have to report it, I think numbly. Won't I? To protect myself. Although I can already see Liz Pollard smirking at me, making it my fault somehow, asking if I'm sure about what happened, maybe I misread the situation? Anthony will do the same; I can tell he doesn't like me. And if Allan hears anything, which of course he will, he'll be annoyed. *Couldn't you have just driven him to the hospital without incident, Laura? Is that too much to ask?*

But if I don't say anything, isn't that worse? More dangerous in the long run, to keep some sort of secret? Except nothing actually happened, I remind myself. And I will most certainly keep a very large distance between me and Ben Lane from now on. I decide to stop thinking about it and worry about his concussion instead. That feels easier, or at least simpler.

We sit in the ER waiting room for half an hour before he's finally seen, and since he's a minor, I have to accompany him into the cubicle, the nurse pulling the curtain closed with a rattle of rings before she leaves us alone. Around us, I can hear various sounds typical of an ER—groans, murmurs, someone quietly weeping.

"How's your head, Ben?" I ask gently.

He shrugs, not looking at me, and then mutters, "Sorry."

Since I don't actually know what he's sorry for, I decide not to answer that one.

They deal with the gash on his leg first, which is still oozing blood; someone must have clobbered him with the spike of a cleat in the scrum.

"We'll need to do a few stitches," the nurse informs him briskly.

Ben looks alarmed. "Stitches?" he exclaims, his voice rising to something close to a squeak, and she looks nonplussed.

"Yes, you need stitches. We'll numb the area first."

"It's not that." He swallows hard, and the nurse looks surprised and a little rueful at his seemingly over-the-top reaction. He's more man than boy, biceps bulging under his rugby shirt, body tall and powerful, but right now the expression on his face is one of childish fear. He gulps once, twice. "I don't... I don't like needles," he says, and then turns to look at me, his face a picture of silent, beseeching torment. "Please..."

I give him a quick, reassuring smile before I turn to the

nurse. "Is there any way you can close the wound without using a needle?"

She hesitates, looking as if she wants to be annoyed by the request but not quite having the heart to, and then she shrugs. "I could use butterfly stitches, but it might not heal as neatly."

"I don't care," Ben says. His face is pale, a sheen of sweat making his skin glisten. What, I wonder, is his deal with needles? It seems like a proper phobia, and one I wouldn't have expected from a confident, athletic guy like him.

"All right," the nurse says, in the dubious tone of someone who really wants to say *on your head be it.*

I give Ben another reassuring smile, and he smiles gratefully back, no knowing smirk, no teenaged sneer, just a child in need of comfort.

When the nurse starts to stitch his leg, with no more than a swab of numbing gel to dull the pain, he reaches one hand convulsively, an act of instinct, for mine, and just as instinctively, unthinkingly, I take it.

He squeezes my hand the whole time the nurse puts the butterfly stitches in his leg, hard enough that my fingers ache, my wedding ring pressing into my skin painfully, and I wonder if I'll be bruised.

Afterward, he's referred to a neurologist to be assessed for concussion; we don't speak as we wait, and an hour passes in mostly silence. Finally, he is examined, asked questions, and it is decided he will stay in overnight for observation, with a CT scan tomorrow morning. If all is well, he can go home then. I am relieved; I want to go home as soon as possible. I want to go somewhere by myself and untangle what has been a very difficult and demanding day.

Still, I feel guilty leaving Ben alone here, even though I know it's the norm. I escort him up to a room on a pediatric neurology ward, its walls covered in murals of zoo animals, the kid in the room next to him only six or so. It all feels reassuringly childlike.

"I'm sure this is all just to be on the safe side," I tell him as he sits on the edge of the bed, and I stand by the door. "How's your head?"

He shrugs and then nods. "It's okay. Got a mother of a headache."

"Well, that's to be expected, I suppose."

I smile at him, a firm, fixed smile, the smile of a kindly stranger.

He glances down at the bedsheet he is twisting between his fingers. "Thanks," he mutters. "For, you know."

I'm not exactly sure what he's thanking me for, or what I should say in response, so I just keep smiling.

"I really don't like needles," he tells me after a moment, his voice low.

"Yes, I gathered that." I keep my voice light, gentle. *He's just a boy*, I remind myself. *Just a little boy, really.* It's easier to realize that, to believe it, when I'm looking at a mural of a giraffe on the wall, and there is a sign by the door that says *Smiles Are Contagious!* with a big, beaming yellow smiley face. "I suspect it's a fairly common phobia," I tell him.

"It's not that," he replies, his voice so low, I strain to hear it.

I hesitate, and then ask cautiously, reluctantly, "No?"

"No." He pauses, his head bent, his gaze still on the sheet. "One of my foster moms used to stab me with a sewing needle, sometimes. When I was little."

I stare at him, utterly appalled, completely shocked. It takes me a few seconds to think how to respond, because there is so much to unpack from that one statement. *Foster mom? Needles? Stabbing?* I didn't know Ben's background, but I would have assumed he was from privilege, maybe with a bit of your average middle-class trauma—divorced parents, a weekend dad, a depressed mother on Xanax, something like that.

"When you were little?" I finally manage.

"Yeah, like five, six. I don't know. I wasn't there that long." He shrugs again and lets go of the sheet, smoothing it out with his hand. "Anyway," he says, and he sounds like he's regretting telling me about any of it.

"I'm sorry, Ben." I don't know what else to say, but that doesn't feel like enough. "I can't imagine..."

"Not many people can." He shrugs. "It's fine. It was a long time ago."

I nod, saying nothing more, because even though I feel desperately sorry for him in this moment, I don't particularly want to share confidences with this boy.

We remain in silence for a few more seconds before I half-turn to the door. "I should probably get back to school. Unless there's anything you need?"

He looks bereft for a moment, and then his expression irons out and he straightens. "Nah. Nothing."

"Okay, then. One of the boarding staff will pick you up tomorrow, after your CT scan."

"I'll have my scan by myself?" Again he sounds like a little boy, lost. I steel myself against it.

"I don't know. I'll speak to the boarding staff about it." I have no idea of the protocols, but judging from the shambles of today, the school does not have the best procedures in place for this kind of situation. I, however, am *not* going to be the one to accompany him, if someone has to. "See you in class, Ben," I say. "Sleep well." And then I walk quickly out of his room, without looking back.

In the parking lot, I let out a shaky breath and cover my hands with my face. For a moment, I feel like crying, but I don't. I breathe in and out a couple of times and then I get in my car and drive home.

It's past five by the time I get back, and Allan is in his study. He comes out as I close the front door, letting out a sigh of relief but also of sorrow. I'd hoped the hour-long drive would clear my head, but I found myself simply staying blank instead. I was too tired, too overwhelmed, to think about anything, but it's starting to rush over me.

"Laura." Allan comes downstairs, his arms held out. "How was it? How is…?" He pauses.

I fill in a little flatly, "Ben. Ben Lane."

"Yes, Ben! Great rugby player. How is he?"

"He's staying overnight. He had to have stitches and he probably has a concussion. One of the boarding staff will have to pick him up tomorrow."

"Oh, that's too bad." Allan frowns. "We're a little light on boarding staff at the moment, unfortunately. One of the matrons has just had to leave rather abruptly."

I shrug, because that is not my problem, and I am not going to let it be. I'm a teacher, not a houseparent, and I don't want to get any more involved than I already have.

"Are you all right?" Allan asks, and I hear genuine concern in his voice that makes me want to tell him what happened. Yet what can I say?

I was cleaning Ben's leg and there was a bit of a weird moment. He put his hand on mine…

I can't win in this situation, I realize. Either Allan will think I've made too much of the incident, and I'm the one who was weird and possibly inappropriate, or I don't make enough of it, and I'm negligent and dangerous. Besides, I need time to process that moment, make sense of it. Maybe I'm not remembering it the way it actually happened. Part of me almost wonders if it happened at all, and yet I know it did. When I let myself think about it, my hand still tingles.

"It's just been a long day," I tell him as I take off my coat.

"Bill Wyatt is giving a hundred grand to the school for a new library," Allan tells me, and it takes me a second to realize he means one of the alumni he was sweet-talking earlier. He sounds ebullient.

"Wow, that's great." I manage to inject a note of enthusiasm into my voice, which shouldn't be that hard because I am pleased. This is an early win for Allan, as headmaster. "How much will a new library cost?"

Allan's smile falters at its edges. "Well, a million, if we want to do it right," he says. "But it's a start."

"Yes, a very good start. *Fantastic*." I smile warmly at him. "What a great thing to have happen your first week as headmaster."

Allan's smile returns and he nods, rocking back on his heels. For a second, he looks like a little boy who has just won a lollipop. I have an urge to walk into his arms, to hug him tightly, press my cheek against his chest. I stay where I am.

"I thought we could go to Mario's," he says. "To celebrate."

"Mario's?" I repeat, even though I know where he means.

"The Italian place in town."

The only restaurant in town, I think, but then I nod. "Okay. Great."

Half an hour later, we are seated in the pizzeria, perusing the laminated menus. I've ordered a large glass of Pinot Noir and I've already drunk half of it by the time the waiter comes to take our order. Allan has been talking about the donor, and the library, and I am trying to listen, but there is a buzzing in my brain, a kind of mental tinnitus.

Then, quite suddenly, Allan puts his hand over mine, just as Ben did hours ago. I tense, jumping a little in my chair, and he lets out a soft laugh.

"Sorry, I didn't mean to startle you." I just shake my head and he continues quietly, "Laura, I don't want you to think I don't realize how hard this move has been for you, how much you've given up to come here, to support me. I want you to know I really do appreciate it." He pauses as he squeezes my hand. "I don't think I've shown or said that enough, and I'm sorry. I know that I've been pretty tense and stressed, trying to get everything right, hit the ground running, start as I mean to go on and all that. I am sorry for the cost it's had on you."

The apology is clearly sincere and heartfelt, and a few days ago it would have made all the difference. Now, for a reason I don't want to consider too closely, I feel like a fraud. I have to shake off today, I tell myself. Move on. Nothing happened, after all.

"Thank you, Allan," I reply, and I squeeze his hand back. "That means a lot." I am reminded, suddenly, that I need to check in tomorrow about Katherine's sleepover see how it went, what happened.

Right now, the world feels like a precarious place, everything off kilter, threatening to slide away. I squeeze Allan's hand one more time and then I reach for my wine.

CHAPTER 12

RACHEL

When I so breezily accepted Tamara's offer, I assumed everything would simply fall into place. Busy Bees had said they had space, after all, and if I can be a teacher, I can certainly be a matron. But, of course, nothing is ever that simple.

I call the daycare center as soon as I get off the phone with Tamara, trying to sound confident and matter-of-fact, and falling at the first hurdle.

"It has been some time since you last inquired," Maureen, the director, states in a rather cool tone, "I assumed you no longer had any interest."

I hold onto my temper, not liking her teacherly tone. "I do, now," I tell her.

"Are you returning as a teacher?"

"No, I'm taking another position, until January," I reply, trying to sound patient.

"*Another* position?"

Why does she care, I wonder, even as I force out, "Yes, as matron of one of the boarding houses. Someone left abruptly, so I'm covering until they can hire a permanent replacement."

A tiny, frozen pause greets this statement. Is Maureen

wondering why, as a qualified teacher, I am willing to be a matron? I am not about to explain.

"I didn't realize your son would be so young," she says finally, her voice taut with disapproval. "Is he even six weeks old yet? Because, legally, we cannot accept a child under that age."

"He'll be eight weeks on Wednesday," I tell her. My tone is cheerful but with an implied *so clearly we don't have a problem.* Why hasn't she mentioned any of this before?

"That's still very young," she says, like she's lecturing me. "Is he being breastfed?"

"Yes, but I'll bring bottles." I'll have to express milk, maybe try formula. Before I had Nathan, I was intending to breastfeed for six months, but now that sounds like a life sentence. Still, I realize with a lurch of panic, I haven't tried him on a bottle yet. I know some babies have a problem adapting. "It's only for seven hours, twice a week. He'd only have one or two feeds during that time."

"And what are the hours you are requesting?" Maureen asks, like it's all a bit too much, as if I'm asking for a favor rather than paying—through the nose—for a service.

"Tuesdays and Fridays, twelve thirty to eight," I reply. Technically, my shift ends at eight; it's about a ten-minute walk from the boarding house to the daycare, so I'll have to arrange to leave a little early.

Maureen lets out a long sigh, which sounds like a no. "That's a problem," she says, and I grit my teeth. "Currently, the last child is picked up at seven on a Friday. We can't stay open an extra hour just for one infant."

"But your hours are till eight p.m.," I say as pleasantly as I can. "Don't you have to stay open until then?"

"Not if there aren't any children."

But there would be a child. I realize I am not going to get anywhere with her; she's decided to be difficult, maybe because she's judging me for putting my almost eight-week-old into daycare.

"Okay, that's fine," I tell her as brightly as I can. "I'll make arrangements for him to be picked up at seven." I don't know how or who I'll ask, but somehow, I'll have to make it work. "Can he start this Friday?"

Maureen makes a sound like a hissing between her teeth. "Normally, there is a settling-in procedure," she tells me. "He'd stay for an hour on the first day, two hours on the second, and build up from there."

Seriously? But that would take over a week.

"I could come in tomorrow?" I offer. "Maybe he could stay for two hours tomorrow, three on Wednesday, five on Thursday, and then the full seven on Friday?" I can't believe I'm having to negotiate with her. I'm *paying* for this, after all. And, I realize, it's going to cost a lot, even before I'm earning anything.

"Very well," Maureen relents, like she really is doing me a favor. "Why don't you come in tomorrow at twelve-thirty, and we'll take it from there?"

"Thank you, I will," I reply, and as I get off the phone, I feel a sudden rush of exultation—and terror.

Nathan will be with someone else for *two hours* tomorrow. It seems, suddenly, like an unimaginable amount of time. I have never left the house without him, since he's been born. I've never gone anywhere, done anything, without him, except sleep or maybe have a shower, when he is sleeping. For the last seven weeks, my life has been completely entangled and enmeshed with my son's, and all I could focus on was getting some freedom. Being able to breathe.

But now I realize how unsettled just the prospect of it makes me feel. What will I do without Nathan? And what will he do without me?

I also know I need to talk to Kyle; he's not going to be pleased with these developments. I decide to wait until after

I've taken Nathan to Busy Bees at least once, seen how it's all gone. If it really is a disaster, I can tell Tamara I can't do it after all, even if I dread the thought of losing this opportunity. Being a boarding house matron is hardly my dream job... but it's better than staying at home. I don't know what kind of mother that makes me, but I do know that it's true.

It takes me over an hour to get ready for our big outing the next day.

I've showered, dressed, blow-dried my hair, and attempted to squeeze into a pair of my old workpants—they don't fit—before choosing my least maternity-looking maternity jeans, wearing a tunic top to disguise both the elasticized waist and my poochy belly. I've changed Nathan twice, fed him three times, and am feeling both frazzled and fragile as I make my way toward Busy Bees. I wanted to present a glossy, professional appearance—my old look—but it feels paper-thin. I didn't manage to put on any makeup, and my hair is flat on one side. My tunic top already has a spit-up stain on one shoulder.

Maureen is a woman in her fifties with a no-nonsense manner and, somewhat incongruously, hair dyed bright pink. Her disapproval from yesterday seems a little less evident today, at least, as she coos at Nathan, who has decided, for a few minutes at least, to act like an angel baby.

"What an absolute cutie," she tells me as I hand over the freshly packed diaper bag and the bottle of formula I mixed up. I tried to give him a bottle last night and he drank a few sips before spitting it out and starting to scream, but I'm hoping if someone else gives it to him it'll be okay. I haven't been able to try expressing breastmilk yet; I bought a pump on Amazon at an eye-watering eighty-four bucks—the cheapest one available—but it hasn't arrived yet.

Still, he might not even need the bottle. I've fed him so much, he's got to be full, and it is only two hours.

As Maureen takes Nathan into the nursery's baby room, I feel a sudden lurch of alarm, a squeeze of terror. The toddler room is full of snot-nosed kids screaming or staring blankly ahead, and while I know it's all normal, it still feels terrifying. One kid is rhythmically banging a wooden block against the wall, and no one is stopping him; the nursery worker is trying to negotiate with two preschoolers about sharing the dress-up clothes.

The baby room in the back has cribs lined up one side and swing seats on the other, reminding me a little bit of an upscale orphanage. One baby is swinging in his seat, looking completely zoned out, and another one is screaming her head off. I have an urge to snatch Nathan from Maureen, and then I tell myself not to be ridiculous. The place is reviewed well online, it looks clean, and has capable, kindly staff, from what I can see. There is no problem here.

I wave to Maureen and a blow a kiss to Nathan and then I walk out of the baby room, out of the daycare. Outside, take a deep breath of autumn-scented air; the leaves have already started to turn ochre and russet. The sky is bright blue, and the air is crisp and cool, and I have two hours to do whatever I want. I didn't actually plan for this; I was so focused on getting Nathan ready that I didn't think about myself.

What should I do? Where should I go? The questions, after eight weeks of being tethered to a small human being, feel overwhelming. I decide to head to Hawley's one coffee shop, on Main Street next to the old movie theater. I order a latte and a brownie, and I sit at a table by myself and revel in a moment's peace and quiet. I am so used to listening for Nathan, to feeling tense and ready to spring into action, that it takes me a good twenty minutes before I can relax into it and sip my coffee rather than bolt it down.

The only other people in the café are a couple of moms I don't recognize, with babies in strollers, chubby, round-cheeked children who look like overfed giants compared to Nathan. When one of them cries, I feel a tingling in my breasts and then the telltale dampening of my shirt.

I zip up my jacket and walk out of the café, heading towards the park on the other side of town. I don't know what to do with myself; half an hour into my cry for freedom and I am already adrift. The trouble, I realize, is that I thought that if I was away from Nathan, I'd recover my old self, but I already know it's not that easy. My old self—that smart, sharp, accomplished woman —is gone, maybe for good.

And what is her replacement? I know, intellectually at least, that I won't be this... this *lump* forever. That Nathan will grow up, and I will go back to work, and even if I can't get my old self completely back, some of me will return, maybe even quite a lot. I do know that deep down, and yet I don't feel it. I feel as if I have fallen into a deep, dark pit with straight, smooth sides and there is no way I am climbing out of it on my own.

I end up sitting on one of the swings in the town park, a dilapidated little square of green on the way to the Price Chopper. It's empty now, and I push myself back and forth, annoyed that I am just killing time, yet not having the energy for anything else. I could go to the grocery store and wander down the aisles, deliciously baby-free. I could go home and tidy up, vacuum without worrying I'll wake up Nathan with the noise, scrub the grouting, do the jobs, the many, *many* jobs, I haven't been able to do since he was born. If I felt like being decadent, I could run myself a bubble bath and soak in it for an hour. Treat myself to a good book, maybe even a glass of wine. Why not?

But I don't do any of those things; I feel as if I physically can't. I simply sit on the swings and push myself back and forth, back and forth, until it's two-fifteen and it's time to get Nathan.

· · ·

"He was good as gold," Maureen tells me, almost smugly, as she hands me Nathan over the counter at the front of the nursery like she's giving me a parcel. "Not a peep out of him! We popped him in the swing, and he absolutely loved it. Didn't even need his bottle. I changed him ten minutes ago."

"Wow, wonderful." I am gratified that it was so easy, and ridiculously proud, as if I had something to do with it, but I am also a tiny bit annoyed. Two hours when he was good as gold and as soon as I get him home, I simply *know* he is going to cry and fuss and need to feed. He'll be up all night, and all I did with my precious time was drink a coffee and sit on a swing.

Still, it's *progress*, I tell myself as I head back home, to the little subdivision of ranch houses behind the movie theater. It means I can take the job, I can go to work. I can be me again. Maybe.

Later that night, I call Kyle. I'm semi-dreading it, because I know he won't be thrilled that I'm taking a job. In fact, he will be decidedly less than thrilled; he might even be angry. As it turns out, it's even worse than that. He's disappointed.

"You're taking a job at the school?" He sounds completely flummoxed, like I'm speaking a foreign language, and maybe I am. "But not as a teacher?"

"No, as a matron in the senior boarding house. They needed someone, just for a month or two, and it's only two days a week."

I keep my tone bright and matter-of-fact, even though I'm already starting to have doubts. I tried to give Nathan a bottle tonight, and once again he spat it out after five seconds, started screaming. Plus, my breast pump arrived and I tried to use it, with a complete lack of success. I felt like a dairy cow, and I managed to extract a measly half ounce from my overfull, leaking breasts. I stain every shirt I have with leaking breastmilk, yet I can't manage to pump so much as a single sip? It's infuriating.

"Aren't matrons, like, maids for the kids?" Kyle asked. "Don't they do the housework and stuff?"

"Among other things."

"How much are you getting paid?"

"Fourteen dollars an hour." Which is significantly less than a lot of jobs, but the school has never been generous when it comes to salaries.

"And how much is the daycare?"

I hesitate and then admit, reluctantly, "Eighty dollars a day." When Maureen told me how much, I struggled not to wince. *Eighty bucks?* Apparently, it's because he's so young. Toddlers are much cheaper.

"*Eighty* dollars a day," Kyle repeats flatly. Neither of us speaks for a few seconds. Then finally Kyle says, his voice soft and sad, "Rachel, I don't understand why you're doing this." I'm not sure how to answer that so I stay silent. "I mean, for what, twenty bucks a day, after paying for the care?"

"Eighteen, actually." I'm trying not to sound flippant, but I hear Kyle swear under his breath.

"So, for sixty-four bucks a week you're putting my son into a nursery."

Anger flares through me, high and hot. "My son, too, Kyle, he's *our* son. And I'm the one who is here, day in and day out, taking care of him, not *you*. You shot off to frigging Aroostook and left *me* here holding the bag—"

"You mean the baby—"

"You don't know," I cut across him, "how hard it can be. I just want a little bit of a break."

"And wiping the piss off teenagers' toilets is your break?" he demands. "You're going to break your back for eight hours twice a week cleaning up after some strangers' kids, rather than look after our—yes, *our*—son? Why, Rachel? Why?" His voice breaks on the last syllable, and I close my eyes.

When he says it like that, it sounds nonsensical. It *is* nonsensical, on one level. I know that full well. And yet... I *need* this. I can't explain it any better than that, and I already know Kyle won't understand.

"It's not just about the money," I say quietly. It's not at all about the money, but that's something else I know Kyle won't understand.

"What is it about then?" he demands.

"Just... having a break." My voice is quiet, almost sad. "Doing something different."

"Okay, fine." He breathes out. "I'll call my mom and ask her to come over during her afternoon off." He speaks levelly, in problem-solving mode, my can-do fixer guy. I love it when he's like this with a lightbulb, but not with my life. "You can have a whole afternoon to yourself to do whatever you like, and she'll take Nathan. How about that?"

I let out a small, soft sigh. "I don't want your mom to come over, Kyle."

"So, you'd rather send him into some daycare situation that's run like a... like an *orphanage*?" His voice rises again, not in anger, because Kyle doesn't actually get angry all that much, but in pain.

"It's a perfectly nice facility," I say wearily, even though I had the same thought earlier. "And plenty of people—most people even—send their kids to daycare. It's not such a big deal."

"At six weeks old?"

"Eight weeks, actually, and yes, some do. Some have to." I know instantly saying that was a mistake, and sure enough, Kyle fires back.

"But you *don't*! We're okay for money, Rachel. You were already planning to go back full-time in January. I mean, what is this? What is going on?" His voice breaks again, tearing at me. "I don't understand this at all."

"Why is it such a big deal to you?" I ask. I want to summon the energy to fight back, but I feel too tired. "It's just two days a week, and I'm going crazy sitting at home all the time on my own, okay? It's *hard*, Kyle." My voice catches and I force myself to continue steadily, "I am finding this really hard." It's the first time I've said it out loud, as simply as that, and I find myself holding my breath, craving his understanding, his sympathy.

"And cleaning a boarding house will be easier?" He sounds not just skeptical, but completely confused.

"Yes, actually, it would." I believe that completely. "Anything would be easier, Kyle. Anything." I know how that sounds, how *terrible* it sounds, because what kind of mother thinks that way? But it's the truth. God help me, it's the truth.

Kyle lets out a long, weary sigh.

"It's not like I can stop you, is it?" he asks.

I don't reply.

"If you need help, Rach, if this really is too hard..." He trails off, and I realize he doesn't know how to finish that sentence, just as I don't. If it really is too hard... *what*? What do you do? "I'll try to get home soon," he says instead. "Maybe next weekend."

"Okay," I say, although he'd originally been planning to come home every other weekend. That hasn't happened so far, and I'm not sure whether to hold out for next weekend, either.

Still, by next weekend, I hope I am coping better than I am now. I hope I am feeling energetic and excited about life, about motherhood even, because the truth I haven't told Kyle, haven't even wanted to admit to myself, is that these two days a week feel like the only thing that can save me.

CHAPTER 13

LAURA

The next few days of teaching go better. Ben is subdued in class, thanks to the concussion, and he seems to avoid even making eye contact with me, which suits me perfectly. Without him watching me—and I hadn't even realized how much it affected me, until he stopped—I can be the teacher I've always been, brisk and cheerful, with a hint of easy humor, enjoying my classes, my students, my life.

Things are better with Allan, too. Since getting that hundred grand from a donor, he's been buoyant; I think he needed an early win to feel confident in his position, and I'm glad he got one. The only stumbling block is the sleepover Katherine went to—I texted her on Sunday and asked how it went, to which I got the unenlightening response "fine", and I forgot to check in with Elise until Wednesday. When I do, the reply I get does not inspire confidence.

Can I call you?

I'm about to head into class, so I tell her to call me afterwards. I don't have time to go back to the house, so I end up taking the call outside the humanities building, my body angled away from the students streaming by.

"Elise?" My voice comes out too sharp. "Did something happen at the party?"

"No, no, nothing happened," she says quickly, too quickly, with an emphasis I don't like on *happened*. "Nothing too bad, anyway." That makes it sound even worse.

"Why don't you just tell me," I say as calmly as I can.

"Well, some boys stayed over. They slept in a different room, and I honestly don't think it was a big deal. They're all just friends."

I think briefly of Ben Lane, sprawled in his seat, the hormones raging through every classroom, the jokes and jostling that accompany every crowd of boys, the side-long looks and smirks.

"Okay," I say as neutrally as I can. "Anything else?"

"There was some alcohol," she admits, and I close my eyes. "But they *are* sixteen—"

"As I recall, the drinking age is twenty-one." The harsh words come out before I can stop them. "I'm sorry," I say quickly. "That's not fair, I know, but..." My voice wobbles and almost breaks. "It's hard for me, Elise, to be so far away." I take a steadying breath. "And I know it's hard for you, too. Harder, even, to parent another mother's child."

"It's not easy," she agrees after a moment, her voice taut with tension.

I close my eyes briefly. All the positive strides I've made over the last few days slip away in an instant. I shouldn't be here. I should be back in Connecticut, with my daughter. "I'm sorry," I tell her. "I wish..." I don't even know how to finish that sentence.

"It was just a couple of six-packs of beer," she states quietly. "They got a little tipsy. I wanted to be honest."

"Thank you," I say, even though I am still struggling not to feel angry, and worse, betrayed by the choices she made in regard to *my* daughter, knowing or at least suspecting that I would not have made the same ones. I want—I *need*—my friend to be honest. I can't have her keeping things from me, because she's afraid I'll be angry. "I really do appreciate your honesty, Elise, and your willingness to be there for Katherine. I hope you know that. I'm sorry if I don't always seem like I understand that."

"I know it's hard," Elise replies, her voice gentling. "I do get that, Laura, please believe me."

I manage a shaky laugh. "I guess it's taking me aback a bit because Katherine has never really gone to parties before."

"Well, she is in tenth grade," Elise remarks. "This is the year when the parties start."

"How did they get so old?" I force another laugh even though I hate the thought of Katherine going to yet more parties, without me there. "Look, why don't I come down next weekend?" I'd been planning to wait until the end of the month, give both Katherine and me a chance to settle into our new lives, but I think that's a bad idea now. I want to see my daughter, and maybe she needs to see me. "I could stay with you, if you don't mind—"

"Well." Elise pauses uncomfortably. "Dave and I are going to New York for the Friday night, staying over."

"What are Molly and Katherine doing?" I blurt.

Another pause, this one longer. "I thought they'd be okay on their own for one night."

I close my eyes briefly. So, this is her being honest? Was she ever going to tell me she planned on leaving them alone for the night? "That's fine," I say, and my voice is definitely cool now. "I can come down and stay with them instead."

"Will you be able to get here in time?" Elise sounds decidedly unenthused about the idea.

The earliest I can leave on Friday is three, and the trip takes seven hours. Still, ten o'clock is better than not at all, especially if Katherine and Molly know I'm coming. "I won't be too late," I tell Elise.

She lets out a sigh. "Well, it's not like I can stop you, is it?"

I stiffen, surprised by her words, her tone. "Elise—"

"It's just, I don't like you checking up on me, you know?" she continues quietly.

"Elise, I'm not checking up on *you.*" Even if she's disregarded most of my rules in the first *week.* "I'm checking up on my daughter, if anything, but really, I just want to see her."

"Okay." Now Elise sounds resigned, and I can't believe things have deteriorated between us this quickly. "It's just..." She blows out a breath. "Laura, you're going to have to trust me, okay? If this is going to work." "This" being her having parental care of my daughter. "I thought we'd hashed it all out."

We had, sort of. A boozy evening with a bottle of wine, our arms thrown around each other, declaring that we were best friends, just like our daughters were best friends, how much better could it get. Elise did warn me, I remember, laughingly shaking a finger in my face, telling me she wasn't as strict as I was. Three glasses in, I'd laughed back, said maybe that would be good for Katherine. I don't think I really believed it, even then, but I didn't have any other options. I still don't.

"I do trust you," I tell her, and I don't think she believes me. I don't entirely believe me, either, but I have to make this work. "I'm sorry. This really is an adjustment. It's going to take some time to figure it out, get used to the new normal." And even though it pains me to say it, I make myself offer, "If it's not convenient for me to come this weekend, I won't. No big deal."

Elise lets out an exasperated sigh, mingled with, I hope, some affection. "No, no, I'm sorry. Of course I want you to come this weekend. I'm only sorry I won't be there for a good part of it."

"Are you sure?"

"Yes, I'm sure."

"Okay." I feel as if we've averted a disaster, but only just.

I've just ended the call, expelling a shaky breath as I cradle the phone against my chest, when I hear a voice boom from behind me,

"All right there, Laura?"

It's Liz Pollard. Perfect.

Slowly, I turn around, trying to give myself enough time to pin a cheerful smile on my face. "Yes, everything's fine."

Her gaze narrows as she takes in my phone. "Making a call?"

Obviously, and it is allowed. Students aren't allowed their phones during the day, but I'm a teacher, not a student. "Yes, I was." I don't offer any further information, and she frowns.

"I was going to speak to you, as it happens. We need to have a meeting about the fifth-form trip to Boston."

"Oh?" I know the eleventh-grade top set English class goes to Boston in October, to see some plays and museums, but I assumed I would have nothing to do with it, as the newest teacher on the block. "What about it?"

"You and Anthony will be chaperoning."

"What?" I stare at her. "Why? I mean, I'm new, I'm still learning all their names—"

"Great way to get to know them, don't you think?" she replies breezily. "Rachel would have gone, if she hadn't gone off on maternity leave." She speaks slightly accusingly, like it's Rachel's fault for having a baby. I think of Rachel as I last saw her, eyes narrowed in suspicion, my hand on Ben Lane's thigh. *No.*

"Sorry, I just didn't expect it," I tell Liz. "Is anyone else going, as a chaperone?"

"It's only twenty boys." She speaks reprovingly. "I think the two of you should be able to handle that, don't you?"

I can already picture it—Anthony will take himself off to

the bar every night; his idea of discipline will be to tell the boys to knock it off once and then ignore them. But more alarmingly, Ben Lane is in the top-set English class.

"Of course," I tell Liz with a rictus smile, because what else can I possibly say? "No problem. I... I'm looking forward to it."

She lets out a booming laugh like she can see right through me, and then starts to move off. "Good, good. We can talk about arrangements next week, during our department meeting."

I head back into the building for my next class, my mind a blur of worry—Katherine, Boston, Ben Lane. In my classroom, a dozen or so ninth-graders are milling around; two of them are tossing a pen between then.

"Stop that," I say sharply, and they all fall silent, stare at me warily. It's not how I usually behave. I'm the laidback teacher, the one who takes everything in her stride, who smiles and shrugs, laughs and teases.

Why am I so rattled—about everything? My mother would tell me it's because of the menopause. I remember, on my fortieth birthday, she intoned, as if offering a funeral dirge, "Your forties are very difficult as a woman."

I know she had a tricky few years of menopause herself, plus her own aging parents, and my brother and I were both teenagers at the time—not too difficult, as I recall, but probably not a walk in the park, either. I can't remember much beyond a few vague bursts of tears or temper, the occasional inexplicable drive, at night on her own, returning around nine or ten o'clock, silent and stony-faced, while my dad looked on, bemused, baffled.

I have no idea what she was contending with, or if it was anything like what I am now. I should visit them, I think, maybe this weekend—then I remember I need to visit Katherine. I think about Tucker, too. He might be at this school, but I never see him outside of class, talk to him. Maybe Allan and I could take him out to Mario's one evening...

"Um, Mrs. Haile?"

I open my eyes, not actually having realized I'd closed them. "Yes?"

A boy is looking at me uncertainly. "Are you going to teach us?"

Two hours later, I drag myself back to the headmaster's house —*my* house, I keep telling myself, even though I can't yet think of it that way. I feel tired and dispirited, and I think it has to do with Ben Lane.

This thing with him—whatever it was, and I keep telling myself it wasn't anything—has blown over, and the trip to Boston isn't for another month. As for my worries about Katherine, she may have gone to a party with boys and alcohol, but Elise seemed certain that nothing bad had happened, and I knew these days of partying were coming, just as they had for Tucker. Allan handled the guy talk about responsibility and all that, but I did my fair share of 2 a.m. pickups from houses on the other side of town, music blaring from the windows, drunken teenagers stumbling on the driveways, red plastic cups of beer held aloft. I'm neither naïve nor stupid. I know what teenagers get up to... which is why I am so worried for my daughter, without me there to guide and protect her.

As I let myself into the house, I hear a clatter from the kitchen, and I walk back to see four catering staff loading up trays of cheese and crackers.

"Is there an event tonight?" I ask, stupidly, because obviously there is, and I've forgotten about it.

"Yes, a wine and cheese evening for community supporters."

Ah, yes. I remember now. In order to foster good relations with Hawley's tiny community, Allan organized this welcome event. He invited anyone remotely notable—the town librarian, the guy who runs the movie theater, the woman in charge of the daycare. Most of them will probably come out of curiosity more than anything else, but it means two hours of mingling and chitchat. I do my best to smile at the staff.

"Wonderful," I say, and tell myself it will be nice to meet some locals... even if the thought of a bath and an early night is infinitely more appealing.

Why, I wonder wearily, did I think I could manage a full-time teaching job and all the duties of my role as headmaster's wife? Because I know it's important for me to be there tonight, at Allan's side. I also know I have thirty ninth-grade essays to grade, and I want to check in with Katherine, maybe even with Tucker, whom I've barely seen since we got to Wilderness. I've asked him to come for dinner twice, and he's prevaricated both times. I also need to call my parents and arrange a visit...

With a departing smile for the catering staff, I totter upstairs to sprawl on the sofa for a few minutes before I change.

I am still lying there, sprawled out, staring at the ceiling, and blissfully thinking of absolutely nothing when Allan comes into our living room. I didn't even hear him come up the stairs.

"Laura?" His voice registers concern. "Are you all right?"

"Yes, I'm fine." I know I should sit up and pin on a smile, otherwise he might say something like *maybe it's all getting a bit much for you*, with a slightly superior note in his voice, and I don't think I could handle that on top of everything else.

But my husband surprises me. Better still, he reminds me of who he has been, who he really is. He perches on the seat opposite and rests a hand on my knee. "The wine and cheese evening isn't for another hour and a half. What if I run you a bath?" I blink at him, and he smiles. "Deep, with bubbles, the way you like. Bring a book and soak for an hour. I'll sort out dinner." He tilts his head, his smile deepening into dimples. "Don't look at me like that."

"Like what?" I genuinely don't know how I am looking at him, but already I am smiling back.

"Like you can't believe I'd ever suggest such a thing. I hope I haven't become that much of a self-absorbed jerk."

"Well..." I tease, smiling all the more, although I think we both know I'm not actually teasing. Not entirely.

"Seriously, Laura." He squeezes my knee. "Relax. Come to the wine and cheese thing late, if you want, or not at all. It's not that important."

"Isn't it?" *Everything* has seemed important, so far.

He shrugs. "Not really. There will be other opportunities. You don't need to go to every single thing."

It occurs to me then, for all my so-called support of my husband, I haven't actually asked after him all that much since we moved here. My attendance at most Wilderness things has been with reluctance, which I fear he has seen right through. In fact, I realize uncomfortably, ever since we first contemplated this move, I have acted as if I am going, as if I am here, on sufferance. I've tried not to, and I've done my best to put a cheerful face on it... but Allan has known, all the same.

Looking at his kindly face now, the way his eyes crinkle at the corners, the faint smile that quirks his lips, I feel a sudden, painful shaft of guilt. I also feel, in light of his kindness and consideration, the need, and even the desire, to give something back, finally.

"How is it all going, do you think?" I ask him as I sit up, push my hair away from my face. "I know you got that big donation, but everything else? Is it what you expected? Are you... are you happy here?" I smile to take any potential criticism or sting from the words; I genuinely want to know. This is what he's wanted for so long; I hope it's living up to his expectations.

Allan pauses, looking reflective, maybe a little guarded, although thankfully that drops away. "Well, it is early days," he says after a moment. "So, who knows what's coming down the pike. There have been a few surprises already, and some of the teachers are decidedly old guard—"

"Like Anthony Weiss?" I fill in, and we give each other the kind of secretive, complicit smile that reminds me of how we used to be.

"Like Anthony Weiss," he agrees with a chuckle. "And David Makin, head of physics. *Yikes.*"

I stifle a giggle with my hand. "That bad?"

"Let's just say political correctness has not infiltrated his thinking one iota."

"Sometimes I feel that way about this whole place," I venture, my tone turning cautious. "It feels a little bit like the Land That Time Forgot."

"Minus the dinosaurs," he agrees with a small smile. "But, yes, I know what you mean. 'The Wilderness School is a different country,'" he quotes whimsically, paraphrasing the opening line to L. P. Hartley's *The Go-Between.* "'They do things differently there.'"

"Too true." I grimace slightly, thinking of Liz Pollard telling me the same thing, in a far smirkier sort of way. "But in any case," I persist, "your initial gut feeling, it's good?" I smile, and Allan smiles back and then nods slowly.

"Yes," he says, feeling his way through the word before he says it again, more firmly. "Yes, it's good."

He pauses while I nod back. We're not saying all that much, but it still feels like we're getting somewhere.

"And what about you?" he asks. "It's good? The teaching? It's not too much?"

"Sometimes it feels like it is," I admit, compelled to uncomfortable honesty. Right now, I don't feel like he'll hold it against me. "But I'll get there. And it's only till January, anyway."

"Yes, although she might want to stay home with her baby. New mothers often do."

I think of Rachel as I last saw her, in the boarding house,

hanging around, Nathan left in the hall. Why was she there? What did she want? I certainly didn't get the sense that she's loving staying at home with Nathan.

"Maybe," I reply, knowing I sound unconvinced.

"Would you want to stay in the role?" Allan asks. "If it came to that?"

Would I? I think of Liz Pollard and Anthony Weiss; both seem determined if not to outright dislike me, then maybe just dismiss me.

"I don't know," I admit, which right now is the truth. I put my hand over his, smile. "I guess we'll cross that bridge when the time comes, if it ever does."

"Worth thinking about it, though," Allan says, sounding far more cheerful about the prospect of me teaching than he has before. "Especially if you enjoy it."

Enjoy it? I think, unwillingly, of Ben Lane, how he's made every class he's in difficult in a way I can't articulate to anyone, even myself, and definitely not to Allan. *Why* does he bother me so much?

And why do I let him?

CHAPTER 14

RACHEL

My first day on the job doesn't start well, which is just typical. Kyle called me the night before to tell me he couldn't come home this weekend after all, but *definitely* next weekend. I wasn't convinced. Then Nathan wakes up at 4 a.m., and when I finally settle him it's close to six and I can't get back to sleep. I lie in bed, trying to relax, feeling tense—and not sure of anything. Suddenly, a seven-hour shift in the dorms feels like a very long time.

I tell myself it's only two hours more than yesterday, which was fine.

On Wednesday, Nathan did three hours at Busy Bees, and instead of frittering those hours away wandering around town, I was proactive. Purposeful. I did a blitz shop at the Price Chopper, even buying some more pudding cups for Gladys. I cleaned the house, dusting and vacuuming and scrubbing out the toilet and tub. It wasn't until I had finished, sweaty and tired, that I realized I'd done it all as if someone was watching me, as if I was waiting for their silent, grudging approval. I don't know if I thought that person was Kyle or my mother or an invisible audience of sanctimonious mothers. Probably all three.

When I returned at three-thirty to pick up Nathan, he was fussing a bit, and Maureen told me, disapprovingly, that he hadn't wanted his bottle.

"He's still getting used to a bottle," I admitted, an apology. "But he is getting there, I promise."

"If he won't take his bottle, we'll have to call you to come get him," she said, a warning, and I nodded and smiled, like that would totally be okay when I already knew it wouldn't.

That night, I tried my hardest to get Nathan to take the bottle, but he simply wouldn't, arching his back and pushing his head away, screaming and flailing and even spitting up in his fury, until I had to put him down and pace the room, my knuckles pressed to my eyes.

A tap sounded at the door. Gladys. A breath escaped me in a rush as the knob started to turn. I really needed to start locking the door, but I always forgot, what with holding Nathan in one arm as I unlocked it, closing it with my butt as I moved onto the next thing.

"Hello, dear," Gladys said as she shuffled into the room. "Is everything all right? I heard poor little Nathan crying."

"I'm trying to give him a bottle, and he doesn't like it." I tried to smile, although I felt near tears—tears of frustration more than anything else. I just wanted *one* thing to work.

"Oh, well, that won't do," Gladys clucked. "Mommies can't give their babies bottles, can they?"

I tensed, waiting for the usual breast-milk-is-best diatribe, although, as I recalled, Gladys's generation were all about the bottle.

"Babies won't take it from their mothers," she explained kindly. "Why don't I try?"

She was already holding out her arms, and I felt too frazzled to resist. I scooped up Nathan and handed him to her, laying him carefully in her scrawny arms. Her face flooded with light, like an ageing Madonna, as she brought him to her chest.

"Now there's a good boy," she murmured, and held out her hand, a bit imperiously, for the bottle.

A few minutes later, Nathan was guzzling like a champ, while I looked on in tearful amazement.

"Gladys... you're *wonderful*," I said, utterly sincere, and she beamed up at me.

"It's been a long time," she replied with a satisfied smile creasing her wrinkled face, "but you always remember, don't you? It's like riding a bicycle."

Nothing about motherhood has been like riding a bicycle for me, but I was certainly grateful to Gladys.

The next day, Nathan went to Busy Bees for five hours, and I headed to school to have a meeting with Tamara. There were forms I had to sign, the usual HR rigmarole. I'd managed to squeeze into a pair of non-maternity pants, if only just; I couldn't do the button and the zip only went halfway up, but another tunic top covered the bulge.

Still, it didn't help my self-confidence to come face to face with Tamara, who wasn't even thirty, tall and leggy and blond, dressed in a tight-fitting power suit, an extra blouse button undone, not the usual workwear for Wilderness. I had upped the fashion stakes with nothing more than a tailored skirt; Tamara took it to a whole, rather ridiculous, new level. She'd come to Maine for the hiking last year, but like our new headmaster, I suspected she'd move on pretty quickly, to bigger and brighter pastures that appreciated her snappy dressing, the way she flicked her long, blond hair. In the meantime, though, she made me feel like a lump of unformed clay.

"Rachel." Her smile was bright and fast. "How's mommydom?"

Who, I thought as I sat down, says *mommydom*? *It's not*

even a word. I doubt Tamara will ever have children. She doesn't seem the type.

"Great," I replied, a bit flatly.

"Good, good. Well, this is all routine, as you know, and we certainly appreciate you helping us out, when we were left in the lurch so suddenly." She cocked her head to the side, and I could see the question in her blue eyes, just as if she'd said it out loud. *Why on earth are you doing this?* "Just a few forms to sign," she said.

"Great," I said again.

I signed the forms, barely listening to Tamara drone on about HR procedures. "Now, you've never been a matron before," she began, and I had to clamp my lips together to keep from saying *no, duh.* "So, it's a little different from teaching." Again: *no, duh.* "But, basically, a matron is there as a support, a mainstay, a backstop." Did she even know what all those words meant?

"Right," I said, nodding. "Uh-huh."

"The first part of the day will be taken up with making sure the boarding house is tidy and welcoming for the boys to return to, after class. So, cleaning the bathrooms, folding the laundry, that sort of thing." Again, with that flash in her eyes—*why are you doing this?* I was starting to wonder myself. "When the boys return from sports, you will assist the housemaster in making sure they're doing their homework, delivering their clean clothes to their rooms, getting them to dinner." She smiled, tightly. "The schedule is on the bulletin board in both the kitchen and the office, so you can check to make sure you're adhering to times. If you have any questions, ask Mr. Garlock."

Andrew Garlock, the housemaster, fortyish and sporty, briskly capable. I figured we'd get along, although we've never worked directly together before.

"Sounds good," I told Tamara and managed to smile. "There's just one thing..."

She tensed, instantly alert and wary, like a predator sniffing prey. "Oh?"

"Busy Bees, my son's daycare, closes at seven on a Friday. Would it be okay if I left a little early, to pick him up?"

Tamara's eyes narrowed slightly, nostrils flaring. *Uh-oh.* This wasn't, I knew, an outrageous request; Wilderness wasn't run as the tightest ship, by any means. There was usually plenty of room for people to be flexible, but I could already see Tamara, the bright, shiny new head of HR—department of one —wasn't going to play that way.

"Well, actually, Rachel, that *is* a problem." She folded her arms, her smile steely. "Because, as I'm sure you'll understand, we're only employing you for two shifts, and missing a whole hour of one shift, well, it's a bit problematic."

Is it?

"The boys will be in their rooms, for a study hour until eight," I said as mildly as I could. "So, I'm not entirely sure that I'd be needed."

"But we're *paying* you to be there, Rachel, to be available for any emergencies. For example, last week, a student had to be taken to Cary Medical Center with a suspected concussion, and there was no staff available to do so, so the headmaster's wife drove him." She spoke as if this had been a shocking development, and remembering that weird moment when I came into the kitchen and saw Laura with Ben, maybe it was. "She's a teacher at the school, so it isn't as out of the ordinary as it sounds, but still. The reason we employ staff is so they can be available as and when they're needed."

Wow, thanks for the lecture on common sense, I thought, but of course did not say. I knew I couldn't argue the point. Penny, the old HR person, would have laughed and told me it was no problem. She would have said I could nip out, get Nathan, and bring him back to the boarding house. "Let the boys have a cuddle before you go. That is, if they want to!" Cue a hearty laugh.

Tamara was a different sort of animal entirely.

"So, is this going to be a problem?" she asked, and I had the urge to slap that supercilious smile right off her painted face. The anger I felt surprised me; I still wasn't used to this kind of rage.

I took a careful breath, let the tide recede.

"Not a problem," I said as cheerfully as I could manage. "I just thought I'd ask."

That evening, the problem was solved for me, anyway. Gladys had offered to try a bottle with Nathan again, while we were watching *Jeopardy*. I told her my predicament and her face lit up.

"I can get him for you, Rachel," she said, and I jumped a little, because I really hadn't expected that. I hadn't been fishing for her to offer; I hadn't even considered it. Gladys was... well, *old*. And even though she'd had a child herself, it had been a long time ago, and she didn't always seem like she knew what to do with a baby, even if she'd been able to get Nathan to take a bottle. In any case, it was only for an hour, and most of that time would be simply collecting Nathan and bringing him back.

Besides, looking at her cradling him in one arm while he guzzled the bottle... well, it inspired confidence, certainly. And, more importantly, it wasn't like I had any other options.

"If you're sure?" I said, and she nodded happily.

"Of course I'm sure."

Now, the morning of my first shift, I feed Nathan before I shower and dress, feeling gritty-eyed with fatigue, like I'm moving in slow motion, my fingers thick as I fumble to button my blouse and pull on my socks. Not a great way to start a seven-hour shift of housework, laundry, and managing thirty or forty rowdy boys, but I tell myself I can do it, simply because I have to. There's no way I'm backing out now.

I feed Nathan again before I leave, and then check in with Gladys to make sure she remembers to pick Nathan up at seven.

"Oh yes, dear," she tells me. "I'm looking forward to it."

"You know where Busy Bees is?" I've already asked her, but I feel like I need to check.

"Yes, out on the way to the Price Chopper." The smile she gives me is full of understanding. "You don't need to fuss or worry at all. Nathan and I will have a wonderful time, won't we, peanut?" She stoops down to chuck his chin with one gnarled, arthritic finger.

I do my best to feel reassured.

The drop-off at the nursery is surprisingly easy, with a staff member I don't recognize, a young woman with hair dip-dyed blue and a warm smile, scooping Nathan from me in one easy armful. I pass over the diaper bag with its bottles and two changes of clothes, wondering why I feel, now, more than yesterday or the day before, as if a limb is being amputated, leaving behind a gaping, messy wound.

I'm fine, I tell myself. *Nathan is fine. I wanted this*, I remind myself as I turn away from the sight of Nathan being deposited into the seat of a swing. I *chose* this.

When I arrive at the boarding house ten minutes later, it's as quiet and empty as it was the night I came in looking for Laura. Emptier, in fact, because nobody is here at all, except for me. Andy Garlock is most likely teaching, and the boys are all in class. They won't be back for three hours, which gives me plenty of time to get on with all the jobs I'm meant to do.

I put on the blue coverall I was given, the same kind I've seen other matrons wear, hardly able to believe it is now my uniform. I don't think I've ever been a snob—I grew up working class, after all—but after getting my bachelor's and master's and

teaching for ten years, wielding a mop and pail feels a bit...
humbling.

But it's quiet, and no baby will cry, and I find I enjoy the
rhythmic routine of it all—swish and mop, swish and mop, as
my mind empties out.

I clean the kitchen, mop all the downstairs floors, fold the
four loads of laundry the other matron, Denise, put in this
morning, and then brave the bathrooms upstairs, which aren't as
bad as I feared, since they are cleaned every day. Really, I
reflect, having the second shift of the day is a piece of cake. It's
quiet, the boys are all at class, and Denise has done the heavy
lifting cleaning-wise, so I'm just doing a mop-up.

That is, until the boys return at four o'clock, like a cloud of
locusts, a horde of invading barbarians. They burst through the
doors as I am putting the mop away in the closet in the downstairs hall, flinging off bags and shoes and coats, tearing through
the lounge and the kitchen, thundering up the stairs, their boisterous laughter, shouts, and jeering ringing through the whole
house. I am instantly overwhelmed.

"Who are you?" one boy I don't recognize asks me as he
wanders past, peeling open a chocolate bar. He doesn't bother
to wait for my reply; he's not really interested in who I am.
None of them are.

I recognize at least half of them from my classes, but they
don't seem to recognize me, or if they do, they're not admitting
as much. Their gaze skates over me without interest or curiosity,
without seeing me at all. Besides, Mrs. Masters the English
teacher from last year is a different person to *this* Mrs. Masters,
the dumpy, near invisible matron.

I check the schedule and see that most of them go out for
sports till five-thirty; the rest have free time until dinner, and
then it's study hall until eight, when I get off shift. I can manage
that. I think.

Boys are continuing to thunder up and down the stairs;

some of them have changed for sports, but they've forgotten something, so they run back up again. Doors open, slam, open again, slam again. A dozen boys are sprawled on the sofas in the lounge, music blaring along with the TV, which is hooked up to a games console. The sound of machine-gun fire echoes through the room and I step inside.

"Shall we turn that down a bit?" I ask brightly, and a couple of them gape at me silently; the others ignore me completely as I hunt for the remote control, find it, and then fumble to figure out where the volume is. I turn it down several clicks while the boys continue to play, utterly ignoring my interference.

I thought I felt invisible when I was with a baby, but it's nothing to what I feel like now, wearing a blue matron's coverall in a roomful of rowdy teenage boys. Now I feel like I actually don't exist.

I push the thought away, make myself a cup of tea, and go to the office, where they're meant to come and find me if they need me. I have maybe five minutes of quiet before a boy comes in, a senior I haven't taught before, needing the first-aid box; he's burned himself on the kettle. I bandage him as best as I can; I did a first-aid course years back, but it's not in date and Tamara didn't ask whether I had the qualification. He stands there dolefully; despite my attempt at cheerful patter, he doesn't say a word.

Five minutes after that, another boy can't find his sweatshirt. Then it's something else, and something else again, and before I know it, it's five-thirty, and they're all trooping out to dinner, thank *goodness*.

I eat by myself in the cafeteria; there are a couple of science teachers eating at another table, but I simply don't have the energy for the chitchat, or to explain why I, an English teacher, am now working as a matron. I really didn't think through that element, I realize. I didn't consider how others would perceive me, or even how I would perceive myself.

My thoughts turn to Nathan, and I wonder how he is doing. My breasts feel heavy and tight; I'd been planning on expressing milk at some point in the afternoon, but I haven't had a chance. I also forgot how awful the cafeteria food is—a wedge of meatloaf and a pile of sweetcorn on a plate of thick white china. It looks like prison food.

Back in the boarding house, the boys head to their rooms for study hall and Andy Garlock has returned, doing an unnecessarily theatrical double take at the sight of me.

"*Rachel*! I was surprised to hear you were subbing in as matron."

"Well, anything to help out," I reply rather tightly. I have a feeling I am going to be fielding a lot of those kinds of remarks.

"Good for you," he says, seeming sincere. "Can you check the boys are actually studying in their rooms? I have to answer a couple of parent emails. And remember, no phones while they're working."

"All right."

I head upstairs, dreading going into each of the rooms, asking for phones. As Mrs. Masters, English teacher, I'd have no problem with it. But as Mrs. Masters, matron? I feel like my armor and weapons have been taken away; this blue coverall might make me as good as invisible, but perversely it also makes me feel exposed.

As I'm coming to the first room—Ben's room, I realize, along with his roommate's—I hear voices floating into the hall.

"She is *hot*. Like, genuine MILF."

I still, tense. I think I know what MILF stands for, and it takes me aback.

The same boy continues, "Wearing those skirts! And she can't take her eyes off you, man, in English class."

A chuckle from the other boy, who, I realize as I listen, is Ben.

"Seriously," his roommate continues. "I think she's hot for

you. She's always looking at you and then acting like she isn't. It's pretty funny. Like, does she think we don't see it?"

"Shut up, Tom," Ben says, but there is a satisfied smugness to his tone; he might as well be agreeing with him.

And, I realize with a strange, hollow feeling I don't recognize, the woman they're talking about, the woman who is *hot* for Ben Lane, is Laura.

CHAPTER 15

LAURA

When I step into Elise's house on Friday night, I breathe a sigh of relief. I didn't realize how much I needed to be away from Wilderness until I was. Every mile down the highway toward home—and yes, it's still my home—has me breathing a little easier, a little freer. The tightness in the back of my neck and between my shoulder blades started to loosen as I drove.

"Mom!" Katherine comes barreling toward me, Molly hanging a little behind.

I open my arms for her enthusiastic hug, gratified by her response. I was worried she might be annoyed I was coming, thinking I was checking up on her, but she seems thrilled to see me. This is the homecoming I hadn't dared to hope for. The homecoming I needed.

My arms close around her and for just a second I bury my face in her strawberry-scented hair. "I missed you, sweetie," I say, trying not to let my voice choke. Teenagers never do well with too much emotion.

To my further gratification—as well as a little maternal alarm—Katherine just hugs me harder. "I missed you too," she replies, and hers is the voice that chokes.

I hug her for a moment more, wanting to imbue her with both my love and strength, fighting a terrible fear that being away is even worse for her than I thought. I glance back at Molly, who smiles uncertainly, and after a couple of sniffs, Katherine steps back, managing a small smile.

"Tell me what you've been up to," I say, pitching my tone upbeat, and we all head back to the family room adjoining the kitchen. For a second, I simply stand in the doorway and savor the scene—a normal house, a family's house. The rigid rooms of the headmaster's house, the industrial kitchen, the unfamiliarity and *coldness* of it... well, I knew all that, of course, but I didn't quite realize how it affected me, until I'm standing in a cluttered kitchen with magnets on the fridge and books piled on the table, a sense that this is a place where life is *lived*, where children are. *My* child.

I don't know how much of my sorrow is tied up with Tucker and Katherine being out of the house, and how much with the move to Wilderness, but right now it feels like a pressure in my chest, an ache in my heart. I've only just arrived, and already I feel like I don't want to go back.

The three of us curl up on the sofa in the family room and Molly and Katherine tell me about the start of tenth grade, the changes at Leabrook, which already sound legion, even after just a few weeks. Katherine becomes more animated, and I am relieved to see her seeming more like herself.

"They're talking about changing the uniform—can you *believe* it?" she exclaims, rolling her eyes.

Molly fills in, "Pants instead of skirts for girls, to be gender-neutral."

"Well, maybe there is some sense in that," I say as mildly as I can, thinking of the skirts that are rolled up the girls' waists until they barely brush their thighs.

Both girls snort in derision.

There are other changes, too—small things, about teachers,

classes, this club or that sport, and I listen to it all, I lap it all up, because Leabrook feels like my home, and I miss it. I miss it all so much.

Nearly two hours pass without any of us noticing, and it's nearly midnight before I finally decide we all need to head to bed. As we go upstairs—Katherine and Molly to their rooms, and me to the guest room—Molly peels off and Katherine hesitates in front of my door.

I wait, sensing she has something to say, my eyebrows slightly raised, a faint smile on my face, determined not to nag or push, but simply to be present.

"I thought you'd be mad," she says in a low voice as she twirls a strand of hair around one finger.

"Mad?" My eyebrows lift a little higher and my smile stays in place. "Why?"

"Because of the party."

I pause, trying to decipher what she isn't saying. Finally, I ask gently, "Did something happen at the party?"

Katherine shrugs. "Well, you know there was drinking. And boys."

"Did you drink?" I do my best to keep my voice level, light. Katherine shrugs, and I reply in the same tone, "I'll take that as an affirmative."

"Just a couple of beers," Katherine protests, but she doesn't sound annoyed. If anything, she sounds scared.

"Katherine," I tell her, keeping my voice gentle but firm, "the reason I'm concerned about you drinking alcohol, besides the fact that it's illegal, is because you have no experience with it—rightly so—and it makes you vulnerable in an unknown situation. Were there people there you didn't know?"

She nods. My heart lurches.

"Did you feel vulnerable? Did... did something happen?" Please God, nothing did, but every mother—at least every mother of teenaged girls—hears the stories of drunk girls at parties, boys who take advantage in the most horrific ways. You just pray those kinds of stories don't happen to your daughter. You tell them to be careful, you lecture and warn and sometimes you scold, but in your heart you are simply desperate for them to be safe.

"No," Katherine replies, but it's after a pause.

"Katherine, you can tell me if something did," I tell her steadily. I know there's no point pushing, but I have to keep myself from it. "I really hope you would tell me, because I'd want to be able to help and support you. And I wouldn't be mad, I promise."

She stares at me, wide-eyed, and then she just shakes her head. I know I am not going to get anything more from her now, if there is even anything to get, and in any case, it is after midnight. We'll have to leave it for another time.

"I love you," I say, and I hug her again, and then I watch as she walks to the guestroom that now is her own; it feels as if she is taking my heart with her.

Elise and her husband, Dave, come back after lunch the next day. I took Molly and Katherine out to brunch, and then they disappeared to do homework while I worked on some lesson plans. Flicking through the next unit of poetry didn't fill me with the usual excitement, just an uneasy sense of dread, as well as a certain ennui. I wonder if I am tiring of teaching, or just tiring of teaching at Wilderness, and after only two weeks.

"Hel-lo!" Elise sings out as she comes into the house, Dave behind her. After a quick wave, he disappears into his study, while Elise hugs me and air-kisses both my cheeks. "You made it!" she exclaims, as if I somehow wouldn't.

"Yes, it's been great to spend time with the girls. How was New York?" I keep my voice upbeat, but it takes effort, and I know it's because of this awkward, impossible position I've put us in. I can tell by the way Elise reacts, with a quick, overly bright smile, that she's feeling it, too.

"So fun," she replies, dumping her purse on a stool by the breakfast bar. "And *so* needed. The start of a school term is always intense, isn't it?"

"Yes, it certainly is." More than usual this year, but I'm not about to go into any of that with Elise right now. "Katherine and Molly both seem to be doing really well," I tell her, and I know it's a kind of apology, although not an entirely sincere one. I haven't had a chance to talk privately with Katherine any more about that party, and I'm not sure I'm going to get the opportunity this weekend, but I have to believe that if something really had gone wrong, she would have told me. She would have trusted me.

"I think they are," Elise replies cautiously. I nod, and then she confesses in a rush, "Look, I'm sorry about the party. I should have handled that better, been more on the ball. I'll do better next time, I promise."

"It's okay, Elise. I know I shouldn't have been so prickly about it. We're both still figuring this out. It doesn't seem like anything terrible happened." I pause as I catch some emotion flickering across Elise's face. Guilt? Or irritation? "Nothing did happen, did it?" I ask, half-joking, half-serious.

"No," she says, and just like Katherine, it's after a pause. "I mean, all right, yes, they both got a little drunk. I could still smell the beer on them the next morning. But other than that..." She trails off and it takes me a few seconds to realize she doesn't know what, if anything, happened, so she can hardly give me any reassurances. Maybe my own daughter doesn't know, if she was that drunk. Is that what's worrying her? What she can't remember that might have happened?

"Well..." I try to smile, but my lips feel stiff. *If I were home... if I hadn't had to go to Maine...* But I know I can't think like that. There's no benefit to it at all, because I've made my choice and I have to live with the consequences. "Maybe no parties for a little while?"

Again, there is a flash across Elise's face—annoyance?

This is too fraught, I realize wearily. I am basically asking her to parent my child and I don't want her to. Maybe it would be better if Katherine was in boarding, even though we can't afford it. I try to suppress the stab of annoyance and even anger I feel for Allan, for putting me—us—in this situation in the first place. Again, not helpful. I need to find a way to move on, for everyone's sakes.

Fortunately, Elise and I manage to find our equilibrium throughout the afternoon; the girls come down and we all chat, and then they do some TikTok dance together while we watch and cheer them on, and after that we all go out for dinner and it almost feels like any other weekend, except my heart is so heavy because I know I'm leaving. I'm going back to Maine, and I don't want to. Not at all.

The next morning, I say goodbye to Katherine, promising to come again soon, hugging her extra tight, and to my gratification, as well as my worry, she returns the hug just as tightly. Then I get in my car to visit my parents on the way home. As I drive toward Boston, I try to prepare myself for another, different kind of reunion.

Just like with Elise, when Allan accepted the position at Wilderness, I had to ask something of my parents that I didn't want to, and I know we both resent it, even if we never would admit as much.

The gracious house I grew up in, a three-story Colonial in Wellesley, has been replaced by a condo with eye-watering maintenance fees in an assisted-living community, that allows, according to its advertising, "a seamless transition from independent, community-spirited living to gentle as-needed assistance, to full-time nursing care by a dedicated staff." The result is unavoidably grim: one half of the manicured compound is attractive, shingled condos with single parking spaces and tiny yards that are maintained by staff. The other half holds a behemoth of a building that tries to look like an overgrown farmhouse but actually contains locked memory wards. Going through the gates of the place feels like driving toward death.

I haven't visited my parents here since they moved six weeks ago, although I did help them unpack their stuff, so I think I know what to expect—except that I don't. It's jarring, to see the selected pieces of furniture—a few tasteful antiques and comfortable chairs, from my childhood home—crammed into the soulless modernity of a two-bedroom condominium with low steps and handrails.

As I greet my parents, they both seem somehow diminished, as if their reduced surroundings have in some way reduced their very selves. They seem older, too, in just a matter of weeks—was my father always so stooped? Did my mother always blink that way, slowly, in a sort of squint?

My parents were towering giants in my childhood—my mother an academic, fiercely feminist and intelligent, my father a titan of the business world, yet with a gentle, almost whimsical manner. Both of them eminently successful and confident in their separate fields, and as much as I have always loved them—and I truly have, and do—I have felt I've disappointed them with my comparatively lackluster choices—stay-at-home mother turned English teacher, with no great career ambition, especially not now, when I chose to follow my husband for his career and more or less abandon mine.

"You look tired," my mother says after she releases me from a hug, frowning. "Is everything all right?"

Already, a lump is forming in my throat. *No,* I think, *everything is not all right, and I don't even know why it feels so wrong, only that it does.*

"Yes, just a lot of adjustments," I tell her, as brightly as I can, but my mother is a smart woman and she's not fooled.

"I'm sure," she harrumphs, and my father beckons me toward their little galley kitchen, a far cry from the soaring space of granite and marble that marked their old kitchen, with its adjoining family room and double skylights.

"Your mother made a pot roast," he says. "And mashed potatoes." He beams at me, as happy as a child. He's seventy-nine and was once the CFO of a Fortune 500 company, but right now he's rubbing his hands together over the prospects of vegetables and gravy. It makes me smile and feel sad, all at the same time.

We chat comfortably over dinner; I keep to the basics, as well as to the good bits, telling them how Tucker's enjoying school—at least I think he is, based on the few brief conversations we've managed to have—and that I'm teaching full-time until January.

"And then what?" my mother asks, cutting to the nub of it with ruthless precision, as she always does. "You'll pour tea for prospective parents?"

"I don't know," I admit. "We'll see what comes up, I suppose."

My mother makes her classic harrumphing noise. "And what about Katherine?" she asks after a moment. "How is she managing, living away from you?"

"All right, I think." But as I say it, I recall how tightly my daughter hugged me, the way her voice choked. "She's a little homesick, maybe."

My mother just shakes her head.

Later, when my father is dozing in his chair, and I am helping my mother clear up after dinner—stereotypical roles she wouldn't have let either of them take on a decade ago—we talk even more openly.

"Dad seems a little tired," I venture, and she purses her lips.

"He's almost eighty."

"Nothing's wrong, though, is it? I mean, health-wise?" I hear the panic in my voice, the child-like obduracy. My father may be nearing eighty, but I don't want him to become sick. I can't have him die. Especially not now.

My mother sighs. "He's just slowing down, Laura. We both are. That's why we moved here."

She speaks with a resignation that tears at me. "Do you like it here, Mom?" I ask quietly.

She shrugs twitchily as she stacks a plate in the dishwasher. "I don't know if anyone *likes* it here. It is what it is."

"But there are lots of activities on offer—"

"As if I ever played tennis," she sniffs. Then she turns her gimlet stare on me. "What's wrong?" she asks bluntly. "Because something clearly is."

Instinct has me prevaricate. "I told you, it's an adjustment —" I am silenced by a shake of her head, and I realize I *want* to explain it to her. I need someone else's perspective, and my mother might be ruthlessly blunt, but she is also incredibly wise. "There's been something of a situation at the school," I admit slowly. "In my classroom. It's made me... uneasy."

She arches an eyebrow, waiting for more.

"There's a student. A junior. He..." I pause, already half-regretting telling her this much. How can I explain it? How can I explain how it made me feel? "He's flirted with me a bit, I guess," I tell her as I stack a plate. "I took him to his boarding house after a rugby injury and when I was tending to an injury on his leg, he grabbed my hand."

She stares at me for a few seconds. "Is that it?"

"Mostly." Suddenly, I feel stupid. "He made a remark about it later, saying no one saw. It made me feel... I don't know." I blow out a breath. "In this day and age, you can't be too careful, you know? And he's very... bold, in some ways."

"Did you put him in his place?"

"I tried, but it rattled me. More than I expected it to, to be honest. Maybe because of the newness of the place, and I don't feel like the other teachers are overly friendly."

My mother nods slowly. "I've always said your forties are hard on a woman," she begins in a pious tone, and I only just keep from rolling my eyes.

"I know, Mom."

"Well, it's true," my mother replies equably, unfazed by my response. "Your parents grow old, your children leave home, your male colleagues start to see you as irrelevant and the men in the street don't even notice you. You're not a daughter, you're not a mother, you're not even a woman. What are you?"

I swallow. This isn't where I expected our conversation to go, but I realize I want to know more. "So how do you make peace with that?" I ask her. "What happens when you hit your fifties?"

My mother smiles and shrugs. "Some women fight it and keep trying to turn back the clock until they look like malformed Kewpie dolls. Other women accept it, learn to move on. Realize the advantages of not being ogled in the street, and embrace this next chapter of life, one toward the end of the book, as it were. But do you miss that spark of interest sometimes? Of desire?" She's quiet for a moment, letting the silence settle between us. "Of course you do."

"*Mom.*" I shake my head. I see where she's going with this, and I'm not comfortable having this conversation with her, not, at least, in relation to what I've told her about Ben Lane.

"I'm assuming this student of yours," she remarks shrewdly, "he's not some scrawny, spotty little thing? I assume he's good-looking? Tall, muscular? Manly?"

"*Mom.*" To my annoyance, I find myself blushing, remembering my hand on Ben Lane's thigh, which I immediately want to stop thinking of, and banish from my mind forever.

My mother smiles and nods. "There's no shame in it, Laura. You *are* a woman."

"He's *seventeen*," I say between my teeth. I checked his file; his birthday was in September.

"So? It's not like you're going to do anything about it, right?"

"Of course I'm not!" I am practically shaking with outrage now.

"How are things between you and Allan?"

So now my mother is going to be my *sex therapist?*

"Fine," I say, shaking my head to discourage further discussion, although I'm not sure things are fine, at least not entirely.

My mother nods again. "Well," she says. "Be careful."

Her warning, so glibly given, clangs right through me.

I'm trying, I think, but somehow it doesn't feel like enough.

And it isn't enough, because on Monday morning, when I head back into my classroom, determined to set the right tone, find an equilibrium as well as distance, I stumble at the first hurdle, because there is a rose on my desk—a single, long-stemmed, blood-red rose. I stare at it like it's a snake, and then I see the note attached to its thorny stem.

It's a line from "Annabel Lee", one we discussed on that first day.

But we loved with a love that was more than love—I and my Annabel Lee.

It's written in Ben Lane's handwriting.

CHAPTER 16

RACHEL

I am four shifts into my matron's role, and I am realizing more and more that I didn't think this through properly. I didn't consider how it would look, and worse, how it would *feel*, to work as a matron, wearing a blue coverall, while my former colleagues bustled around me, busy and important. I didn't think how the students who recognized me as Mrs. Masters, their smart, savvy English teacher, would react to seeing me as the dumpy, nameless housekeeper who empties their trash and folds their clean underwear. I am humiliated in a thousand tiny ways every day, and it is excoriating; I feel raw and exposed and invisible all at the same time.

This time, a boy—Chris Fielding, in tenth grade—runs into the kitchen with a pair of muddy shorts, saying, "Can these be washed before practice?" only to have his jaw drop at the sight of me. "Mrs.... *Masters?*" he asks in disbelief, as I wipe my hands on a dishcloth and give him what I hope is a sunny smile.

"Hello, Chris."

"What are you...?"

"Just helping out." It's been my mantra, my motto, something I chant in a singsong voice, through gritted teeth. "I'll see

you in English class in January, though." I am reminding myself
as much as I am him, because I need to hear it. To believe it.

He holds out the pair of shorts. "Um, can you wash these?"
he asks again, his tone an apology. I take them in silence.

I'm not sure if the teachers' reactions are harder to bear; the
look of undisguised glee, along with a sort of horrified fascina-
tion. The look on Liz Pollard's face, when she came by the
boarding house to drop off some homework, was certainly tough
to brazen out.

"I'd heard you'd taken a matron position," she said, unable
to keep from sounding delighted, "but I didn't really believe it."

"Well, here I am," I replied, rictus smile in place.

Liz shook her head slowly. "Is maternity leave that bad?"

"It's a little boring," I admitted as mildly as I could. "I like
being busy."

Fortunately, she left it at that, still shaking her head, still
looking gleeful.

My shifts were hard, but leaving at the end of them felt, in
some ways, even worse. Stepping out into the dusky night, every
muscle aching with tiredness, and knowing I'd be up until the
small hours with Nathan. Taking him into my arms from
Gladys or someone at Busy Bees, feeling him snuffle against me,
was both a homecoming and a prison sentence, the two inextricably entwined. Did every new mother feel this way, I
wondered, or was it really just me?

I tell myself it will all get better, both being matron and
mother. I tell myself that, because what else can I do?

At the end of my third shift, when the boys are all studying in
their rooms and I am picking up dirty socks and plumping
pillows in the living room, I am surprised by the sight of Laura
standing in the doorway, looking uncertain.

"Rachel!" She looks just as surprised to see me.

We haven't laid eyes on each other since the day Ben Lane hurt himself, and it almost seemed like I'd walked in on something between them, although I've told myself I had to be imagining things. I haven't forgotten what I overheard Ben and his roommate say on my first shift, about how hot Laura was and how she couldn't keep her eyes off him. Part of me was appalled, another part of me was weirdly jealous, which made me feel even more appalled, and the last, overriding part of me insisted it was just boys boasting and being stupid, as they often are.

But now, as I see a faint blush rise to Laura's cheeks, and how discomfited she seems, I wonder...

"I didn't know you were working here," she says.

"Yep." I try to sound cheerful, but my voice comes out a little flat. I'm tired of having this conversation, over and over again, with that look of either uneasy surprise or unabashed delight crossing people's faces. "Do you need something?" I ask, because teachers don't go into the boarding houses all that often, if they're not working in boarding themselves.

"I was hoping to have a word with Andy Garlock," she says, and now she sounds really uncomfortable.

My curiosity is sharpened. I place the last pillow on the sofa.

"Sorry, he's had to step out for a little while. Some meeting or other." I raise my eyebrows. "Maybe I can help?"

"Oh, I don't know..." Laura lets out a funny, unhappy sort of laugh.

I take a breath, and then a chance. "Is it about Ben Lane?" I ask bluntly, and her eyes widen, her expression freezing, before color floods her face.

"How..." She pauses, licks her lips as she stares at me. "How did you know?"

I shrug. "Just a gut sense, I suppose. You get a feel for these things when you work at a small school like this. There was a weird vibe between the two of you, that day he got hurt."

I pause significantly, let my words soak in. Even though I'm feeling my way through the dark, I'm pretty sure I got it right. Something is going on with Laura and Ben. The question is, what, or, really, how much?

I do my best to keep my tone casual. "Is he giving you trouble?" I ask.

"Not exactly." She pauses, glancing behind her, as if to check for eavesdroppers.

"All the boys are upstairs," I reassure her. "But we can go into the office for privacy, if you want."

"I don't know..."

I realize then just how much I want to hear what she has to say. I don't even know why; is it simple curiosity because my life has become so mundane and monochrome, or is it something a little more complicated than that? I can't deny that the thought of Laura struggling in *my* job, having some sort of trouble with *my* students, delights me on some level. I know that doesn't reflect well on me, but at least I can acknowledge it.

I start walking toward the office, with the obvious expectation that she'll follow me, and she does.

"So, what's going on?" My tone is friendly, and, of course, there is no reason for it not to be. I might resent Laura for taking my job, but I know that wasn't her fault, and she *has* been kind to me. If she has a problem with a student, I want to help her.

Don't I?

"Oh Rachel, it's so... strange." She lets out another unhappy laugh as she sinks into a chair, and I perch on the one by the desk, my hands resting on my knees, my expression alert and interested. She's going to confide in me, I know she is, and I feel a thrill of expectation.

"What is, exactly?" I ask.

"Ben. He's... he's been a little bit... *flirty* with me, I guess." Her face is still flushed, and she bites her lip. "More than any other student I've ever encountered, and maybe it's because I'm new, and everything feels a little different than I'm used to, but it's really thrown me off track. I wanted to ask Andy about it, because I'm not sure how to handle it, and I figured he'd know more about Ben."

"How to handle it?" I let my forehead crinkle, as if confused. I don't know why it feels as if I'm playacting; maybe because I've forgotten how to be with other adults, or maybe because I no longer know how to be sincere with Laura, not since she took my job. "Nip it in the bud, I'd say."

"Yes, I thought so, too, but that only seems to encourage him. You can't be too careful these days, can you?" She shakes her head, and I can see how this has eaten her up.

"So, what has he done, exactly?" I ask, genuinely curious. *How juicy is this gossip?*

She hesitates, and I feel her withdrawal. She doesn't want to tell me, which makes me wonder all the more just what has happened between them. "Just little things," she says at last. "Comments, looks, smirks... you know what I mean?"

"Yes, but that's teenaged boys for you, isn't it?" I shrug, unsure whether this really is all there is or Laura has more to confess. "Haven't you had that kind of thing at other schools?"

"Not... quite like this."

I know there must be more than she's telling me. Every female teacher of teenaged boys has had their fair shares of all those things, and we all either shrug it off or smack it down. Once again, I think of that boy telling Ben how Laura couldn't keep her eyes off him. Maybe there was more truth to that observation than I'd originally thought.

"I know Ben is one of the school's students drawn from foster care," she says slowly. "I wondered if that had anything to do with it. Maybe he feels the need to test boundaries, or maybe he's looking for a mother figure..."

Those are two very different things, and I'm not sure how Ben flirting with her relates to either possibility. "I don't know that Andy would be able to give you more information about that, or at least information that would be helpful," I tell her. "I've known Ben a long time. I taught him for the last two years, since he started at the school. He was shy at first, but when he discovered he was good at rugby, it gave him a confidence boost —one he might not have needed, in the end. It's probably made him cocky, especially when he grew into himself—would you believe when he started in ninth grade, he was only five two?" I smile, and Laura smiles back faintly, although she still looks troubled.

Underneath Ben's seeming arrogance, I think, is a deep insecurity. I once found him hiding in the library, sitting on the floor, knees drawn up to his chest, because it was a parents' weekend and he had no one to visit him. He tried to shrug it off, but I could see how he was hurt, and it made me like him more. Still, he is a cocky kid, and maybe Laura doesn't know how to handle that, although I would have thought she'd have got plenty of experience at Leabrook.

"I think you just have to be very firm," I tell Laura, "and ignore any looks or remarks. I find these things usually subside if you just rise above them."

She nods slowly. "You must have had some similar issues, especially when you were younger," she remarks. "Is that always how you dealt with it?"

"Usually. If they don't get a reaction, they tend not to continue."

And the truth was, when I was younger, part of me sort of *liked* the smirks, the sideways looks, the whistles under the breath—or, if not precisely liked, then at least I didn't entirely mind them. I ignored them all, yes, but the attention helped to make me feel confident. Powerful, at least at first, when I was struggling with my own insecurity. Is that what's going on with Laura, now that she's in a new place?

"To be honest, ignoring it just seems to make it worse," she says on a sigh. "And I'm afraid things could become... well, misconstrued."

Misconstrued? Now we're getting somewhere. "How so?" I ask.

But once again she closes up, shaking her head as she rises from her seat. "I just want to be really careful," she states, sounding as firm as she might with a potential brush-off of a boy. "You read stuff in the news about teachers and... well, inappropriate contact, and it just seems like such a minefield sometimes. I want everything I do to be absolutely above reproach."

"Well, I'm sure it is," I tell her, and she doesn't meet my eye as she fumbles for the door of the office.

"Thanks, Rachel," she murmurs, and then she is gone.

I sit back in my chair, my mind whirling. That was definitely an unusual conversation, and one I haven't had at Wilderness before. It isn't as if Liz Pollard is attracting any admiring stares from the boys, and even my friend Deidre—who was younger than me—didn't really get that kind of attention. If she did, she certainly wasn't fazed by it, while Laura seemed seriously rattled.

Guilty.

The thought filters through my mind, settles. Has Laura done something inappropriate? Something that could be *misconstrued?* Or maybe she's just thinking about it. Of course, I know I shouldn't jump to any conclusions. Teenaged boys have febrile imaginations, not to mention dirty minds. Some boy saying that Laura is a MILF is a far cry from her acting on that awareness.

And yet...

Almost immediately I feel a sudden sense of crashing guilt. Why am I thinking this way about *Laura?* She's gone out of her way to be nice to me. Yes, she took my job, but far from maliciously, and, frankly, I don't think I could have coped with a full-time job right now. Two days a week simply being a matron is already just about killing me.

Why am I letting these thoughts roost, fester?

A sigh escapes me, long and low and lonely. I want to go home, curl up on the sofa with Nathan, my head resting on Kyle's shoulder. I want to feel part of a family again, something I never felt until I met Kyle, until he changed my light-bulbs and showed me what caring really looks like. I miss him now, with a hungry desperation I haven't felt in a while. Since Nathan was born, I've struggled so much with guilt— for not being the mother and wife Kyle expected me to be— that *I* expected me to be. But, right now, I just want his arms around me. I want to feel safe and loved, away from all of this.

I certainly don't want to care about Laura Haile and any potential inappropriate relationship with Ben Lane, or anyone else, she may or may not be having.

I hear the boys start to stir upstairs now their study hall is coming to an end. My shift is almost over, and I'm starting to wonder why I'm here at all, why I even took this job.

At five past eight, Andy comes in, looking only slightly sheepish. "Sorry to keep you, Rachel. The meeting ran long."

I nod, a bit tightly, because it's a Tuesday which means Nathan is at Busy Bees rather than with Gladys, and even though I called them to let them know I'd be a few minutes late, they were furious, and they're charging me a dollar for every minute that I'm late, which certainly eats into my paltry pay.

I grab my coat and head out into the night; now that it's heading into late September, there's a nip in the air. It takes me ten minutes to walk to Busy Bees, and by that time they've charged me fifteen bucks for being late, which is more than I make an hour. As I hurry inside, one of the nursery workers—

Debbie, I think—thrusts Nathan toward me. He's both sobbing and sodden.

"You didn't bring enough diapers," she states flatly, making me wonder why she couldn't have used one from their own stash.

"It's okay, buddy, it's okay." I try to soothe him, but he's screaming, and Debbie is glaring at me, and I wonder why on earth I agreed to this stupid job in the first place. It's only for four more weeks, but right now that feels like forever.

Nathan screams the whole way home and when I get inside the house and change him, I see he is red and chafed with diaper rash. I am furious with the daycare center, but also with myself. I should have brought more diapers. I should not have put him there in the first place. I try to nurse him, but after a day of having the swift ease of bottles, he arches away from me, screaming all the more, until I break down and feed him from a bottle, taking shallow breaths to keep the tears from slipping down my face.

Then, to my surprise, there is a sound at the door. I look up from the sofa, caught between alarm and a weary resignation that Gladys has probably come to visit. But then I hear the sound of a key in the lock, and the knob turns, and Kyle is standing there. He's got a month's growth of beard and his hair is dark and shaggy. He smells of chain saw oil and woodsmoke. For a second, I can only gape.

"I... I thought you weren't coming till Friday," I say. I'm surprised, because he's delayed coming home several times already.

"I asked if I could come home early."

"Why..." I shake my head. "Why?"

"I just wanted to." He steps toward me, and a shuddery sound escapes me, almost like a sob. "Rach." He frowns, his expression tender but also concerned. "Are you okay?"

"I..." For the first time, I realize the truth, and it feels like both freedom and failure. "I don't know," I confess quietly, a tremor in my voice. I have to blink a few times.

Kyle comes to sit next to me on the sofa, putting his arm around me just as I'd longed for him to, and I lean my head against his shoulder and close my eyes as I breathe him in, grateful beyond belief that he is there.

CHAPTER 17

LAURA

I don't know what to do about the rose. It's been two weeks since I found it on my desk, and I still haven't done anything about it besides that awkward conversation with Rachel, where I stopped short of telling her the truth. I'd gone there to see Andy, hoping he might have some wisdom, but in the end, I think it was probably better I didn't talk to him. I don't want to make this a bigger deal than it has to be, and I'm not sure a male teacher would understand. And yet I feel guilty.

I don't have anything to hide, so why do I feel like I do? Why do I feel as if I am keeping secrets—except, now I am, because I haven't told anyone, not even Allan, about the stupid, stupid rose.

It was a mistake not to, I realize that now, two weeks later, but once you've decided *not* to tell something, it feels worse to come clean far too late. How would I explain my silence to Liz Pollard, to Allan, to anyone? I have tied myself in knots over this one stupid boy, until I feel like I am obsessing about him, about what he does, or says, or even thinks, and I don't even want to.

I find myself tracking him when I see him walking around campus, as discreetly as I can, but sometimes I think he notices, a prospect which makes me inwardly cringe and squirm with humiliation as well as fear. Even in an assembly, I know where he sits. It's as if I'm physically attuned to him, an internal antenna always on alert, and that scares me. I don't want to feel this way. I don't even want to *think* about feeling this way—or why I do.

I tell myself it's just the nervousness of knowing he's something of a wild card, but what if it's more than that? I think of my mother, guessing that Ben was good-looking, that he wasn't some scrawny sprout of a spotty-chinned kid. How did she know? Why does it make a difference?

It doesn't help that Allan is too busy even to ask me how my day is, or that Liz Pollard still treats me with an insufferable kind of condescension, while Anthony ignores me, and John, while nice enough, just keeps his head down. I have no friends here, no one to confide in, no one to understand something I can't even understand myself. I text Katherine, trying to maintain our connection, and she answers three days later, just a couple of words. I ask Tucker if he wants to come over for dinner, and he tells me he has a lot of homework. I text Elise, and her reply seems cautious, guarded; the affection we once had has been tarnished by this change to our relationship—the dependency I have on her, the lack of trust. I think about asking Rachel for another coffee, because she's the closest friend I have in this place, but something stops me. Is it my own sense of guilt?

I feel almost unbearably lonely, like a cancer eating me from the inside out. Allan closets himself in his study or is hurrying off to endless meetings, and so I spend most evenings alone. We barely get a chance to debrief about basic things, so I'm not even sure when I could have told him about the damned rose.

And so, what I ended up doing with the rose was wrapping it in a wad of paper towels and stuffing it deep in the trash, far from my classroom... which also felt wrong.

I've spent a fair amount of time thinking of better ways I could have handled the whole thing. I could have perched on my desk, a wry smile on my lips, and lightly commented to my class that *somebody* seems to be taking poetry pretty seriously, but no more gifts on my desk, thank you very much. I could have shown the rose to Liz Pollard and rolled my eyes, clearly taking it in my laidback stride, and said, "Boys, eh? What will they think of next?" I could have told Allan all about it, and made an official safeguarding report, and spoken to Andy Garlock about Ben, raising my concerns about inappropriate contact before anyone else does.

Why didn't I do any of those things? Why didn't I *think* about doing them?

My mother told me to be careful, and I know I'm not following her advice, at least not enough. I'm being foolish and frightened, acting out of instinct rather than sense. A student having some sort of crush on a teacher is not a big deal; at least it doesn't have to be. It happens all the time, I know it does, and while in today's age of power imbalances and informed consent and all the rest, teachers have to be very, *very* careful, it's still understood and accepted that these things happen, that teachers can't help it if their students fall a little in love with them, or at least think that they do.

Rachel seemed to think it wasn't a big deal, at least what I was willing to tell her about—the comments, the looks. Maybe one of the boys, even Ben, has given her a rose or something similar. Maybe all the female teachers have similar anecdotes, laugh about them over a bottle of Merlot at Mario's. *Why* am I so freaked out? Why am I always checking where Ben Lane is, wondering what he's doing, *feeling* his presence like a laser, a brand?

And then I realize why when Ben comes and finds me in my classroom. Classes have finished, and all the other boys have left the building, heading outside or back to their boarding houses to change for sports. It's only the beginning of October, and it already feels deep into fall; there was frost on the ground this morning, tipping every blade of grass, every leaf. In just a few weeks, I'll be taking Ben and his class to Boston for two nights, and I am already dreading it.

I've stayed in the classroom to mark some seventh-grade essays before heading back to Webb House; Allan has a meeting tonight and I don't feel like being alone in that big, empty house.

After the easy win of a hundred-grand donation early on, he has become stressed about money. He's intimated that the school's finances aren't as strong as he'd thought, and worried that he's going to have raise tuition simply to make ends meet, never mind find the funds for a new library.

My head is bent over an essay, pen in hand, when I hear the door open. Footsteps, slow and deliberate, so awareness prickles over my skin. I look up. Ben is standing there, looking a bit hang-dog, a bit somber. His hair is ruffled, his tie askew, his shirt untucked. It should make him look younger, like a schoolboy, but as he closes the door behind him, I am conscious only of how tall he is, how strong. He's several inches over six feet, with wide shoulders, a broad chest. It's four o'clock and already he has a shadow of beard, stubble glinting gold on his jaw, his chin. I notice all these things, even as I wish I didn't.

I have done my best to act as if I am ignoring him over these last few weeks, even as I've been constantly aware of his presence. My gaze always skims over him in the classroom; my comments on his essays are deliberately impersonal. I act as if he is invisible in class, and I know I'm probably making too much of a deal of ignoring him, so it has become obvious, but he feels dangerous to me—and no more so than when he is standing right here in my classroom, the sound of boys' laughter drifting on the breeze through the open window, his gaze lingering on mine in a way that feels not just bold, but brazen, and yet also strangely, unsettlingly tender. The smile softening his mouth isn't a smirk or a sneer; it's almost gentle, and it terrifies me.

"Hello, Ben." Already I sound stiff. I put down my pen and fold my hands on my desk, my spine perfectly straight, everything about me as prim as could possibly be. "May I help you?"

He takes a step toward me, and then another, until he is only a few feet from my desk. When he speaks, his voice is a low, gravely thrum. "I wanted to apologize."

I raise my eyebrows, still playing prim. "Apologize? What for?"

"For the rose."

I think I see a faint challenge in his eyes, maybe even a flare of excitement. He's said it out loud, acknowledged what I have refused to for the last two weeks, so it's right there between us. The mood, which was already taut, turns electric. My heart starts to thud, but when I speak, my voice is thankfully calm.

"*You* put the rose on my desk?" I make it a question, one of faint, surprised disapproval, but either I'm not a good actor or Ben is, because he looks as if he doesn't believe my little show of ignorance.

He smiles, a slow, knowing curve of his lips, and then takes another step toward me, so he's right in front of my desk, blocking my view, taking up the light. "You know I did," he says, his voice dropping to little more than a murmur, so it sounds intimate, a secret we share, which essentially it is, because I made it so. Once again, I curse my stupidity, my cowardice.

My heart is racing now, and I stand up from my desk, even though it means Ben can see I'm rattled. "I'm glad to see you're taking your poetry seriously," I say, trying for something of a laugh and not quite managing it. "But let's not get too carried away, all right?" As some sort of set-down, it fails spectacularly. Ben looks completely unbothered; in fact, he seems as if he is enjoying my distress.

He puts his hands in his pockets and rocks back on his heels, creating something of a pelvic thrust. I quickly avert my eyes.

"Was there something else you needed to speak to me about, Ben?" I ask, still not looking at him.

He laughs softly, like another secret. "Why are you scared of me?"

A sudden pulse of rage fires through me. This boy, this *child*, is toying with me. Deliberately. And I'm letting him.

I swing my gaze back to him. "I'm not scared of you," I state coolly. "Far from it, Ben. But your behavior is starting to feel inappropriate. So, unless you have anything else to say to me that is relevant to English class, I'd advise you go and get ready for sports." My heart is thundering now, a pain in my chest, but I keep his gaze as he continues to rock back on his heels, a small, smug smile on his face that I want to slap off.

Then, suddenly, it drops. His shoulders slump and he hangs his head. He looks like a little boy again. "You were really nice to me, at the hospital," he says, his voice soft, his tone turning dejected.

The sudden switch in conversation, in tone, puts me at an utter loss. I need him to go, but now I feel uncertain in an entirely different way. He's a child in need of comfort, and yet...

"I don't dislike you, Ben," I say after a second's pause. "But there are rules and boundaries between students and teachers for a reason."

"You didn't tell anyone about the needles, did you?"

I blink slowly, surprised at yet another turn in the conversation. Is he actually worried that I might have told someone about his fear of needles? "No, of course not," I reply quietly.

"I haven't told anyone else about that," he confesses in a low voice. "Ever. No one knows but you." He lifts his head, his bright golden-green gaze blazing into mine. "I trusted you. You helped me." He issues these statements like sacred vows.

I swallow dryly. I am so out of my depth, and I think Ben knows it. I certainly do. I feel it in every atom of my body. What do I do? What do I say? *What do I feel?* "I'm glad your head is better," I tell him helplessly. "Now, I really think you should go."

He leans slightly over the desk, so I have to brace myself not to step back. "You really don't need to be scared of me." His voice is gentle now, like he's soothing a skittish horse. "You know, I wouldn't tell anyone about... *us*."

My heart freezes in my chest, my breath bottling as I stare at him in shock while my mind reels and I cannot think of how to reply.

"That's because there's nothing to tell." I am finally jolted into action, my voice coming out high and sharp. "Really, Ben, this has got to stop." I point to the door. "I'd like you to go now." My finger is shaking, and he notices.

The air between us feels as if it is expanding, pressing down on me. I struggle to breathe. Ben doesn't move.

"I know you're lonely," he says quietly. He places his hands flat on my desk as he leans toward me, close enough that I breathe in the smell of his deodorant, typical teenaged body spray, cheap and cloying. "Your husband works all the time. Tucker hardly ever sees you. You haven't made any friends here." He shakes his head in seeming sorrow, and again I feel that stab of rage. How does he see these things? How does he have the audacity to say them to me?

Because he's right, and we both know it.

"You don't know anything about me," I tell him. "Now, get going, please."

He doesn't move. "I see how sad you look, when you don't think anyone's watching you," he replies. "You get this faraway look on your face, and you put one hand up to your cheek." He imitates me, pressing his hand to his face, but there's nothing mocking about it; again, I feel that tenderness from him, and this time it confuses me. "At rugby practice," he says. "That first time, I saw it. I still see it. *I see you.*"

And some part of me, I realize, is desperate to be seen—but not by this boy, a student of mine. Never.

"Don't, Ben," I say unsteadily. "Please. If you're not going to leave, then I will." I gather up the pile of essays, stuff them, crumpled, into my bag before throwing it over my shoulder. As I move past him, he grabs my arm, his fingers wrapping around my bare wrist.

"Laura," he says, and his fingers are warm on my skin, the tips of them pressing into the inside of my wrist, making my pulse jump. "I'm lonely, too. That's what I was trying to say. You know I was in foster care? Still am, technically, not like my foster mother even cares." His lips twist in a sneer of something like despair, his hand still holding onto me.

Somehow, I can't move. Can't shake his hand off my arm as I know—I *know*—I should. "Yes, I know you've been in foster care," I say through stiff lips. It feels as if my voice is coming from outside my body. I can't manage to say anything more.

"It sucks," he states, and I hear the throb of truth, of hurt, in his voice, and his fingers briefly tighten on my wrist. "Everyone else here has got their parents, their tennis classes, their vacations to the Virgin Islands."

"You're not the only student here in foster care," I reply weakly, and he lets out a huff of something like laughter.

"Yeah, there's around twenty of us, and we never talk to each other, because if we did, we'd become this *group*, you know? Of outcasts. Pa-pariahs." He speaks the word hesitantly, like he doesn't know how to pronounce it, and I am reminded of how young he is. How *dangerous* this is, simply being alone here with him, his hand on my arm, and I am not doing anything about it.

"You don't seem like an outcast, Ben," I tell him. "You're a popular boy, you do well in school and in sports." I tug my arm from his hand, but he holds on, his fingers pressing into my skin. I know he's just saying this stuff to try to gain my sympathy, and yet he already has it. It has to be tough, to be a charity case at a private boarding school. I feel for him, but that's all. That's all it ever will be. "Let me go," I say quietly, and somehow that makes it worse. It turns this moment into something intimate, and it *isn't*.

I force myself to stare at Ben, trying to command him to release me, to intimidate him somehow, or at least compel him, but it doesn't work, because as I look at him, I am noticing how green his eyes are, I am hearing his uneven breathing. Or is it mine? I feel trapped, frozen, spellbound.

He tugs me toward him, and I take a single step, transfixed for a mere second. I watch Ben's eyes widen, his lips part, and then I wrench my arm away and practically run from the classroom, slamming the door behind me.

My whole body is shaking, my stomach heaving, and for a few seconds, I think I might actually be sick. I practically sprint down the hallway, hurtle through the front door of the humanities building, and nearly smack straight into Liz Pollard.

"Laura!" Her voice is an irritating mix of jovial and disapproving. "You look like you're in an almighty hurry. Is something wrong?"

"No." The lie springs to my lips before I can think it through it. I should tell her what just happened, and yet I can't. I physically can't. Bile gathers in my throat, pools in my mouth. *What the hell just happened?*

Meanwhile, Liz's eyes are narrowing, lips thinning. She's already suspicious of me and she doesn't know anything. And, I remind myself semi-hysterically, nothing happened. *Nothing happened.*

"I just... want to get home," I tell her.

"Oh?" She tilts her head to one side, looking at me in an assessing sort of way, and then the door behind me opens and

Ben Lane saunters out, hands in his pockets, smug smile firmly on his face.

"Bye, Mrs. Haile," he says in a knowing tone, and I'm not sure whether I am about to vomit or sob.

I don't reply.

Ben walks past while Liz continues to stare at me.

"What were you doing with Ben Lane?" she asks, sounding more surprised than suspicious. At least, I hope she does. "He should be at rugby."

"He was asking about his essay." Another lie. I know I'll only spin an even more complicated web if I let her ask me any more questions, and so I lift my chin, force a smile, my stomach still churning. "I'll see you later," I say, and I walk past her on shaky legs, clutching my bag to me. I don't know if it's just paranoia, but I feel her stare burning into my back all the way down the road, until I turn the corner.

Back at the headmaster's house, I close the door and slump against it, my legs too weak to hold me up and so I slowly slide to the floor. Why am I entrapping myself in this web of lies, making everything seem worse than it is? I'm innocent, and yet I feel guilty. I've got to talk to Allan, I decide, before this gets out of hand.

Before I do something even stupider than I already have.

CHAPTER 18

RACHEL

Having Kyle home settles me. Lying there with my head on his shoulder, his arm around me, I felt as if I'd found myself again, without entirely realizing just how lost I was. How lonely.

"How long can you stay?" I asked him, and his arm tightened around me.

"A week."

A whole week. It felt outrageously extravagant, to have that much time together. We so rarely did. And while I'd never thought I'd be the kind of woman who needed a man to make her feel safe—my father walking away without a backward glance when I was two years old put paid to that idea, or so I thought—the truth was, I *did* feel safe with Kyle in the house. I felt loved. And I no longer felt alone, like I was slowly slipping into a dark hole where there was no way out, no way even to see the glint of light at the top.

The next morning, Kyle slips out of bed when Nathan stirs a little after five—he'd been up at one, and two-thirty, and four already—and tells me to stay in bed, that he'll give him a bottle.

I snuggle under the covers with a huge, gratified sigh, slipping back into sleep as if a delicious undertow is tugging me downward and I can let myself surrender to it. When have I last been able to sleep without having to listen for Nathan? To trudge wearily to the nursery to settle him yet again?

I sleep for four more hours. When I finally wake, surfacing slowly, stretching languorously, I can hardly believe the time. I feel both sleepy and sated, the sunshine pouring into the room like a benediction. For the first time, I feel as if I can see, and even feel, a future that isn't tainted with despair. Nathan won't be a tiny, needy, crying baby forever. He is already almost three months old; I can see he is settling a bit more, waking up just that little bit less. By January, when I return to work, he might be weaned off breastfeeding and sleeping through the night. The possibilities of such an existence, the glorious freedom of it, feel overwhelming, and I can finally glimpse it, just a little, dancing just out of reach of my fingertips.

I climb out of bed and pull on my bathrobe and slippers, self-consciously running a hand through my bedhead as I go out to the living room. Kyle is watching the news, Nathan cradled in the crook of his crossed knee, swaddled in a blanket, and looking angelic.

"Wow, I can't remember the last time I slept for so long," I remark, rubbing my eyes.

Kyle looks up at me, his eyes crinkling at the corners as he smiles. "You needed it, Rach. There's coffee in the kitchen."

"Thanks." I pour myself a cup of coffee and sit on the sofa. Just looking at Nathan is making my breasts tingle; I need to feed him soon, and yet I also want to enjoy this moment, sipping coffee in the sunshine, feeling relaxed. "It's so good to have you here," I say, and Kyle smiles again briefly and nods.

"Yeah, it's good to be back."

Am I imagining a slight undercurrent to his tone, a certain somber import? I'm afraid he is going to want to talk about my job, about having Nathan in daycare, about money. I take another sip of coffee. I don't want to think about any of that now. It is only Wednesday; I don't have to work again until Friday. I tilt my face toward the sunshine slipping through the window and close my eyes.

"I thought you could go to that mom and baby group at the library today?" Kyle suggests after a moment, his voice mild, yet also holding a certain, steely determination. Is this the trade-off? I wonder. He let me sleep in and now I have to show him I'm a good mother by going to the baby group? I decide I don't want to fight him about it.

"Sure," I tell him, opening my eyes and trying to smile. "I'll go."

It is amazing how much stuff is required, simply to leave the house with a baby. Kyle stands over me while I pack the diaper bag, and I can't tell if he's just trying to show his interest and involvement, or if he thinks I need checking up on. He's been nothing but kindness and consideration since he came home, and yet something about his presence, as soothing as I first found it, is starting to make me feel edgy. Like I'm playacting at being a parent, instead of showing my natural maternal talents. Or maybe just like Kyle suspects I am.

I take extra care, folding two extra changes of clothes— onesies and sleepsuits—into the bag, as well as six diapers, two bottles of formula, two burping cloths, and even a tube of diaper rash ointment, all just in case. I am being overly conscientious, like I need to prove something, and I'm not sure why. I'm a good mother, aren't I? Surely Kyle believes I'm a good mother?

"You'll have fun," he tells me as I tuck Nathan into the seat of his stroller and buckle the straps. I can't tell if it's a command or a promise.

It's a beautiful day, at least, sunny and crisp, as I dutifully push the stroller toward the library. I've gone to this group twice and both visits were not unmitigated disasters, but they sort of felt like it. I felt like I should fit in to this group of women just like me, new mothers, every one of us so wanting to get it all right, and yet the simple truth of the matter is, I didn't.

I don't *want* to talk about teething or diaper brands or when it's best to wean. I don't want to listen to the anxiety, or worse, the sanctimoniousness, of other mothers as they recite their many sacrosanct commandments of mothering—let babies self-soothe or pick them up if they so much as whimper, feed them on demand or on a strict schedule, co-sleeping is a danger or the only way to bond with your baby, all of it depending on who you ask, all of it believed utterly by someone. All of it making my teeth itch. It's bad enough having to stay at home all day with a human being who can only communicate through cries. But do I really want to talk about the deadly dull minutiae of that life, as well, as if it's the key to the meaning of life? Today, it seems, I have no choice.

Thanks to Kyle, I am early to the baby group in the community room at the back of the library. It is always better to come to these things a little late, when everything is already hopping—toddlers in meltdown, babies crying or gurgling or needing to be changed. Then you can sidle in quietly without anybody noticing. As it is, there are only three other moms present, and they all swivel to face me as I shoulder my way through the door, grasping the car seat with one hand; I learned the first time that there is a strict rule about leaving strollers in the library vestibule.

"Hi there!" one of the mothers, a pert-looking thirtyish woman with a blond bob and very white teeth greets me, a few seconds too late. "Are you new?"

"Sort of." I smile, hating the charade of this already. "I've come a couple times before, but not for a while."

"And how old is this little guy?" She comes over to peer down at Nathan, who blinks up at her solemnly.

"Um, nine weeks, I think?" I try for a laugh, but she gives me a stern look, like I should know my child's age down to the day and maybe even the hour. "Three months on November sixteenth," I add, and she nods, looking moderately appeased that at least I know that much. Already I want to leave.

What is wrong with me? I wonder, as I take a seat towards one end of a horseshoe of folding chairs, while the mother who greeted me drifts back to the other two. Why can't I interact normally with the women here? Why does it all feel so hard, and why do I feel so fake, like I'm an impostor?

I bend over Nathan, fussing with his blanket, murmuring to him, simply to have something to do. A few more moms come in, and by the way they are all greeting each other, they're old friends, or maybe new ones, but their laughter rings out, while I twitch Nathan's blanket this way and that and resist the intense impulse to check my phone, look like I'm busy.

"Hey, are you new?"

Not again.

I look up, my smile edged with irritation, to see another mother. She's holding a baby against her chest, a little girl dressed in pink, no older than Nathan. She's holding her awkwardly, elbows out, the baby's arms flailing, although at least she's remembered to cup her head. But I feel a flicker of sympathy for her; she's young, maybe early twenties. There is a stain on her shirt and her hair could use some brushing.

"Pretty new," I tell her. "I don't come here all that often, I'm afraid. What about you?"

"Yeah, it's my first time." She lets out an uncertain laugh. "Can you tell?"

"Well," I reply with a little laugh of my own. "Sort of."

To my surprise, she collapses into the seat next to mine, positioning her daughter a little more securely against her. She smells a bit like sour milk overlaid with perfume, and I can relate. "I feel like I've run a marathon," she confesses. "And I live two blocks away."

I laugh and nod in return. "I feel like I've packed for a month-long vacation," I tell her. "And I only live a couple of blocks away, too."

A bubble of laughter escapes her, and I feel my smile relax into genuineness. She gets it, or maybe I get it, but for once I feel like I'm on the same page as somebody else.

As she introduces herself—her name is Nina—and tells me about her daughter Lizzie, rolling her eyes over the sleepless nights and the spit-up, I realize that talking with her reminds me of talking with Laura—except this time I'm in the Laura role, the mom with a little more experience, a sanguine sympathy, simply because Nathan is all of three weeks older than Lizzie.

"It does get better, right?" Nina asks, her laughter tinged with desperation.

I smile and shrug, although her question feels like a hole opening inside me. "Truthfully?" I answer. "I don't know."

The next two days slide by, far too fast. Kyle continues to be involved, taking Nathan in the mornings and letting me sleep, holding him while I make dinner, giving him a bottle for the "dream feed" at eleven at night. I know he's only doing his fatherly fair share, but after weeks on my own, I feel pathetically grateful.

On Friday, Kyle tells me he'll stay with Nathan, so he doesn't have to go to Busy Bees.

"We'll have to pay anyway," I tell him, more warning than apology. "That's how it works."

He shrugs. "I don't care. I want to be with my son."

I wonder how Kyle will manage with Nathan for seven

whole hours; he's never had sole responsibility for him for that long. But I decide not to worry about it as I head to my shift at the boarding house, wishing, with a sudden, surprising ferocity, that I didn't have to leave them.

The first few hours are peaceful, at least, as I tidy up and fold laundry, restock bathrooms with toilet paper and check the emails from parents. I see a bundle of printed-out permission forms on Andy's desk, and as I scan them, I realize it's the AP English trip to Boston next week. If I hadn't taken maternity leave, I would have got to go on that. Instead, I see as I read the information letter, Laura is taking my place. I feel a stab of envy, of jealousy, unable to keep myself from it. I wonder if she's managed to control the Ben situation, or if he's still teasing her, flirting. He never flirted with me, I think, and uncomfortably, I realize I don't know how that makes me feel.

I turn away from the forms and focus on cleaning.

By the time I get back home, I'm tired, my feet aching, my head pounding from navigating the noisy chaos of forty boys on break—their study hall on Friday ends at seven, and so for the last hour of my shift, they are bouncing around the boarding house, wrestling in the hallways, shouting in the living room, looking for snacks in the kitchen. I kept an eye out for Ben, just to gauge his mood, but I couldn't see him anywhere.

As I open the front door, I hear Nathan screaming and I close my eyes.

"He's been freaking out for hours," Kyle tells me, clearly at the frayed end of his rope. I hold my arms out as he thrusts Nathan toward me. "Is he hungry or something? I gave him a bottle. I changed him—"

"Sometimes he's just fussy," I reply.

Kyle rubs his hand over his face, looking tired and frustrated. "He just wouldn't stop. Gladys came over and held him for a little while just so I could get some dinner."

"He might be tired," I tell Kyle. "Has he had many naps?"

My husband shrugs. "He's dozed on and off, I guess?"

"Well, maybe that's it. I'll feed him, just in case." I lower myself onto the sofa and Nathan latches onto my breast with greedy alacrity. I close my eyes.

"I made some pasta," Kyle says, "if you want it."

"It's okay, I ate at school."

He doesn't reply, and after a long moment of silence, I open my eyes to see him looking at me, a look on his face I can't quite read.

"What is it?" I ask.

"I didn't realize how hard it was," he says, somewhat grudgingly, and while I know I should feel gratified by this admission, I just feel tired. I've been telling him this all along, or trying to, but maybe he wasn't able to hear it. But at least now he's saying something, I tell myself. At least now he realizes.

But if I think this is the start of some new chapter, I am mistaken. The next morning, Kyle's explosive shout startles me from a deep sleep. I scramble up in bed, clutching the duvet to me.

"Kyle, what—"

"What the *hell*," he demands furiously, storming into our bedroom, "is *this*?"

He's glaring at me, and I feel guilty, and I have no idea what is going on. "What are you talking about?"

"Look at Nathan."

"Where is he?"

"I was changing him—"

"You left him alone on the changing table?" I can't keep the accusation from my voice. "Kyle, he could fall off."

"He's not even three months old. He can't roll yet. I checked."

"Still." I lurch out of bed and run to the nursery. Nathan is lying on the changing table, kicking his legs, happy as a clam.

My heart is still racing. "You can't just *leave* him, Kyle," I say, and my husband glares at me.

"Like you do?"

What? I stare at him. "What do you mean?"

"Look at him."

I step closer to the changing table, and a gasp escapes me. There are two bruises on my baby's stomach, one on either side of his ribcage. They are the shape of thumbprints.

"Who did that to him?" Kyle demands in a low voice.

I turn to him slowly, my stomach hollowing out. "You don't think I...?"

"Was it someone at the nursery?"

A shuddery breath escapes me. "I don't think so. He wasn't even there yesterday." A sudden realization pierces me. "Gladys," I say slowly. "You said she watched him last night?"

"Yes, but just for twenty minutes—"

"Sometimes she holds him a little funny. She doesn't mean to, but—"

"You knew this, and you didn't tell me?"

So now it's *my* fault? I stare at him in disbelief.

"I didn't know you were going to ask her to watch him!" I protest, sounding more self-righteous that I actually am. This is definitely not the time to mention that Gladys has been picking Nathan up on Friday evenings. I'll have to figure something else out, I realize, but that is a problem for another day. Right now, all I can think about is that my baby has bruises—and that, for a second, I thought my husband was accusing *me* of causing them.

Even worse, for a second, I wondered if he might be right.

CHAPTER 19

LAURA

I am determined to talk to Allan about Ben, but, of course, it's not that easy.

When he comes back that evening, he is rushing to a meeting, and by the time he returns, I am already in bed, although admittedly not asleep. But he sighs heavily as he undresses, and as I glimpse his silhouette from squinting eyes, I decide to leave it. When he comes to bed, he turns away from me, hunching his shoulders. I close my eyes and tuck my knees to my chest.

The next few days pass in a similar pattern, with Allan never home, and when he is, he seems distracted, irritable. I have work to do, marking essays, making lesson plans, and so we exist side by side without really interacting, and meanwhile I have to deal with the situation, with Ben himself, every single day, in class.

I decide the only thing I can really do is take Rachel's advice, and try to rise above the situation. Above *him*. And so, for the next week, after our interaction—I don't know what else to call it, what else I *want* to call it—I ignore him with intent, with effort, more than ever before. For the first three days, I make too much of it, dressing frumpily, acting prudish, and never even glancing in Ben's direction in class. He might as well be invisible—except, of course, he isn't, and he knows it full well. I can tell he does, simply by the way he saunters into the room—I see him out of the corner of my eye, conscious of him even when I am trying my utmost not to be. Once, he dropped a pencil on the floor, let it roll toward me before he slowly bent to pick it up, thighs crouching, muscles flexing, hand reaching. I did my best not to watch, while holding my breath.

So much for ignoring him.

I start to wonder if my overreaction might actually be making things worse—*the lady doth protest too much*—and so I revert, somewhat self-consciously and with even more effort, back to my usual self, or at least a facsimile, a *façade* of it. I am playful and wry in the classroom, I make jokes, cock my head, put my hand on a hip, a parody of how I usually am, a *satire*, but I hope it works.

I even call on Ben on occasion, keeping eye contact, smiling, and trying not to falter when I see the knowing glint in his eye as he returns my smile and lounges back in his chair, legs akimbo in a confident man spread, as if we share a secret—and the trouble is, we *do*.

We share that secret every time I glance at him, and then quickly away, betraying myself. Once, he has the audacity to wink at me—in *class*—and to my horror and shame, I feel myself blush. I stumble in what I'm saying. And, worst of all, I glance back at Ben, who smiles at me in sympathy, his head cocked, his eyes soft, as if he knows what I'm feeling, as if he's sorry for it. I lose my train of thought completely.

It's one episode of several, *many*, all of them so insidious I wonder—I *hope*—that I am imagining them, but I know I'm not.

All of this is, of course, utterly exhausting, and it feels as if it costs me everything—my sense of sanity, my sense of *self*. How I have become this emotional, nerve-bitten shell of a woman, obsessing over a teenaged student, of all things, of all people? How have I let a mere boy turn me into this pathetic caricature of a lonely and desperate, middle-aged, menopausal woman? I hate it. I hate myself.

With every day that passes, the opportunity to talk to Allan, to come clean with this situation and to *deal* with it once and for all, slips away. Not only that, but the dreaded trip to Boston looms ever closer, with all its potential pitfalls and dangers, most of which I try not to think about in any detail. At least I haven't found myself alone with Ben again.

I make sure he has no opportunity to approach me—I am out of the classroom the second the bell rings, walking swiftly, and I make sure not to be alone between classes, falling in step with other teachers or students. It's ridiculous, as well as demeaning, like I'm a scared little girl in need of chaperoning, but I don't know what else to do. It's gone far enough already that I am well and truly frightened—not just by Ben's actions, but by my own.

I've had a lot of time to think about Ben Lane, and more significantly, my reaction—or, really, my overreaction—to him. Why has he been so bold with me? And why have I been so meek in my response, which has surely only emboldened him further? Rachel was right, you have to rise above it, ignore it all to make it go away, and I haven't done that. I've *pretended* to, even to myself, but in the seething disquiet of my own soul, I know I haven't. Some part of me—some very small part—has craved the attention this boy gives me, just like my mom said it might. Some part of me has *relished* it, which is so utterly shaming.

If I feel anything for him, and I recognize, with a discomfort that borders on the excruciating, that I *do*, it is no more than a maternal affection, a longing for the children I no longer have, with Katherine in Connecticut, Tucker so busy with his own life. I crave a connection, an affection, and Ben, in his own, twisted, immature way, has offered both.

I know you're lonely. How was he, of all people, able to see that? Say it? *Dare* to say it? *I'm lonely too*. Because, on some level, he understands, and that makes him tempting—not as he'd like to think, in a crass, physical way, but in a far more alarming, emotional one. And *that* makes him even more dangerous than he thinks he is. I do not trust myself with him, and that scares me more than anything else, so much so that I can hardly bear to admit it, even to myself.

Liz Pollard has definitely noticed something is amiss, ever since I nearly bumped into her when I was leaving the building, and then Ben came sauntering out. I feel her watching me, in the staffroom, in the hallway, across the cafeteria. She gives me long, considering looks, sometimes a shrewd remark—*You look tense, Laura. Are you sure you're all right?*

Yes, I'm fine, I reply through gritted teeth, forced smile. *Absolutely fine*.

But who else is going to notice, eventually? Who is going to say something—student, teacher, parent, staff? Every day, my nerves fray a little more, the fear that gnaws my stomach hollows me out even emptier. I start to have trouble sleeping, afraid to surrender to unconsciousness, when my mind has free, mortifying reign.

Once, I dream of Ben, a vague shapeless sort of dream, just images and sensations more than anything else, but it is enough to make me lie gritty-eyed for the rest of the night, staring at the ceiling, sick with shame and fear. What is wrong with me? Why is this happening? Why am I allowing it to?

I manage just over a week of trying to act normal and ignore Ben, and feeling utterly exhausted by it all, before I decide I simply have to talk to Allan. I can't live like this any longer. It's destroying me from the inside out.

Allan and I have been the two proverbial ships passing in the night for weeks—or really, I feel as if I'm stagnating in dry dock while Allan sails around the world. But in the middle of October, he finally has an evening at home, and there are no mandatory receptions or wine and cheese evenings or anything like that to distract us from each other.

I find Allan in his study, staring moodily at the screen of his laptop as he rubs his chin.

"Busy week?" I ask lightly, and he merely grunts in response. He was in Boston for two nights earlier in the week, meeting with some trustees of the school, not that I ever got a chance to talk to him about it, and, I acknowledge, not that I actually bothered to ask. "Is everything all right?" I ask now, more as an opener than a genuine question, but, to my surprise, Allan looks up from his laptop, his expression bleak.

"As a matter of fact, no," he says. "Everything is not all right."

"What?" I am surprised by his tone, by the grim certainty of it.

For a fleeting second, no more, I wonder if he's heard something about Ben, but then I realize I am being ridiculously paranoid.

I move into the room, perch on a chair in front of his desk. Now that I'm looking at him properly, I can see how anxious he looks. How *old*—the crow's feet that fan out from his eyes and have always made him look distinguished are deeper now, and the grooves between his nose and mouth deeper still. Is his hair grayer? How did I not notice before? I was so wrapped up with my own problems, with stupid *Ben Lane*, that I didn't see how strained and unhappy my husband has become.

"What's going on?" I ask gently.

He lets out a weary sigh and leans back in his chair, steepling his fingers together. "This school," he states matter-of-factly, "is going under."

I stare at him in slight bemusement, because surely it can't be as bad as that? Surely he would have known if it was, everyone would be talking about it, worrying about their jobs? You can't hide those kinds of numbers, can you?

"Everyone knows the smaller schools are having a hard time of it," I offer hesitantly. Covid, inflation, cost-of-living crisis... all of those have made schools like Wilderness struggle to survive. Corners are being cut at an alarming rate, which is why, I acknowledge grimly, *I* ended up treating Ben for an injury, in an empty kitchen. No nurse, no matron, not enough staff anywhere. It never should have even been allowed to happen.

"We're not just having a hard time here, Laura," Allan states, an edge to his voice like I should have known this already. "We're going *under*. There's not enough money in the bank to see through even this school year. Best-case scenario, we'll have to shut the doors after spring break."

"What..." The word escapes me in a breath. That really is bad, far worse than I thought, and yet, treacherously, I feel a faint flicker of hope. If Wilderness closes, we can leave this place. We can go back to Leabrook, or somewhere, *anywhere* else... As much as I told myself I was going to give this place a chance, the thought of going home is dizzyingly intoxicating. To leave and never have to come back, never have to see this place, these *people* again... "So, what are you going to do?" I ask after a moment.

"I don't know." He rakes both hands through his hair as he shakes his head. "I've been looking through the budget numbers and no matter how many cuts or adjustments I make, they still don't add up. Besides, at some point you've got to ask yourself, why would parents pay for a product that is so obviously mediocre?"

"Other schools can make it—" I begin, only to have him cut me off.

"Other schools have big, fat endowments and donors with deep pockets. Wilderness doesn't have either."

I am silent for a second, acknowledging this fact. Leabrook's endowment is upward of three hundred million, thanks to legacy gifts from its two-hundred-year history. I'd assumed Wilderness had *something* in the bank, but apparently not.

"What about the alumnus who agreed to donate a hundred grand to the library?" I ask. "Couldn't you use those funds for operating costs instead, at least to close out the year?" It means Allan wouldn't have made his mark as he longs to, but at least the school wouldn't have to close under his leadership.

"I already asked, and he refused. It's a donation for the library, or nothing." He smiles without humor. "I'm not the only one who wants to make my mark on this school, it seems."

"I'm so sorry, Allan." I don't know what else to say, so I put my hand on his. I know anything I could think of he's thought of already, and the kind of cash the school needs isn't going to be raised by some silent auctions or bake sales.

"I am not going to allow this school to close the first year I'm headmaster," he states grimly. "I simply am *not*."

But you might have to. I don't say it. I try not to think it.

Allan wearily rubs his hand over his face before blinking up at me. "Did you want to talk to me about something?" he asks. "I'm sorry I've been so distracted lately, but I guess now you can see why."

There's absolutely no way I can tell him about Ben now, I realize sickly. I can't add to his worries, to the *school's* worries, not when everything seems to be circling the drain. Do the other teachers know? I wonder. Do the parents suspect? If the school has to close before the end of the year, that will be disastrous for everyone, especially Allan.

"No," I tell him, trying to smile. "I was just checking in."

"Okay." He nods slowly, trying to smile, and I walk around the desk and bend over to put my arms around him, my cheek pressed to his. He pats my arm and closes his eyes, and for a second we are in solidarity, in step.

I will take care of this thing with Ben, I decide. I'll write everything down, file a report, even if I don't show it to anybody. At least it will prove I was being responsible. The last thing this school—or my husband—needs is a scandal.

CHAPTER 20

RACHEL

The bruises on Nathan's tummy feel like an almighty wake-up call, a clarion call of anxiety and alarm. I can't stop thinking about those faint purplish marks on his ribcage, worrying about them, wondering how they were caused. Was it Gladys? Was it someone else?

Was it... me?

Sometimes, in the middle of the night when Nathan wakes up crying, everything is a blur of fatigue and frustration. I'm exhausted, stumbling around in the dark, reaching for him blindly, trying not to give way to that howl of impotent rage inside me, even though part of me wants to scream and scream. Could I have...?

But no. *No.* I have to believe I couldn't have. Ever. I would never cross that line.

In any case, I have to tell Kyle not to march over to poor Gladys's house and shout at her, which is what he wants to do.

"She didn't mean any harm!" I insist, while he growls at me.

"All right, fine, but how do we even know it was her? What if it was the nursery?"

"Nathan hasn't been at Busy Bees since Tuesday," I remind

him, doing my best to sound calm, even though inside I am
fizzing with panic. *Bruises... on my son!* On my tiny, vulnerable
not-even-three-month-old baby. And I don't know how—or who
—caused them. "And it's Saturday now," I continue. "I didn't
see any bruises on him in all that time. I'm sure it must have
been Gladys, and she didn't mean to hurt him. We just won't
have her hold him anymore." Even if she loves to. Even if I'm
not one hundred percent sure it *was* her.

"I think we should take him to the doctor," Kyle says,
shaking his head, looking stubborn. "Get him checked him out.
What if he's got a broken rib?"

"Kyle, we can't do that." He looks at me, nonplussed, and I
try to speak calmly even though my heart is racing at the very
thought of inviting the authorities to examine my son, examine
me as a mother. "If you take your baby to ER for bruises, you
know what happens? They start investigating you. They open a
case with social services, you're in their system. Forever." I stare
at him unblinkingly, willing him to see the seriousness of it, but
Kyle looks skeptical.

"Rachel, I don't think—"

"It's true." My voice is high, thin. "They'll think you've lost
your temper with him. Shaken baby syndrome, that kind of
thing."

"But we haven't!" Kyle protests, and I shake my head,
convinced, a zealot.

"They won't know that. They certainly won't assume it.
They'll have to make a report, and the next thing you know
we've got social workers crawling all over us, asking us all kinds
of questions." It happened that way to my neighbor, growing up.
Admittedly, the mom was something of a deadbeat, but once the
social workers started knocking on the door of our shabby low-
rent apartment building, they never left that mom alone. Eventually, the child—a boy a couple of years younger than me—was

taken away. I never saw him again. Who even knows if his mother did?

"All right," Kyle agrees reluctantly. He's no friend to government agencies, certainly. Self-employed, living up here in the woods, he and his family are pretty skeptical of anything and everything government related. I breathe a little easier.

"I'll talk to Gladys," I promise, and he nods.

The rest of the weekend goes more smoothly, as long as we steer clear of discussion of Gladys or bruises, which thankfully fade very quickly. On Saturday, we go apple picking, Nathan in a baby carrier on my chest, and on Sunday, we drive to Dover-Foxcroft for brunch. Sunday night we lie in bed together, legs tangled, my cheek on his chest, as Nathan thankfully sleeps.

"I'll come back the weekend after next if I can," Kyle says as he twirls a strand of my hair around his finger. "I won't leave it too long."

"Are you worried about me?" I ask. I meant to sound teasing, but it comes out as a serious question, and I realize it is one.

"This is all harder than I thought," he admits. "The adjustment, I mean, to us being a three, being a family and having a kid." He pauses. "I don't know that I should have left you alone to deal with it so soon."

I'm glad he understands, but I feel a contrary flicker of affront, that he is afraid I can't cope. Even if it's true, I don't want him to believe it. I want to be the capable person I was before I had Nathan, and I want Kyle to see that. To believe and trust in it, even if I can't.

"I'll be okay," I tell him, and he smiles in a way that makes me think he doesn't believe me. But then, despite the progress I've made—a friend at baby group, Nathan sleeping better, the bruises fading—I'm not sure *I* believe me, either. Even if I want to.

But I'll do my best to convince my husband of it, no matter how I really feel.

On Monday evening, the night before Kyle has to head back up north, I leave him at home with Nathan bathed, dressed, and fed, and walk through the soft twilight, a frosty chill to the air, to the headmaster's house. It's the beginning of October and the evening is still, crisp and clear; I feel its peace like something that is barely out of reach, just beyond my grasp. If I didn't feel so unsettled inside, I'd enjoy it—the stars coming out in the indigo sky, the silence that permeates the night, soaking in. Even after ten years in northern Maine, I can still enjoy the changing of the seasons, the quiet evenings and the sense of stillness. Almost. At least, I can remember how it felt.

Laura answers the door. "Rachel!" She looks surprised, flummoxed, even, and doesn't hide it. Can't, maybe.

I smile. "Hey, Laura. Is this a bad time?" It probably is, but with her schedule and mine I don't have any others.

"No..." She sounds hesitant, but then, seemingly recklessly, she steps aside to let me through. "Actually, it's a great time. Allan has a meeting *again*, and I was thinking about opening a bottle of wine. Now you've given me the reason I need." She smiles at me, too brightly, and I am intrigued as well as tempted. This is not the kind of reception I was expecting at seven o'clock on a Monday night.

"Great," I say, and step into the hall.

Laura leads me upstairs, and then goes back downstairs to fetch a bottle of wine, while I prowl the room I was in before, the little living room with its comfortable sofas and soft throws. The photos are on the wall now—two children, gorgeous and mostly grown-up. I am envious, not of their gorgeousness, but their grown-upness. No diapers, no sleepless nights, no exhaustion, no emotional emptiness. What could Laura possibly have to worry about?

"Here we are," Laura sings out, and comes into the room, brandishing a bottle of Pinot Noir and two wine glasses. "Is it wrong, do you think, to open a bottle of wine on a Monday night?" she muses, more to herself than to me. "Well, I don't care. I have this trip to Boston tomorrow and I need some fortification." She fills the glasses both nearly to the brim.

Oh-kay. I am surprised, but I realize I am totally willing to go with this. Why not? It's not like I'm hitting the bottle every night. I can't remember the last time I touched a drop of alcohol, thanks to pregnancy and breastfeeding.

"Thanks," I say as she hands me a glass. I take a sip; the wine is rich and velvety and slips down easily. "So, what's brought this on?" I ask as we take seats on opposite sofas. "Hard day?"

"Hard day?" Laura leans her head back against the sofa and closes her eyes. "Hard day, hard week, hard month, hard *year*. Take your pick." She lifts her head to take a sip of wine, and then lies back again, closing her eyes.

"That's a lot to choose from," I reply wryly. Two sips in and I feel myself unspooling like a thread, relaxing into the sofa, into my drink, into the surprising mellowness of this unexpected evening. Laura wasn't the only one who needed this.

"Tell me about it," she says, and tosses back half her glass in one long swallow.

"Seriously," I say, leaning forward, alert now, interested. "Tell me about it."

Laura opens her eyes, straightening, her wine glass still held aloft. For a second, I think she's going to backtrack, prevaricate. I am bracing myself for the seeming sting of rejection, but then a sigh escapes her in a long, lonely gust and she shakes her head. "Where to begin?"

I settle back into the sofa and take another sip of wine. "Well, maybe at the beginning," I suggest.

Laura is silent, and with a jolt, I see the sheen of tears in her eyes before she blinks and sighs. "I didn't want to come here," she admits slowly. "It feels disloyal to Allan to say that, although I know he already knows, and in any case, it's true. I didn't want to come here at all." She blinks rapidly, and brushes at her eyes, and takes a sip of wine.

I try to think how to respond; half a glass in and my mind is moving slowly. *Is here so bad?* I think and then immediately after, some elemental part of me answers, *Yes, it is.* Why did I not realize how the isolation here has affected me? Feel it, after all these years? Or did it take having a baby to make me understand?

"Sorry," she says, brushing at her eyes again. "I know that sounds awful, and Hawley, Wilderness, it's all perfectly…"

She hesitates and I fill in instinctively, "Awful."

And then, suddenly, surprising us both, we are laughing, deep guffaws, near hysteria. Maybe it's the wine. Maybe it's us. It's certainly unexpected, because ever since I walked in on Laura and Ben in the kitchen, there has been a certain tension between us. But right now, it feels like we're just two women—wives, mothers, teachers—and maybe even friends, of a sort.

"You know," Laura chokes out between gasps of laughter, "it is. It *is*." She wipes at her eyes; this time, the tears are ones of laughter, or at least I think they are. "I mean, the town is literally one street—"

"Well," I say in the tone of someone being generous, "technically, two."

Laura lets out another guffaw. "And *Mario's*. Allan is determined to see it as the height of haute cuisine."

I roll my eyes, and we burst into giggles again.

"As for the school," Laura continues, drawing herself up. "I mean, Liz Pollard—"

"Oh my *goodness*," I interrupt her. "Don't get me started."

And then we are laughing again, except it sounds like wheezing—or maybe even close to sobbing. There is something both wonderful and terribly sad about it, but I don't even care. It feels so good, to talk like this, like a pressure valve finally, necessarily released; I am sagging, spent, and yet happier than I've been in a long, long time, practically fizzing with it. How is that even possible, and especially with Laura, who I have struggled not to resent this last month?

"So why did you move?" I ask, when our laughter—or tears —has finally subsided.

Laura lets out another heavy sigh and collapses back against the sofa. "Allan," she says, and I feel like she doesn't even need to say any more. I could say *Kyle* in the same resigned tone, and I think she would understand. Men. *Husbands*. Their dreams and desires, their ambitions and expectations. You can be the most liberated woman in the world, fierce and freethinking, and it still comes down to that. I wouldn't still be in Hawley, Maine, if not for Kyle. I would have taken up a position at another school, a better one, one like Leabrook. I would be head of department, earning more money, *something*.

Laura and I are both silent, absorbing all we haven't had to say.

"My daughter is still in Connecticut," Laura says after a moment. "At Leabrook. And Tucker's here, but it feels like he isn't. I barely see him. He came for dinner the other night, but it was like he was here on sufferance, he barely spoke. But he's obviously happy at school... I should be glad, right? I should be *glad*."

I know she isn't. I don't answer, just sip my wine.

After a second's pause, Laura continues. "I feel like I've lost everything," she says quietly. "*Everything*. My children, my job, my parents, my *life*. I don't know who I am in this place, Rachel.

I'm... nobody. I'm a cipher, a nothing. Invisible. Do you know how that feels?"

Wordlessly, I nod. I can't manage to say anything, but *yes*, I certainly know how that feels. Since having Nathan, I have felt as though I am slowly but surely ceasing to exist. I didn't realize Laura understood it, so completely.

She closes her eyes. "And this... situation with Ben," she whispers.

A jolt of awareness shoots through me. I'd almost forgotten about Ben, talking about all the other stuff, and yet now, realization slams through me. If she's felt so invisible... has *Ben* made her feel seen?

She opens her eyes to look at me bleakly. "I feel guilty, even though I haven't done anything wrong. I know I haven't." She leans forward, an eager penitent. "I shouldn't feel guilty, right? Why are women the ones who always feel guilty?"

My brain feels fuzzy, fuddled, but I manage to ask the question burning inside me. "What happened with Ben?" Because obviously something did, more than I realized, or even suspected. But what?

Laura sighs again. "I don't know why, but he's got it in for me, you know? He's always there. Looking at me. The other day in class, he *winked*." She shudders. "And he left a rose on my desk—a rose! I mean, what the hell, right? What the *hell*." Clumsily, she reaches for the bottle and pours us both more wine, sloshing some onto the table. "I haven't known what to do about any of it. I mean, you said to rise above it and I'm trying. But he's..." She draws a hitching breath. "Persistent."

I take my full glass, sip it slowly, letting her confessions trickle through me. This is more—a lot more—than anything I've ever experienced—a few flirty looks, some questionable comments. But a wink? A *rose*? And who knows what else Laura isn't saying?

I can't figure out how I feel—disquieted, yes, concerned, too, but also a bit, just a very tiny bit, yet alarmingly so, jealous. Why didn't Ben Lane, my favorite student, one I felt such an affinity with, ever give *me* a rose? A wink? I didn't want him to, of course, I didn't even think about such a possibility, but... *What's so special about Laura?* It's both humbling and shaming, to resent her for *this*, as well.

"Sorry," Laura whispers, looking abject, a little afraid. "I shouldn't have said all that. I'm just... I don't know what to do, Rachel. I don't know what to *do*." The last is said in something close to a wail, but my brain has stalled out.

"Rise above it," I finally say numbly, falling back on my tried, tired line which rings hollow now.

"I am, I'm trying," Laura exclaims, "but it's so *hard*. It takes so much effort—and I don't even know why. I mean, he's a stupid, snot-nosed kid, right?"

She talks about him like he's six, and we both know he isn't. He's a near-adult male, potently virile. We can acknowledge that, surely? Except, of course, we can't. We don't dare. Women aren't allowed to think that way, and certainly not about someone as young as Ben, no matter how adult he can appear. Men are allowed, no problem, maybe with a bit of an eyeroll, but not women. Women have to be saints, mothers and virgins all at once, always, *always* above reproach.

Laura lets out an unruly sob. "You must hate me," she exclaims, clapping her hand over her mouth. "Listen to me. I sound like... like a *predator* or something. You must really hate me. I'm sorry." And then she's crying, silently, the tears slipping down her face as she shakes her head and sips her wine, utterly disconsolate.

"I don't hate you," I protest, because that much is true. My own emotions are in a tumult, but I am sure of that. I am jealous of Laura, yes, and I resent her, but I also feel sorry for her. And I am horrified that her life is hard, because mine is, too. Isn't it supposed to get easier? Shouldn't Laura be reassuring me of that? *Wait till they're grown up, you'll have so much time on your hands...*

"You don't?" Laura wipes her face, sounding tremulous, hopeful, and my heart aches for her, even as my mind seethes with all this new information.

"No, not at all." I smile, recognizing that I am more than a little drunk. "No, Laura. I don't hate you at all. The truth is, I came over here to ask you for a favor. To pick up Nathan on Friday nights while I'm working at the boarding house—Ben's boarding house, as it happens." I grimace, and she lets out a wild, hiccuppy laugh. "I need your help," I tell her. "And I trust you—with my child. Of course I don't hate you."

And in that moment, I really do believe I mean it.

CHAPTER 21

LAURA

I am sitting on a bus that smells of gym socks and sweat, one hundred miles outside of Boston, counting every minute that passes with agonizing slowness. My head is already pounding, and in the seat across from me Anthony Weiss is dozing, slack-jawed and snoring, as he has been almost since we started this trip over three hours ago. Behind us, twenty boisterous boys are alternately glued to their screens or screeching at each other. I don't know which is worse.

What I do know is the last two weeks have felt endless, but not as endless as this trip. And yet I don't want to reach our destination, a Holiday Inn on the outskirts of Boston, where I'll basically be in charge, even as Anthony acts like he is.

And then there's Ben. *Ben.*

He is sitting halfway down the bus on the right, by himself, although many of the boys are paired up, jostling in seats together. He doesn't, I have come to realize, have many friends, real friends. He has boys he talks to or partners with in class or sports, but not *friends*. How do I know this? Because I watch him too much. I am attuned to him in a way that feels abnormal.

I am already starting to regret sharing a bottle of wine with

Rachel last night. As fun and even necessary as that evening was, I regret it now. I shared way too much. I told her about the *rose*, for heaven's sake. I mocked the town, the school, Allan even—and I *cried*. How could I have been so foolishly indiscreet? And yet I didn't tell her the whole truth, thank God. I didn't tell her how I really feel.

I'm not even telling myself that, because the truth is, I don't know, and that uncertainty is terrifying enough.

I turn to stare blindly out the window, willing the minutes away. Ever since Allan told me about the state of the school's finances, I've been counting down the months, weeks, days, hours. Come March, we could be out of here. Spring break, and we're gone. Forever. I have to believe that.

"Hey, Mrs. H."

I whirl away from the window, shock drenching me in icy waves, even as part of me has been expecting this. Ben has slid into the seat next to me; his thigh is nearly nudging mine and his smile is soft, yet also cocksure, that frustrating yet beguiling combination of arrogance and tenderness. A surge of hatred fuels me, mixed with a treacherous, shaming longing. My hands curl into fists and I scoot toward the window.

"Go back to your seat, Ben," I hiss through gritted teeth.

Across the aisle, Anthony stirs, snorts, and then falls back asleep.

Ben gives me a wounded look. "I wanted to see how you were."

"Go back to your seat." It's all I can manage. For nearly a month now, I've done my best to ignore him, practically fleeing my classes, trying never to be alone, struggling to meet his gaze, answer his questions in class, everything such an *effort*, that it's sucking the very life from me, and he sits here and wants to know how I am?

And I want to tell him?

"Go back to your seat," I say for a third time, brokenly. I

can't summon the outrage anymore, as much as I want to. I am so, so spent.

"Laura." He speaks softly, so softly. I feel his hand touch my thigh, rest there possessively, his palm warm and sure through my skirt. There are twenty boys on this bus, and a teacher right across the aisle, and a seventeen-year-old is stroking my thigh. I push it away, but a second too late. How on earth did I find myself in this position? How did I let myself get into it? Because, surely, this is my fault. Surely Ben Lane wouldn't have targeted me in this way if he hadn't sensed something in me—some weakness, some inkling of desire.

I rise from my seat, moving past him roughly, kicking him in the shin simply because I can, and I *need* to. I lean over Anthony's seat and shake his shoulder, none too gently. He startles awake, dribbling a little. I feel nothing but contempt, and weariness. So much weariness.

"I think we need a rest stop," I state flatly, brooking no arguments.

Anthony blinks at me rheumily. "Are you... are you sure?"

"Yes," I reply. "I'm sure."

I walk down the aisle of the bus, leaving Ben behind.

"Put your shoes on," I instruct the boys sprawled in their seats, smelling of sweat and cheap deodorant. "Screens away. We're stopping."

At the rest stop, while the boys mill about and buy candy and sodas, I sneakily buy a pack of cigarettes and smoke one behind the building, furtive and desperate, sucking in the nicotine like my life depends on it, and maybe it does. I'm not even a smoker; I never have been. The smoke floods my lungs and makes me dizzy and sick, but I don't care. It's a respite, of sorts. It's what I need, to stave off the loneliness, the longing, the terror. They're all mixed together, and it's a potent cocktail of emotions I don't have the strength to deal with.

I check my phone to see if Katherine has texted me; it's been nearly a month since my weekend visit, and she's fobbed me off from coming again, although I've asked twice. I think of how tightly she hugged me, and I choke back a sob. Why do I feel like I'm losing her? I feel like I'm losing everything.

"Hey, Mrs. H."

I jerk around, taut with shock, and yet not even surprised when Ben saunters up to me. I'm hiding by the dumpsters behind the rest stop, and yet somehow he's found me.

"Can I have one?" he asks, and holds his hand out for a cigarette, confident that I'll give him one.

I don't, because I am still that much in control, but it doesn't matter because, with a little smirk, Ben plucks the pack from my fingers and takes one for himself. He fits the cigarette between his lips, an expert at seventeen. Of course.

"Why are you doing this, Ben?" I ask quietly.

He takes a lighter out of his back pocket and cups his hands around the flame, lighting the cigarette with fluid ease, and then inhaling and blowing out smoke in one natural movement.

"Doing what?" he asks as he pockets the lighter.

"Stalking me. Hounding me. Making my life a misery." The words come wearily. I'm too tired to care anymore, even though I know I should. I do, if I can remember how to feel. How to fear.

Briefly, he looks hurt. "Is that what you think I'm doing?"

I wonder what he thinks is happening between us. Does he believe we share some emotional connection? Because, in my head, I know we don't, no matter how lonely we both are. He's a child and I'm a nearly fifty-year-old woman. Of course we don't.

"That's what it feels like," I tell him bluntly. I drop my cigarette on the ground and grind it to ash with the heel of my boot. "Why are you doing this, Ben? Pursuing me? Do I remind you of your mother or something?"

For a second, he looks furious, a flash of rage turning his eyes the color of jade. "I never even knew my mother," he tells me, "so, that would be a no."

I am curious, even though I know I shouldn't be. "What happened to her?" I ask.

He shrugs. "The usual. Drugs. I last saw her when I was about five or so, but I don't really remember."

I am silent, absorbing this. "I'm sorry," I finally say, quietly, because I am.

He shrugs again. "That's not what this is about."

"What is it about, then?" I realize I am genuinely curious. "Because you singled me out from the start. Why?" I can't believe I'm being this honest, and yet I want to know the answer. *Why me?*

"Because the first time I saw you, by the rugby pitch on that first day..." He pauses, inhaling deeply and then blowing out smoke. "You looked like I felt."

I am unnerved and trying not to show it. Touched, too, which is far worse. "What is that supposed to mean?"

"Alone," he says simply, and when he turns to look at me, there's no pretense, no smirk, no sneer, just honesty, and it shakes me to the core. It reaches something inside me I don't want to be reached. Touched. I want to look away, but I can't.

"You know I could lose my job over this?" I ask him unsteadily. "What you're saying. How you're acting. I could be *prosecuted.*"

"How *I'm* acting?" he replies, raising his eyebrows. "And over what, exactly?" There is a challenge to his voice, a dare. He wants me to name it. *Us*, and I can't bear to even think that way. I am disgusted, my stomach roiling with it, and yet I don't move.

"This," I say, and gesture to the space between us. But maybe that's the problem. I no longer know what *this* is. I don't want to think about it, even as I keep obsessing about every aspect. "I just want you to leave me alone," I whisper. "Please. *Please*."

Ben takes a step closer to me. I can smell the cigarette smoke on his breath. "Are you sure about that?" he murmurs.

I take a step back, a breath of much-needed air. "Yes," I reply flatly, and I turn away, back to the bus. I haven't given up yet, thank goodness, but I feel as if I am drowning, the waves already closing over me as I walk away.

Somehow, I survive the next few hours on autopilot. We arrive in Boston, and I shepherd the boys off the bus, help them find their luggage. I check in, sort out room assignments, check on our tickets for a play tonight—Shakespeare, even though they're not studying Shakespeare this semester, a small, inconsequential detail that still encapsulates everything that frustrates me about this school.

I speak in a brisk voice to the boys, and don't react when Anthony takes the room on another floor and leaves me with the room at the end of the hallway where the boys are, even though, as the male chaperone, he should obviously take that room.

There is a weary inevitability to everything that I no longer have the strength, or even the desire, to fight. I chivvy the boys to get ready for dinner, shepherding them out with their over-gelled hair, smelling of body spray and drugstore cologne, laughing and jostling each other, seeming excited and eager and so very young. Ben is in the middle of the group, and yet he still stands apart. I make sure not to meet his eye.

I arrange taxis to take us to a restaurant near the theater, something cheap and cheerful. A few of the boys try to order a beer; they are firmly rebuffed by the waiter, thank goodness. I sit through two and a half hours of *A Winter's Tale*, while the boys shuffle and fidget, some falling asleep.

It's after eleven by the time we get back to the hotel; eleven-thirty by the time I've checked on the boys in their rooms, not making any eye contact with Ben although I saw him sprawled on his bed, smiling at me. I said goodnight, settled any arguments. Anthony disappeared as soon as we got back from the play.

Back in my room, I let out a gust of a sigh, pure relief, mixed with an exhausted sort of sorrow. If I let myself think of that conversation with Ben at the rest stop... well, I just can't. I do my best to block it from my mind, act like it never happened. At this point, I don't know what else I can do.

I change into my pajamas, brush my teeth. I think about texting Allan, but then I don't. As I curl up on the double bed, the cheap bedspread scratchy beneath me, the loneliness I've been staving off all day comes for me like a crow, swooping down with a cackle, settling on top of me with a heaviness I can't lift.

I miss *everything*. My husband, my children, my parents, my job, the life I once knew, and not just in Leabrook, but anywhere. Anything but this. I tell myself to stop with the self-pity, but it's deeper than that, closer to despair—or something even worse. What is past despair? Hopelessness, perhaps. When I think of Ben Lane, of the way he says my name, his hand on my leg, I feel utterly hopeless.

There is a knock on the door, and I rise wearily, straightening my pajamas. I'm assuming it's one of the boys asking for ibuprofen or complaining about someone snoring, but when I open the door, I see that it's Ben, and I realize I am not surprised.

I shake my head, blocking the doorway. "Go back to your room, Ben."

"I need to talk to you." He sounds anxious, upset even, a catch to his voice that makes me hesitate for one damning second. "Please." His voice hitches, and his expression is one of both worry and sorrow. Is he regretting his actions earlier today? Or is it something else?

I step out of my room, closing the door behind me, and stand there, my arms folded, my expression as forbidding as I can make it.

"What is it?" I ask.

"Laura…" Ben's voice drops to a murmur and then he is stepping toward me, his hands on my shoulders while I freeze, shocked, even though by now I shouldn't be.

And then he is leaning forward, his eyes turning heavy-lidded, and I know he is about to kiss me.

CHAPTER 22

RACHEL

It isn't until Kyle leaves, that I realize, as much I had been missing him, it is a relief. I didn't realize until he went how he'd put me on edge, how I felt as if he were watching me, assessing, judging. I had started acting as a parody of myself, or really, a parody of a good mother. *See me burping him, Kyle? See me rocking him, rubbing in the diaper rash ointment, speaking in a sweet voice?* See me doing everything right, even when inside I feel jumbled up and wrong.

It's another relief to go back to work just a few hours after he's left, to hand Nathan over to one of the nursery assistants at Busy Bees, to let go of him for a little while. The bruises, thankfully, have faded.

The boarding house is quieter than usual that evening, since twenty boys—including Ben—are in Boston. I haven't thought much about what Laura told me last night, about Ben winking at her, giving her a rose. That little frisson of jealousy I'd felt alarmed me enough not to want to think about it anymore, and in any case, I have enough troubles of my own.

But as I tidy up the kitchen and living room while the boys are in study hall in their bedrooms, I wonder. What might

Laura *not* have told me? She seemed quite edgy, upset even. And what slipped out while drinking the better part of a bottle of wine can't be all of it.

Or can it?

I don't know why I'm bothered by it. Maybe Ben is being a bit flirtatious, but who cares? He's nearly eighteen years old, as good as a man, and I don't really think Laura is having some sort of liaison, an actual *affair*, with him. So why, as I scrub and tidy and fold, do I keep thinking about her? About Ben?

Yes, he was my favorite student. I liked that up-to-no-good twinkle in his eye, while appreciating that he never actually crossed the line. I sensed his vulnerability underneath, especially when he was younger, new to Wilderness, feeling like an outsider, the way I had when I first arrived. The way I sometimes still do.

But is something inappropriate or even illegal going on? No, I don't think so. I really don't think so.

A noise at the doorway of the kitchen has me looking up from the sink, where I've been trying to dig out diamond-hard encrusted Cheerios from a cereal bowl. To my surprise, it's Tucker Haile standing there, Laura's son, although I haven't actually thought of him that way. When I work here as matron, the boys become one faceless blob—they thunder in and out, they joke and jeer, they leave their stuff and their smell and they hardly ever look me in the eye or even notice I'm around. Alive.

Tucker isn't looking me in the eye. He's standing there with his shoulders slumped, his hands jammed into the pockets of his khakis.

"Tucker?" I prompt pleasantly. "Can I help you?"

"Do you know when the AP English trip is getting back from Boston?" He mumbles the question, his chin tucked toward his chest.

"Tomorrow evening, I think." They'd better be, because

Laura is meant to be picking up Nathan at seven from Busy Bees on Friday. "Why?" I ask. "Do you need something?"

Tucker shakes his head, his chin still tucked to his chest. "No. I just wondered."

I've worked with teenaged boys long enough to sense when something is wrong. I turn back to the bowl, chipping away at the Cheerio with my thumbnail. I think of asking Tucker how he's settling into school, but I know well enough that that kind of question gets only one monosyllabic answer—*fine*—and then a fast retreat. So instead, I ask casually, "How's rugby going? Are you missing any practices, because of the boys on the trip?"

"Not really. It was a little low in numbers today, I guess."

"When's your next match?"

"Saturday, with Dover-Foxcroft."

I turn to give him a quick smile although he's not looking at me. "Ah, our big rival."

"I guess."

He's still not making a move from the doorway, which is strange. What's going on? What does he want—or need—to tell me? "Have you heard from any of the guys on the trip?" I ask, turning back to my bowl. "Are they having a good time?"

"No." He speaks so quickly, so certainly, I am surprised.

Again, I turn back to him, bowl in hand. "No?"

"I mean, no, I don't know. I haven't heard. Anything."

Hmm. The Cheerio finally comes off the bowl with a lightning shaft of pain under my thumbnail. Tucker still hasn't gone.

"Your mom's on that trip, isn't she?" I ask nonchalantly, I'm not even sure why. Instinct, maybe. I turn back to Tucker, surprised by the sudden look of vitriol that has come over his face.

"Yeah," he says, glaring at me. "So?"

So? Why hadn't he texted her about when they were coming back?

I stare at him as he tries to get his expression back under

control, wondering what on earth is going through his head. "Your mom seems to be missing Connecticut a bit," I venture, and his lips twist into something like a sneer.

"Yeah, I don't think so," he replies, and then he walks out of the kitchen.

I am still thinking about the strange encounter as I hurry to pick up Nathan from Busy Bees an hour later; Andy was late again from a meeting, which means I'll be late, and they'll be annoyed. They are, and worse than that, Nathan is screaming his head off. As I take him into my arms, he doesn't stop screaming.

"He's been fractious all day," the assistant, Cara, says, as if it's my fault, even though he's been with them, not me, for the last seven hours. I pat his back as he snuffles and hiccups against me.

"Maybe he's teething?" I suggest, wishing I hadn't made it so much of a question.

"Babies don't teethe this early," Cara replies in a well-duh tone. "And he doesn't have any of the classic signs of teething, anyway. There's something else going on with him. Babies shouldn't be that fussy."

Babies shouldn't be that fussy? Really? She doesn't know many babies, then. She can't be more than twenty, with hair dip-dyed in blue and four piercings in each ear. Somehow, she's the expert, not me.

Nathan is still crying, but not as loudly, and I buckle him into the stroller, while Cara watches, her arms folded, her face grim. When I fumble with the buckle, she actually tuts.

"Next time," she says as I start to push him out, "maybe you can get here on time? You were five minutes late, and I have a life to get home to, you know."

"Next time," I reply before I can think better of it, "maybe you can be less of a bitch?" I walk out without waiting for her reply.

I am shaking, my fingers gripping the handlebar of the stroller tightly to keep from trembling, as I walk home through the cold and the dark. I don't usually lose my temper like that; in fact, I never do. I've always tried to get along with everybody —I've wanted to be liked too much not to—but Cara's swift judgment cut me to the quick. *Something else is going on with him?* What the hell did she mean by that? Why would she say such a thing?

I am almost to my front door, the street quiet and empty, when Gladys pops her head out of her house. She's in her night-gown and bathrobe, slippers on her feet and her hair in those old-fashioned plastic curlers. "Rachel!" she exclaims. "Kyle's gone already?"

"Yes, this morning." Which she knows, because she stood in her doorway, just as she is now, and waved him goodbye.

"I'm all set for Friday," she chirps at me. "Can't wait to see my favorite boy." She blinks owlishly at me, peering for a glimpse of Nathan, who has thankfully fallen asleep.

I hesitate, key in hand, knowing I need to tell Gladys that she's not going to be picking him up on Friday and yet not having the energy for that conversation now. All the same, I know I can't postpone it. I can't lie to poor old Gladys, even if she did put bruises on her favorite boy... and especially if she didn't.

"Actually, Gladys, I don't need a pickup this week," I tell her, and she stares at me for a second, uncomprehending, before her face collapses in on itself in disappointment and hurt.

"You... you don't?"

"No, someone from school is bringing him to me after I work." More or less, anyway. "Thanks, though. You've been amazing, and I'll come by tomorrow with him, okay? You can have a nice cuddle." I smile, a bit patronizingly perhaps, hoping she'll accept this compromise with good cheer.

"Oh, but..." Gladys looks as if she is at a loss, wanting to argue with me but knowing she can't. Then she draws herself up, her expression turning a little stiff. "As you like, dear," she says, and I hear how offended she sounds, and I am both annoyed and hurt. Now, it seems I might have made an enemy of one of my only friends.

"Tomorrow," I say, like a promise, and she doesn't reply as I unlock the front door and push the stroller inside. As I bump it over the doorstep, Nathan wakes up and starts crying again.

True to my word, I bring Nathan over at ten o'clock, after he's napped and been fed, freshly changed and, most importantly, not crying.

"Really, Rachel," Gladys says as I step into her house, "don't feel you have to bring him over if you don't want to."

"I do, Gladys," I tell her, and realize, to my surprise, that I mean it. I'm not sure what it says about me that Gladys is the person I see the most, besides my own baby. "And Nathan likes it, too."

For a second, Gladys looks like she's going to stay all stiff with me, but then her face softens into a smile, and she holds out her arms. "Give him here, then."

I hesitate, because if Gladys *did* give him those bruises... and for a second, I am overwhelmed by all the choices I have to make as a mother—and how I'll be held accountable if they're the wrong ones. Do I breast or bottle-feed? Do I let him cry it out or do I cuddle him? And when he's older... do I allow sleepovers? Peanut butter? Skateboards? Or older still... parties? Alcohol? What about dating, driving, that crawl to jog to sprint toward independence? It all feels so *fraught*.

And as for right now... do I refuse Gladys the opportunity to hold my son? I don't actually know that she made those bruises. I can sit right next to her, and make sure she doesn't hold him too tightly, and take him back if she does. And yet I know Kyle, as well as the invisible chorus of mothers who always seem to be silently watching me, would say not to. Never.

"Here you go." I offer my son like a sacrifice, and Gladys takes him with a smile.

As she cradles him close to her chest, awkwardly perching him in her scrawny arms, I realize her fingers aren't anywhere near his middle. She's not holding him that way at all.

I'm still figuring out how I feel about that, when she glances up at me and says in a tone I can't decipher, "How is my little man? When I changed him the other night, when Kyle was making dinner, I thought I saw bruises."

I stare at her, her eyes opened innocently wide, and my insides turn icy. What? *Gladys* saw the bruises?

"I didn't know whether to say anything to Kyle," she continues. "He's a big man, isn't he? Doesn't know his own strength."

Wait, she thinks *Kyle* caused those bruises? Kyle, my gentle giant, who treats Nathan like he's made of glass?

"Of course," Gladys continues in the same funny, knowing tone, "it's hard being a mother, especially when they keep you up at night. My William didn't sleep through the night until he was four." She lapses into silence, looking down at Nathan, while my mind reels.

I can barely keep up with what she is saying. Now is she implying *I* caused them?

"I never put William in a nursery," she finishes as she croons to Nathan. "The girls who worked in them seemed so young. I was never sure if you could trust them, not really."

So Busy Bees caused them? Is Gladys messing with me on purpose? I have no idea, and I can't tell anything from the benevolent smile she gives me as Nathan gurgles in her arms. I resist the urge to snatch him out of Gladys's grasp and run back to my house. I don't know what to think about anything, or anyone, anymore.

I feel like I can't trust anyone, not even myself.

That sense of unreality, of uncertainty, is only compounded when I take Nathan to Busy Bees on Friday afternoon. I've been dreading going there, after my altercation with Cara on Tuesday night, but I only have a few more weeks working as matron, and I don't have any other childcare solutions.

As I come in, Maureen is waiting for me, already glowering as I close the door. "I need to speak with you regarding Tuesday," she pre-empts me before I've even managed a greeting. "Do you have a moment?"

I don't, actually, because I'm running late, but I can tell I'm not going to get out of this, and it doesn't really matter if I show up to the boarding house a little late. It will be empty anyway, and all I'm doing is cleaning.

"Yes, of course." I give her a cool smile, tensing for the expected telling-off, and I get it.

"It's important that you know we have a zero-tolerance policy towards verbal, physical, or emotional abuse toward our staff," she tells me, as if she's reciting from a staff handbook, but with a decided edge to her voice. "We view Busy Bees as a partnership between families and staff to care for the children, and if you recall, you signed an agreement to uphold all our policies when you first registered Nathan to be cared for here. If you cannot abide by the policies, then I'm afraid we'll have to ask you to withdraw Nathan from our nursery."

She's giving me a warning, so *not* a zero-tolerance policy, then, I think, but of course don't say.

I smile through gritted teeth and nod. "Sorry. It was a tough day."

"You seem to have a great number of tough days," Maureen

replies with asperity. What is *that* supposed to mean? "Maybe you need to rethink your work commitments."

"Actually, I'm giving notice until January," I tell her, my tone saccharine sweet. "Next week is my last week of work until the new year."

Maureen glowers. "We require four weeks' notice for termination of care," she informs me. "So, you'll need to pay for that regardless."

Even though she just told me to rethink my work commitments? I stare at her, and she glares back, and I wonder if it is something about me that is making this woman dislike me. Was it something she saw in me right at the beginning, something I lacked? I've always wanted people to like me, and I've always been afraid that they don't.

Maybe it's from my dad walking out, or my mother's continual, weary disappointment, but I've lived in the push-pull of that desire and fear for so long, it's become normal, a part of me. It's what motivated the glossy, confident image I've tried to portray to the world, even as I often wilted and cringed inside, because that's the kind of person people like. It's what drives me now, I realize, because I'm afraid my own *child* doesn't like me. I'm afraid I'm getting this motherhood thing completely, awfully wrong—and Maureen knows it.

"Fine," I say, several beats too late. "Consider this my notice."

"We'll need it in writing," she fires back, and I decide that I don't care if she doesn't like me. I don't like her either.

I'm in a bad mood all afternoon, and nothing helps alleviate it.

Denise, the morning matron, forgot to change the laundry, so there are three loads of wet, smelly clothes that need to be rewashed. Some boys came in during their lunchbreak, right before I arrived, and left the kitchen a disaster zone, with cereal spilled all over the counters, the milk left out. Everything chafes, rubs me raw.

By the time the boys thunder into the house at four, I'm already stomping around, hurling clothes into the dryer. At five-thirty, when they head to dinner, I'm banging cupboards in the kitchen, where they've made a mess again. And at seven, when they head upstairs to study hall, I want nothing more than a cup of tea and some peace and quiet.

As I wipe down the kitchen counters, Andy closeted in his office answering emails, I hear a ruckus from upstairs—laughter, some shouts, more laughter, another shout. They're all meant to be quiet in their rooms, no talking, never mind shouting, and right now I am feeling like a showdown.

I march upstairs, ready to yell at the offenders, only to stop when I hear Ben's voice.

"Come on, man. Don't!"

"This is frigging *hot*—"

"Don't!" Ben says again, more insistent this time.

More laughter, some scrabbling or tussling. Then: "So did you actually *do it* with her? The headmaster's wife, man?"

What?

"Shut *up*," Ben says, his voice low, fierce.

I march down the hallway and into their room, my hand held out. "Give me that phone," I command in the voice of a teacher who will not be disobeyed.

Ben's roommate smirks at me, but Ben, I see, looks horrified. Terrified, even, his face pale, his eyes wide, in a way I've never seen before. He shakes his head. "We're just joking around—"

"Give it here," I say again, coldly, and with a shrug, the other boy hands it over. The screen is locked, so I gesture to him with my other hand. "Unlock this phone and show me what you were looking at."

"*Chris*," Ben says in a low voice, a plea.

Chris shrugs again, then takes the phone, swipes a few times, and hands it back.

It takes me a second to focus on the screen—a video of two people in an anonymous-looking hallway. It's Ben and Laura, I realize sickly. Ben is talking to her, and then Laura is pressed up against the wall, and her hands come up to Ben's shoulders. It looks... it looks as if they are about to kiss. I feel icy with shock, with horror, but with some other seed of an emotion I refuse to name.

The video lasts for three seconds, most of it of them just talking, and it cuts out before they make any contact, but still... it looks bad. It looks *very* bad.

My stomach roils as I stare down at it, play it a second time, just to make sure.

Ben makes a small sound of something like distress while Chris says under his breath, "What was I supposed to do?"

"Not take the video, maybe?" Ben snaps in return.

"You wanted me to—"

"I *didn't*."

"Enough." I look up, the phone still in my hand, the video on pause, Ben and Laura frozen together in the start of what seems could be a passionate clinch.

I can't quite believe it, even as the damning evidence is right there before me—and I have no idea what I should do now.

CHAPTER 23

LAURA

When the call comes, I am actually expecting it.

For six days, ever since Ben almost kissed me, I have been living in a numb, defeated daze of terror, knowing it will come out. It will have to. I can explain away a lot of things, but I don't think I can explain away almost kissing a student, even if it was obviously his idea. Even if I pushed him away, before he actually managed to kiss me. Even if I hissed at him to leave me alone. Even if he then did.

I know none of that matters. At least, it doesn't matter to me. I feel sick with guilt as well as dread, absolutely consumed by both, like they're eating away at my insides, a cancer I cannot stop. The rest of the Boston trip is a blur; somehow, I chaperoned and shepherded the boys for the next thirty-six hours. I went through all the motions; I talked and listened, smiled and nodded. Ben tried to speak to me once, when I'd taken the boys shopping in Faneuil Hall. Anthony, predictably, disappeared before we'd even walked through the doors, to do his own thing. I'd originally arranged to meet my mom there, since the boys were going around by themselves in groups, but I canceled at the last minute, knowing I couldn't handle it. Not without breaking and telling her what had happened, and I didn't want to tell anyone.

And so, I was alone when Ben approached me, without the usual confident swagger, the smirk or even the smile. He looked both young and uncertain as he slid into the seat opposite me in the Starbucks just outside the market hall, his gaze level yet questioning. I was clutching a latte and I nearly put my head right down on the table when I saw him. I managed to keep myself from that, but I did close my eyes.

"I thought you liked me," he said in a low voice. He sounded sad.

"Ben, you're a student, and I'm a teacher." I spoke wearily, my eyes still closed because I couldn't bear to look at him. "I'm *thirty* years older than you, for heaven's sake." As well as in a position of responsibility, not to mention married, with children the same age as him.

"So?"

As if none of that even mattered.

"I don't like you," I stated flatly, my eyes still closed. "I never liked you, and I never will. Not like that. Not as anything other than one of my students, *any* of my students."

He was silent for a moment and then he said in that low, knowing voice I recognized, *hated*, "Then open your eyes and tell me that."

I kept them closed.

"You can't," he said, a hint of hope in his voice, of triumph.

I forced myself to open my eyes. I looked right into his face —the slow smile curving his mouth, the glint of excitement in his eyes, and I had the urge to cry.

"It doesn't matter whether I can or can't," I told him, "because I *won't*. What... what almost happened in that hallway, Ben, it never should happen. It never should even come close to happening, and I can assure you, it will never happen again." My voice started to shake. "I would rather resign from my job than have something like that *ever* happen again."

His face crumpled like a child's. "Laura..."

"*Don't* call me that."

"You like me, I know you do. We're similar, we're both lonely." He reached for my hand, and I yanked it away from him hard and fast, knocking my barely drunk latte off the table in the process. Foamy coffee spilled all over the floor, splashed onto other customers. I felt the icy shocked silence of a scene being made, and one, I knew, of my own making: the indrawn breaths, the condemning stares and the covert glances.

Ben sat there, simply waiting, while I scrambled up from my seat and walked swiftly away, without looking back or even picking up my spilled cup.

Fortunately, I managed to avoid him for the rest of the trip, but I knew it didn't change anything. No matter how much I kept my distance—skirting around him, hanging back, never looking him in the eye, I knew the truth would still come out.

When I got back to Wilderness on Friday night—Rachel had arranged someone else to pick up Nathan, so at least I didn't have to worry about that—I felt too heartsick and tired to tell Allan anything about what had happened—not that he even asked. He was closeted in meeting after meeting, trying to save the school, and meanwhile I was contributing to—*creating*—its worst scandal in years. I curled up on my bed and tried to sleep; I must have, because hours passed, but I didn't feel as if I did. And somehow, I got through the weekend.

Then, on Monday morning, as I'm dragging myself to my first class, Tamara Watson, the school's HR person, calls me on my cell.

"Laura?" Her voice is brisk but with a hint of something almost like excitement in it, and I know immediately that she must know. This is probably the most thrilling thing that has happened in her career. "I need you to come to my office as soon as possible, as a matter of some urgency," she tells me. "An issue has arisen that needs to be dealt with immediately."

I have a class in five minutes, but I don't even bother to mention that fact. "Okay," I say, and I know I already sound defeated.

When I walk into her office in Westcott House, she is sitting primly behind her desk, hands folded, blond hair blow-dried to a gleaming sheet. "Laura," she says, and tilts her head in acknowledgement.

I slide into a seat in front of her desk and wait. I'm surprised there's no one else here, although I'm not sure who to expect. Liz Pollard? Allan? The police?

Tamara clears her throat. "Some distressing information has come to light," she states, and then waits for me to respond.

I say nothing, because I simply cannot summon the energy.

Something like triumph flickers in Tamara's eyes; my silence is as good as an admission of guilt in her eyes.

"About you and a student," she continues portentously. "Ben Lane, with whom it seems you have an inappropriate relationship."

I stare at her, too tired even to blush, never mind attempt to prevaricate. "I do not have an inappropriate relationship with Ben Lane," I finally say, but my voice sounds wooden.

Tamara turns to her laptop, clicks the mouse a few times, and then angles it so the screen is facing me. A video is playing, and it only takes me a second to realize what—*who*—it is of. Ben and me, almost kissing in that hotel hallway. Watching it as an observer is even worse than experiencing it as a participant. My hands are on his shoulders; I was pushing him away, but from a distance, it looks as if I am embracing him. He's closer to me than I remembered, far too close, and the video cuts out before I did push him away, hard enough to make him stumble. It looks as if we're about to kiss, and we never did. That, and only that, perhaps, is my saving grace, but I am honest enough to admit that's not at all what it looks like.

My life, as I knew it, could be over—my job, my reputation, my marriage, my family. They're all on the line now. I realize that in one sickening lurch, and suddenly I have to double over. "I'm sorry," I manage to gasp. "I think... I think I might be sick."

"There's a bathroom down the hall," Tamara informs me coolly, and I heave myself out of the chair and practically run down the hallway, dropping hard to my knees in front of the toilet. I want to retch, I *try* to, but nothing comes out. It's as if I am physically, as well as emotionally, completely empty.

I rest my cheek on the seat of the toilet and close my eyes. I don't know how long I sit there, utterly spent, but it must be too long, because eventually Tamara raps sharply on the door of the bathroom.

"Laura? Laura, are you in there?"

"Yes." My voice sounds watery, wavery.

"You need to come out," she tells me forcefully. "This is a very serious matter, you know. For both you and the school."

Does she think I don't realize that? That I don't know it, feel it, with every fiber of my being?

Slowly, I rise from the cold, tiled floor and open the bathroom door. Tamara is standing there, her arms folded, her expression stony.

"Are you ready to come back into my office?" she asks, like she's speaking to an unruly child. I nod.

Back in her office, Ted Lytton, the deputy head of diversity and inclusion, is standing in the room, looking deeply uncomfortable but also terribly grim.

"This is Ted Lytton, our designated safeguarding lead," Tamara says, as if I don't know him.

I nod at Ted and then I slump into a seat, fold my arms, and wait.

Tamara and Ted both take seats.

"Laura," Ted says, and his voice sounds surprisingly gentle, which is almost worse than if he were stern, "why don't you tell us what happened?"

Tamara glances at him sharply; I can tell she wants to treat me like a criminal. Maybe it gives her a power trip.

I release a pent-up, shaky breath, knowing I am far too close to tears.

"While I was on the trip to Boston with the eleventh-grade AP English class," I state as factually as I can, my voice wavering a little, "Ben Lane knocked on my door and asked to speak to me. It was late and I was ready for bed, but he seemed upset. I came out into the hallway and asked him what was wrong. He tried to kiss me, I pushed him away before he could, and I suppose someone filmed it, editing it to make it look like something happened, when nothing did." I nod toward Tamara's screen; for the first time, my weariness is coalescing into something stronger, something closer to anger. Did Ben *arrange* the video? Was it all a set-up, a stupid game kids play without realizing the devastating consequences for those involved? "The video doesn't show it, because, of course, it stops before this happened, but I pushed him away as soon as I realized what he meant to do and told him to go back to his room." I glance at Ted, ignoring Tamara. "That's what happened. That's *all* that happened."

"Why didn't you report the incident to anyone?" Ted asks.

A sigh escapes me. "Whom should I have told? Anthony Weiss, who was also chaperoning the trip, not that you'd even know it?" An edge enters my voice, surprising them both, as well as me. "He should have had the room on that floor, with the boys, but he took the more private one instead. He spent the evening in the bar. He was completely checked out in terms of chaperoning, actually doing his job, for the entire trip."

"This isn't, Laura, about what Anthony Weiss did or didn't do," Tamara interjects with sanctimonious sharpness.

"No?" I challenge her. I am really angry now, and it feels good to feel this rage. I've been so stupidly meek for so long, and I don't want to be anymore. "Because the whole point of having more than one chaperone on a school trip, *Tamara*, is to avoid situations like this—for both the students and the teachers' sakes." I turn to Ted, who is looking troubled. "Ben Lane targeted me from the start of the school year. He continually attempted inappropriate contact, and I continually rebuffed it. But now I'm the one getting the blame."

"He *continually* attempted it?" Tamara repeats, sounding triumphant. "And you never reported it?"

Briefly, I close my eyes. How stupid can I be? And yet, all right, fine. I'll be honest. What do I have left to lose? I know the answer to that—*everything*. But I can't keep these secrets anymore. I don't even want to, because they have been destroying me.

"Yes, he did," I say flatly. I turn to look at Ted again. "It was mainly looks at first, held a little too long. Smirks, suggestive smiles, that kind of thing. Nothing I could actually report or put my finger on, and every female teacher"—I think of Rachel— "has had their share of that stuff, so I did what another female teacher advised me to do, and I tried to ignore it. Rise above it. But that only seemed to encourage him."

"What happened then?" Ted asks quietly.

I hesitate, because even though I have determined to be honest, I'm not sure how honest I really want to be. Do I want to talk about the moment Ben trapped my hand on his thigh? No, I don't think I do. "It escalated," I finally say. "He acted as if there was something between us, told me he wouldn't tell anyone about us—but there was nothing, absolutely nothing, to tell. And one afternoon, a few weeks ago, he left a rose on my desk."

"How could you tell it was from him?"

I blow out a breath. "I recognized his handwriting."

"And you didn't think to tell anyone about this?" Tamara demands, sounding incredulous.

"I wanted to," I admit. "But I didn't know how. I was freaked out by it all. In twenty years of teaching, I've never dealt with something like this. And, truthfully, I was afraid I'd be blamed somehow, that he'd make it seem like more than it was—because it wasn't anything." I stare at them both. "I have never, *ever* initiated inappropriate contact with Ben Lane," I state firmly.

Of that, at least, I am one hundred percent certain, but neither Ted nor Tamara seems appeased by this. Both of them have clocked the word *initiated*. Which doesn't mean I didn't respond in some small, infinitesimal way, because, even if I'll never admit it, even if no one, not even Ben, could tell, I know I did.

I look down at my lap, unable to meet either of their gazes any longer—Ted's troubled one, or Tamara's vindictive stare. Why, I wonder, does she seem to have it in for me—or is this just the most interesting thing she's ever had to handle, a chance for a power play? The anger I felt is receding like a tide, back into weariness.

"The fact that you did not report these incidents," Ted says slowly, as if it genuinely grieves him, "exhibits, as a teacher in this school, a failure in duty of care to its students. A very serious failure."

I say nothing; I don't even look up. I know he's right, even if it doesn't feel fair. What about the school's duty of care to *me*, as one of its staff, targeted by a pupil? Not that I'm going to make that point. It's irrelevant; I am the adult, the teacher.

A silence stretches on, and I force myself to look up. "So, what happens now?"

"We need to conduct a full report into what happened," Ted states unhappily. "Your... your husband will have to be informed, of course. And we will have to talk to the student in question." He pauses. "Were there any other incidences of inappropriate contact that you have not yet mentioned?"

I open my mouth to say no, of *course* not, and then reluctantly admit, "He came to talk to me the next day, while we were still in Boston. In public, at a Starbucks. Nothing inappropriate happened, but we did have a discussion about it."

"And what was said?"

"I told him that he never should have tried to kiss me, and I would ensure that kind of situation would never happen again. I asked him to leave me alone, and then I left."

Tamara almost looks disappointed, Ted even unhappier. "Why didn't you report that, Laura?"

"I was in Boston."

"You got back on Thursday."

What did I even do between Thursday and today? Four days and I can't remember a single thing about them. "Like I said, I was scared," I tell him. "You have to be so careful these days, and honestly, I was trying to be careful, but Ben—he *targeted* me."

"Students can't target teachers," Tamara fires back, and I turn to stare at her in disbelief.

"Oh, *no*? What about that TikTok trend a few years ago, where students filmed teachers and then pretended they were pedophiles? The fact that his trying to kiss me was filmed at all —it was obviously set up. The video was *circulated*. Do you honestly think I had anything to do with that? Why would I want that?"

They are both silent.

"How did you find out about the video?" I ask, although I'm not sure it really matters.

"It came to the attention of a member of staff," Tamara tells me with a sniff.

I wonder who turned it in. Anthony? Liz? There's no love lost between any of us, I know, and yet there is still an unacknowledged code between teachers, to have each other's backs. Why didn't they talk to me first? Give me a chance to explain? But then *they* would have failed in their duty of care.

There's no easy way out of this. There's clearly a right answer, I know that, but no one seems to appreciate just how hard it is to give it.

"I don't know what else to tell you," I finally say on a tired sigh. "I know I should have reported it, but it all happened gradually, and I didn't want to make more an issue of it than it was. Seem as if I was overreacting to normal teenaged behavior."

"But the incident in Boston," Ted presses, still sounding unhappy. "Surely at that point—"

"Yes, I *know*," I cut across him. "I should have said something then. I really do know that. It's just... I think I was in shock. I can't even remember the last four days, to be honest. I think I spent most of them sleeping, just... shutting the world out." I suddenly find myself near tears again. "The truth is," I tell them, my voice catching, "this move has been really hard for me. My daughter's back in Connecticut, my parents had to move into assisted living, I haven't made any friends here..."

I trail off when I catch sight of the expressions on their faces. Ted looks embarrassed; Tamara coldly sneering. I'm making excuses, I realize, and I shouldn't even need to, because yes, *yes*, I should have reported it, I *know* that, but I also truly believe I didn't do anything wrong.

Don't I?

CHAPTER 24

RACHEL

I tell myself I don't need to feel guilty, that I didn't do anything wrong, but my stomach still churns for days after I've handed over the phone to Tamara Watson. I realized belatedly, after I'd already given it to her, that I should have actually shown it to Ted Lytton, the school's safeguarding lead, but Tamara's the person I've been dealing with lately, and all I could think was that I had to give it to *someone*. It felt like a hot potato, one I didn't want to touch, never mind hold for any length of time. The last thing I wanted was to endanger my own position at the school, by turning a blind eye to something that absolutely had to be dealt with.

And yet... Laura. *Laura.* Should I have tried to talk to her first? Attempted to handle it privately? But you read the articles in the papers, clucking your tongue, shaking your head, thinking, *why didn't they just come clean with it?* Cases of historic abuse handled privately, inappropriate relationships swept under the carpet, heads turning the other way, false promises that it won't happen again, as if that could ever be enough. I couldn't be party to anything like that, and yet...

Laura. The one person who truly *got* me, in many ways.

Who welcomed me and was kind to me, right from the beginning, who had her own fears, fears she shared with me, about Ben Lane and his inappropriate contact. How could I do this to her?

How could I not?

When I handed Tamara the phone, I saw how her eyes widened as she watched the video, and then, for a second, her lips curved in a tiny smile. It was only for a flash, and then she looked appropriately serious, saddened even, but I still saw it. What is it about other peoples' misfortune that makes us turn into the worst versions of ourselves? Schadenfreude, it's called, but it feels darker than that. What could Tamara Watson, head of HR, for heaven's sake, possibly gain from exposing Laura, the whole school really, to scandal and shame?

She pocketed the phone as she turned to me briskly. "Thank you, Rachel, for handing this in. I'll deal with it now."

"If there's anything you need me to do..." I felt I had to say it, but Tamara gave her head a firm shake.

"There isn't. Thank you."

It was clearly a dismissal. Well, fine. I didn't want to get any more involved than I had to.

I left to pick up Nathan from a frosty Cara at Busy Bees—she clearly hadn't forgotten my unfortunate comment and never will—and then went home and googled the laws about inappropriate contact between teachers and students, and what the consequences could be for Laura.

For a minor, it was clear-cut—a sexual relationship was always inappropriate, of *course*, but with someone under eighteen, it was also a criminal offense, potentially punishable with time in prison. If the student was eighteen or over, it was still inappropriate, still a sackable offense, but not necessarily a criminal one.

But did things between Laura and Ben get that far? And if it was just a kiss—and that was not even on the video—what does that mean for her? Would she be fired? Suspended? Or, as the headmaster's wife at a school that certainly hasn't minded bending a few rules in the past, would it just be a slap on the wrist as everyone agreed to look the other way this one time?

I find out on Monday afternoon, when I am rocking Nathan to sleep, and my cell rings in the pocket of my jeans. I forgot to turn it to silent and its shrill ringtone startles him awake. I see that it's Tamara, and so I put Nathan in his crib as he starts to cry in earnest, and close the door. In the kitchen, away from his shrill cries, I swipe to answer the call.

"Yes?"

"Rachel." Her voice is terse. "As you know, we have something of a situation at the school." She sounds like she thinks she's a CIA operative. "I was hoping you could cover Laura Haile's English classes for the foreseeable future."

Laura's classes? *My* classes. My heart leaps into my throat with both excitement and trepidation. "Yes, of course," I say. "Has she... has she been suspended?"

"Pending an inquiry," Tamara replies, "and I'm afraid that's all I can say about it. Are you able to start tomorrow?"

"I'm meant to be on duty as matron—"

"Never mind about that."

"Yes," I say immediately, although it will mean calling Busy Bees and having to beg to rework Nathan's hours. "Yes, of course I can."

I feel dazed, as if I am in a dream, as I end the call. Tomorrow I'll be teaching again. *Teaching.* And yet...

My stomach is still churning, and there is a sour taste in my mouth.

Nathan is still screaming, and I hurry to his nursery, grab him from his crib, try to shush him, and all the while, my mind races, and I have no idea how I should feel.

. . .

Predictably, Maureen is sanctimonious about taking Nathan for the whole day tomorrow.

"But you have space!" I insist when I call her, because I know that is not in question.

"You already gave your notice—"

"Situations change, and you have *space*."

She sighs. "What times are you hoping for?"

I tell her, and after more coaxing and begging, she finally agrees. As I get off the phone, a shudder escapes me and again I feel that restless churn inside me, as I struggle to know how to feel.

I did the right thing. Didn't I?

I have to be at Busy Bees by eight the next morning, and I am still feeding Nathan at seven-forty. He woke up four times in the night, and I'm tired and stressed, already tense with frantic energy. This is, I am realizing, all going to be a lot harder than I thought it was.

Somehow, breathless, sweating, my hair still wet from my shower, I get Nathan there at five to eight, and I'm in my classroom at ten after, still breathless, still sweating, and my hair now sticking to my face. I can't believe I did this five times a week, without any problem at all—but then I didn't have a human being to look after, and I was getting eight hours of sleep a night.

I take a few moments to compose myself, brush my hair, put on some lipstick. I look down at my outfit—my best pair of maternity pants, a sweater that covers my stomach. It's a far cry from what I used to wear, but at least my clothes are not sporting any stains or sweat patches. I look decent.

I flick through the syllabus, which I am familiar with; last night, Liz Pollard sent me a rather brusque email informing me what Laura had got up to in the semester's unit on poetry. She's done Gothic, Romantic, and has just started Victorian poetry—

Tennyson and Browning. I can do this in my sleep, I think, but then, as I review the text of Browning's most famous poem, "My Last Duchess," an unease starts to steal through me.

Oh, sir, she smiled, no doubt,
Whene'er I passed her; but who passed without
Much the same smile? This grew; I gave commands;
Then all smiles stopped together…

The poem is a monologue by the Renaissance-era Duke of Ferrara, musing on the portrait of the wife he had killed, his cold and callous cruelty toward her slowly and shockingly revealed through the text. In the past, I've enjoyed teaching it to my students, guiding them through the difficult and often archaic language, helping them to see how the duke slips in his dark references with such chilling casualty—*E'en then would be some stooping; and I choose/Never to stoop*—but now I hesitate.

It all feels a little too *close*, somehow, even though I know the situations are completely different. Laura is not some young, innocent duchess framed in a portrait, with *"the depth and passion of its earnest glance."* And Ben Lane, all of seventeen years old, is not the nefarious and scheming duke, who can poison a wife without batting an eyelid, who mentions the *"half-flush that dies along her throat."*

And yet… I am uneasy. I find that I'm not questioning Laura, or Ben, but myself.

I did the right thing.

A sound at the door makes me jump; it's still ten minutes to class, and the boys shouldn't be coming in yet, but one boy is.

Ben.

I put the poetry anthology back on my desk, my heart fluttering with nerves. I actually feel a little scared to see him, in part because of the hard look on his face, brows drawn together, eyes narrowed, lips pressed into a straight line. He looks very tall and strong, and I am aware of him in a way I've never been before.

"Hello, Ben."

He stares at me for a moment, and then he closes the door behind him in a way that feels vaguely menacing. I tell myself I'm being fanciful. He's a *child*. And I did the right thing.

"Why are you here?" he demands in an unfriendly tone.

Just like that, I am catapulted into a situation I didn't expect, but maybe I should have—this animosity, this *aggression*, and from a student I thought I had a good rapport with, once upon a time. I know I should do what I told Laura to do, and rise above it, and yet somehow, in this fraught moment, I can't.

"What do you mean?" I ask, and he takes a step toward me. It takes effort to stand my ground, keep a faint, inquiring smile on my face.

"Why are you teaching Lau—Mrs. Haile's class?"

I don't miss the fact that he almost called her *Laura*, and I feel vindicated. If he can call her by her first name to *me*, something more must have gone on. It gives me the sense of authority, of superiority, that I need, and I straighten.

"That's none of your concern, Ben," I tell him briskly, my tone turning a little supercilious. "Now, maybe you should go get ready for class."

I look down, uselessly rearranging the books on my desk, until he stops me with a palm slapped flat on top of the poetry anthology, the suddenness of it making me jump a little, the noise echoing through the still classroom. I look up, my heart starting to race.

"*Excuse* me—"

He is scowling now, and it feels threatening. I am conscious of how tall he is, how wide his shoulders, in a way I never have before. "It *is* my concern," he tells me in a low, growling sort of voice. "You *know* it is, because you turned the video in, didn't you?" His face twists, his voice filled with venom. "You just went and *narced* on her."

"Ben." I recoil, but keep my tone firm. "Do *not* use that tone with me."

"Why not?" He leans over the desk, seeming even more menacing now. "It's true. What, were you *jealous*?" His lip curls in a sneer. "Did you want some of that action, maybe, Mrs. Masters?" He says my name like it's an insult.

Rage fires through me, along with fear. I can't believe how quickly this has escalated, how unprepared I am for any of it. I have a sudden, surprising shaft of sympathy for Laura; right now, I can see, all too clearly, how she might have been backed into a corner.

And yet Ben is just a boy, a vulnerable boy, who has spent his life in care. Even if that is not how he is coming across now... at all.

I take a steadying breath.

"I'm not jealous, Ben, and this conversation needs to stop right now. I suggest you go and get ready for class." I place my palms flat on the desk and hold his gaze, even though my heart is beating wildly, my face flushed.

Ben rakes me up and down with his contemptuous gaze, seeming to dismiss me not just as a teacher but as a woman, a human being, and then he shakes his head. "Whatever," he says, a sneer, and walks out of the classroom, slamming the door behind him so loud it rattles in its frame, and a book falls off my desk.

I find my legs are trembling, so I have to sit in my chair. A sound escapes me, something almost like a sob. I cover my hand with my mouth, just as boys start trickling into class.

They look at me in surprise when they see me, but I can tell they are not *that* surprised. They know what has happened. How many just saw Ben storm out of my classroom? How many of them have watched the video of him and Laura? I find myself again feeling that surge of sympathy for Laura, for how exposed she must feel, how vulnerable.

But Ben is the vulnerable one. Isn't he?

Somehow I manage to get through that class, teaching "My Last Duchess" in a dispassionate way, droning on the way Liz or Anthony might, not caring if I sound dull. I get through the next class and the next and the next after that, but all the while, I feel as if I am apart from myself, as I am observing this pale-faced, lank-haired woman, wondering what she is thinking. Feeling. Wondering why she is here at all.

At lunchtime, I go into the female staff bathroom to express milk, because my breasts are so full and aching. I do it clumsily, because I have yet to get the hang of a breast pump, but the relief I feel as my breasts begin to empty out is palpable. Halfway through the laborious procedure, Kate, the PE teacher who was so friendly with me once, comes in and does a double take.

"Rachel..."

"Sorry." I try to laugh as I gesture to the pump, my boob. "Needs must."

"Oh, don't worry about that." She waves me away, my sweater rucked up and the plastic pump with its suction cup attached to my breast, with a small, understanding smile. "I guess you're here because of Laura?" She sounds unhappy, and so I simply nod. "I feel bad for her," Kate tells me, like a confession. "I didn't know her that well, it's true, but she seemed nice. And you just wonder... is there more to the story?"

I have no idea what to say.

I think Kate takes my silence for some sort of disapproval, because she ducks her head. "Sorry... but do you know what I mean?"

"Yes," I reply, sincerely, because I do. There *is* more to the story, and I know at least some of it. I know Laura was anxious about Ben's attention. Should I have taken that into consideration, before handing over the phone? I detach myself from the pump and cover up, because you can't have any kind of real conversation while you're being milked like a cow. "It seems like a complicated situation," I offer.

"Do you know who turned in the video?" she asked. "Because that seems like such a hard call... I mean, why not just give it to her? Let her be the one to turn it in, at least?"

For a second, I simply stare at her, stricken, because while I had, briefly, thought about that after the fact, it's galling to know other people are, as well. Is that what I should have done? Is it what everyone thinks I should have done? "I don't know," I finally murmur. "I guess... I guess they must have had a reason."

"I guess," Kate replies, but she doesn't sound convinced.

I fix my rumpled sweater, my cheeks heating. *Should* I have shown Laura the video? I wonder again. Given her a chance to explain, to turn it in herself, at least, which would have had far better optics? That feels fair, reasonable, and yet it didn't even cross my mind.

Why? Was some part of me *trying* to get her into trouble? The thought is troubling, shaming. I'm not that kind of vindictive person. I know I'm not. And yet I doubt myself, my motives. Since having Nathan, I don't know who I am anymore.

"Well, good to see you again," Kate says, and she sounds as unconvinced of that as she was of the backstabber who turned in the video. That is, me.

By the end of the day, I am absolutely wilting. I forgot how exhausting teaching was, except maybe it wasn't, it didn't used to be, because I wasn't doing it on less than four hours' sleep and I also wasn't wondering if I'm just about the worst person in the world, for turning that video in.

And that feeling only gets worse when I start walking

toward town, to pick up Nathan, and Laura herself opens the door of the headmaster's house as I pass and beckons me.

"Rachel." She's whispering, like we have a secret, or she's a spy.

For a second, I am tempted—*so* tempted—to pretend I don't hear her. I want to keep walking; I *need* to, but I can't do that to her—or maybe to myself—and so I slow. Stop. Turn around.

"Hi, Laura."

She looks terrible. Pasty-faced, her greasy hair in a ponytail, but with hanks of it falling down, half-obscuring her face. She's wearing a gray sweatshirt and sweatpants, both hanging off her frame, reminding me of a prison uniform.

"You're covering for me?" she asks, and I manage a nod. Her face collapses in on itself, reminding me, of all things, of a sunken soufflé.

"Do you want to come in for a minute?" she asks. "I know I'm *persona non grata* right now, but..." She trails off pathetically.

I do not want to come in. I feel horribly, wretchedly, guilty now, as I look at her looking so defeated, so *destroyed*. "I'm sorry," I say, "I have to get Nathan."

"Oh, of course. Is he at Busy Bees?"

I nod.

"I was thinking you wouldn't want me to pick him up anymore—" For a second, her voice trembles and I think she might cry. "I never even got a chance to, but I guess you don't need me to now? You're not matron anymore."

I swallow, unable to look her in the eye. "No." I realize I have to say something. "Laura," I begin, "I'm sorry..." I mean to say I'm sorry this happened to her at all, but something in my voice betrays me; maybe part of me, subconsciously at least, wanted to be betrayed. For her to find out, so I could at least have the possibility of being exonerated. Absolved.

She frowns, confused, and then realization dawns slowly,

like a mist lifting from her face. "Wait..." she breathes. She takes a step toward me, and then stops.

I stand still, ready to take it. Knowing I need to.

"It was you," she says softly, her voice reminding me of something broken—a bird, perhaps, or a toy. "It was *you*."

"Laura..." I stop, because there is nothing to say.

"*Why?*" she whispers. She's not angry, she's *hurt*, and that is so much worse. "Why didn't you come to me first?" she asks, her voice growing stronger. "Why wouldn't you give me a chance to explain, to go to Tamara or Ted first myself? Instead you... you..."

She's at a loss for words, but I'm not. "Narced on you," I state dully, thinking of Ben.

She looks startled, and a little confused again, and then she just shakes her head. "I thought we were friends," she says, still shaking her head. "I told you things. I thought you understood what was really going on."

"I *did*—"

"And yet you turned that video in without a word to me? Knowing how concerned I was, how I was afraid that he'd do something pretty much exactly like that? I *trusted* you."

"Laura, I had no choice—" My tone is strident, the words feeble.

She shakes her head harder this time, the look of despair on her face turned to one of disdain. "Go to hell, Rachel," she spits, as she turns away. "Go to *hell*."

And as she retreats back into the headmaster's house, slamming the door behind her, I wonder if I am already there.

CHAPTER 25

LAURA

I honestly didn't think things could get any worse, but clearly they can. Of *course* they can. Had I really thought I'd reached rock bottom? My husband can barely speak to me; my son refuses to. The school is still deciding whether criminal charges might be pressed against me. I'm not at rock bottom at all. I've barely glimpsed its dark depths, yawning below me. And now Rachel... *Rachel*, the one person I counted as a friend in this place, betrayed me—and I'm not even surprised.

She was there from the beginning, wasn't she? I recall the look of surprise and suspicion that crossed her face for an instant when she walked into the boarding house kitchen, when Ben was first injured. The way she asked me for details when I came looking for Andy Garlock, to discuss the situation. How willingly and even eagerly she listened to me talk about Ben, the wink, the rose. She knew pretty much all of it, and she clearly didn't hesitate to turn that damned phone over to Tamara Watson, of all people.

I close my eyes, my arms wrapped around my waist as if I need to physically hold myself together, and maybe I do. The last twenty-four hours have been, absolutely, the worst of my life. After the torturous meeting with Tamara and Ted, I was told that I would be suspended, effective immediately, pending an inquiry into my actions. I felt cold and numb inside, which was better, I supposed, than feeling terrified, although I knew I felt that, too, even if I was trying not to acknowledge how it was poised to swamp me, if I let it.

As I walked from Westcott House to Webb House just across the street, I felt as if everyone was staring at me, whispering and pointing, even though there was hardly anyone around, as first period had already started. How many students had seen that video? Had *Tucker*? I shuddered to think of him watching it. I hadn't known, of course, that Ben's almost-kiss—because it *was* his, not mine—had been filmed. Had he planned it? Had it all been a set-up to mock me? Stupidly, the thought hurt, even though I didn't want to let it. Ben Lane meant nothing to me. *Nothing.*

The next few hours passed in a haze of dazed incredulity. I curled up on the sofa upstairs, the cashmere throw that had been a wedding gift—the same one I had lent to Rachel when she'd been nursing Nathan—draped over me. I closed my eyes against the world, even though I couldn't sleep, my knees tucked to my chest like a child. Ted and Tamara would have told Allan by now—how had he responded? What had he thought of me? I imagined his face hardening into disgust, or worse, crumpling into hurt, and I pushed the image away because I couldn't bear it.

Then I wondered if I should contact a lawyer, if I needed to make plans and provisions just in case, but I couldn't even move. I lay there, my eyes scrunched closed, my knees tucked up to my chest, until Allan finally came home, somewhere around four o'clock.

I heard the click of the front door closing, and then a few

seconds' silence. I imagined him simply standing there, his head lowered, shoulders bowed. I hadn't checked my phone for any messages or texts, but I doubted he would have sent any, once he'd been told. I hoped he didn't believe that I'd had some sort of affair. I hoped he trusted me that much, at least, despite the seeming evidence right before his eyes.

He came slowly up the stairs, each footstep sounding so labored, so weary. I told myself to sit up at least, but I couldn't even manage that much.

I heard him come to the doorway of our living room, and I didn't even open my eyes.

"Laura." His voice sounded heavy, sad. "How are you holding up?"

Relief coursed through me, that he was asking me this. I realized I'd half-expected him to fly at me, for creating this scandal that might threaten the school even more than it already was.

"I'm..." After lying still and silent for so long, my voice sounded croaky. "I'm pretty crap, actually," I said, and then I tried to laugh, except I ended up crying, a hiccough escaping me before tears slid silently down my face.

"Oh, Laura." Allan came over to sit on the edge of the coffee table, reaching out one hand to stroke my hair.

"I'm sorry," I choked out, and his hand stilled on my hair.

"For what?" he asked, and I heard the wariness in his tone, the suspicion.

"For creating such a scandal for the school," I told him, my voice sharpening, rising. "Not for—Allan, did Tamara tell you what I said? Ben Lane was *targeting* me. Nothing happened between us. I mean, nothing, you know—"

"I know." His voice was quiet again, and sad, but not entirely convinced, either.

I made myself scramble up to a seated position, pushing my

hair out of my face, wiping the streaks of tears from my cheeks. "I know I should have told you what was going on. And other people, too. I kept meaning to make a report, but Liz Pollard has always been so... so *sneering* and suspicious of me, and I felt like it would make everything worse, a bigger deal than it was, if I mentioned it to her. I honestly thought it would all blow over, that he was just testing my limits." I risked a glance at him, hoping he understood. Needing him to believe me, but I couldn't tell anything from his expression, his eyes downcast, his lips pursed. "Allan, *say* something."

"I don't know what to say." He looked up, and the bleakness in his eyes stole my breath. "What do you want me to say?"

"That you *believe* me."

"That Ben Lane targeted you in some way? I do believe you." But the way he said it made me feel like that was maybe the *only* thing he believed.

"What did they tell you?" I asked. "Tamara and Ted?"

"Just that they were required to open an inquiry into your behavior with Ben. They showed me the video and they told me that you were suspended until it was resolved. And, considering our relationship, I would naturally not be involved in the inquiry. One of the trustees is overseeing it."

"Oh..." I felt leaden at learning that. The trustees who Allan was appealing to, to save the school. Both our reputations have suffered, and I know Allan will feel that even more than I do. "Did they say how long it will take?"

"I have no idea." He rose from the table where he'd been sitting, loosening his tie and shrugging off his suit jacket, which he tossed, crumpled, onto the sofa. It was so unlike him; Allan always took good care of his clothes, especially his suits, kept the jackets and trousers neatly pressed on padded cedar hangers.

"I'm sorry," I said again, in little more than a whisper. "I never meant for this to happen."

Allan was silent for a moment, his back to me, his head lowered. Then he shoved his hands in the pockets of his trousers and turned around. "How *did* it happen, as a matter of interest?" His tone had become decidedly cool, and I tensed.

"I told you—"

"No, you didn't," he cut me off. "You told Ted and Tamara, although I imagine you left out a few details." He eyed me appraisingly. "Why don't you tell me, Laura? Everything. Not as a headmaster, but as your *husband*." His voice throbbed with hurt, and I felt a tear slip down my cheek.

"I'm so sorry," I said again, barely able to get the words out of my throat, which had turned painfully tight. "I'm so sorry."

"For what? Don't talk about the scandal again," he warned me, his voice rising; I realized he wasn't just hurt, but angry. "Talk to me about how Ben Lane, a seventeen-year-old student, was able to send you a rose, practically kiss you in the hallway, without anyone else knowing. What else happened between you two, Laura?" His voice throbbed now. "What else?"

"Nothing..." I sounded abject, feeble, and my husband wasn't convinced.

"Please don't lie to me."

I closed my eyes. "I'm not," I whispered. "Allan, nothing else physical happened between us. I swear to you on my life, on our *children*'s lives, that is true. You have to believe me."

A ragged gust of sound escaped him, and he lowered himself onto the sofa, dropping his head into his hands.

"I *do* believe you," he said in a low voice. "But you must know that's not just what I meant."

I eyed him uneasily, waiting for more.

"I've been a teacher for a long time, Laura," he said finally. "So have you. We both know that kids get crushes. They act inappropriately, they push the boundaries. Sometimes they even cross the line."

He paused, and I waited again, wishing I knew where he was going with this. Wishing I knew how I was meant to respond.

"But when that happens," he continued steadily, "the teacher in question makes a report, makes sure it's all transparent, totally out in the open for everyone to see, to show they have absolutely nothing to hide. You didn't do that, and don't give me that crap about Liz Pollard again, because I *know* you, and I know it's more than that. I can see it in your face right now, even if I didn't sense it, from everything I was—and wasn't—told." He was breathing heavily then, his gaze more tormented than angry, before he dropped his head into his hands again, a sound escaping him that was far too close to a sob.

"Allan... *Allan.*" I gulped back a sob of my own. "It really wasn't like that."

He shook his head, still dropped into his hands, wearily. "What was it like, then?"

All day, all semester, I'd been tormenting myself with what I did—and didn't—feel for Ben Lane. Because I'd known all along that there was a kernel of something—affection, awareness, attraction, even—burrowed deep inside me. I'd been too afraid to acknowledge it even to myself; how on earth could I tell my husband?

And yet it seemed he already knew.

Allan lifted his head. "Laura?"

"I... I don't know," I admitted, and I saw his face crumple a little, as he swallowed hard, and I hated myself more than I ever had before. "It wasn't anything, Allan. I mean... I was so thrown, the first time he—" I stopped, and he narrowed his eyes.

"The first time he *what?*"

"The day he was injured in rugby, and I took him back to the boarding house." I spoke in a rush, and Allan looked shocked.

"Back *then?*"

"It wasn't... it wasn't *anything*. He had a cut on his leg, and I was cleaning it for him and he just... he put his hand over mine while I was cleaning it." I gulped. "I moved away immediately, of course. But later he said something about how he wouldn't tell anyone about *us*, and I... I panicked."

Allan looked at me wearily. "Even if you panicked in the moment, which I can understand, you should have reported it the next day, or the day after that, or the one after that." His voice was rising again. "Come on, you *know* this. If you didn't report it, it was because some part of you, no matter how small, felt complicit."

I closed my eyes, because I knew he was right. "I did," I admitted in a suffocated whisper, my eyes still closed, "but I don't even know why. Nothing happened, I swear. The truth is, we barely spoke. I felt sorry for him sometimes, because he'd grown up in foster care, and he seemed to... to understand how I felt." I was ashamed to admit it, because it sounded so pathetic, so *wrong*. How could a seventeen-year-old boy possibly know how I, a middle-aged woman facing menopause and an empty nest, felt?

"How you felt?" Allan repeated neutrally.

"He said he knew I was lonely."

Allan gave a snort of disbelief, maybe even disdain, and suddenly I was the one who was angry.

I opened my eyes to glare at him. "It was *true*, Allan. You've had no idea how hard this has been for me. How lonely and isolated I've felt, all alone, with Katherine back at Leabrook, and Tucker barely talking to us anymore, and this place, this place is so remote, all these *trees*—"

"You think I don't know?" he interjected in a hard voice. "Laura, did it not occur to you that *I* felt just as lonely?"

I goggled at him, because it genuinely hadn't crossed my mind. "But your job..."

"Just made me feel more alone," he filled in flatly. "It's not like I can confide in anyone here, is it? They're all under my authority, and most of them seem as if they're waiting me to fail, or maybe just to move on. Who knows. It's not like I've found a bunch of kindred spirits here, though."

"You could have confided in me..." I whispered.

"I tried—maybe not as hard as I should have, I admit—but you were so set against this place, Laura." His face crumpled again, just a bit, before he ironed out his expression. "Did you think I didn't see that? Did you think I didn't *feel* it?"

I had no idea what to say. I looked down at my lap, feeling ashamed and guilty—guiltier, perhaps, than I should have felt, considering what I had—and hadn't—done.

But maybe that didn't matter so much to Allan. What I'd done, what I'd told him, was enough for him, and I could understand that. If I'd been in his position, how would I have felt? Devastated, I knew. Devastated, even if I knew nothing really had happened.

Enough still had.

"So there's going to be an inquiry," I said dully. "Will there..." I swallowed hard. "Will there be a criminal investigation?"

Allan glanced at me sharply. "There would only be a criminal investigation if there had been sexual activity." He paused, and I could almost hear the unspoken question hanging in the air.

Was there?

"A student trying to kiss doesn't count as that, I presume?" I asked, determined not to lower myself by denying something so offensive and absurd.

"I wouldn't think so, but Tamara in HR was pretty close-lipped about it all. *There's* someone on a power trip," he said with a hint of his old wryness, the jokes we used to share. "She's absolutely adoring all the attention, the sense of importance this gives her, no matter what damage it does to the school. She's out of here in a year or two anyway, I'm sure of it.' He sighed. "They interviewed Ben this afternoon." He was quiet for a moment. "I wasn't party to that interview, but I got the sense that he didn't say much to them."

"He didn't?" I realized I was surprised. Part of me expected Ben to go into full swagger mode, bragging about how he hooked up with his English teacher, how into him I was, even if I wasn't. I *wasn't*.

"No, he didn't," Allan confirmed with another tired sigh. "The sense I got was that he was pretty upset about the whole thing. Ted let it slip that Ben said he really didn't know the two of you were being filmed."

I squirmed inwardly at that—the two of us. There *was* no two of us. None at all.

"I just want this to be over," I told Allan, and he rose from the sofa, turning toward the door, dismissing me, or at least that's how it felt, but maybe there was simply nothing more to say.

"Well, it will be over, soon enough," he told me. "There's no way the school, in the current financial crisis it's in, can survive something like this."

The next day, after my conversation with Rachel, I am not thinking about the school's financial crisis, or the looming scandal, or even Allan or Ben or anyone, as I walk slowly upstairs. I am thinking only of how I can survive this moment, and the next, and the one after that, endlessly onward. I've never ever contemplated suicide, and I don't think I am now, but at the same time, I can see the sweet relief of not having to feel this way anymore.

I haven't even ventured out of Webb House, haven't dared to, because watching the students and teachers from the upstairs window is bad enough. I've seen people whispering, shooting glances at the house before I step quickly away so I can't be seen. Everybody knows. Everybody is talking about it.

Will I be arrested? I think Tamara would like me to be, perversely, since surely the point of an HR department is to handle these things discreetly, for the sake of the school, if not my own, but, like Allan intimated, she loves the drama.

But even if the inquiry resolves the situation, acquits me as much as I can be acquitted, I know everything has still changed. I know I won't be able to go back to my job. This morning, I steeled myself to look online at similar cases, ones of teachers who were accused and eventually cleared, and there's no way I'll ever be able to teach again. This is a blot on my copybook that will never be rubbed out.

But besides that, there is the thought of how Allan will be affected. If the school closes, and he has a wife who has been accused of inappropriate contact and barred from teaching, will he ever get a headship again?

It's doubtful. Very doubtful. And I hate that I have ruined things not just for myself, but for him.

And what about Tucker? I texted him as soon as this all blew up, asking to see him, and he told me he didn't want to. Allan said to wait till he was ready, but it is tormenting me, not being able to talk to my son, to explain. I hate to imagine how he's feeling—the hurt, the *humiliation*, which feels worse at that age. I ache to talk to him, but I satisfy myself with texts, telling him I love him. He doesn't reply. Katherine hasn't been in touch, either, but I'm hoping she hasn't heard anything from Tucker. I'm not brave enough to reach out to her, though. Not yet.

Again and again, I've asked myself, why didn't I make a report? Be transparent, as Allan said? I think of Ben Lane's hand trapping mine on his thigh, that first night. It started right there, and I knew it, and I didn't do anything, and the truth is—the truth that I can barely bear to face—is that I didn't because part of me, a very tiny, treacherous part, was thrilled at being noticed. Being *seen*.

And I will never, ever forgive myself for that.

CHAPTER 26

RACHEL

I cannot shake my guilt. It eats at me, even as I tell myself —again and again—that I did the right thing in turning over that phone. But just when I am convincing myself of that, my own life starts to unravel in a way I never expected.

Except maybe I did.

It starts when I pick up Nathan, right after leaving Laura. Cara is holding him, waiting for me to arrive, while he wails in her arms, his face screwed up and bright red.

"What—?" I am breathless, anxious, as I hold my arms out to my son. Cara doesn't give him to me.

"He's been fractious all day," she tells me flatly. "I told you something was wrong with him."

"He's a *baby*," I say, my voice sharpening with both fury and fear. "There's nothing wrong with him. Now, can I have my son please?" I keep my arms held out as I glare at her. She shifts him to her other arm.

"You're a single mom, aren't you? Maureen told me."

"What does that have to do with anything?" I demand. "But, as it happens, I'm not."

"Why has your husband never dropped him off, then?" she challenges.

"You have no right to ask these questions." My voice is shaking, along with my arms, from the effort of holding them out for so long. "Now give me my son."

"He has bruises on either side of his ribcage," Cara says quietly. "As mandated reporters, we have a legal obligation to make a report of any bruising in a baby under six months old to the Office of Child and Family Services."

I stare at her, slowly drawing my arms downward as I feel the blood drain from my face. "What..." The word escapes me in a long, low exhalation.

"There were bruises, in the shape of *thumbprints,* on either side of his stomach," she states in that same flat voice, "as well as on his back in the shape of fingers. We took photographs and filed a report. It's up to OCFS to decide whether the report mandates an intervention, but based on what I've seen, I'd think a caseworker will be visiting you in the next day or two." And then, with a face like thunder, she hands me my son.

Nathan stops screaming when he comes into my arms, which is something, but I am both terrified and humiliated, my fingers trembling as I buckle him into his stroller. I press a kiss to his forehead, and Cara lets out a huff of sound, something close to a snort of disbelief.

I cannot believe this is happening. I am going to have to tell Kyle. *I might lose my child.*

And meanwhile I'm meant to be teaching tomorrow.

I don't bother saying goodbye to Cara; I just start pushing Nathan home, one foot in front of the other, my mind a buzzing blank, at least at the start, but by the time I am halfway back, it is seething with suspicions and fears. What if the bruises were caused by someone at Busy Bees, and they made a report to cover themselves? Or what if Gladys knew she caused them, and that's why she said what she did to me the other day?

Maybe she held him differently then for that reason, too. It's hard to believe Gladys could be so calculating, but I'd rather think that about her than believe it was me.

I would *never* hurt Nathan. I know I wouldn't.

But I might have done so, by accident.

It's a possibility I can't bear to consider, and yet I know I have to. Those sleep-fogged nights, when I stumble into his nursery, when I pick him up and sink into the glider, barely aware of my own movements...

But to give him *bruises*?

And yet I can't deny that he's had bruises, and if he has them now, they've most likely been caused by either me or someone at Busy Bees.

But why *shouldn't* it be someone at Busy Bees? How can they prove that it isn't them?

How can I prove that it isn't me?

I make it back home, thankfully without seeing Gladys, because right now I don't even know what I'd say to her. I take Nathan out of his stroller and lay him, as gently as if he's a precious antique, on his changing table. I unbutton his sleepsuit and onesie and then, holding my breath, lift it to see his tummy.

And there they are, two purplish bruises on either side of his ribcage, definitely in the shape of thumbprints.

Still holding my breath, I very gently press my thumb to one of them. It matches the shape perfectly, and my breath rushes out in something close to a sob.

No. No...

Nathan looks at me, unblinking, quizzical, and then he gives me one of his big, beaming gummy smiles as the tears slide silently down my face.

The social worker calls me the next day, while I'm at work. I brought Nathan to Busy Bees this morning, both stony-faced and trying to act humble; Maureen was there, her head cocked to one side, her expression closed yet so clearly judgmental, bordering on contempt. I hated handing him over to her, yet I had no choice.

I'd thought about calling Wilderness and telling them I couldn't come in, but somehow that made me feel as if I knew I was guilty, as if I had something to hide. Better to brazen it out, I decided, but I was regretting that decision when I saw the look on Maureen's face.

"I didn't hurt him," I told her quietly, hating that I had to say it.

"We are dutybound to report any signs of abuse or neglect," she replied in something close to a monotone. "We could lose our childcare license otherwise."

"But I *didn't*," I said again, and she didn't bother to reply.

I handed her my son.

I see the missed call after my second-period class, and I listen to the voicemail with a sense of slightly removed horror, like it's an emotion I can take out and examine, study from all angles.

"This is Shelley Stevens, with the Office of Child and Family Services. Could you please give me a call back at your earliest convenience?" Her voice is calm and measured and scares me half to death.

I teach my next class on autopilot, in a daze. I have a twenty-minute break afterwards, and as my classroom empties out, I close the door and, my heart starting to thud, call her back.

"Ms. Stevens?" My voice comes out in a croak. "This is Rachel Masters. You left me a message?"

"Yes, thank you for calling back." There is a professionalism to her voice, but also a surprising warmth, and that heartens me a little. "I was hoping we could meet, Ms. Masters, and discuss the report I received from Busy Bees. Do you have some time today?"

I register a steeliness to her voice that suggests I'd better.

"Yes, during my lunch period. I teach at The Wilderness School, in Hawley..."

"I'm in Dover-Foxcroft, so about an hour away. I can be there for one?" She makes it sound as if we're scheduling a coffee.

"All right," I reply woodenly. "I don't teach until one-forty-five—"

"That should be enough time," she assures me, and even though her tone is still warm but professional, I am chilled to my core.

I can't concentrate on my last lesson before lunch, and I lose my train of thought completely several times, and a concerned eighth-grader has to prompt me.

"Mrs. Masters?" one of them, a boarder named Harry, asks me once the boys are trickling out of the classroom. "Are you okay?"

I blink him into focus, and then find I can't answer. "Yes," I say finally, having to grope for the word. "Yes, I'm fine, Harry. Just a little tired..." I manage to smile at him, even though I realize I am, quite suddenly, far too close to tears.

Shelley Stevens meets me at Hawley's one and only coffee shop, where I had a latte and a brownie what already feels like a million years ago. She is kind enough to order our drinks—I ask for an herbal tea, knowing I'm already too jittery to handle caffeine—and we take a table in the corner.

"How are you, Rachel?" she asks, her tone so kind and concerned that I am suddenly, shockingly defenseless. "Do you mind if I call you Rachel?"

"No." I gulp, my hands clutching my paper cup of pepper-mint tea. "I'm..." I find I can't finish that sentence.

"You're finding things hard," she says, and while her tone is still warm, the words are not.

"Finding things hard as a new mother doesn't equate to *hurting* your child," I say stiffly. "And that's why you're here, isn't it? To figure out if I'm the one who put those bruises on my son that Busy Bees reported?"

"I'm here," Shelley answers carefully, "because there was a report, yes, that I am required by law to investigate. But why I'm really here, Rachel, is to figure out the best way to support you and Nathan. OCFS exists to help families, not to hinder or hurt them. Our goal here, our absolute *priority*, is to keep you with your son, with both of you healthy and thriving."

If she thinks those words are going to reassure me, they don't. *Keep me with my son?* Which means there is a distinct possibility that he might be taken away.

"I don't know what to tell you," I say, my tone turning a little stubborn, even truculent. "I didn't hurt my son."

"Let's talk about your situation," Shelley replies easily. "You have a partner?"

"Yes, a loving and devoted husband, who *adores* Nathan."

"Does he know that we're meeting?"

I hesitate before admitting reluctantly, "No, I haven't told him yet. He's a logger. He's in northern Maine for the winter, but he comes home some—*most*—weekends." Not quite, but he said he'd come home more often.

"You didn't tell him about the bruises?" She pauses, not long enough for me to reply. "You've seen them, haven't you?"

"Yes. I saw them last night, after Busy Bees alerted me to them." I decide not to mention the earlier ones. I jut my chin out a little. "Have *you* seen them?"

"Yes," she replies calmly. "I visited Busy Bees before I came here, and I saw Nathan. What a cutie, by the way."

I swallow hard and say nothing, because I don't know what to say. I feel as if everything in me is drawn so tightly, I am going to snap, and I have no idea what that will look like if—when—it happens.

"How do you think he got those bruises, Rachel?" she asks.

I no longer like that she says my name; it feels too *personal*, like she's trying to tell me she knows me, when she doesn't. Is she hoping I'll let something slip? Is she trying to catch me out? I don't want to be suspicious of her, but I am— of course I am. I grew up with an angry single mom who would never let a government official past the threshold, I saw a boy being taken away when I was a kid, and my infant son has bruises in the shape of my thumbprints. I am very suspicious.

And so is Shelley Stevens—of me.

"Well." I swallow dryly and then take a sip of peppermint tea to wet my throat. "There are a couple of options, unfortunately." I sound flat, and I realize I should be panicked, *traumatized*, determined to get to the bottom of this, to find the monster who did this to my baby, and see them prosecuted.

The trouble is, I sound guilty, because I feel guilty. What if *I'm* the monster? Not that I'll ever admit as much to Shelley, because I don't believe I am.

I can't be.

"Obviously, someone at Busy Bees could have done it," I say, and Shelley does not reply. "I mean, even without meaning to," I continue hurriedly. "Babies are fragile, and Nathan is so small." For a second, I am picturing him, the smile he gave me, the way he kicks his legs when he's happy. My eyes fill, and I have to brush at them to keep the tears from slipping down my face.

"It's been hard, hasn't it?" Shelley says, harping on that *one* theme, and I realize that right now my tears make me look as guilty as my lack of them did.

"Yes, it has been hard," I tell her, having to gulp back yet more, "but I didn't hurt him. I promise, I really didn't."

"Do you think you could have without realizing?" she asks gently. "Just like someone at Busy Bees could have?"

"I..." What on earth can I say to that? "I don't think so. I mean... I'm careful. I'm always careful. No one will tell you any differently."

"I've spoken to your neighbor, Gladys Hocker," Shelley says, and I feel my face freeze.

Gladys...?

"She mentioned seeing bruises on Nathan's tummy, in approximately the same place as they are now, on Friday October thirteenth, a day when he wasn't at Busy Bees, and hadn't been since the Tuesday before." She falls silent, giving me time to absorb the fact that while I might have *narced* on Laura, according to Ben, my kindly old neighbor Gladys has narced on me.

It doesn't feel good.

"I actually thought Gladys caused those bruises," I tell her stiltedly, and I hear how feeble, how *forced* it all sounds. "She liked to give him a cuddle sometimes, and I started noticing that she was gripping him pretty hard around the stomach. I don't think she meant it or anything, but... Kyle noticed it, too, and we both agreed we wouldn't let her hold him anymore."

"So, you'd stopped Gladys from holding Nathan since then?"

I can tell where she's going with this, of course. If Gladys hasn't held Nathan since, who caused the second round of bruises?

"Look, I don't know," I say helplessly. "I really don't think I caused them. I'm a good mother. I try to be."

"No one's calling that into question, Rachel," Shelley says with a gentle smile, which I have the sudden urge to slap off her face.

Really, I think, *because it certainly seems as if you are.*

I glance at my watch and see that I am teaching in ten

minutes. "I'm sorry, but I need to get back to my class," I inform her. "Can you tell me what happens now? You've obviously opened an inquiry."

"An investigation," she agrees with a nod, which sounds worse. "Well, I'd like to talk to you again, and I'll also be talking to the nursery workers at Busy Bees, as well as your colleagues at your place of work. You said you teach at the Wilderness School?"

"Yes, but..." The prospect of a social worker asking my colleagues questions about whether I might have hurt my own child is a potential nightmare scenario, almost as bad as what Laura is facing now... a scenario, I realize, that I basically caused.

"Considering the nature of my work," I tell Shelley, "that could be quite problematic for me, especially if you conclude, as I'm sure you will, that I wasn't involved in Nathan's bruising."

Her eyebrows lift a millimeter. "If that is the conclusion I draw, then surely it won't be a problem?"

"You must know," I tell her, my tone sharpening, "that accusations of this nature stick, even after you're cleared, in a school setting." *Like they will for Laura.* Did I realize, on some level, how devastating it would be for Laura, when I handed over that phone? I can't really remember. I was so shocked, so... condemning. Maybe I shouldn't have been.

She spreads her hands wide. "I have to do my job, Rachel, just as you have to do yours."

There is pretty much nothing I can say to that.

"I have to go," I tell her, and she smiles.

"I'll be in touch."

I'm sure you will, I think, as I head back toward school, my head down, walking fast. I know I need to call Kyle; I need to get him involved. I need to talk to Gladys too, although I'm not sure I trust myself not to scream at her, for basically turning me in. She couldn't have talked to me first? No wonder Laura was so angry, I think, when she was in more or less the same position as I am now. It's terrifying, and humiliating, and infuriating all at once. Is that how Laura feels? I think of apologizing to her, but I have too much else to worry about now.

As it turns out, Shelley isn't the one who gets in touch. I have just finished teaching my last class when I get a call from Nancy, on the school's reception desk.

"Rachel?" She sounds nervous. "Can you come to the front desk? There's a police officer here to see you."

An icy frisson of terror goes through me, but then I tell myself that it is almost certainly to do with Laura. She is far more likely to face criminal charges than I am; Shelley Stevens is just opening an inquiry, anyway. An *investigation*. But there's no way she'd involve the police already, is there?

But when I see the officer standing grim-faced by the reception desk, I know it's me he's come for, and has nothing to do with Laura.

"Rachel Masters," he says, stepping toward me. "Do you have a moment to come down to the station and answer a few questions?"

It's clearly a rhetorical question. "Sure," I say, my throat paper-dry, my lips numb. "Can I just make a call, to let the nursery know who will be picking up my son?"

The officer nods, and I angle myself away slightly as I call Busy Bees first. Maureen sounds sanctimonious, and she says she'll have to check if someone else can pick Nathan up, "now that the police are involved." Did the police go there first, I wonder, and then realize it doesn't matter. They're here now.

"He hasn't been taken away from me," I tell her in something close to a snap, knowing I shouldn't lose my temper. "Not yet."

Then I make another call, praying she'll pick up. She does.

"Laura... it's Rachel. Please don't hang up," I say hurriedly as I hear her indrawn breath. "Please, Laura. I'm in trouble. I... I need you to pick up Nathan for me." Another indrawn breath, and I can tell she's so surprised, she can't find the words. "Please," I whisper. "I need you to help me. I have no one else I can ask."

CHAPTER 27

LAURA

When I step out of the doorway of Webb House to pick up Nathan, it's the first time I've left the house since this whole thing happened. I've showered and brushed my hair and put on clean clothes for the first time in days, but even so I feel like some shell-less thing, squinting in the lights, raw and pink-skinned and exposed. Fortunately, no one is around, and I am able to walk swiftly off the school campus without seeing anyone.

I have no idea what to think, that Rachel asked me to pick up her son. She sounded terrified on the phone, and I wonder if something happened to her husband. Or could it possibly be something to do with me? Surely not. Surely, she wouldn't ask me to pick up her child while she was getting me into even more trouble. But considering what's happened so far, maybe she would.

But she wouldn't sound scared about it, would she?

I find my way to Busy Bees—somewhere I've never been or needed to be—and give the woman who comes to the front desk a sunny smile, or as much as I can, but she's looking at me with something like suspicion, her brows drawn into a scowl beneath her hot pink-dyed hair.

"Hi, I'm here to pick up Nathan Masters? I think his mother Rachel called. My name is Laura Haile."

"Yes, she called. Do you have some ID?"

"Oh, ah..." Thankfully I remembered to take my purse, even if I don't recall grabbing it. "Yes." I fumble for my driver's license and show it to her.

She scans my photo and then my face, and I just about hold onto my fixed smile.

"All right." She gives me back my license. "I'll go get him. But you should know that you might be contacted by a caseworker with OCFS."

"With—*what*?" I stare at her blankly.

"The Office of Family and Child Services. Rachel Masters is under investigation. At the moment, I have no choice but to give Nathan to her designated provider, but the situation is ongoing and may change. OCFS can invoke Title 15, which would mandate a temporary emergency interim care provider."

She might as well be speaking a foreign language, I understand so little of what she is saying, except that somehow Rachel —*Rachel*—is under investigation. For what? "Sorry," I say helplessly. "I have no idea about any of this."

"If OCFS decide that it is necessary to remove Nathan from Rachel's care for his own safety, they have seventy-two hours before they have to apply for a court order." She fires off the words like bullets. "That would mean taking Nathan to a safe place, either into foster care or with relatives. Are you willing to be that person?"

"For seventy-two hours?" I am jolted. There's no way I can take care of a baby for seventy-two hours. I don't have the equipment, first of all, and with my own life the way it is... "Yes," I say, because what else *can* I say? "But what about Rachel's husband? He's a logger, he works up north, but I'm sure he'd come back for this—" Even if I've never met him, have no idea what he's like.

"Generally speaking, in situations such as this, the child must be removed from both parents, assuming they are still together."

"They are," I tell her, then hesitate. "Well, at least, I think they are—"

"Then Nathan will be removed to another relative or person." She lets out a sigh. "But that's not my problem, frankly, and I have a lot of other kids to deal with. It's up to the caseworker to decide whether Nathan can stay with you or needs to go into care. Can you please give me your cell and landline numbers in case the caseworker needs to contact you? And your address."

"Okay."

I give her all the information, and then she gives me Nathan. He looks fine, awarding me a gummy grin as I take hold of him. I collect Rachel's stroller and spend an anxious few minutes trying to get Nathan into his seat, straps and all, underneath the woman's beady stare. I can't believe I'm doing this. I can't believe Busy Bees is letting me. And where on earth is Rachel?

My mind is whirling as I leave the daycare and then push Nathan back toward Wilderness's campus, garnering a few curious looks from students and teachers along the way, although I keep my head down in case I see Ben.

I don't, though. I see Tucker. My son. He is waiting by the front door to Webb House, looking furious.

"Can you believe I don't even have a key to my own house?" he spits at me as a greeting before he glances down at Nathan, doing a double take. "Why do you have a *baby*? Have you added kidnapping to your criminal portfolio, Mom?" His words are sneering, his voice vibrating with pain. I knew he'd be angry, but I still didn't expect this level of hostility.

"Tucker, I'm sorry. Of course, we'll give you a key. I'm so glad you're here. Come in." I usher him into the house and then bump Nathan's stroller up the stairs and into the hallway. Tucker has only been in here briefly before, once when we were taking him out for dinner and another time for an exeat weekend; he stayed two nights and spent almost all his time in his room. I have not talked properly with my son since before he started at this school.

Nathan is happy in his seat, so I leave him there for the moment, pushing any thoughts of Rachel out of my mind in order to help my own child.

"Tucker," I say, "I'm so sorry about what happened."

He takes a step toward me, aggressive, hands clenched into fists. "So, what *did* happen?"

I take a deep breath, let it out slowly. "I assume you've seen the video."

"*Everyone's* seen the video, Mom." He's trying to sneer again, but this time he doesn't quite manage it; he sounds like a little boy on the verge of tears. "Every single person in this whole school. I saw it before you'd even got back from Boston. *That* was fun, let me tell you. Everyone telling me Ben Lane had scored with my own *mother*."

I fight against the urge to close my eyes and keep my gaze on my son. "Tucker, it wasn't like that, at all."

"That's what it looked like."

"I know. But I pushed him away before he... before he could kiss me." It is excruciating, to talk about this with my son. "I was shocked by the whole thing, Tucker. Maybe it was—I don't know—a dare or something. But there's no relationship between us. There never was, not remotely. And if he's saying differently—"

"He's not saying anything. He won't talk about it with anyone." Tucker sounds sulky now, as he stares at the floor.

It's what Allan intimated, but I am still surprised. I would have thought Ben would have bragged, at least a little, to his friends, if not to teachers, but maybe not, considering he does seem to be something of a loner. "This is all going to be cleared up," I tell him. I have to believe that. I can't be criminally prosecuted for a student trying to kiss me, even if I can be fired.

He looks up. "Will you teach again? Will Dad still be headmaster?"

"I... I don't know." His lip twists in disdain and I continue as steadily as I can, "The truth is, I should have reported what happened immediately, and I... I didn't. I think I was so shocked, I... shut down, I suppose. I just couldn't..." I stop, start again. "But that failure to act means I probably won't be able to teach again, and for that I am truly sorry. As for Dad... I really don't know what will happen. He didn't do anything wrong, not anything at all, but whether the school trustees will feel he can stay in his position, considering..." A breath escapes me. How could I have screwed up so royally? "I don't know."

Tucker frowns, folding his arms. "And will I be able to stay here, if you guys have to leave?"

"You're on an athletic scholarship, Tucker, so yes. That is, if you want to." Have I ruined my son's chances at this school, along with my husband's and my own?

He shrugs, and I have no idea what that means. I suspect he doesn't, either. Is this all going to blow over in a few weeks or even days as another scandal of some sort takes hold—maybe even one around Rachel being investigated? Or will it linger and fester and become something that stays forever, a subject heading on the school's Wikipedia page—*School Scandal Involving Headmaster's Wife and Student*.

"I'm sorry," I tell him again, helplessly, meaning it so much but knowing it's not nearly enough. "I'm so sorry, Tucker."

He nods, not looking at me, and then Nathan starts to cry. "Why do you have a baby, anyway?" he asks.

"It's a long story." And one I don't even know the details of.

Is the caseworker going to call? Will I hand Nathan over to her?
"But please, Tucker," I continue as I unbuckle Nathan from the stroller, "please, please believe that I never meant for this to happen. I was completely shocked when Ben—well, when that happened. And right now, I'm wishing I never took the teaching job here." I could have stayed as the headmaster's wife, in my twinset and pearls, pouring tea for prospective parents. I wish I *did* do that, more than anything. What's a little boredom compared to what I'm facing now?

"Yeah."

I don't know if he's accepting my apology or just agreeing with me; the word comes out grudgingly.

"Are other people making things difficult for you?" I ask, and, once more, he shrugs, unwilling to reply.

I draw Nathan to my chest; he is snuffling in my shirt, and I am guessing he needs to be fed. Hopefully, there is a bottle of formula in the diaper bag.

"I should go," Tucker says. "You're busy."

With Rachel's baby. The irony is not lost on me. "Okay," I say reluctantly, because as much as I want to work this out with him, I know now is not the time. "But—come back, okay? Dad wants to see you. I want to see you. Maybe for dinner..." He's already heading to the door, and I feel like I am losing him. "Tucker—I love you."

He nods and leaves without looking at me.

Fortunately, there is a bottle in the diaper bag, and I manage to give it to Nathan without any mishaps. I remember the fleeting peace of a feeding baby, when they drink so avidly, their gaze unblinking, fastened on mine. It gives me an ache of nostalgia, for those simpler days, hard as they were. They were nothing like this. I picture Katherine and Tucker when they were little, all chubby cheeks and dimpled elbows, wide eyes and beaming smiles. I need to talk to Katherine, I realize. I haven't spoken to her since this all happened. I don't even know if she's heard or not. I don't think Tucker would have told her, but maybe in his anger, he did.

After I've fed Nathan, I decide he could do with a diaper change; I forgot what a rigmarole it is, to get out the changing pad, the wipes, the diaper, all while keeping hold of a squirming baby. It's been so long, and he's so small. He kicks his legs as I undo the poppers on his sleep suit, a shocked gasp escaping me as I see what can only be bruises—on his ribcage, but also all down his legs, mottled and blue. He's *covered* in them.

No wonder OCFS has become involved, I think. I am truly shaken by the sight of those bruises, on such a small baby. Could Rachel have actually caused them? I don't want to believe it, and yet...

There they are, right in front of me.

By the time Allan comes home two hours later, I am feeling both exhausted and frazzled, yet strangely glad to have had something else—someone else—to focus on. Nathan was fussy for a while, and then he fell asleep, and I managed to make some dinner while he dozed in his stroller seat, although I wasn't sure when Allan would be back, or if he'd want to eat.

When he walks in the door, he looks tired, but he offers a small smile when he sees me. We have barely seen each other since our painful confrontation; he's been out of the house, and I've been hiding in it.

He leans against the doorframe as I stir some spaghetti sauce—from a jar, but I still feel like I've achieved something simply by heating it up.

"The inquiry has been resolved," he tells me. "They wanted to deal with it quickly."

My breath catches in my chest. "And?"

"No criminal charges will be filed. Your failure in duty of care means your contract will be terminated immediately, but no further disciplinary procedures will be taken. Tamara will contact you tomorrow, to schedule a final meeting, to tell you the terms."

I stare at him in disbelief for a few seconds. "You mean... it's actually over?"

Allan nods. "The board of trustees is meeting tomorrow to decide whether they will ask for my resignation."

I flinch, my stomach swooping. "Allan, I'm so sorry..."

He holds up a hand to forestall me. "I know. I am, too. I wasn't entirely blameless in this, Laura. I get that. I'm just sorry it happened this way. For both of us."

"And Ben Lane?" I can't quite keep an edge of bitterness from my voice. "Will anything happen to him?"

"He refused to talk about the situation at all, except to say there had never been a sexual relationship, he'd been the one to try to kiss you, and you weren't to be blamed."

"Oh..." I don't know how I feel about any of that. Relieved, yes, and even touched, but also wary.

"Tamara intimated that he was protecting you, but as there's no proof of any crime being committed..." He shrugs. "The school can only act on the evidence it has."

"She really has it in for me, doesn't she?"

"She doesn't care about the school. She just wants to make her mark." He sighs. "Like I did. I'm sorry." He is quiet for a moment, his lips pursed in thought. "I never should have accepted this position. I knew you didn't want to come here."

I shake my head. "I should have been more supportive..."

"I shouldn't have been so desperate to prove myself." Another pause as he gazes unseeingly into the distance. "I've always been desperate to prove myself. You know how I've never actually been part of this world. Maybe I need to give it up. Recognize I don't belong in these types of schools, and I never will."

He's never, ever talked like this before, and I ache for him. "Allan—"

"I'm not being sorry for myself," he cuts across me. "I'm being serious. I think back to my first job at that private day school in New York, when we were just married. I so wanted to be let into that world, that *club*. Not the wealth, but the know-how. The sense of privilege people wear—not even like a cloak, but like a *skin*. It's so much a part of them, they're not even aware of it, but I always was. I felt like I was walking around, pretending all the time. I never really belonged, and I still don't. It's all an act, all the polish and charisma, the easy laugh and the shaking hands. It's just a role I play." I must look surprised because he smiles wryly. "Don't tell me I even fooled you?"

"Sometimes, maybe," I admit, and he lets out a hollow laugh.

"And yet, the older I get, the harder it is to keep it up." He lets out a long, low sigh. "You'd think it would get easier, that I'd start to believe in myself a little bit, but I never have, and I'm not even sure I want to anymore."

I have never heard Allan talk like this before, and it both heartens and moves me. There is a new honesty, right here, between us, and amidst all the devastation, it gives me a faint flicker of hope.

I open my mouth to reply, although I'm not even sure what to say, when Nathan, waking up in his seat, starts to cry.

Allan looks almost comically startled.

"What on earth..." He peers around the corner of the kitchen, to the nook where I've tucked Nathan's stroller. "Is that a *baby*?"

CHAPTER 28

RACHEL

So here I am, in Hawley's little Podunk police station, waiting for an officer to talk to me. The guy who brought me here didn't speak much, and left me sitting in a hard seat, staring at the wild-eyed crazy guy who is wanted, I see, for armed assault and robbery. Wow. I'm keeping good company—except I'm not, because he's on the run while I've been arrested. Or maybe not arrested, no, but brought in for questioning, at least. What happens next, I have no idea. I'm afraid to guess.

"Rachel Masters?"

The police officer who emerges from the back of the station is a woman, fortyish and solid-looking, unsmiling, arms folded. Yes, she has definitely already passed judgment.

I rise from my seat on legs that feel watery and weak.

"Do you know why you're here?" she asks when we're in one of those little interrogation rooms you see on TV—a table, two chairs, a window of opaque glass that is probably one of those one-way mirror things they have on crime shows. I almost want to laugh. Is this even for real? And yet, unfortunately, horrifyingly, it is.

"I don't, actually," I tell the police officer, in as polite a tone as I can manage. "I spoke with Shelley Stevens this morning about OCFS opening an investigation into the bruises that were found on my son, but I wasn't under the impression that the police were going to get involved." I speak far more calmly than I feel; inside, I am shaking.

"You're here because this afternoon we were alerted by your daycare provider to the further bruising that was discovered on Nathan Masters' body," the officer informs me. "There were concerns that he would be in danger if released to your care, and the level of bruising indicated a criminal offense."

I stare at her, having to swallow a couple of times. "What *further* bruising?"

"Did you hurt your son, Mrs. Masters? Did you get angry with him?" She waits a beat while I simply stare, and then continues, "I understand you've been on your own. Your neighbor mentioned that Nathan has been difficult—he hasn't slept very much, he's often crying."

Gladys *again*. I wet my lips, which have suddenly become bone dry.

"Busy Bees has reported that you have been aggressive and verbally abusive with their staff."

I feel as if I am falling; as if this officer, with all her words, is getting smaller and farther away. I still can't speak.

"Mrs. Masters? Do you deny this?"

I open my mouth. Nothing comes out.

"Mrs. Masters?"

"I want to talk to my husband."

"I'd like for you to answer my questions." Her tone is brusque.

"I didn't." I wet my lips again. "I didn't hurt my son." But *someone* did, I realize, if he has further bruising from just a few hours ago, when Shelley Stevens looked at him, and this time, I know that wasn't me. It couldn't have been me. "Please." I lean forward. "Where has he been bruised? Is he okay? Can he be checked out at Cary? Please—"

A flicker of something passes across the officer's face, and I am desperate to believe it is sympathy.

"Please, I'd like for him to be examined," I say as firmly as I can. "I want to make sure he's okay."

"You can do that shortly," the police officer says, back to being brusque. "Now, can you please answer my questions?"

I take a deep breath. I need to cooperate, I realize, and only then will I get out of here. "I did lose my temper with one of the nursery workers at Busy Bees," I tell the officer. "It had been a long day and she was rude, saying there was something wrong with Nathan, because he was crying. I called her a... a bitch. I was sorry for it, but I was never aggressive—in fact, I'd say she was. And I never threatened anyone physically or anything like that."

I take a breath that hitches audibly. "As for the bruising... I told Shelley, the caseworker, this afternoon that it might have been my neighbor, Gladys, because she was holding him funny. The two bruises on his ribcage, like thumbprints. And I admit —" I hesitate, because I'm not sure whether I should say this, and I so wish Kyle was with me, giving me strength.

I decide to keep going. "I admit, I initially wondered if I might have caused those bruises, accidentally. Absolutely accidentally. In the middle of the night, when I'm half-asleep and he's screaming, I wondered if maybe I grabbed him a bit too hard." I lean forward, my voice breaking, tears spilling from my eyes. "But I didn't think I had. I honestly didn't think I had. It's just—it's so easy to doubt yourself, you know? Because you're so *tired*, and it all feels so endless. And it feels like the world is saying you're a bad mother, if you don't do everything *exactly* as you're supposed to, and act like you're absolutely loving it the whole time. It was *hard*." My voice throbs as I beg her to understand. "It's been really hard. But I love my son, and I would never willingly hurt him, and I know—I absolutely know —if there is further bruising, I didn't cause it. I definitely didn't, and I want him checked out." I try to meet her gaze, even though I am quaking, and tears are trickling down my cheeks.

The officer gives a small, resigned sigh. "I believe you," she says, and I would take it as victory, but she still looks grim. "Look, it will be up to OCFS as to whether they decide to file for an emergency court order, to take Nathan into care for seventy-two hours. At this point in time, I do not see sufficient reason for criminal charges to be filed, but that could change, depending on OCFS's ongoing investigation."

I nod, gulping, and the police officer nods in the direction of the door.

"For now, you're free to go."

I totter out of the station like I've been walking across a desert, dying of thirst, exhausted and completely spent, which I am. I half-collapse onto a park bench and take out my phone. I don't know who to call first—Kyle or Laura. I decide Kyle, because I need to talk to him, even if I am dreading the conversation.

"Rach?" He sounds busy, slightly harassed, and everything in me wilts, shrinks. How can I possibly explain this?

"I need you to come home." My voice is small yet resolute.

"Come home?" Kyle's voice sharpens with anxiety. "Rachel, what's happened? Is it Nathan?"

"Yes. He's okay. At least, I think he's okay—"

"*Rachel*—"

"Kyle, please. Listen, I need to explain." And then I do my best, in a halting voice, hating myself, to tell him everything, or as much as I can remember in my dazed state.

At the end of it, Kyle is silent.

I feel like a dried-out husk now, too spent for tears. "Kyle, please. Say something."

"I'm sorry," he says at last, his voice heavy, so heavy. "I should have been there. For all of it."

That, I realize, was one of the last things I expected him to say. I was bracing for him to blame me, the way I've blamed myself. To tell me that good mothers—real mothers, even—don't do this kind of thing. Don't even think it. That I'm a failure, a reject, a *criminal*. It's what my mother would have said, or at least what I think she would have said—always disappointed in me, always blaming me for my dad leaving.

But Kyle isn't blaming me. He's blaming himself, and that actually, in its own way, feels worse.

"I should have been more honest," I whisper, "about how hard it was for me. But, Kyle, please, please believe me. I never meant to hurt him. If I even did. I don't know that I did—"

"I know, Rach." His voice is achingly gentle. "Of course I know that."

A sob escapes me, an unruly bubble of sound. Apparently, I have more tears left in me. "I'm so sorry. So sorry."

"So am I."

We are both silent; I have to press my fist to my mouth to hold back the sobs.

"What do I do now?" I ask, when I finally trust myself to speak without crying.

"Take Nathan to the medical center," Kyle says. "And get him checked out. He's the most important part of this right now. It'll take me about three hours for me to drive there, but I can meet you at Cary."

Relief fills me, at the thought of Kyle facing this with me. "Thank you," I whisper.

"Rachel," Kyle says, his low and deep and strong, "I love you."

.   .   .

Feeling immeasurably heartened by my conversation with Kyle, although still wobbly, I call Laura next. She answers on the second ring, sounding worried.

"Rachel, are you okay—"

"Do you have Nathan?" I cut her off, needing to know.

A tiny pause. "A caseworker from OCFS is coming right now to pick him up."

My blood freezes—at least that's what it feels like, everything in me going icy. "I'm coming over," I tell her, and I hang up before she can reply.

It's only a ten-minute walk from the station to school, but by the time I arrive at Webb House, looking imposing and imperious in the oncoming dusk, Shelley Stevens has already arrived. When she sees me, she doesn't look nearly as friendly as she did just this afternoon, when we were having coffee.

"I've applied for an emergency interim order," she tells me. "Under Title 22. It's only good for six hours, but I want to use that time to take Nathan to Cary Medical Center and get him checked out."

"That's what I want, too," I tell her. "That's why I'm here."

She stares at me for a moment, looking tired and jaded, and I imagine the scenes she's seen—the parents who are out of their minds on drugs, who systematically and calculatingly abuse their kids, burning them with cigarettes in places teachers won't see, knowing how to inflict pain without causing a bruise or a mark. I'm a teacher, I've gone to safeguarding classes, I've heard the statistics, seen the pictures. I know what to watch out for, when it comes to signs of abuse or neglect, and I know, with an absolute certainty, that I am not like that. I am not like that at all.

I am a tired, stressed mother of a three-month-old baby, yes, and it might be that I've been struggling with some postpartum depression or anxiety, but I am *not* an abusive parent. I know it absolutely, and all my doubts fall away, leave the truth blazing in me like the sun. I love my baby boy. I'd do anything for him. I will fight for him now.

"This order," I tell her, my voice steady and strong, "does it allow me to accompany you to the hospital?"

She hesitates, and then replies with a nod, "You can follow in your own car."

Except I don't have a car. The only car Kyle and I have is the truck he is driving down from Aroostook right now.

"I can drive you," Laura says quietly, and I am stunned. *She's* going to drive me, after everything that's happened between us?

"Thank you," I tell her.

Just five minutes later, we are in Laura's car, driving north to Cary Medical Center. My hands are clasped together tightly in my lap; neither of us speak, probably because we have no idea what to say to each other. To call this an awkward and bizarre situation is something of an understatement.

"You know," Laura finally says in a funny voice whose tone I can't quite decipher, "the last time, the *only* time, I've driven to Cary Medical Center was with Ben, when he had that concussion." I'm not sure how to reply, so I don't say anything, and she continues stiltedly, "After you saw us in the kitchen. I know you noticed something. The truth is, I'd been cleaning his cut and he put his hand over mine, kept it there. It completely shocked me." She is silent for a moment, her lips pursed as she gazes out at the darkened road. "In the car, on the way there, he told me not to worry, that you didn't see anything. He made it seem as if we had this secret, and I let him, because I was so... stunned, I guess. Totally stunned. But I think that, really, was my first mistake. But I know I made a few."

I'm not sure why she's telling me this, until, with a jolt, I realize how similar our stories are.

"I made a few, too," I say, looking out the window. "Starting with not being willing to admit to Kyle that I was struggling with being a mother. Wanting to prove I could do it all on my own, when I actually knew I couldn't."

She nods, like she's not surprised, but also like she understands—and remembering how she first was with me, back at that barbecue, I know she does.

"Why is life so *hard*?" I demand, the words suddenly exploding out of me.

Laura smiles faintly. "Because it's *life*," she says, "and also because we're women, we're mothers, and maybe we care too much about everything."

I turn to look at her. "I didn't hurt Nathan."

She glances at me, her expression unreadable in the twilit darkness. "I didn't have a relationship with Ben Lane," she replies.

And yet somehow, in those statements, there is an admission, or at least a recognition, of not *guilt*—no, not that, not quite, but perhaps responsibility. That neither situation is as clear-cut as we would like it to be, as the world insists it should be. That we both know that, even if we don't say as much.

"The inquiry has finished," she tells me after a moment, her tone matter-of-fact. "The school wanted to wrap it up quickly, to avoid any scandal. No criminal charges or anything like that, but my contract is being terminated immediately. Understandably."

I wonder if my contract will be terminated, too, considering. "You could sue," I venture. It feels strange, suggesting such a thing, when I was so clearly part of the problem. "Wilderness bears some responsibility, surely. They failed in their safeguarding measures, from having you take Ben to the hospital, to the chaperoning of that trip." My voice rises in indignation. "They've always been lax about stuff like that, and they let someone else take the blame if something goes wrong."

Laura shakes her head, the gesture firm and very decided. "No, I'm not going to do that," she says quietly, and I hear what she isn't saying—that she still blames herself, at least a little bit, for something.

Just as I do.

No matter how innocent we truly are, we will both feel guilty. Is it simply because we're mothers, and that's what mothers do, how they feel?

Or maybe it's because it's the truth. Sometimes innocence and guilt go hand in hand.

By the time we arrive at the hospital, Nathan is already in the ER, being assessed. I haven't even seen the bruises on him, the further ones, and when Shelley comes out to the waiting room, as Nathan is being taken for X-rays, I ask her about them.

"Where were these bruises? And when did they appear? Because you saw him this morning and they weren't there then, were they?" I am trying to sound logical rather than aggressive, but I'm not sure it's working.

"Bruises can take some time to appear," she tells me levelly. "And these ones were, according to the mandated reporter, all down his legs."

His *legs*? I've never touched Nathan's legs hard enough to cause a bruise. I know I haven't. "Where on his legs?" I demand. "And in what kind of pattern?"

"I couldn't tell you, because I didn't see them myself," Shelley replies, sounding tired. "But based on what I heard, I had to make a judgment call to have him examined, which I did."

"And involve the police," I interject bitterly, and she frowns.

"I didn't involve the police, Rachel, not at this point. I wouldn't, not yet. Busy Bees called me this afternoon and I got the order, but I haven't called the police."

What? I stare at her in confusion. "The police showed up at my school. They said they'd been alerted, and they took me in for questioning."

Shelley shakes her head slowly. "That had nothing to do with me." She frowns before suggesting, "Maybe someone else in my office..." She trails off before she finishes that thought, shaking her head again "This is not yet a point at which OCFS would involve the police."

"But *someone* involved them."

"The lady I picked Nathan up from seemed to know about it," Laura interjects quietly. "Not that she said as much. But she didn't seem surprised that Rachel couldn't pick Nathan up herself."

"I can't think why that would be," Shelley says, but I know I can.

Maureen, or maybe Cara, called the police on me. Maybe even called in a favor from someone they know on Hawley's tiny police force; this is a small town, and that's often how it works. But why would they do that? Because I was rude to Cara, or did they have it in for me before then? Maureen has never seemed happy to have me there, right from the beginning. I assumed she was just being grumpy and difficult, but now I wonder if there is some other, complicated reason.

"How did you know Nathan was with Laura?" I ask Shelley.

"Maureen at Busy Bees told me," Shelley explains. "She gave me Laura's number. I'd gone there as soon as I could after she'd reported the further bruising."

Further bruising. They are words that will always haunt me.

"I don't know that it matters, anyway," I say tiredly. "They said criminal charges couldn't be filed."

"Still..." Shelley continues to frown. "That shouldn't have happened. I'll look into it."

I don't know whether to be heartened or not by this; while

I'm certainly glad I'm not in imminent danger of being arrested, the reality remains that someone has been hurting my son, and I no longer think it is me. So, who is it?

Twenty minutes later, a nurse calls Shelley's name, annoying me, because she's not his mother. "There's no reason I can't hear what he has to say, is there?" I demand, and Shelley looks like she wants to object, before she gives a shrugging sort of nod.

"I suppose not... considering."

Considering I never should have been questioned by the police? I want to ride high on a tidal wave of self-righteous rage. However, I find I can't summon the energy or emotion. Like Laura, I don't want to pursue some kind of revenge. I just want my son back, so I can move on.

But as we move toward the doctor, I don't know if that will happen. I don't know if that will happen at all... or whether this is the beginning of even worse things to come.

CHAPTER 29

LAURA

A week after I have been cleared of wrongdoing, my contract has been terminated, and I don't know if I'll ever teach again, I am packing up our things. It is surprisingly bittersweet, to put books into boxes when I feel almost as if I just unpacked them. We have been at the Wilderness School for just two months, and we are already leaving. I didn't even have time to get settled, I am realizing, I was still in the adjustment phase, and now it's all over.

Allan offered his resignation last week, and the trustees accepted it with an alacrity that was, for my poor husband, humbling. He did the right thing, though, or so he says; his position at the school was untenable, mainly because of me. It's something I'll have to learn to live with, the sense of blame, of guilt, I feel. I know Allan doesn't blame me, not entirely anyway, but it's still hard to accept, even though I'm trying. I had a responsibility, and I failed in it. That doesn't make me a bad person, but it still *is*. We make mistakes and we learn to move on. Both statements are true.

Tucker is staying at the school, at least for now. If it really does have to close by the end of the year, we'll have to figure out something else. We're not ready to think about that yet, but he told us he wanted to stay, and his anger toward me has abated, at least a little. I have to believe we'll be okay, eventually.

Two weeks on from the Boston trip, at least, and the scandal has already started to blow over, at least for the students. They've moved onto the latest TikTok trend, the newest YouTube craze. Ben being so tight-lipped helped, I think, in keeping it from becoming even more of an event. And, of course, he doesn't have interested, invested parents to potentially make a fuss or file a complaint, a realization which just makes me sad.

Allan's and my plan is to move back to somewhere near Leabrook. We have enough in savings to rent a place for a few months, figure out our next move, and Allan can get some substitute teaching before he figures out whether he wants to continue in academic work or think about moving into a new sector; he's thinking of charity work, maybe for disadvantaged students, like the kind he was. I'm going to look for an office job, something simple and undemanding, which right now sounds like bliss. None of it is ideal, it's true, but it *is*. It could be worse; at least we'll have Katherine, who needs us now more than ever.

I called her a few days ago, to explain the situation, knowing I needed to be honest even though it was hard. She was incredulous, near tears, but, amazingly, she didn't blame me for any of it.

"We all make mistakes," she said through her tears. "We all do things we regret, Mom." There was a wealth of implication in that statement, of *sorrow*, and I knew, with that gut-level mother's instinct, that something *did* happen at that party.

"Katherine..." I began, and she let out an unruly sob.

"Yeah, that party," she said. "I didn't tell you..."

My heart lurched, but my voice remained steady. "What happened, sweetheart?" I asked.

Katherine sniffed. "I got drunk. Really drunk. I knew I

shouldn't have, but... there was a guy... he started kissing me and stuff."

And stuff? "Katherine, if something happened without your consent—"

"I don't remember. And he doesn't either. I mean, I didn't... you know, I wasn't *that* far gone, Mom."

I closed my eyes. I felt unbearably sad for my daughter, and yet grateful that she'd finally told me... and that I could finally be there for her. "We'll be home in a few days," I told her. "We'll be together again really, really soon." I hope I'll have the opportunity to find out more about what happened, when we're back together. And together we will help each other to heal.

"I'm glad you're coming back, Mom," Katherine confessed in a rush. "I've missed you so much. I didn't even realize how much, until..." She trailed off, and I couldn't wait until we were together, and I could look into her eyes, take her into my arms.

"I've missed you too, Katherine," I told her, my voice choking. "And I love you. So much."

I hear the front door open, and then footsteps on the stairs. Allan comes into the doorway of our living room and watches me for a moment as he loosens his tie. His hair is ruffled and he looks weary and sad and yet still like my charismatic husband, with so much charm and potential.

"I can't believe this is actually happening," he says quietly.

I give him a sad smile of both acknowledgement and apology before putting another book in the box. "I know. Me, neither."

"Here's a little twist in the tail," he tells me, and fortunately he sounds more amused than annoyed or hurt, his eyebrows raised, a slight smile curving his mouth. "An anonymous alumnus heard about what happened through a nephew who is currently at the school, in Ben's boarding house, and this alumnus became concerned about the state of the place, so he decided to look into it himself."

"Oh?" I am wary, unsure what to expect.

"He's donating *three million* dollars to get the school back on its feet, all because the place was drawn to his attention because of the stupid thing with Ben. So, really, Laura, it's because of *you* that the school isn't closing." I let out a huff of incredulous laughter and he smiles. "I'm not sure the trustees would appreciate that irony, but it's still true."

I shake my head in total disbelief. "Well, silver linings and all that, I suppose." And now Tucker's education won't be disrupted.

Allan smiles at me, his shoulders slumped, his eyes sad, and I know exactly how he feels because I feel the same way. Bruised, battered, battle-weary. We both have scars, because you don't go through life without getting them. Some are of our own making, some of others', but in the end, it doesn't really matter, because you're still scarred, and that's okay. We'll both be okay… in time.

The doorbell rings. I turn. "I'll get it," I say, because the last thing Allan needs right now is a conversation with some staff or teacher about why he's leaving.

When I open the door, however, it's not a teacher or trustee or staff member standing there, wanting to offer commiserations or simply get the gossip, it's Ben. Ben Lane, dressed in his uniform, hair ruffled, looking both grim and uncertain. I haven't seen him since the Boston trip, and I am jolted by how *young* he seems, just another school boy, nothing else. Not anymore.

I stare at him wordlessly, and he flings a hand out to keep me from closing the door, even though I haven't even tried.

"I won't come in," he says. "I won't do anything but stand here. I just…" His breath hitches and then he rubs a hand over his face. "I just wanted to say that I'm sorry."

I stare at him for another few seconds before I manage to get my brain into gear. "I'm sorry too, Ben."

"It's just... I really liked you. I wasn't just messing around. I had no idea some idiot was filming us, you know, *when*... I really didn't." He stares at me intently, pleadingly. "I need you to believe that."

"Ben," I say as gently as I can, "it doesn't matter what I believe."

"But—"

"I do believe you," I tell him. "But it really doesn't matter. I never should have allowed things to... I should have made a report. I'm the negligent one."

"I *liked* you," he says, and I just shake my head. I don't want to hear this, because it just reminds me how young he is. How vulnerable. And how I was the adult in charge. I don't blame him, but I can't make any more mistakes.

"I really am sorry, Ben," I say quietly. "I should have handled things better."

"Laura—"

"Don't," I tell him quietly but firmly, "call me that. I am sorry, for how things happened and my part in them, but I really do think this must be goodbye."

And with that, I purposefully close the door on Ben Lane, my breath rushing out of me as I sag, pressing my forehead against the door.

My heart aches for him—this young boy, so lost, so alone, and so confused. And I had my part to play in that. I know I did. But it's over now. For good.

After a few seconds, I hear a noise from behind me. When I turn around, Allan is there, standing by the foot of the stairs. I can tell by the expression on his face that he has heard the entire, brief conversation, and without a word, he opens his arms and I walk into them.

CHAPTER 30

RACHEL

Acute thrombocytopenia. That's what the doctor told us in ER, probably as a post-viral symptom of the cold Nathan had back in September. A condition that can manifest in children as easy and extreme bruising, due to a low platelet count, often as the result of a viral infection, usually resolved within a few months.

The lightest touch could have caused any of those bruises.

Could have.

Because, the truth is, after Shelley became shamefaced, after the investigation OCFS opened up was dismissed, after I find out it was Maureen who called the police, who had it in for me from the beginning, because her sister was matron before, and was fired for suspected stealing, after Kyle came home and we are a family of three again, safe and secure, I know the truth.

I could have caused those bruises, acute thrombocytopenia or not. In the middle of the night, when I was exhausted and even angry, I could have grabbed my son. I think that's what Gladys was trying to tell me, in her elderly, befuddled way. She apologized later, wringing her hands, genuinely upset that she might have caused some distress. I assured her she hadn't, and we watched three episodes of *Jeopardy!* back-to-back and ate a six-pack of pudding cups between us, a sleeping Nathan cradled gently in her arms.

Motherhood is hard. Life is hard. We all make mistakes, some worse than others, some with worse consequences. The only thing we can do is choose to learn from them, to move on stronger, wiser.

Or weaker, as the case may be.

"I need help," I told Kyle, when we were back at home, when all the struggle and danger had seemed to have gone away, and our happily-ever-after was waiting for us, with a bow. "I can't do this on my own. I'm not sure I even know how to be a good mother. My own mom wasn't the greatest example, and I need help to learn."

Kyle, to his credit, didn't look fazed by my admission. "Then we'll get help," he said in his slow, steady way, and I could have cried—not with sorrow, not with regret, but with relief. With gratitude for this man, who has never wavered from my side.

I went to see Laura the week after it all happened, hoping she'd be there, although I wasn't even sure what I would have said to her. But they'd already gone, as I'd heard they would, back to Leabrook and their life there. They were a two-month blip in the life of Wilderness; in a year they'd be remembered as "the headmaster whose wife..." A year after that, they wouldn't be remembered at all, or barely. That's how life is sometimes.

I don't know if I'll be remembered. I told Wilderness I was taking another year of maternity leave, after all, and teenagers have short memories. I realized I needed a total break; Liz Pollard was surprisingly understanding. I think she was shaken by the way everything played out with Laura and Ben; she certainly seemed a little less pompous when I spoke to her. Maybe she—like Laura, like me—was wondering what her responsibility in all this was.

I knew I needed a chance to recalibrate, to adjust, to figure out who I was as a mother, as a person. If I was no longer the sophisticated, savvy teacher I'd been before Nathan, and if I wasn't the smiling, perfect mother of my dreams—or the carelessly evil one of my nightmares—then who was I? I'm still figuring that out.

I'm in therapy, and I'm also on antidepressants. Both help. Kyle isn't going back up north; he's going to plow snow in the winter, here in Hawley, and figure out the rest as he goes. We'll make it work.

I wish I could have told Laura I was sorry for my part in what happened. I wish I could have explained to her how trapped and lonely and confused I felt, but I'm pretty sure she understood anyway, because we both felt the same. Still, it would have been nice to say goodbye. To make amends, as best as I could.

In April, when the snow has finally melted and spring feels like a hint of promise on the air, when the leaves are barely starting to bud, and Nathan is nine months old, a chubby, happy baby who squeals with laughter, loves toy cars and tickles, I get a postcard from Connecticut. It's one of those silly cartoon ones, a black and white drawing of a Victorian-era mother looking both thoughtful and tired, her chin in her hand, her hair in a big, sweeping updo. The caption reads: *My daughter is going to change the world one day. I just have to survive raising her first. Daughter* has been crossed out and *son* written above. On the back, all it says is, *I'm doing so much better than I thought I'd be. I hope you are, too.* It's not signed, but I know, absolutely, that it's from her—Laura—and I am moved.

I take the postcard to the playground, where Nathan now loves going on the swings. As I push him up toward the pale blue sky while he shrieks with laughter, I take the card out and study it.

I am too, I think, hoping Laura somehow hears me, and knows. *I am too*. And I smile.

A LETTER FROM KATE

Dear reader,

I want to say a huge thank you for choosing to read *The Mother's Secret*. If you enjoyed it, and would like to keep up to date with all my latest releases, just sign up at the following link. Your email address will never be shared and you can unsubscribe at any time.

www.bookouture.com/kate-hewitt

This story was somewhat inspired by my own family's experience of working and living in small boarding schools, although in our case the schools were in the UK, not the US, and nothing untoward happened! But it made me think about how the close-knit community of a remote place can be both wonderful and threatening, and I wanted to explore that in the context of this story.

I hope you loved *The Mother's Secret* and if you did, I would be very grateful if you could write a review. I'd love to hear what you think, and it makes such a difference helping new readers to discover one of my books for the first time.

I love hearing from my readers—you can get in touch on my Facebook group for readers (facebook.com/groups/KatesReads), through Twitter, Goodreads or my website.

Thanks again for reading!

Kate

KEEP IN TOUCH WITH KATE

www.kate-hewitt.com

 twitter.com/author_kate

ACKNOWLEDGEMENTS

As ever, there are so many people who are part of bringing a book to fruition! Thank you to the whole amazing team at Bookouture who have helped with this process, from editing, copyediting, and proofreading, to designing and marketing. In particular, I'd like to thank my editor, Jess Whitlum-Cooper, as well as Laura Deacon, and Sarah Hardy and Kim Nash in publicity, Melanie Price in marketing, Richard King in foreign rights, and Sinead O'Connor in audio. I'd also like to thank my husband, who was my go-to for questions about safeguarding protocols in schools, and to my children, who have weathered our many moves—and many schools—with aplomb. I love you all!

Printed in Great Britain
by Amazon

28317122R10178